Summoned

Summoned

A From Smokeless Fire Romance

M.A. Guglielmo

TULE
PUBLISHING

Dedication

To my daughters, Chiara and Sabrina.

Chapter One

C OMING OUT OF the lamp was such a rush. One minute
Zahara was nothing but vapor, swirling in the icy
storms of the last level of hell. The next, she streamed out
into the mundane air of the human sphere. Her flesh
solidified into a floating upper torso, while her lower body
remained only a tail of black flames licking up around the
brass vessel used for the summoning.

And what flesh it was.

Zahara pinched back her shoulder blades and posed with
her hands on her hips to better accentuate her breasts. They
were huge, because she liked her first impression to be a
lasting one.

The resounding crack of thunder that marked the transition into the world of man faded away. With a fanged smile,
she faced the sorcerer who had dared to call her, the most
notorious *jinnayah* this side of Baghdad.

"Behold. It is I, Zahara, dread spirit of the endless desert." She'd made that up on the spot, and it sounded great.
"I have journeyed, o' child of mud and dirt, from the land of
smokeless fire to your dreary realm. What do you call
yourself, and what is it you demand of me?"

She had decided to put as much formality into her
speech as possible, to further impress upon him how fortu-

nate he was to have summoned such a powerful jinn to do his evil bidding. Not too traditional, of course, since she was speaking in flawless English, not classical Arabic.

The twenty-something standing outside the pentagram stared back at her, his mouth hanging open wide enough for a vulture to fly inside.

His first time, obviously. Perfect. This was the one time she wanted an inexperienced man.

"Daniel." He managed to get that much out, then circled around her, rubbing his eyes as if he couldn't believe what he was seeing. Either that or she had gone a little too heavy on the clouds of brimstone. "Daniel Goldstein. And you're... floating."

Zahara had chosen to appear in her favorite human manifestation, a voluptuous female with black hair that spilled around her bare shoulders. As for clothing, this was the only aspect of Zahara's life where she preferred minimalism. Two scanty triangles of crystal-encrusted silk clung desperately to her breasts, and a veil of silver mesh provided some limited coverage to her nether regions. Which were, currently, still in the nether region. From the waist down, she was only a twisting funnel of smoke and fire. It was a hard trick to keep up for more than a few minutes, but the stunned look on humans' faces when she did always made it worthwhile.

"I mean," the sorcerer stammered, "you don't have legs, or feet. You really did just float up out of that lamp."

He wasn't the brightest evil magician Zahara had ever encountered, but not the worst looking, by a long shot. A little taller than average, with amazed hazel eyes framed by a mop of curly hair. For the occasion of his first summoning, he had chosen to wear a New York Mets T-shirt and plaid pajama bottoms. Smelled like he had been doing a little drinking before her arrival, too.

Sorcerers these days. Always trying to seem nonchalant. He should be striving to awe her with his power and mastery of dark magic—for self-preservation, if for no other reason. Back in her mother's heyday, one wrinkle in a human's formal set of Magi robes would have led to an immediate and gruesome death. This Daniel character was fortunate Zahara wanted to be conjured up, and was willing to overlook a few procedural details.

The summoning space Daniel had chosen didn't exactly exude competence, either. They were inside a small apartment, with a window looking out onto a nighttime cityscape of glittering lights against a dark sky, with occasional flashes of color from passing police cars. Inside, a clumsy pentagram had been poured out in sand over a woolen Berber rug. Some tastefully dull black-and-white photo art hung on the walls, and the room's Bauhaus replica furniture had been neatly pushed aside to allow extra room for the ceremony. No weeping naked virgins in chains, no bowls of blood, not even a severed goat head. For candles, he had selected congealed wax set into squat glass containers better suited for jams and jellies. Zahara gave the air a sniff. What was that smell? Pumpkin spice?

Well, the last thing she had wanted was a skilled practitioner of the dark arts who might be able to outfox her in negotiations. This modern setup all but screamed newbie magician, which meant he'd be easier to trick. Her first goal was to loosen him up a little.

She solidified the lower half of her body and stepped out onto the rug. Her long, shapely legs ended in razor-sharp stiletto heels—a concession to the modern world; Zahara loved human shoes. A belt around her waist dipped below her jeweled belly button to hold her metallic slit skirt in place. She rotated around to show him the rear view. A narrow strip of filigreed silver plunged over her bottom and fell to the floor.

"There you go." Zahara gave her best flesh-jiggling shimmy before twirling around to slink toward him. She used the sharpened tip of her fingernail to lift up his shirt and get a better look at his chest. "So, what do you want to do first? A little French, perhaps?"

"French?" He stared back at her, puzzled.

Zahara undid the drawstring on his pants and parted her lips to show him her forked tongue.

"Oh, God, no." Daniel stumbled backward, yanking his pajamas back up.

Wait. Was he *refusing* her advances?

She made a sweeping gesture up and down her body. "What's wrong with you? Don't you think I'm beautiful?"

With a snap of her fingers, a roaring wall of flame shot up behind him, cutting off his escape. She narrowed her eyes in fury. Rejection wasn't something she handled well.

"It's not you, it's me." Daniel tried frantically to bat down some of the flames with a couch throw before turning back to face her, his hands raised in surrender. "You're stunning, gorgeous, a vision of pulchritude. But I'm gay."

"You're gay." Zahara folded her arms over her chest. Well, there went the plan to cloud his mind with lust. "Do you have any idea how long I worked on these breasts?"

"So, so gay." He raised a shaking hand toward the back of the room. "Do you want to see a picture of my ex-boyfriend?"

Zahara pursed her lips, then nodded. No need to panic. All she had to do was find another method to break through his defenses. The flames died down, and he rushed over to the corner to retrieve a framed photograph. The background was all blue waves and white buildings, and the man standing next to him in the picture combined a dour expression with a polo shirt to ill effect.

"This was taken in July. Anton and I spent a weekend in Provincetown. I looked for some art, and he complained about the stock market. It was wonderful. But since then we've grown apart. It was a mutual decision. We both needed to take a break for a while." He stopped and took a breath, as if even he realized he was babbling.

"Your lover spurned you." Zahara deepened her voice to give more dramatic emphasis to her words. She leaned over him. Even without the heels, she had given herself a form two meters tall. Who needed a short jinn? "He rejected your affections, disregarded your burning passion for him."

"Okay, yes, maybe the breakup was his idea. But I'm over it at this point. I'm surprised I still have this old picture hanging around."

Zahara flicked her fingers at the coffee table, which held three additional framed photographs of the two men. "Don't worry. When I'm through with him, he'll be writhing on the ground, blood oozing from every orifice as he begs for the merciful death you'll refuse to grant him."

Daniel gasped. "No, I don't want to hurt Anton. I didn't call you to do anything like that."

"Of course not." Time to shift tactics. Zahara flicked her fingers again and the picture frame in his hand shattered into a spray of glass shards that fell to the floor. For added effect, she made the photograph inside burst into flames. "That worthless worm is nothing compared to the hordes of beautiful young men who will fight for your attentions once you have the power that's rightfully yours." She brushed by him to admire the skyline soaring up outside the window. As magicians' lairs went, it had a decent view. "Shall I assassinate the leader of this city and place you in his palace?"

"No, thank you, I don't want to kill off the mayor of New York. Or even my city council member, who's totally annoying. I'm not interested in politics."

She decided to drop the ancient jinn speech and explain things to this dim-witted sorcerer in words he could understand. With a stomp of her foot, she started to tick off topics on her fingers. "No kinky sex, no bloody revenge, and no palace coup? If you've summoned me to lead you to hidden treasure, you've got the wrong girl. I love the Big Apple, but with my knowledge of New York City's ancient past, I'd be lucky to scare up some wampum and pottery shards."

"I don't want money," he said. "I called up a jinn because my *bubbe* told me I had to save the world before two fallen angels destroy it."

That sounded wrong on so many levels, Zahara didn't know where to start. Humans often confused some jinn, like the peri of Persia, with angels, assuming any human-appearing creature with a pair of giant bird wings was on their side. But Zahara knew what total bastards those peris were, and she wanted nothing to do with a fight against not one, but two of them. Besides, what sort of sorcerer called up a jinn like herself to *save* people?

"So Daniel Goldstein's *bubbe* told him to call me." Zahara emphasized the correct pronunciation of the Yiddish name for grandmother, since she could. She spoke hundreds of human languages, not that any of them were much use in understanding Daniel's drunken ramblings. "And you want me to help people, not haunt them. I think you're getting your infernal servants confused. Try a golem. They're not too bright and a much better cultural match."

"My grandmother was from Morocco and she believed in the jinn." Daniel's voice had an edge in it now, as if her comment had stung him into sobriety. He walked back over to the pentagram and picked up the lamp Zahara had emerged from. "She sent me a letter with instructions and then this arrived. I didn't think any of it could be real at first. But strange things kept happening..." His voice trailed off, and he reached out to touch her arm. "I can't believe this worked."

Zahara took a step back. She had been waiting for this opportunity for years, hoping to answer the call of a greedy sorcerer whose base desires would lead to his downfall. Now she had to deal with a do-gooder whose extended family had magical chops. For a moment, she considered vanishing in an offended puff of smoke and waiting for her spells to reveal another, more standard summons. But it wasn't like the world was crawling with magicians these days, and she wanted—no, *needed*—to make this arrangement work.

For once in her life, Zahara wanted her mother to take her seriously. Tricking a human sorcerer into giving up his soul would be the perfect way to do that.

"If your grandmother was from *Al Maghreb*, then she's your *jeeda*, not your *bubbe*." Zahara took the oil lamp from him and studied it. A cheap modern replica of an antique, not to mention a ridiculous cliché. Still, casting a summoning spell on such an ordinary object took skill.

"I know. My father's Catholic relatives called her bubbe, and she thought it was hilarious, so the nickname stuck."

Great. Now he wanted to tell her his entire life story. After tossing the lamp back on the floor, she walked over to the couch and took a seat, crossing her legs and swinging one high-heeled foot back and forth. "What's a demonic spirit got to do to get a drink around here?"

"Sorry." He rushed over to the kitchen and hunted through a few cupboards. "What exactly do you people drink? I tried to do some research, and it said something about eating bones, or certain types of rocks."

"Bring something expensive with bubbles, and make it snappy." Zahara leaned back. This was the critical part. He had summoned her, but so far he hadn't outright asked her for anything. Once he demanded something from her, the bargaining started. Unless he structured the agreement perfectly, he would pay far more for this magical favor than he had ever imagined. "Didn't this grandma of yours teach you anything about us?"

"When I was a kid, she told me stories about the jinn. I hadn't thought about this stuff for years. But if you're here and real, then what she told me in the letter is true." He gave an audible gulp. "I really do need to work with a powerful spirit to prevent disaster from falling upon the human race."

He returned, struggling with two glasses under one arm and a magnum of champagne in the other. "I'm not sure if I got all the instructions right. She wrote something about a great *marid* with a giant sword who could do battle with the forces of evil. You're not quite what I expected."

"Well, I was expecting a horny old sorcerer who wanted to do something fun, not an uptight geek who's not even up for a quick tumble in bed." Zahara tapped her razor-sharp nails against a pillow, sliced through the fabric, and admired the cloud of feathers that emerged. "Hurry up with that drink."

"I was saving this bottle for Anton. Our five-year anniversary would have been in September." He propped the base of the bottle against his stomach and aimed the neck away from him as he tried to peel the foil off the top, frowning. "I always get a little nervous popping open one of these."

Zahara gave a sigh and rose to her feet. She reached out her hand, willing her sword to materialize. Her weapon had been a hideous, blood-encrusted present from her mother to celebrate her arrival into jinn adulthood. As soon as she could master the magic, Zahara had transformed its blade into a graceful curve of silver, then set it off with a hilt embossed with lapis lazuli and as many diamonds as she could get to fit. With a quick slice, she severed the neck of the bottle, sending foaming wine spilling between Daniel's legs.

She grabbed the glasses from under his arm and filled

both of them, handing one to him before taking a sip of hers. "A toast. To your quest."

Daniel grabbed a pillow and tried to dry off his crotch, then gave up and drained his glass. "The problem is, I don't know how to start this quest of mine."

Damnit, he still hadn't asked her for anything. "So what do you expect me to do about it?"

"Well, I'd like you to help me stop whatever evil creatures my grandmother's been warning me about."

Finally.

Zahara licked her finger and ran it around the rim of the glass. "This would be under the standard arrangement, I assume?"

"Does that mean I get three wishes?"

"No, it's one wish, and that's all you get!" She pulled back her lips to bare her fangs, then sent sparks arcing off her fingertips across the room.

Let the games begin.

Daniel jumped up to stomp on a few smoldering spots on the carpet. "That's fine. One wish. And I'll follow all the rules, I promise."

Zahara paused mid-rant. That was it? She had spent more time and dramatic flourish bargaining for a cheap pair of sandals. For a moment, a flicker of doubt threatened to disrupt her new, buoyant mood. Daniel belonged to her, body and soul, once she delivered on the contract. He hadn't even attempted to negotiate with her. But stopping two peris armed with bad intentions toward humanity and whatever magic their race possessed might take some muscle. She was a lover of many things—handsome men, desserts, expensive shoes—not a fighter.

Then a thought struck her, and she couldn't stop a smile from spreading across her face. Of course. She knew just the jinn to help her out with this little adventure. Even better, he would love the part about saving humanity. She raised her glass. "Then we have a deal."

Daniel gave a nervous nod and rushed to refill her barely-drained glass before over-pouring his own, sending foam cascading over his shaking hands. "Great."

Zahara sat back down, stretched one arm over the back of the couch, and knocked back a solid swig of bubbly. Success tasted sweet. Or in this case, semi-dry with a creamy finish and a hint of peach. Daniel had excellent taste in wine. Cleaned up a little, he'd be a wonderful eternal slave. "Did your sweet old *bubbe* give you any idea where to start with this quest of yours?"

"She told me to go to her old house in Marrakech. But once I get there, I have no idea what to do." His gaze traveled to the kitchen. "Her letter had more details in it, I think."

"Fine. Give it to me, and I'll read it myself." The deal was sealed, and Zahara didn't want to lose any time cashing in on it. Not to mention she wanted to learn a little more about this mysterious *bubbe* Daniel kept talking about.

Daniel coughed. "I sort of freaked out and—burned it."

Zahara gave him a long, withering stare. Then she decided to focus on the positives in this situation. If Daniel's grandmother had known enough to tell her grandson to call up a specific type of jinn, she might have told him something about the negotiation process. So the letter was gone. Just as well.

"Call up old granny and tell her to meet us in Morocco. She needs to be a little more specific about what we need to do."

"That's not possible." Daniel fumbled for a coaster, even though the coffee table was splattered with wine, and rested his glass on it. "She died over ten years ago."

Chapter Two

ONLY A FEW hours prior to Zahara's buxom-and-brimstone appearance, the only hint of trouble in the structured rhythm of Daniel's all-work-and-no-fun-routine had been the letter. One simple envelope had been all it took to upend his comfortable existence, grounded in his firm belief in a rational explanation for anything and everything. From comfortable routine to magical anarchy, in less time than it took him to get through his favorite zombie movie marathon.

Daniel threw his daily collection of mail down on his kitchen countertop. If the letter hadn't landed with an odd, soft *thunk*, he might not have bothered to check it out until later. Like Monday. His weekend had begun, and at ten p.m. on Saturday night, it was already half over. His social plans for the evening included Netflix and a chilled glass of that expensive bourbon he had received as a housewarming present.

A recent promotion at his tech company and the success of an augmented-reality game app he had developed meant enough money for a small but nicer-than-average apartment on the Upper West Side. The new position and living space had come with killer work hours, bills, and layers of added responsibility. Adulting was harder than it looked.

He picked up the envelope, running his hand over the creamy, thick paper. His name had been written out in lovely spirals of cursive on the outside. No return address, no postage. Odd. It must have been placed directly into his mailbox in the building's front foyer. Some sort of pretentious welcome announcement from the building's super, maybe? He had received wedding invitations inside less formal stationary.

He slid a steak knife along the top seam of the envelope and extracted a collection of documents and newspaper clippings in a foreign language. He couldn't read any of them. Only one item in the package was written in English, in a fine handwritten script scratched out on paper that felt like skin.

The letter wasn't from the building's super, but it was addressed to him. He skimmed it at first, jumping to the signature at the bottom. Then he grabbed a chair and sat down to read the entire message again.

The note had been signed by his maternal grandmother... who had died when he was fifteen. And that wasn't the strangest thing about it. According to the letter, he held in his hand magical instructions that described how to summon one of the unseen ones and bend it to his will.

Daniel's long-dead *bubbe* had sent him a message from beyond the grave, with instructions on how to call up a genie. A jinn, as she would have put it.

It got better. The letter included details about embarrassing anecdotes from his childhood Daniel would have sworn no one else could know about, and a firm order for him to call up that jinn. He would need a powerful magical servant to defeat the two fallen ones, his grandmother wrote, or a magical war would break out. It went on from there, getting crazier and crazier. Whoever wrote this had either been blessed with a fantastic imagination or had been high as hell.

Daniel put the paper down, rested his head in hands, and laughed himself into a coughing fit. He hadn't been pranked this hard in ages. Maybe his parents were in on it, given the specific references to his childhood. Or maybe not. That would require the type of communication that could ruin a happy divorce.

One thing was for sure. His grandmother would have loved the joke. She had been downright eccentric, with a quirky sense of humor and a tendency to stuff him full of sweets and teach him French swear words every time he visited her. And she had loved telling him stories about the jinn. He shoved the papers into a drawer, vowing to figure out who had punked him tomorrow, after a good night's sleep.

His dead grandmother had other plans.

DANIEL DID HIS best to ignore the first signs of trouble as he slid into bed. His covers short-sheeted? His fault for being too lazy to make his bed properly. The sudden slam of his closet door? Uneven flooring, probably. The cacophony of voices screaming guttural curses and chanting in unfamiliar languages?

Okay, things were starting to get weird.

He sat bolt upright, his pulse thudding in his neck, and

stared into the darkness of the room around him. The screaming died down into discontented grumbles. Someone in the building had turned up the volume on a terrible music collection, maybe. One thing was for sure, he wasn't about to let a prank letter freak him out into believing in ghosts.

His bedside lamp, shaped like a giant light bulb for interior design reasons beyond his comprehension, flickered on, then off again. Daniel reached out to turn it on, only to watch as his hand began to glow, the energy from the bulb transferring to his palm. His skin dissolved away like a sheet of paper set alight. Daniel gasped, waiting for pain that never came. He flexed and extended his denuded fingers in morbid fascination, staring as arteries pulsed and veins wound a blue path around the exposed muscles and ligaments of his hand.

Shaking off his paralysis, Daniel jumped to his feet and ran out of his bedroom. Ghosts did not exist, and his new apartment wasn't haunted by his dead grandmother. That being said, ghosts and hauntings would not exist even better if he slept somewhere else tonight. He paused in mid-flight as he passed the bathroom. The door gaped open a crack, and light spilled around the casing onto the floor in front of him.

He hadn't left that light on.

Daniel took a few hesitant steps closer, then grabbed the handle and yanked the door wide open.

Inside was nothing more alarming than soap scum in the sink. He moved into the brightness, taking the opportunity to examine his right hand. All five fingers present, with skin to cover them. Excellent. For a moment, he avoided staring at the mirror, waiting for the horror movie cliché of a mask-wearing villain to pop up behind his reflection. When that didn't materialize, he leaned closer and tugged down on his lower eyelids, checking his pupils. They looked too small. Pinpoint, even. Maybe that smoothie he drank for lunch had been spiked with more than a protein burst. That would be a nice, simple explanation for everything.

Behind him, a rasp of scratching broke the silence. He jumped and whirled around, his eyes searching the cold smoothness of the tiled walls. Nothing. He exhaled, his heart slowing down to a mild gallop. Then he thought to look down.

At his feet, a solemn line of cockroaches stood in parade formation on his bathroom floor. Hundreds more came to join them, pouring out of every crack and crevice in the room, forming a seething mass that turned the white tile black.

The insects shifted into lines and circles, their hissing bodies spelling out a message for him:

Listen to your bubbe, Daniel.

Daniel ran out of the bathroom and headed for his front door, only to discover he couldn't open it. The handle had melted away, and no amount of frantic shoving made the door budge. The screaming voices started up again, building to an unbearable crescendo.

This couldn't be happening. He was trapped in his apartment with a pissed-off ghost who wanted him to call up a jinn.

He retreated into the kitchen, where he stepped on something wet and squishy next to his refrigerator. Against his better judgment, he reached over and opened the door to the appliance, spilling light onto the scene.

Blood was everywhere.

Gobs of the stuff dripped down into flat puddles on the refrigerator's clear shelves. Little red rivulets splashed over a head of arugula, and thick clots soaked through an old take-out container of Thai food. Even the freezer compartment had gotten into the act. Sticky, half-frozen red globules clung to his last container of mango froyo.

All in all, it was more blood than he had ever wanted to see in his entire life. For several seconds, the only thought in his overwhelmed brain was an uncontrollable urge to research cleaning agents used by serial killers.

Daniel ran to the drawer and pulled out the papers from his grandmother. Rifling through the contents, he grabbed the parchment explaining how to call up a jinn. He carried it over to the kitchen sink, his bare feet sticking to the blood on the floor, and threw it in. After pouring half a bottle of Jefferson's Bourbon on it, he set it on fire.

"Why are you doing this to me?" His words echoed through the apartment. "I was your favorite grandson, remember? Your only grandson."

The voices stopped.

Daniel grabbed the bottle of bourbon and took a solid chug for himself. Then he staggered into his living room to finish it off.

About an hour after his encounter with the Appliance of the Damned, he sat rocking back and forth on his couch, the empty bottle by his side. Drinking the alcohol had led to him to an important conclusion. Trying to summon a jinn would either confirm he was suffering from stress-induced hallucinations, or get the haunting to stop.

The trouble was, the instructions on how to do just that were little more than aromatic ashes in his sink, giving off hints of vanilla and aged oak, not to mention burnt paper.

Then he heard the knocking. A few polite raps on his door. Not frantic, or angry sounding, but it was the middle of the night. Maybe one of his neighbors, worried about all the noise.

Daniel walked back over to his sealed entrance to his apartment, finding that the floor swayed underneath him far more than it should, even given how much he had to drink. What should he do now? He could tell the caller he was under attack by a ghost. But who would believe that? Or maybe whatever was waiting for him on the other side of the door was worse than possessed roaches and an exsanguinating refrigerator.

"Mr. Goldstein?" The voice was smooth, with a courtly tone that suggested its owner had several decades on Daniel. "May I pay you a visit?"

"Sure." Daniel stared at the molten mess of a door handle, which resembled a Surrealist melted clock. "Mind letting yourself in?"

The door swung open, revealing an older man with white shoulder-length hair. "Sorry to disturb you. My name's Reza Gul. I recently moved in on this floor."

"Nice to meet you!" Daniel pumped the man's hand and put as much enthusiasm into the statement as he could, given he was wearing blood-stained pajamas and wasn't entirely sober.

"It sounded like you were awake," Reza continued, returning Daniel's handshake.

Well, that was a diplomatic way to put it.

Reza's fingers were too long for his hands—downright skeletal. Cold as ice, too. Did that mean he had a warm heart? Daniel tried to focus on standing upright and not making an even bigger drunken fool of himself.

"Given I'm a night owl myself, I thought I'd drop by and give you your package." The older man handed Daniel a box. It rattled as he passed it over. "The doorman made a mistake and gave it to me earlier today." Reza ran a long, yellowed fingernail over the label. "See? It has your name right here."

Daniel accepted the cardboard box and ripped it open on the spot, swaying a little. "Thanks."

Inside was a polished brass oil lamp. Like the ones in the movies. His grandmother's ghost was not giving up on this. Well, she hadn't been the type of woman to take no for an answer. If she wanted him to call up a jinn from a lamp, maybe he should.

"So all I need to do—" Daniel paused to hiccup. "Is rub this baby, and poof! My genie appears."

Reza laughed. "No harm in trying, I suppose. Well, it was a pleasure to meet you, Daniel. I hope you get your wish."

He gave a half-bow and walked back down the hallway. Daniel clutched the lamp to his chest and made his way to the living room. An eerie silence greeted him. Was his grandmother pleased?

Only one way to find out.

Daniel opened his laptop, executed the most unlikely

internet search he could ever have imagined, and scrounged up the items necessary to raise an infernal spirit. He placed the lamp inside what he hoped was a respectable pentagram at 3 a.m. At exactly 3:13 a.m Sunday morning, Zahara floated up out of the lamp, cleavage and all.

Chapter Three

ZAHARA PERCHED ON the café's high-top stool and watched Daniel stumble inside. The clean shirt and khakis, along with the lack of stubble on his chin, made it clear he had at least taken the time to shower and dress, hangover or not. Excellent. She'd never had a human thrall before, but she had already decided he would need to dress well.

Daniel made his way to the counter without any sign he noticed her and fumbled inside a canvas messenger bag that hung by his side.

"The usual, Jake." Daniel pushed his hand around in the bag again, then flipped the flap open to stare inside. "Wait a minute, I think I lost my wallet."

"Your brew's already at your table." The scrawny young hipster behind the bar gave him a goofy grin and jerked a thumb in Zahara's direction. "Dude, I had no idea you got married. I didn't even think you were straight."

Daniel whirled around. Zahara scrunched her fingers into a wave and patted the seat in front of her with as suggestive a wink as possible. Her new sorcerer came over and collapsed into the chair across from her, barely able to get out a sentence, much less touch the steaming cup of coffee in front of him.

"You look—" He tried to untangle his tongue. "Normal."

Zahara's skills in human transformation had few equals amongst jinn. Sure, every liver-munching *ghula* she had ever met loved to brag how she well she could pass for a sweet young human thing—at midnight and half-hidden in the shadows of a deserted graveyard. Let her try appearing as a curvy brunette in a sleeveless top and jeans, in the full daylight of a New York City fall morning. Zahara didn't look normal, she looked awesome. And totally human.

Daniel shot a glance back at Jake, as if to confirm that Zahara was, in fact, real to someone other than himself. "How did you know I would be coming here? Magic?"

Now that Zahara had bound Daniel into an unbreakable contract, there were spells she could use to locate him. Difficult, boring incantations that would have taken far too long. Fortunately, when Zahara had rummaged through Daniel's apartment last night, she had found all sorts of useful items. "I didn't have to use *magic*. You have a frequent buyer card with the coffee shop's address on it. Punched every Sunday."

Daniel open his mouth a few times, then closed it. "You stole my wallet?"

Zahara beamed at him and tossed it onto the table. She had also taken his phone, hoping to find a few nude selfies. No such luck.

Daniel took back his wallet and shot another glance at Jake. "Why does the barista think we're married?"

"Because I told him so." Zahara jabbed her thumbs at her breasts. "You seemed a little freaked out last night so I toned down the ta-tas. Still a slamming double-D, though."

"I don't care what your cup size is." He shoved his wallet back into his messenger bag. "Stop telling everyone you're my wife. I don't need a beard, thank you very much." He frowned, rummaging in his bag again. "Wait. Did you take my phone, too?"

Zahara pushed Daniel's cell across the table. "It's easier to book a hotel room for a married couple in Morocco. This is where we're staying." The screen lit up with a photo of a majestic tiled building overlooking a sparkling blue pool. "So now all you have to do is get our plane tickets. Daily flights, LaGuardia to Casablanca. And don't even think of trying to make me fly coach."

Daniel rubbed his eyes, still bleary and red. "I need to give work notice I'm taking vacation. It's not like I can tell them I'm jaunting off to Morocco to do battle with two evil angels because my grandmother's ghost told me to."

Zahara flicked her hand at him. "Tell them your *bubbe* died and you have to go to the funeral. Problem solved."

Daniel shifted in his seat, his expression uneasy. "How safe is it to travel there, anyway?"

Zahara bit back a remark that the trip would be a whole lot safer if he didn't plan on picking a fight with two peris—or angels, as he insisted on calling them. Daniel had summoned her to do him a favor, and once she did, he belonged to her. But if he dithered around and didn't give her more information, she wouldn't be able to keep up her end of the bargain. Of course, this whole battle idea *did* sound like a lot of work, even if her friend Zaid would be doing all of it for her. Maybe she could talk Daniel into something simpler.

"My earlier and far more entertaining offers are still on the table," Zahara said. "Money, power, revenge on your ex—I can get you all three of those things without even leaving New York."

"If the jinn and magic are real, then my dead grandmother really reached out to me last night." Daniel took in a deep breath and rested his hands on the table. "She was a good person, and there's no way I would use some magical gift she gave me to do the wrong thing. And you have to do what I say, right?"

There was no arguing with this do-gooder of a sorcerer, apparently. Fine. Zahara sprinkled sugar over the top of her latte. Jake had swirled the foam into a coffee-art display of concentric hearts.

"That's right." She dragged a finger over the cup, smearing the symbols of love into a blur, then licked the foam off a scarlet-red nail. "And after you get your wish, I get what I want."

"Good." Daniel stared down into his coffee, as if hoping to find something to support his decision. At Zahara's request, Jake had shaped his latte surface into a rough approximation of a sexual position from the *Kama Sutra*.

Daniel took a gulp, then raised a finger. "I thought of something. My grandmother's letter—the one I burned—mentioned a special date I had to watch out for. Something about the moon being in the house of sad Bula. I'm not sure who Bula is, or why he's sad. Or what the moon has to do with anything."

Zahara paused mid-sip. "I don't know what online scam university you paid to get your sorcerer training from, but you should sue them. Seriously, you've never heard of the Mansions of the Moon?"

"There isn't even a permanent space station on the moon, much less mansions."

Zahara let out a long-suffering breath. Granted, the golden age of human sorcery had long since passed, given the rise of technology, but Daniel needed remedial classes in the basics of spell-casting and prophecy. "Think of it as the lunar zodiac. The House of Sa'd Bula refers to a position of the moon against the stars."

Daniel slurped his coffee again. "I'm not sure what my sign has to do with anything. And let me guess, you're an Aries."

Zahara slammed her cup down on the table. "Certain days of the month are best for certain types of magic, okay? The House of Sa'd Bula usually controls dark magic. Getting lovers to hate one another, allowing slaves to escape, that sort of thing."

"So when is the moon in sad Bula's house?" Daniel asked. "I need to know if I have some sort of deadline here."

Zahara held up her fingers to count, staring upward for a moment. She had never paid much attention to her tutors about this topic. Or to any of her lessons about complicated spells that didn't involve clothing or dessert. "For this month, in Morocco? Next Saturday."

"I have to save the world from two monster angels by Saturday?"

"I have a friend in Marrakech." Zahara added more sugar to her remaining coffee, then drank it down. "He owes me a few favors. We'll fly out tomorrow night. That'll give us plenty of time."

"I need to pack, get money, figure out a travel itinerary…" Daniel rubbed his head. "We've got a lot to do before we leave."

"You're telling me? I need new clothes, shoes." She wagged the fourth finger of her left hand at him. "And since I'm now Mrs. Daniel Goldstein, I expect a rock on here by this afternoon."

ZAHARA PRESSED HER hands against the jewelry store window and parted her lips to breathe vapor over the glass. "Sparkly!"

Daniel leaned over her shoulder and groaned. "A crystal gargoyle with a golden collar? It's a Halloween decoration."

Her new sorcerer hadn't been as enthused as she was about their pre-quest shopping trip. For one thing, he had begun to complain about carrying the ever-increasing number of bags filled with her purchases. Even more annoying was his endless stream of questions about the jinn and her world in general. A cute, naïve sorcerer was one thing; a total magical virgin something else entirely. If he was that clueless about the children of smokeless fire, too much information might scare him off this crazy fight he wanted to pick with two peris. She didn't want that to happen.

Ignoring his question, she headed for the store entrance.

Daniel sighed and held the door open for her. "Another thing. I'm all for being culturally sensitive, but I know a guy in Brooklyn who'll sell us some fairly convincing cubic zirconia for that engagement ring."

"Well, great quests to save the world take some start-up cash." Zahara spotted a young woman behind the ring counter brighten at their approach, and made a beeline for her. "I offered you treasure. You chose to save the world. Try to look like an eager fiancé, please."

After a red-faced Daniel sputtered his way through a ring fitting, they left the store with the gargoyle, along with a set of gold-plated wedding bands. Daniel started in on the questions as soon as they stepped onto the sidewalk. "Were you in that lamp for a long time? Because you seem to know an awful lot about the modern world."

"You thought I lived in that thing?" Zahara doubled over in laughter, recovering in time to reach out and grab the buttocks of a handsome passerby wearing headphones and an overly-tight business suit. He glared at Daniel, then marched away.

"Stop doing that!" Daniel's face turned crimson. He grabbed her arm and moved them further down the sidewalk. Granted, impulse control had never been one of Zahara's strengths, but Daniel needed to learn how to let loose once in a while.

"Don't pull anything like that overseas. So where do you come from then?"

"Anywhere I like." Zahara moved ahead to ogle a group of construction workers. Unlike the guy in the suit, they didn't seem to mind the attention. "Beirut's always hopping, and I love Cairo. When I feel like serious shopping, I spend a little time in Paris, or maybe Dubai."

Daniel's face scrunched into confusion. "But I thought

the jinn come from that land of smoke-free fire and deserts of dread, like you talked about. Why don't you live there?"

"Some of us like it here, that's all."

She had no intention of telling Daniel the real reason she avoided the Mountains of Qaf, and her family. She yanked at Daniel's arm as he tried to pause at a no-crossing sign. One quick spell, and the light switched colors, trapping confused drivers in the box of the intersection and sending a flurry of pedestrians into the path of irate and honking taxi drivers.

The malfunctioning traffic sign now featured a suggestive set of pixels jiggling to an unheard tune. People nearby stopped, laughed, and took pictures of it with their phones. And humans always complained that jinn like her were bad news.

Daniel winced, but pushed his way through the crowd to follow her. "This friend of yours in Marrakech you want me to meet. Is he one of you?"

"No. He converted." Zahara shrugged at Daniel's blank expression. Zaid's religious beliefs were his own business. Unlike her mother, she had no problem with them. "That's why he lives in this world. Plus, he can't travel through the seven levels, so he's sort of stuck here at this point."

"What are the seven levels?" Daniel asked.

"The seven levels of hell." My, but this interrogation was getting tiresome. Still, she had to give him *some* information. No sense in letting him get suspicious. Zahara swiveled her head to give a blatant once-over to an attractive Asian woman strolling by in a short skirt and cowboy boots before continuing. "If I travel through each one I can pop out pretty much anywhere I want. Don't you know anything?"

"Until last night I didn't even believe magic existed."

So her summoning had been Daniel's first spell ever. It was so perfect. All she had to do was jaunt over to Morocco with him, let Zaid rough up those two birdbrains, and she had her first human thrall. That would show her mother a thing or two.

Daniel came to an abrupt halt, his body tensing. "We need to turn around. Now."

Right after the sidewalk café in front of them, a high-end fashion store beckoned. Zahara had no intention of missing out. "Why?"

A man sitting at one of the outside tables stood up—a Wall-Street type, wearing a suit even though it was the weekend. No less than six water glasses stood on the table in front of him. He liked to stay well-hydrated, apparently.

"Midtown on Sunday, Daniel? Not your usual stomping grounds." Pale, with red hair combed back into a severe part, he reminded her of someone. Someone she didn't like.

Then she pictured him wearing a scowl and a polo shirt.

Anton. The ex-boyfriend in the picture frame. Something about him sent the fur on the back of Zahara's neck on end. No, not fur. Long, glossy black hair. She was in her full human form, and no one could see through her disguise spell. Well, almost no one.

Daniel clenched his jaw a few times, then stepped around the tables to join the man, as Zahara pressed herself up against him. "I'm shopping with a friend." He nodded at her, his face set into the worst imitation of a cheerful smile she had ever seen. "This is Zahara. She's new at the office."

"And his new wife." Zahara flashed the gold band they

had bought, which she hadn't been able to resist slipping on her finger. That store clerk had been so taken with her breathless story of love at first sight. "So you're Anton. In case he changes his mind, what size do you take in hand-cuffs?"

"Is this a joke?" Anton shifted his eyes from Daniel to her, his mouth tightening.

Did he suspect something? Of course not. Another stupid modern human, unable to grasp anything outside his safe, rational world.

"Of course it is." Daniel rearranged the position of the bags he was carrying. "Zahara's traveling with me on a work trip overseas. It's a Muslim country, so she's going to wear a wedding ring, just in case."

"Massachusetts is a foreign country as far as you're concerned." Anton gave an awkward laugh; Zahara bristled. Patronizing chump. "Do you even have a passport?"

"Of course I have a passport." Daniel turned to Zahara, his face a few shades paler. She had a feeling she would need that useful magical trick she had learned to enchant human forms of identification. "I've visited Canada. And once I almost decided to visit Mexico. Anyway, I'll be away for a week or so in Morocco."

Anton shot another glance at Zahara, this one even less friendly. He sensed something, she could tell. Maybe he had the sight. Even so, by adulthood most humans with it had talked themselves out of the ability to recognize jinn. It was those pesky little toddlers she had to watch out for.

"I'm not sure if I'd advise that trip right now." Anton's voice grew smooth. "My uncle owns some property in

Marrakech, and he's been talking about renewed terrorist activity along the border with Algeria."

Zahara paid little heed to human politics, but she had visited Zaid in Morocco recently, and the biggest issue facing tourists in the country was deciding which rug to bring back as a souvenir. "For your information, my fiancé is more than capable of taking care of himself and me while we're there. On our *honeymoon*."

That prickling on the back of her neck returned. Something wasn't quite right about Anton, but she couldn't figure out what. The man had to be human. She refused to accept that any supernatural creature could do as good a job as she did enveloping itself in a human form in the light of day. Regardless, she didn't need anyone trying to talk Daniel out of this trip. She couldn't claim her prize until the contract had been completed. They had to go to Morocco.

"I'm sure we won't be going anywhere near Algeria." Daniel appeared too flustered to correct her about the honeymoon part.

"Since when has your company asked you to travel overseas?" Anton asked. "In your line of work, you should be able to handle any problems from your apartment. In your pajamas."

Daniel had told her what he did for a living, but Zahara had tuned him out after a few seconds. Something about computers, and creating little digital monsters.

Unlike most of her kind, Zahara had no concerns about human technology. She had used a computer once, and found it to be an exceptionally useful way to view pornography.

She rested one hand on her hip. "For your information, our personal presence there is critical to the important, techie work that needs to be done."

This Anton had become a major problem. Could she use a compulsion spell on him to stop him from trying to talk Daniel out of the trip? She couldn't pull that on Daniel. The contract protected him against any of her magic unless he agreed to it in advance.

Daniel's face flushed, and for a moment she thought he might give in to his ex-lover's objections. Instead, he squared his shoulders. "Actually, Anton, that computer game work you told me I was wasting my time on has turned out to be quite interesting to our overseas business partners. I'm flying out tomorrow to seal a big contract. And I won't be wearing my pajamas."

Good. A nice, confident lie. Turned out her newbie sorcerer had a backbone after all.

"Watch out for yourself over there." Anton didn't press further. Not a man who wasted energy on a losing strategy. He eyed Zahara again, his lips pressed into a thin line. "And watch out for your new friend."

Chapter Four

D ANIEL SPENT THE long flight from New York to Casablanca, and the shorter hop to Marrakech, doing three things. The first was adjusting his noise-cancelling headphones to drown out the chorus of screaming babies incensed by rapid changes in air pressure. The second involved slapping away Zahara's hands whenever she grew bored and tried to play the role of horny newlywed. And the last, sandwiched in between those exhausting activities, was reading up about his destination. Marrakech, the Rose City.

The hotel Zahara had selected warranted several glowing paragraphs in his hastily purchased tourist guide and, as they stepped out of the private car she had insisted on, he spotted a few wide-eyed tourists in horse-drawn carriages snapping photos of the palatial complex. A few minutes later, the two of them made their way past the hotel's front gate, oasis-like grounds, and rushing fountains to stand at the foot of tiled steps leading to the entrance. A pair of courtly valets in traditional clothing swung open massive doors to usher them in.

They were inside the gilded lobby—dominated by a statue of a warrior on a camel—for only a few seconds before a stunning woman with dark brown hair piled on her head in a chignon came to greet them. She wore a tailored white pantsuit and a discreet tag with her name in French and Arabic. "Mr. and Mrs. Goldstein?"

"That's us." Zahara reached over to squeeze Daniel's hand, ignoring his attempts to wiggle out of her grip.

The brunette flashed them a brilliant smile. "Welcome to Marrakech. We've been expecting you."

"It's a German name," Daniel broke in, wondering if he should have checked in under an alias, or his grandmother's maiden name, or any name less Jewish than "Goldstein". He was about to continue when Zahara's well-placed elbow cut him short.

"We sent our luggage ahead. Could you check to see it arrived? And we were expecting a message at the front desk."

"Your bags are already in the honeymoon suite. Congratulations to both of you." The woman gave Zahara's ring hand an appreciative glance. "And Monsieur Al Nemr is waiting for you in Le Bar Churchill."

Zahara's posture relaxed. Apparently, she had worried her local contact might not show. Did this mystery man know or care that she could pop out of a bottle in a puff of smoke any time she wanted? Daniel had no idea how many people knew Zahara and her kind were more than a myth, or what kind of guy might want to be associated with this sorcery stuff.

Zahara beamed back at the woman and spent the next few minutes admiring her bottom as she walked away to check them in at the front desk. "Now that's an ass to write home about."

"I thought you liked men," Daniel whispered.

"Unlike you, I'm not picky." Zahara accepted a pair of

room cards from the woman when she returned, and motioned for him to follow her through the lobby.

Daniel stuffed his hands in his pockets and stayed put. "Who is this Al Nemr guy, anyway? I can't go around telling everyone about this. They'll think I'm crazy."

"Relax." Zahara tucked her arm in the crook of his elbow, the very picture of a love-struck bride. "When I told Zaid about your little quest, he couldn't wait to meet you. I'm sure the two of you will get along just fine."

AT FOUR IN the afternoon, the opulent hotel bar was almost deserted. Padded leather panels and plush wingback chairs upholstered in leopard print reflected back in the darkened mirror behind the gleaming bar. Only one seat in the cool, cavelike interior was occupied, by a black-haired man in a blazer draped over a white shirt open at the collar. He rose to his feet as they approached, his dark eyes alight with a grin of welcome when he saw Zahara.

"*Cherie.*" He took a few quick, fluid steps toward them and pressed his lips against her outstretched hand. "A new look for you. I like it."

Zahara preened. "Thank you, Zaid. I spent a lot of time getting the breasts perfect." She ran her fingernails along his lapel.

This close, the man's physique was more apparent. His sculptured chest, broad and well-proportioned, tensed under his clothing. He was only a few inches taller than Daniel, but with his compact, muscular frame, he gave the impression of someone much larger and more powerful, like a big cat poised to pounce.

"And you're wearing a suit. What's up with that?"

He extended his arms to indicate the dimly lit space around them. "Dress code. My friend here knows me well enough to give us a nice dark space to meet, but Le Bar Churchill has its standards to maintain." Zaid regarded Daniel with an appraising glance. "And what does your latest plaything call himself?"

"Daniel Goldstein." Daniel stiffened at the sarcasm in the man's voice. "And I suppose you're the mysterious Monsieur Al Nemr."

"Is that the name Ibrahim gave the staff?" Zaid chuckled. "Appropriate, I suppose. So, a Goldstein from New York City? I guess you're not here to tour the mosques."

"Yes, I'm a Jew." Daniel stood up straighter. "Try not to freak out."

Zaid's grin, wide and wicked, faded for an instant before his mouth shifted into a feline smile. His teeth elongated into a set of fangs and his visage shifted, flickering between the handsome face of a man and the ghostly image of a leopard, his yellow eyes glowing with menace and hunger.

Daniel stumbled backward, too overwhelmed with shock and panic to keep his feet underneath him. He recovered enough to dash toward the room's exit, making it to within a few feet of the threshold before both doors slammed shut. A pair of animal eyes materialized in front of him, and Zaid shimmered into view around them, like an inverted Cheshire cat.

"And I'm a jinn. Try not to freak out."

Hysterical giggles broke out behind him. Zahara bent over laughing, unable to catch her breath for a few minutes.

Daniel got enough control over himself to ask a question. "How did you do that?"

Zaid shrugged. "Magic, of course." He motioned to the table he had recently vacated. "Welcome to Morocco. Have a seat, and I'll bring us all a round of the local drink. Berber whiskey, we call it."

Daniel slumped into one of the padded chairs, hoping his heart didn't pound right out of his chest, as Zaid busied himself behind the bar. Zahara perched on the edge of her seat and pulled a mirrored compact out of the designer handbag she had picked out during their New York shopping trip. "Don't worry. Zaid is quite reformed these days." She applied another layer of lipstick. "Years ago, when he was a bad jinn like me, he was very, very bad."

Zaid appeared from behind the bar bearing a brass platter, buffed into a golden sheen.

"What changed you from awful to merely terrifying?" Daniel asked.

Zahara's friend was intimidating enough in his present incarnation; Daniel could only imagine what she meant by his jinn version of a misspent youth.

"Religion." Zaid rested the platter on the table and distributed a set of jewel-colored tea glasses. "I converted a few hundred years ago to Islam. Now, *cherie* here"—he motioned to Zahara—"she's still a *shaytana*." With a smooth, practiced motion, he tipped the spout of an ornate silver teapot until steaming liquid filled the base of one of the cups, then elevated the vessel above the table, sending a golden stream several feet long crashing into the glass without spilling a drop.

"I follow that old-time religion." Zahara regarded the cup in front of her with a pout.

The drink didn't smell anything like whiskey to Daniel.

"Mint tea." Zaid completed the same ceremony for Daniel, then himself. He handed a container of sugar cubes to Zahara with a wink. "With sweetener or without. Get used to it. You'll be served it often."

Daniel leaned forward, curious despite himself, and took a sniff of the frothy green liquid. It had a pleasant, herbaceous odor. He took a sip and shifted in his seat. "So there are pagan jinn and Muslim jinn?"

"Christian ones, too." Zaid arched his eyebrows. "Even Jewish jinn. And you don't want to mess with that tribe, believe me. But enough questions about us. Why did you seek out our kind? I'm far from perfect, I'll admit, but I won't help you if you have a dark purpose."

Daniel drained his glass and gave Zahara a questioning glance. "I summoned a jinn because I received a letter from my dead grandmother. Well, I said no at first, then crazy things started happening in my apartment." Daniel shivered, not wanting to relive those particular memories. "It's been a rough week. Zahara told me you could help us track down more information here in Morocco."

"*Cherie*, as usual, told me nothing and everything." Zaid smiled at Zahara and leaned back in his chair, his legs apart. Although he had transformed back to human form, he had missed one detail—his muscular legs ended in razor-clawed spotted paws. "Feel free to start from the beginning."

Daniel didn't trust Zaid one bit, and was sure he would end up liking him even less, no matter how good-looking he was. He fished through his messenger bag and pulled out the sheaf of papers and the oil lamp he had brought from his apartment.

Zaid gave the lamp a sniff. "Dev magic. Dangerous stuff. Why did you use it?"

"What's a dev?" Daniel asked.

"You don't want to know." Zahara pushed her tea glass away. "Trust me."

"Persian jinn." Zaid ignored Zahara and answered Daniel's question as he leafed through the documents. Instead of expanding on that statement, he tapped his fingers against one of the papers. "Botbol. So you do have Arab blood. From your grandmother, you said. English is so imprecise. From the father's side or the mother's?"

"My mother's mother, yes."

Zaid grunted. "It *would* come through the maternal side for you people."

"You people?" Daniel repeated, indignant. "And what exactly comes through this special Jewish blood of mine?"

"The sight, perhaps, or the ability to cross over." Zaid examined more of the documents. "So for your first demonstration of your inherited abilities, your grandmother told you to summon a jinn. Ambitious, to say the least."

"She wanted him to raise a *marid*," Zahara said.

Zaid coughed out some of his tea, laughing. "Well, that would have been an enjoyable bargaining session to watch. I doubt it would have ended well for you. You can't even handle my sweet *cherie*, here." He grinned at Daniel. "What arrangement did you make with her, if you don't mind me asking?"

Daniel didn't see how Zahara's insistence on granting him one wish instead of three was such a topic of fascination. He was about to say as much when Zahara interrupted.

"Details, details. We can talk about all that later. For now, let's focus on you."

"When you summon a bad jinn, you have to make a bad bargain." Zaid reached out and refilled Daniel's tea glass.

Was Zaid playing along with Zahara, trying to scare him off? That didn't make sense. Turning into a giant cat had been more than enough to send Daniel running in a panic. If Zaid was serious about his religion, maybe he needed Daniel to prove he didn't have evil in his heart or something like that.

Zaid pushed more of the papers around, then paused. He unfolded another item and smoothed out the creases. "This newspaper article. Why didn't you mention it?"

"Well, for one thing, I can't read it." Daniel craned his neck to look at the clipped-out article again. Flowing foreign script outlined a large photo of what looked like the scene of a ski slope accident. "I don't read Arabic."

Zaid sighed. "That's obvious, since you can't even recognize when you're not looking at the language. This article is in Farsi, not Arabic. From the *Tehran Times*, six months ago." He squinted at the lettering. "*Cherie*, help me out here. Blasted modern Persian isn't my strong suit. If the old language was good enough for Ferdowsi, it's good enough for me."

Zahara grabbed the newspaper from him and ran her

fingers along the lines. "It's about a hiking expedition lost on Mount Damavand, in Mazanderan. Investigations underway, families in grief, that sort of thing." She crinkled her nose at the photograph. "They could have at least provided some nice close-ups of the mangled bodies to spice up the article a little."

"And that's it?" Zaid asked.

"Well there's something here at the end about the sole survivor stumbling into a ski resort, screaming he'd seen giants hanging in a huge cavern, suspended by their feet."

"There's skiing in Iran?" Daniel asked.

"Mount Damavand is the highest peak in the Middle East." Zahara popped a sugar cube in her mouth. "Nice powder at the resort, too."

So, some jinn were into winter sports. In that case, Zahara was definitely an après-ski kind of girl.

"And?" Zaid asked, gesturing again to the clipping.

His face had darkened at the name of the mountain. Maybe he wasn't fond of wintery weather, or maybe there was something else about the location that concerned him. Either way, he looked even more dangerous, if that was possible.

"And then he died." Zahara yawned and stretched out her arms. "Well, that was a nice cheery story. But I'm bored now. This tea isn't going to cut it much longer. I need a real drink."

"Fallen angels, hanging bound in a hidden cavern." Zaid drew in his breath. "Humans have sought out the cave of Harut and Marut for centuries, to force them to reveal the secrets of dark sorcery."

"Yes. My grandmother's letter said there were two angels. Two brothers." Daniel leaned forward, excited. "They've been released into the human world and they want to do something bad. Get back at humankind in some way."

"Harut and Marut would have little love for the children of mud." Zaid's expression held something even more concerning than anger—fear. "If you seek to fight those two, you won't find me helping you. Zahara needs to abide by the old laws, and stand beside you until the contract has been fulfilled. But you have no such power over me."

"You said you'd help me as long I wasn't planning anything evil." If some sort of magical showdown was brewing, the shape-shifting man in front of Daniel would be a lot more useful than a sex-and-shopping-obsessed genie diva. "What could be more of a good deed than trying to save humanity?"

"Saving my own skin." Zaid rose to his feet, shaking his head. "The two fallen ones have no reason to go after the children of fire, unless we're crazy enough to provoke them. Something wicked this way comes, Daniel Goldstein, and I plan on staying as far away as possible."

DANIEL RUBBED HIS eyes and took another gulp of his coffee, hoping the combination of caffeine and the brilliant sunshine of a Moroccan morning would help him wake up. He sat at one of the cafe-style tables next to the hotel's enormous zero-entry pool, a plate of food from the sumptuous breakfast buffet in front of him. Despite all the luxury, his first night in Morocco had been far from restful. He had spent most of it awake, trying to figure out what to do next. Their meeting with Zaid had been jarring, and not just because the male jinn could turn into a leopard whenever he felt like it. Daniel and Zahara had only a few days to come up with a plan to stop the two fallen angels Zaid had identified as Harut and Marut. They couldn't count on Zaid for help, and the last known location of the two angels was in Iran, of all places. And as of this morning, he had no idea where Zahara was either. She hadn't been in the hotel room when he woke up, so he had said her name three times, tried mumbling some magical-sounding phrases, then settled for leaving an angry note on her pillow to meet him for breakfast.

He finally spotted her walking toward him, taking her time as she strolled along one of the shaded paths around the pool's crystal-blue water. She had changed into a coral bikini under a short silk cover-up. A sweeping sun hat in matching red and large dark sunglasses completed the ensemble. Time was running out to save humanity from two monster angels, and she was dressed for a day of lounging by the pool and ordering drinks.

She plopped down in the seat across from him and snapped her fingers to call over one of the waiters.

A young man dashed over, his face growing pale as he recognized her. Ibrahim, Zaid's friend—or perhaps more—had come up to check on Daniel while Zahara flitted down to check out the hotel's high-end fashion shops. Either in New York or here in Morocco, everyone seemed to regard Zahara as nothing more than a strikingly attractive woman who liked clothes far too much. Not Ibrahim. He had spoken of Zaid in tones of awe and respect, but had been practically incapable of saying Zahara's name without stuttering in fear.

"May God protect you from one such as she," Ibrahim had said, pressing the small package he had come to deliver into Daniel's hand.

"Mimosa, *s'il vous plait*." Zahara flashed Ibrahim a smile as crisp as his starched shirt. "And extra sugar cubes, too."

"It's only eight a.m. and you're already drinking." Daniel didn't know whether to be annoyed at her lack of concern over their current predicament, or relieved she had shown up at all. "And why do you need all that sugar, anyway?"

"Sweets for the sweet," she said. "Anyway, I deserve a treat after all the great work I did last night."

"All I remember from last night is what a mistake it was to stay with you in a room with a king bed. You need to learn how to keep your hands to yourself." Daniel pushed a golden pastry with a foamy surface around on his plate as the shaken waiter rushed off to get Zahara's drink. "Should I eat this? Ibrahim recommended it."

If Zahara had any concerns about the young man who so obviously knew the truth about her and Zaid, she didn't show it. She reached over, selected a silver container next to Daniel, and poured the contents out over his dish. Golden syrup flowed into a puddle, soaking the entire plate of food. "*Beghrir.* They're pancakes you eat with honey."

Daniel grabbed two cloth napkins and tried to block the flow of the thick liquid dribbling over the lip of his plate, off the table onto his lap. "Great. Now I'm covered in this sticky stuff."

Zahara ran her tongue over her lips. "Sounds like fun to me."

He abandoned his effort to mop up the mess. "What sort of work are you talking about? I didn't even see you leave the room."

"You're still not getting the part about jinn being the unseen ones. Anyway, I was busy. First I visited Zaid and taunted him about being a coward for not helping us."

"Making fun of a guy like that doesn't sound like a good idea to me." Daniel nibbled at the pancake, then stuffed the rest of it into his mouth. "Maybe I'm in over my head. If a jinn who can turn into a giant cat is nervous about this Harut and Marut duo, I don't think I'm up for the job."

Finding out more details about the two angels had involved nothing more complicated than a quick search on his computer. Several different versions of the legend existed, but the Persian one spoke of two angels so contemptuous of mankind's immorality that they were sent down to earth to live as mortals and experience temptation. There was even a Zahara in the story, a married woman who refused the brothers' advances as they devolved into a series of sins. Hung by their feet to await the apocalypse, Harut and Marut were said to be a source of terrible, dark magic. Call it a hunch, but Daniel guessed they probably weren't in the best of moods after that experience.

"That's exactly what I told Zaid." Zahara dabbed her fingers into the dish of honey and began to lick the syrup off them, one by one. "If someone like you is brave enough to take a quest like this on, he needs to man up."

Daniel gave her a sideways glance. "You certainly know how to destroy whatever shred of self-confidence I have left. So, are the two of you some kind of supernatural item, or what?"

"Zaid prefers men." Zahara broke off their conversation to accept the mimosa from Ibrahim's shaking hands, giving Daniel a moment to recover from that revelation. "Anyway, after that I found your grandmother's old house in Morocco. So we're all set."

"All set? The two angels I need to stop are in Iran. As in the Islamic Republic of. How am I supposed to go there?"

"On a plane, with a tour group full of other tourists." Zahara took a sip of her drink. "Harut and Marut *were* in Iran. Six months ago. We need to know where they are now. Your bubbe told you to go to her house in Marrakech, and that's what we're going to do next."

"I guess we could start there, yes." It did sound like a better plan than traveling to Iran. "Finish your drink, and let's go."

Zahara wrinkled her nose at the sun overhead. "Not now. My awe-inspiring and terrifying powers peak at night."

"And those powers would be—"

She flicked her hand at him. "I don't like to brag. You'll find out if we need them, let's leave it at that. Why don't you do some sorcerer stuff, like look up how to kill giant angels? Make yourself useful for a change."

"I've already tried. The magic of the internet didn't return that answer." Daniel rose to his feet.

He hated the idea of wasting more time, but his grandmother's letter hadn't been specific about his next step.

Maybe spending the day doing research wasn't the worst idea. Zahara frowned and pointed at the table as Daniel started to leave.

Right. A tip. The guidebook had mentioned a few guidelines on that topic, and Daniel had converted some US dollars to colorful Moroccan *dirhams* at the airport. He reached into his back pocket for his wallet, his hand closing over the present Ibrahim had given him.

"I'm not sure if it would stop a fallen angel, but Ibrahim did tell me to carry this around for good luck." Daniel unpeeled layers of padded newspaper to reveal a stylized hand made from inlaid camel bone set into a bronze base. Semiprecious stones of blue and red outlined a single eye in the center of the palm.

Zahara snarled. For a moment, her face pulled back into a horrified, involuntary grin, fangs showing beneath her red lips. Then she disappeared.

Daniel took a few moments to close his mouth, then sat back down, his eyes scanning the tables around him to see if anyone had noticed that his breakfast companion had vanished into thin air.

The couple at the table closest to him seemed unaware of anything but their cups of tea and the tourist map they were poring over. Both were well into their forties, wearing sensible warm-weather vacation wear. They were accompanied by a young boy around six, clad in a bathing suit, thick eyeglasses, and a pair of inflatable water wings. He hadn't missed Zahara's invisibility trick. The child gasped and pointed at her empty chair, a delighted smile on his face.

"Stop it with the magic games." Daniel lowered his voice

to a whisper. "People can see you out here."

Actually, no one could see her. That was the problem.

"Put that awful thing away and I'll come back out." Zahara's voice came from under the table, and Daniel ducked his head underneath, hoping to find some sign of her. Feeling foolish, he tried to pretend he had dropped something, then sat back up and picked up the amulet. "Ibrahim said the Jews here call it the Hand of Miriam. His mother sells them in her shop."

"Hand of Miriam, Hand of Mary, Hand of Fatima." Zahara let out a decidedly inhuman growl. "The *hamsa* is older than your silly mud-people religions."

Daniel shoved the icon back into his pocket and Zahara materialized in front of him in human form, down to a set of ultra-white, normal-sized teeth.

"That's better." She glared at him. "What else did Ibrahim give you to ruin my day? Why not spike my drink with Syrian rue or dragon's blood sap while you're at it?"

"I have no idea what those two things are." Daniel shot another glance over at the couple next to them. They had risen to leave, mercifully ignoring their child's repeated attempts to turn their attention to Zahara. "But if you keep trying to blow our cover I'll ask Ibrahim to get me bottles of the stuff."

The boy's face fell as his parents walked away, calling over their shoulders for him to join them. Instead, he bounced over to their table to gaze at Zahara with unabashed longing.

"Look, Daddy." He spoke in a childish version of his parents' clipped British accent. "She's the cutest thing ever!

Can I take her home with me as a pet?"

The mother elbowed her husband, who turned the color of a beefsteak tomato and rushed over to scoop up the child. "Sorry about that. He's normally quite a shy boy."

Daniel blinked as the parents scurried away, telling the child in a loud voice that one shouldn't go bothering strange ladies wearing very little clothing. "What was that all about?"

"Nothing." Zahara pushed herself back from the table, her teeth bared again. She caught herself in mid-snarl and continued. "Some young children have the sight. They can see jinn in our true forms, even when we try to hide them. Most of them grow out of it."

"I would think any little kid who could see the real you would run off screaming in the other direction."

Zahara had assured Daniel she was an ancient and powerful being thousands of years old, with a true form so horrific the shock of seeing it could kill him. For his part, Daniel still had a hard time imagining Zahara as anything other than a twenty-something shopaholic with a sex addiction. In any event, she was his only option to fulfill his grandmother's request—or rather, her unearthly demand.

"Did you see the Coke-bottle glasses on their little pride and joy? He could confuse a rabid squirrel with his pet guinea pig. You go run off and put your computer skills to good use. Tonight we'll go to your bubbe's house and find out why she sent you there."

Chapter Five

ZAHARA GLIDED DOWN the narrow alleyways of the old city, pausing for a minute to let out a loud, exasperated sigh and wait for Daniel to catch up to her. The hum and bustle of activity from Jemaa el-Fnaa died down to a low buzz as they walked deeper into the maze of twisted side streets.

"Stop sightseeing and keep up." She resorted to grabbing his collar and yanking him along.

"I'm trying to get my bearings." Daniel shifted the strap of his messenger bag, then spoke to his wristwatch.

"Are you in a relationship with that thing?" Zahara asked. "Or are you just obsessed with checking the time every five minutes?"

"It's a phone and a computer," Daniel explained, slowing his words like he was speaking to an especially dense toddler. "I'm using it to check my GPS location, since I like to know where I'm going."

"You should feel right at home. We're in the old Jewish section, the *mellah*."

Everything around them was narrow and cramped, hemmed in by battered walls illuminated by a few scattered electric lights. The alley they were in was only a few streets away from the leather district, and around them, the reek of traditional animal skin preparation mingled with odors of strong spices and fresh garbage. They turned another corner. A giggling child dashed across in front of them and a scolding female voice barked out orders from a hidden window. Then they were alone.

A man stepped out of the shadows toward them, his arms crossed. Zahara smiled, the tension in her neck and shoulders fading away.

Nothing like questioning someone's manhood to ensure he did exactly what she wanted them to do. Human or jinn, men were all the same.

"Nice to see you finally grew some balls, Zaid." Zahara pushed Daniel forward. "New York City's finest sorcerer is here, and on the case."

Her friend shook his head. "This is a bad idea, *cherie*. I should have known when you called me that nothing but trouble would come of it. A *fitnah*. That's what you are."

There was no higher compliment, as far as Zahara was concerned, than being compared to a source of religious strife and temptation. She gave Zaid a wink and waved her hand at the building behind him. "We're here."

"You're sure this is the right house?" Daniel squinted at the metal door in front of them, secured with a rusted padlock. An ancient air conditioner teetered on a ledge above them, connected by frayed electrical cables to a balcony on the second floor. Black scrollwork, its complex arabesque design partially obscured by sheets of canvas thrown over it, enclosed the tiny outdoor patio.

"This is it." Zahara was sure they had the right address. She was less confident about what they would find inside.

Something about the building felt off to her.

"All the Jews left the *mellah* years ago." Zaid waved a hand at the neighborhood around them. "The ones still living in the city have homes in *la ville nouvelle* now. But this was their neighborhood for centuries. Close to the king's palace, for protection."

"What are we going to do, break in?" Daniel asked.

"Exactly." Zahara nodded to Zaid, who crouched down then leapt upward, his now-clawed toes scratching the cobblestones as his powerful hind legs propelled him into the air. He caught the railing with his hands and swung himself over to land on the balcony.

"Since I can't turn myself into a leaping leopard, I don't think that method's going to work for me." Daniel rotated in a circle, perhaps hoping to find a conveniently abandoned ladder.

Clearly, Zahara needed to do most of the thinking in this relationship. She reached around his waist, giving him a quick goosing for luck, then spread out a pair of wings from her back and launched both of them into the air.

"Holy shit." Daniel grabbed on to the railing as she dumped him next to Zaid on the balcony. "Next time, a little warning?"

"Try to keep your whining to a dull roar." Zaid eyed the chains encircling the handles to the doors in front of them. He raised an eyebrow in her direction. Apparently, Zaid's crazy moral compunctions even forbade the harmless fun of a little breaking and entering. Zahara pointed at the lock and muttered a spell. The chains cracked and shattered and the door creaked open.

The inside of the home gave every sign that no one had bothered to live in it, or clean it, for a few decades now. Dust from their feet kicked up into clouds around them as they stepped into the center of the room. Zahara waved her hand, and the patio doors slammed shut behind them, cutting off even the dim light from the street. She blinked her eyes into their elemental form. They were inside a master bedroom dominated by a sagging bed abutting a hand-carved headboard. As filthy as the scattered furniture around them was, the overall quality of it suggested the home's past inhabitants had more money than the humble exterior suggested. Zahara couldn't imagine why some enterprising young juvenile delinquents hadn't broken in years ago and sold the stuff to the local antique shops.

Daniel walked directly into a charming hand-painted armoire, giving himself a bloody nose in the process. Zaid cursed him in French, Arabic, and English, then sent a glowing fireball up toward the ceiling to flood the room in red light.

Someone had lived here recently, but scoring pricy old Moroccan antiques hadn't been high on their agenda. A pile of munitions lay stacked in one corner. Modern weaponry fascinated Zahara. So much power, so little work. To become a jinn even half as dangerous as Zaid, Zahara would have to spend centuries studying boring spells to kill her enemies, or fight a deadly battle to gain some ugly cursed sword. Modern humans only needed enough money to buy the finest means available to inflict wanton death and destruction. But from the looks of it, the semi-automatic rifles, ripped-apart cell phone parts, and body armor had an eclectic, bargain-basement feel. Whoever had left them here had gone cheap from the get-go.

Daniel knelt down to examine some recording equipment, then leafed through a set of pamphlets. "Can you read what these say? Because I have a feeling whoever left this stuff wasn't planning to shoot a music video."

Zaid pulled out a sheaf of paper and gave a snort of disgust. "If you want to rant about the worldwide Zionist-Crusader conspiracy, you might want to run a spell-check on your message before going public. The losers who wrote this misspelled *jihad*."

"Whoever they are, they like picture books." Zahara giggled as she dug out a set of color magazines with titles in English like *Big Pussy* and *Ass Man*. "But maybe they're reading these for the articles."

"Hypocritical assholes." Zaid picked up a Koran resting on the bedside table and carefully tucked it under one arm.

"We need to call the police." Daniel stood up, the glow from Zaid's night-light giving his pale, freckled skin an unnaturally ruddy glow. "There's nothing supernatural going on here. Whoever left this stuff, criminals or terrorists, broke into my grandmother's house and is planning something bad. My bubbe would be spinning in her grave if she found out."

"I thought the problem was she's already not staying put in her grave." Zahara cocked her head, her next remark slipping from her thoughts as the moaning reached her ears. Low and sobbing, as if the source had long ago given up hope anyone would hear. "Someone's in the house."

Daniel gave her a blank stare for a few moments before

the crying built up to a volume even his human ears could hear. "That sounds like a little kid. And he's hurt."

With that, Daniel flung open the bedroom door and dashed out into the darkness. Zaid gave Zahara a quick look of surprise, then sent his glowing sphere soaring out of the room as he jogged after him.

Great. Some entertaining second-story work had turned into a rescue mission. Zahara grabbed one of the guns, a cheap, Chinese-made Type 56, a rip-off of the original Russian AK-47. Modern human weapons did little damage to her kind, but the semiautomatic might be useful to scare off a common thief. If nothing else, it would make a fun souvenir.

The sobbing noises increased in volume as she made her way down a narrow stairway. Daniel disappeared around a corner and Zaid bounded down the stairs to catch up. With Zahara's more leisurely pace, she took a few extra minutes to join them on the first floor. The two men stood still in front of a closed door—Zaid's face grim and Daniel's a shade of green.

Zaid's ball of red flame floated above them, illuminating the gutted body of a young goat hanging from a stake hammered into the archway. The animal's cracked ribs splayed open to expose an empty chest cavity and white, wormlike intestines hanging from spikes embedded in the animal's blood-spattered skin. Headless, the grotesque offering spun in slow circles on the hemp rope knotted around its extended forelegs.

"What the hell is that?" Daniel clamped his hand over his mouth, suppressing a gag.

"A sacrifice and a sloppy one at that." Zahara circled around the dead goat, breathing in the scent of fresh blood. It was a recent kill. "Crappy black magic. Even your politically correct summoning had more power than this. You'd need to be calling something nasty and desperate for this botched mess to work."

"That might be the case." Zaid pointed to the door behind the slaughtered animal. Nails had been slammed into the casing to seal the entrance. The sobs switched to a high-pitched scream, leaving no doubt what was trapped in the room. A child, crying and begging for his life.

Daniel took off at a run, hitting the door with his shoulder. Zaid tucked the gold-leafed Koran into his belt and pulled out a long, curved sword as the thin lacquered wood splintered and the door burst open on its hinges. They both ran in, leaving Zahara with little choice but to join them.

Inside, the rest of the setup for the summoning was as amateurish as the mess outside. An awkward pentagram scrawled in white paint mixed with goat's blood spread over the tile floor, enclosing a wooden dining set. The overall effect resembled a picnic table surrounded by vomited Pepto-Bismol. On top of the makeshift altar, leather straps held down a struggling human boy who couldn't have been more than three or four years old. The goat's severed head rested on his thin, bare chest. He had spit out the filthy rag that had been crammed into his mouth and was screaming in terror.

And for good reason. As incompetent as the magical setup had been, the twisting tendril of black smoke rising from the floor meant something had heard the call. And a fresh, living sacrifice was waiting.

Zaid's face contorted into a feline snarl at the sight of the captive child. He was on top of the writhing smoke within seconds, the striations of the blade in his hand gleaming like ripples of water in the red light of the fireball above him.

Coming out of the seven levels was tricky. Until one's shape had solidified, they could be killed by any half-assed hero with an enchanted spoon, let alone Zaid's weapon. The Damascus-steel blade had been taking out major paranormal players long before Zahara had been a fiery gleam of lust in one of her mother's hundreds of eyes.

"There is no god." Zaid thrust his sword into the swirling shape coalescing in front of him with a savage grunt. "But God." He withdrew the blade, and the amorphous shape folded in on itself. "And He is great."

Zahara breathed a quick prayer of thanks to her own gods that she had convinced Zaid to join them. Whatever had tried to crawl out of hell and eat the child might have been more than she could handle.

She scanned the room, unfamiliar uncertainty settling into her chest. Something was wrong, but she wasn't sure what. The space around them had been a formal dining room at one time, with an arched ceiling and tiled floors. The far wall held a series of floor-to-ceiling windows draped in dark cloth, no doubt overlooking a central courtyard, or *riad*. Nothing unusual there. Then a prickling sensation of ominous weight above her caused her to look up. An enormous pendant chandelier hung from the apex of the ceiling's curves, its arrow-shaped tip aimed down at the center of the pentagram. Solid iron. No wonder she felt spooked. The light fixture struck her as a more recent addition to the house's decor, with a crude design and no evidence of years of dust collecting on its black surface. "Cut the ropes, Daniel, and take the kid."

Daniel dashed forward and fumbled at the leather straps pinning the child to the table, as the young boy thrashed wildly. He got only one tiny arm free before everything went to hell.

Flames roared over the walls, sealing off any chance of escape. The coil of smoke that had remained after Zaid's sword blow expanded like a black balloon, filling half the room. Then the bubble of darkness shattered and the angel appeared.

The cathedral ceiling of the room was over six meters above them, but he needed to bow his head to fit inside. A pair of feathered wings like a hawk's stretched out behind his back, the wingspan stretching to touch both walls. His face was chiseled, features cold and perfect. Long hair, dark and straight, fell to his shoulders. And where his eyes should have been, there was only fire.

Zahara took the prudent step of fading into invisibility. Zaid took a few precious seconds to recover from his surprise that his initial blow had done nothing to harm the winged giant in front of him. He feinted right, then took a slicing cut at the angel's leg. With an insolent, almost lazy blow, the angel swung a huge fist at Zaid's chest and sent him flying into a crumpled heap across the room. Then the creature bent down, his attention focused on the screaming child beneath him. And Daniel, who had remained crouched next to the table, did nothing but stare up at certain death with slack-jawed shock.

This was all bad and not in any way Zahara liked. Nothing she had ever encountered could have taken a hit from a sword that powerful when barely out of the levels, then come back to defeat Zaid with no obvious effort. And when it came to fight-or-flight situations, her talents laid in running away, not swordplay. But the eerie fire roaring around her had cut off the escape option, and all of them would be dead in minutes unless she did something. Time to bluff, and hope it worked.

"Hey, asshole!" Shimmering back into visibility, she stepped forward, unslung the semi-automatic from around her shoulder, and aimed it at the angel's chest. "Try picking on someone your own size."

He turned the roaring flames of his eyes toward her, sneering condescension twisting his flawless features. She squeezed the trigger, firing a round at his chest. The bullets froze in midair, inches from his body, then dropped to the floor. Useless as it was, it made him step away from the table and advance toward her. He raised his fist and brought it down with massive force.

Zahara darted to one side at the last second. The angel's balled-up hand left a gaping hole in the floor where she'd stood only moments before. Another round from her weapon sent a volley of bullets toward the ceiling. They ricocheted off the chandelier, showering sparks over him. His other fist followed, quicker than the first. She moved even faster to dodge it. Fading back into invisibility, she dashed between the angel's legs, risking a quick glance toward the center of the room.

Daniel had shaken off his paralysis. But instead of leaving her and Zaid to deal with the monster, which was what she would have done, he remained at the table, working to free the child with dogged determination. He was, beyond a doubt, the worst evil sorcerer any jinn ever had the misfortune to be summoned by. If they survived this debacle, which seemed less likely by the minute, she was going to kill him herself.

The oversized angel whipped his head around, trying to spot her without success. Few of even the most powerful jinn could see past her invisibility spell, which she had spent years honing to a fine art. If brute strength and invincibility were the angel's strong points, perception was a weak link. She needed to exploit that to have any chance of getting them out of this.

Zaid lay groaning in the corner and with her disappearance the angel again turned his attention to the altar. The boy stared up at the monster standing over him, and his screams died away. His lips moved in a soundless plea for his mother.

Another unaccustomed sensation constricted Zahara's chest, closing off her next breath and bringing stinging tears to her eyes. Terror, loss, and the death of an innocent. The sacrifice of a living child would give the angel tremendous power in this world—a world in which he was already the most dangerous entity she had ever fought, with the possible exception of her mother.

Zahara needed to be small, fast and airborne. Like it or not, that meant transforming into her hated elemental form. With a running jump, Zahara's true shape soared upward toward the ceiling, her leathery wings flapping silently through the stale air.

The angel reached down for the boy, as Daniel ripped the last restraint off the child and rifled through his messenger bag. What was he thinking? This was *not* the time to hunt for his cell phone.

Daniel pulled out his *hamsa* and held it up with a shaking arm, blocking the boy's body from the monster's grasp with his own. The angel recoiled, a growl bubbling up through his lips. Then a sword the size of a small car appeared in his hand, flames racing along the blade.

The few seconds of distraction gave Zahara time to get into position. Banking left, she soared past the chandelier, extending her claws out and slicing through the chain holding it aloft, a shiver vibrating through her body as she touched iron.

For an instant, the weakened chain strained and groaned under the weight of the light fixture. Zahara folded her wings flat against her tiny body and dove straight down. Slowing her descent at the last second, she gave a sharp kick with both hind legs and knocked Daniel out of the way. Then she reached out with her front paws and pounced on the child, rolling over and over with him until they toppled off the table and onto the floor.

The angel turned his gaze upward, his brow furrowed in confusion and his sword still raised for the killing blow. The tortured chain snapped and the light fixture plunged downward, the pendant tip embedding itself into his chest. With a howl of anger and disbelief, the angel collapsed, shattering the table into a pile of splinters.

Zahara lay panting on top of the child. He reached up, his thin arms tightening around the soft fur of her body in a grateful hug. *"Kitty,"* he murmured, speaking an Amazigh dialect. *"Nice kitty."* Invisibility spell or not, the little boy could see the real her.

The skin around the gaping hole in the angel's chest bubbled and blackened. He raised his head and stared around him, evidently shocked by his unceremonious landing.

Zaid staggered to his feet, dragging his sword behind him, and raised his blade over the winged monster's neck. The angel flung a massive arm out to block the blow and sent Zaid sprawling, but at the cost of a deep slash to his forearm.

Daniel yanked a cardboard box out of his bag and dashed forward; Zaid picked himself up off the floor. The two of them advanced on the angel. Zaid held his sword at the ready as Daniel ripped off the box's cover and poured its powdery contents around the prostrate giant.

Despite herself, Zahara was impressed. Between the trick with the *hamsa* and trapping the fallen angel in a ring of salt, Daniel was proving himself to have something approaching a brain.

With a roar, the angel yanked the chandelier tip out of his chest, pushed aside its metal weight, and rose to his feet. The child wailed in terror, clutching Zahara even tighter.

The walls shook, and an unearthly woman's scream echoed through the room, followed by a series of curses even Zahara wasn't familiar with. As if doused with a torrent of water, the flames roaring over the walls extinguished into a small sizzle. The angel gave them all one last, hate-filled glare from his fiery eyes. Then, with a thunderclap and a hiss of menace, he disappeared back into a swirl of smoke and flame.

Zaid fell to his knees, gasping for breath. Daniel eased himself into a sitting position on the floor next to him.

He waved a hand at the fading echoes reverberating through the dining hall. "I think my grandmother *did* roll over in her grave."

Zahara reappeared in human form, the sobbing child in her arms, clinging to her neck. He stared up at her transformed shape, his brown eyes wide and wondering.

"Angel," he said.

With a jolt, Zahara realized he was talking about her.

Chapter Six

DANIEL STEPPED OUT of the taxi, then turned to scoop the young boy they had rescued into his arms as Zaid murmured something to the driver and slipped him a roll of bills. The child smelled of urine and fear, and he clutched Daniel's hamsa in one grimy fist. Daniel tried shifting him into a more comfortable position, with his head resting against his shoulder, but the child spotted Zaid and screamed. Daniel patted the boy's back to soothe him as he shrieked out a few words in an unfamiliar language and buried his face into Daniel's shirt, sobs shaking his thin frame again.

"Why is he so afraid of you?" Daniel asked.

The child had been as reluctant to be pried out of Zahara's arms as she was frantic to hand him off, but once Daniel whispered some reassuring—but no doubt incomprehensible—words into his ear, he had calmed down. That was, unless Zaid was anywhere where he could see him.

"He has the sight." Zaid sped up to walk a few steps ahead, where the boy couldn't spot him. "He's able to see my elemental form. As you've discovered, I can be a little alarming until you get used to me."

"But he couldn't get enough of Zahara." Daniel found himself whispering, even though they were alone on the

65

darkened street where the jumpy taxi driver had dropped them off. This section of town had a more modern feel, with smart storefronts advertising Western-style clothing mixed in with large concrete apartment buildings. "She told me her true form was so awful I'd drop dead if I saw it."

Zahara hadn't stayed with them for long after their quick exit from his grandmother's house. After a muttered conversation with Zaid, she had disappeared into roiling clouds of smoke while a crack of thunder split the air. That left Daniel alone with Zaid, and the two of them had wasted little time in getting themselves and the child as far away as possible from the house.

Zaid chuckled. "*Cherie* can be quite dramatic. I've seen her true form. It would send far more human men running to her side than fleeing in fear."

"So this little boy can see jinn as they actually are?" Daniel asked. "Maybe that's why he was picked for the sacrifice."

"I wouldn't doubt it." Zaid motioned for Daniel to stop under the flickering yellow glow of a streetlight. "Take his little hand in yours and look at his palm. I don't want to get too close. He's been frightened enough tonight to last a lifetime."

Daniel loosened one of the sleeping child's arms. The boy's hands were large compared to the rest of him, like a puppy with oversized paws. "Are you some sort of a palm reader?"

"There's only one line I care about." Zaid reached out to take Daniel's hand in his, then ran his index finger over the upper part of his palm. The overall sensation was far from unpleasant. "You see here, where you have two horizontal creases parallel to each other?"

Daniel nodded, finding that the smooth touch of Zaid's skin sent most rational thoughts fleeing from his brain. He shook his head to clear it, then looked back at the boy's hand, now limp in his grasp. The child had fallen asleep with the rocking motion of the walk, his chest rising and falling with hiccuping breaths; even unconsciousness couldn't banish the horrors of the night from his mind. "He has one horizontal line, not two."

"As I thought." Zaid released Daniel's hand and resumed walking at a brisker pace. "This is a mark some humans carry."

"I remember reading something about a so-called simian crease," Daniel said. "I have a cousin whose little girl has Down's Syndrome, and that's one of the physical signs of it."

"Mostly boys have this mark," Zaid said. "And it puts them in great danger. Dark magicians associate it with the sight and other powers, although only a few with one transverse crease have special abilities. Children with hands like this are used in black magic, like the sacrifice we stopped. Or they're abducted and butchered, their body parts sold to other sorcerers."

"Dear God." Daniel's stomach churned, and for a moment he thought he might vomit. He got a handle on himself. The child needed his help, and breaking down wasn't an option. "Shouldn't we go to the authorities?"

"When the powers-that-be find what's in your grandmother's house, neither of us wants to be included in the investigation, trust me," Zaid said. "As for the child, don't worry. I know someone who'll help us."

He swung to a stop and pointed at a small home adjacent to a tall tower lit with a glowing green light. "The imam of the mosque I go to lives here. It's not the first time I've shown up in the middle of the night with nothing but trouble for him."

Zaid's sharp knock on the front door went unanswered for several minutes. Daniel squirmed, trying to adjust the little boy's position to get a glance at his watch. It had to be two or three in the morning—hardly the time to drop by for a casual visit.

"I don't understand what happened back there." Daniel paused for a moment, trying to come up with questions for Zaid. Of course, he didn't fully understand it. On some level, he still didn't believe he had been caught up in a magical conflict where actual lives were at stake, including his own. And that of the small child he held in his arms. "I thought I had until Saturday to stop something horrible from happening. *When the moon enters the house of Sa'd Bula*— that's what my grandmother wrote."

Zaid had lifted his hand to knock again, but at Daniel's question he froze and turned to him. "You didn't say anything about a Lunar Mansion connection to this glorious mess."

"That's because I don't know anything about medieval moon astrology," Daniel said. "I asked Zahara, and she figured out the date."

"Celestial magic is hardly Zahara's forte," Zaid replied. "She was off by a few days. The moon is in the twenty-third mansion, the house of Sa'd Bula, tonight."

"That's good, then. We stopped one of the fallen ones,

or whatever they call themselves."

"We barely got away with our lives." Zaid sighed. "I wish I had known this a little earlier. But it makes sense. Tonight is the perfect time for a magic spell to release a captive. At least one of the two angels isn't fully free."

"He was free enough to almost kill us," Daniel said. "And we still have his brother to worry about."

The door creaked open, ending the conversation. An older man with a graying beard stood framed in the doorway. His wrinkled forehead bore a reddened mark in the center, like a chronic bruise. As he recognized Zaid, his eyes, soft and friendly, widened.

"*As-salamu alaykum, ya sayyidi.*" Zaid took a hesitant step forward, and the imam reached out to kiss him on both cheeks before returning the greeting and waving him inside.

Daniel stepped over the threshold, trying not to awaken the boy. Zaid motioned to him and switched to English.

"Imam Youssef, this is Daniel Goldstein, visiting us from the United States. We've run into a little trouble tonight. I took him into the *mellah* to visit his family's old house there. The boy was inside."

Daniel rested the boy as gently as he could on a nearby couch, lifting his hamsa from the child's hand. He stirred but didn't wake. In the direct light of the imam's living room, the bruises and scrapes on the child's wrists and ankles were more apparent. His shirt, stained with goat's blood, was partially torn, exposing a series of unfamiliar symbols scratched into the skin of his abdomen.

Imam Youssef gasped. Shaking his head, he bent over to take a closer look at the marks. The boy's eyelids fluttered open, and he reached out to get a reassuring grasp from

Daniel's hand.

"The ones that did this…" the imam's voice trailed off.

"Enough evidence in the house for the police to track them down, I would hope." Zaid shifted position, trying to avoid the child catching a glimpse of him. "As for the creature they summoned, I'll take care of that problem myself."

"Not alone, you won't." Daniel's firmness surprised even himself.

Imam Youssef pulled a blanket over the child up to his chest and stroked his forehead. Nothing about the conversation, bizarre as it was, appeared to surprise him. "I'll give you a blessing, brother Zaid, for the work you need to do among your own kind." He walked to a nearby table and came back with a rectangular business card he pressed into Daniel's hand. "What you did tonight was a good deed. A *mitzvah*, as your people would say. But for what you might face out there, I would counsel you to seek out religious advice from those of your faith. Here's the card of a friend of mine, a rabbi who does not shut his eyes to the evidence of the unseen world around him."

Daniel tucked the card into his pocket and looked down at the child. "Will he be all right?"

The imam nodded. "There's a ceremony to cleanse him of the dark spirits that gathered around him. And my wife will have him washed up and stuffed with food while I make inquiries about his parents."

"I'll have to excuse myself from your hospitality, then." Zaid headed toward the door, waving at Daniel to join him. "I make your wife as nervous as I make the child, and Daniel and I have a good deal of work to do."

Chapter Seven

Z AHARA PAUSED AT the door of the tea house, trying to decide what unsettled her more—that her mother had journeyed to the human realm, or that she had agreed to meet her daughter in the middle of the day. Both actions were so out of character, Zahara didn't know what to make of them.

As soon as she could get away from Daniel and Zaid, she had traveled through the seven levels of hell to her clan's vast fortress in the far eastern reaches of the Mountains of Qaf, the world of the jinn. Withering criticism of her less-than-demonic lifestyle, her decision to remain in the human world, and, of course, her lack of interest in the host of potential suitors her family had chosen for her—all this she expected upon her return. Not finding her mother home to lead the chorus of disapproval? Now, that was a surprise. Her mother rarely left the fortress, let alone the Mountains of Qaf.

But a host of anxious relatives had informed her that Lilitu, devourer of souls and matriarch of the clan, had crossed over to the world of man. Even more startling was her mother's choice of vacation destinations—Mount Damavand in Iran. The same location Daniel's newspaper article listed as the site of the mysterious mountaineering accident, and the same location that hid the cave of Harut and Marut.

Zahara was quite sure her mother had little interest in either skiing or mountain climbing, although restarting the eruptions of a stratovolcano might be a prank she would find amusing. In any event, the only way to find out was to ask her mother, who was currently in Tehran, about a three-hour drive from Mount Damavand. Not that her mother often chose to take human modes of transportation.

She stepped into the tea house, confident she would attract little attention. Unlike in Morocco, where she had played the role of a Western tourist traveling with her husband, here she adopted the persona of a fashionable Iranian city girl, her hair covered with a loose head scarf color-coordinated with her foreign purse and stylish boots. The *chaikhaneh* held a mixed dinner crowd of older, gossiping men and groups of women and families. The building itself was an old one, with soaring geometric arches covered in mosaics and lit by ornate red chandeliers. The atmosphere and light evening menu had attracted a gaggle of European tourists, who chattered in German at a table under one of the arches and shared puffs off the hose of a tobacco water pipe.

Picking her mother out of the crowd wasn't difficult. Lilitu sat alone in a darkened alcove in the back, dressed in a black chador covering everything but her eyes. Even at this distance, the cloud of gloom emanating from her was all but palpable. Although Zahara knew full well how deaf, dumb, and blind modern humans were to the unseen world, she had to wonder why everyone in the room hadn't run out screaming long ago.

Perhaps her mother had been too distracted to devour any human who caught one of her many eyes. Or, more likely, she had just eaten. Zahara made her way around the diners and slipped into a seat next to her, folding her hands on the table and trying not to look guilty.

Her mother made a sound approximating a hiss, before clucking in irritation at her lapse into one of the many inhuman languages she spoke. A waiter jumped over to the table at the sound, producing a beautiful porcelain and brass samovar and depositing clear glasses and a plate of flatbread before them. A faint tremor in his hands betrayed the fact that he, unlike the oblivious diners around them, had some understanding of who he was serving.

The waiter attempted to leave a plate of rock sugar crystals infused with golden saffron on the table, but a snarl from Zahara's mother made him snatch them back. He beat a hasty retreat, as her mother's eyes flashed into reptilian form, slit pupils dilated in fury. They faded gradually back into a normal human brown.

"Have some tea, dear." Her mother reached out her hand, her gloves outfitted with extra material in the fingers to accommodate her claws. She was terrible at human transformation. "It's been so long. I've missed you."

Zahara lifted the cup of reddish tea to her lips, breathing in the faint scent of rose petals, and cast a longing glance at the other diners, many of whom drank the hot liquid through the chunks of sugar held in their teeth. Her entire clan found sweets repellent to the point that sugar could be used along with certain fragrances to drive them away from a planned attack on a human victim. In this, as in so many other things, Zahara was nothing like her family.

"Nice to see you too, Mother." Zahara gulped down the tea, wishing it had been served scorching enough to burn the pleasantries out of her mouth. Any conversation with her family that started without the actual drawing of weapons meant she was in even more trouble than usual. "I went home to visit, but the husbands told me you had decided to cross over."

Her mother made a habit of collecting husbands, some of whom survived long enough for Zahara to remember their names. None of them was her father. For all she knew, the crushing disappointment brought upon her family by her birth had doomed the man to banishment or death. Husbands had been devoured for far less.

"Unpleasant as it is to visit the land of the mud people, I needed to see certain things for myself." Lilitu lifted up the lower edge of her veil and sipped the tea. Despite her mother's usual insistence that blood spiked with alcohol was the only proper drink for someone of her stature, Zahara had seen her partake of some particularly bitter caffeinated beverages. "I hope you've come to me, my daughter, to tell me you've decided to return home for good."

"Not exactly." Zahara did her best not to squirm in her seat. "But I do have good news. I found a sorcerer performing his first summons and succeeded in tricking him. His soul is mine as soon as the bargain's completed."

Her mother drummed her nails against the table in irritation. The black fabric of the gloves began to tear, revealing the sharpened tips of her claws. Lilitu might have been the master of disguising herself as an alluring seductress in her youth, but centuries away from contact with actual people had taken their toll. Not that she would ever admit it. "You've never demonstrated the ability to carry out a simple demonic possession, much less the skills required to handle a human sorcerer of significant power."

"This sorcerer is totally clueless, so that's not the problem." Zahara played with the flatbread for a minute but didn't eat any. She had been so hungry before she had seen her mother. "It's his wish. I might need the teensiest bit of help with it."

"Take him to a treasure trove." Her mother's two visible eyes roved over the room, as if she was concerned the place might be unsafe. It was, of course—for everyone *but* her. "Greedy creatures, sorcerers."

"He doesn't want money." Zahara gave up on any thoughts of eating and pushed her plate to the side. "I already asked Zaid to help me, since he owes me and all, but this is out of his league."

Her mother growled, and Zahara cursed herself for bringing up Zaid at all.

"I don't approve of your association with that apostate. His clan was right to cast him out of the Mountains of Qaf, and you shouldn't have carried a message to them from him. The *hamar* may be our enemies, but they've always held to the old ways."

As alliances and battles went in the Mountains of Qaf, the *hamar*, or the red jinn, were more likely to be on her family's side than against them. But Lilitu considered everyone an enemy.

Maybe she should change the subject for a few minutes,

get her mother in a better mood before asking for help. "So you went to Mount Damavand? I've been skiing there a few times."

Her mother paused her careful inspection of people entering the tea house long enough to give a confused grunt.

"Humans strap smooth boards on their feet and slide down on the snow, as fast as they can." Zahara pantomimed a skier's moving feet with her hands. "Most of the time they aren't even killed or maimed at the end of it."

"I have little patience for your obsession with trivialities. My trip to the cursed mountain had only one purpose—to visit the cave of Harut and Marut."

Zahara shouldn't have been as surprised as she was. If something awful and diabolical had been unleashed into the world, it stood to reason her mother would be tangled up in it somehow.

"The two fallen ones," her mother clarified. At Zahara's continued stunned silence, Lilitu clucked her tongue in disapproval. "You know every detail of the mud people's sordid little lives and you've not heard of them? They're a source of great magical knowledge, if one wishes to pay the price. Or at least, they were."

"Is one of them the size of a house, with flaming eyes and a terrible attitude?" Zahara decided it would be best to ease into the part of the conversation where she revealed she did, in fact, know something about Harut and Marut. Something even her mother didn't.

"Marut would appear so now, at least after darkness has fallen and he's free to roam the earth." Her mother's gaze fell on a beam of sunlight gleaming through the stained-glass windows of the tea shop. "During the hours of light he remains trapped in the cave, where he and I had a conversation. Harut, his brother, is another matter entirely."

"Oh." Zahara made a great show of refilling her mother's tea glass. "What did the two of you chat about?"

"His desire to tear open every portal to our land and unleash a war between the mud people and those of smokeless fire." Her mother took another sip of her tea and motioned for Zahara to have some herself.

At this point, Zahara had long since lost both her appetite and her thirst for anything that didn't contain a substantial percentage of alcohol. "That sounds a little drastic."

"The dev of Persia agree with you." The powerful jinn of Iran, renowned for their devious plots and the cruel subtlety of their magic, were another group her clan often allied with—or fought against—depending on the circumstances. "They say our world should remain unseen, and feel that Marut should be destroyed before he can bring his plan to fruition."

Zahara lifted her cup, now breathing in relief along with the aroma of roses. This was so perfect. Anyone her mother wanted dead, got dead. Sooner rather than later. "Now, *that's* what my sorcerer wants."

"Marut's death? That's what the simpleton sorcerer you spoke of asked of you?" Her mother leaned forward, gripping the edge of the table so hard her claws sank into the wood. Her eyes morphed again, and the edges of her shape began to blur. Zahara shrank back. What had she said wrong? If her mother got any more upset, she would lose her transformation entirely, and that wouldn't be pretty. Especially for the humans in the teahouse.

"Daniel's grandmother called him from beyond the grave and told him to summon a jinn to stop the two fallen ones." The truth tumbled out of her. "I brought Zaid along to do any fighting for me, but when we took away Marut's sacrifice, things didn't go exactly as planned."

Her mother sat still for a moment, unblinking—another problem with her human transformation. Even people under a powerful spell began to notice a dead stare like that after an hour or so. "Which of the three of you intervened to save the child?"

Zahara thought back to the little boy in her arms, crying and hugging her after she had snatched him off the table seconds before Marut reached out to devour him. She had been invisible then, and even Zaid and Daniel hadn't seen that actual moment. It had been a neat trick. But it wasn't the sort of demonic activity her mother approved of.

"Daniel was the closest, I guess." She beamed at her mother. "That's my sorcerer's name. I mean, he'll be mine soon enough, right?"

"This *Daniel*," Lilitu said, dragging every syllable out for emphasis, "interfered with the sacrifice. If it had been completed, Marut's power would be incalculable. I doubt even I could stop him after that."

Zahara gave her mother a modest wave. "It wasn't that big a deal. Daniel wasn't quite as incompetent as I thought he would be, and his grandmother's ghost helped out." She leaned forward to help her mother yank her embedded claws out of the table and held her hand. "So it should be no problem at all for you to wipe the floor with Marut. I can't wait to see it."

"I planned that sacrifice myself." Lilitu's words were as precise and cold as snow crystals. "I gave detailed instructions to Marut's pathetic human minions. All was as it should be, until the youngest and weakest of my offspring blundered into the whole affair."

Zahara released her mother's hand and collapsed back in her seat. "But I thought you and the dev were working together to stop Marut."

"That's what the dev think, yes." Her mother's transformation had slipped again, and now her eyeballs were burning coals of rage. Honestly, if she would just ask Zahara for help, she could fix that for her. "What I want them to think. As much as I despise his kind, I agree with Marut's plan for vengeance. Humans have grown too numerous, too powerful. A rebalancing of the natural order is required."

"That's crazy." Zahara didn't intend for the words to come out as bluntly as they had, but it was a little too late to worry about pissing off her mother. "You don't know anything about the modern world, Mother. Things have changed, and they continue to change, more rapidly than ever. There are few enough of us as it stands, and you want to start a war with several billion people?"

"I know how few of us there are." One tendril of black wound itself out of her mother's sleeve, then another. Raving fury and a human body didn't go well together, in her mother's case. "What I had to do to produce you all but destroyed me."

"If you've finished explaining to me for the hundredth

time what a terrible disappointment I am, I'll run along." Zahara went so far as to stand up in defiance, even though her knees were shaking. "I'm stuck in a magical contract to stop the two fallen ones from starting a world war between mud and fire. If you won't help me, I'll figure it out myself."

Zahara tilted her chin in the air and turned her body to leave, hoping the bluff would have its intended effect. She and her mother couldn't be on opposite sides of this conflict. They just couldn't.

Her mother remained uncharacteristically silent for a few moments. "Then that is how it must be. You are young, yes, but you are of age. If you entered into a contract with this sorcerer, there's nothing I can do." Lilitu noticed the tendrils escaping from her body and patted them back into her clothing. "The timing of this is most unfortunate. I'm too busy to run off and engage in a blood feud to avenge your death right now."

Zahara's lower lip trembled, but she pressed her mouth into a firm line. "For your information, I have no intention of losing." She yanked the handle of her purse over her shoulder and prepared to leave—for real this time—but her mother spoke again.

"What of Harut, the second brother?"

"Haven't run into him yet."

That was it then. Her last hope, that her mother would get her out of the terrible mess, had evaporated. But Marut wasn't invincible, at least not yet, and maybe she and Zaid could figure out a way to stop him. Maybe if she succeeded, her mother might finally admit Zahara had done one thing right. And if she died in the process, Lilitu would have no choice but to avenge her death, no matter how inconvenient it was for her schedule. "Want me to give him your regards when I do?"

"He's working against his brother, not with him." Her mother's rage faded, and for a moment, she looked like nothing more than an ordinary middle-aged woman, saddened and fatigued after an argument with her daughter. "Stay away from Harut, Zahara. For you, he's the most dangerous one of all."

ZAHARA PUSHED ASIDE the grimy curtain she had materialized behind and stepped out of a storeroom tucked into a remote corner of the Marrakech *souk*. The open-air space was crammed with plastic bags stuffed with dried lizard skins, twisted roots, and fungi more suitable for poisoning enemies than livening up a stew.

On the other side of the narrow alley, a wooden stall filled with similar items was presided over by an older woman, the deep lines of her dark features set off by a white headscarf. Zahara was back in her human persona of a clueless tourist, but the saleswoman clutched a thin talisman to her chest as their eyes met for a brief instant. Zahara's skin prickled. She didn't need a better view of the object to tell it was identical to Daniel's *hamsa*. The woman who gripped its twin so tightly must be Ibrahim's mother.

Zahara tensed for a moment before stalking past the woman, who inclined her head in respect. Nothing more than a local witch, selling charms to protect against the evil eye, but she knew when a jinn crossed her path.

Anyway, what difference did it make that the woman had recognized her? Zahara had bigger problems to worry about. Like *her* mother.

She had stormed out of the tea house in Tehran, then hovered around the area all day and throughout the night, hoping her mother might change her mind and seek her out. When dawn finally came—the least auspicious time to travel through the levels—Zahara had given up and returned to Morocco.

Early morning sunlight darted through the open areas of the mazelike market around Jemma el-Fnaa, depressing Zahara's mood further. Around her, most of the salespeople were occupied setting up their stalls for a busy shopping day. She turned a corner at the last moment to avoid the path out of the *souk* and back to the hotel. Zaid wasn't exactly an early riser, and with any luck Daniel was sleeping in as well. If she was up at this hour and no one was missing her, she might as well swing by grandma's house to see the aftermath.

Several tense-looking soldiers hovered around the entrance as she approached. Slipping by them into the house while invisible would be easy, but she had a queasy feeling about going back in alone.

All of this thinking about subjects other than sex or shopping was making her depressed. After all, the three of them had taken on a monster angel and lived to tell about it. That certainly called for a celebration, since future victories were likely to be in short supply. In fact, a case could be made that she had saved Zaid's life. She should demand some sort of reward from him for that. Jewelry, perhaps, and several free drinks. Or maybe a threesome with him and Daniel.

Buoyed by naughty thoughts, Zahara almost walked right past without noticing him. Then she stopped, enthralled. The most beautiful man she had ever laid eyes on was leaning against a doorway, his smoky green eyes regarding the armed men milling around the alleyway with quiet intensity. Once she focused in on him, everything else faded away. He was tall, with wavy chestnut hair, cheekbones as defined as ocean-side cliffs, and lips that begged to be kissed. She held out an arm and pressed her palm against a nearby wall to support herself as her heart missed a few beats. Zaid, Daniel, and the imminent danger the world was in could wait. This honey wasn't getting past her.

She gathered herself together and took off with a skipping gait along the alleyway, taking care to toss her head from side to side, as if she couldn't get enough of the exotic urban sprawl around her. Then she walked right into him.

"Oh!" She clasped a hand to her mouth in exaggerated dismay. "I'm so sorry. I didn't even see you there."

Close-up, the man was even more breathtaking. His jeweled eyes rested on her for a moment, a look of gentle concern crossing his face.

"That happens sometimes, I'm afraid." His voice was low, alluring, and carried the slightest hint of an accent she couldn't place. Not British. And certainly not American. She could listen to it all night long. And fully intended to, after she was finished hearing his moans of ecstasy.

"You speak English. Great!" She adopted her best "dumb American" accent. "To be honest, I was getting a little nervous. You see, I decided to wander around by myself to see the sights, and now I'm so lost. Do you think you could walk me back to my hotel?"

"You'll be back there before you know it." His tone was confident, commanding and reassuring. For a quick moment Zahara felt herself taking a step back away from him, a smile on her face and a wonderful feeling of contentment settling deep inside of her.

Then the real Zahara returned. He wasn't going to brush her off that easily. Sword-fighting feathered monsters might not be her cup of warmed bloodwine, but seducing handsome strangers was one of her specialties. "I'm worried about being in a strange, foreign city all by myself." She brushed her hand against his arm. He wore a pair of loose white pants and a simple shirt that molded over his well-defined chest and biceps. Easy, casual clothing that would be so easy and casual to peel off of him, as soon as she lured him back to her hotel room. "Tell you what. You help me find my way to the hotel, and I'll buy you breakfast."

"I doubt I'd be of much assistance as a guide. I'm new here myself." His gaze returned to the display of military force across the street. "I'm sorry, Miss—"

"Zahara." She ran her fingers down his arm. His skin was warm and soft, and he even smelled great. Like hot desert sand, mixed with a hint of sandalwood.

He jerked his head toward her, focusing in as if seeing her for the first time. "Your name is Zahara?"

"Yes, do you like it?" She sidled up a little closer so he could look down her shirt, if he wanted. "What's your name?"

"I was known as Harut, once." His gaze fell to the ground, his face somber.

A nagging thought intruded into her expansive and wonderful new mood. Where had she heard that name before? It sounded awfully familiar. It had to do with something important she needed to deal with. Yes, something important and depressing and awful.

Well, then. Maybe she should forget all about it and focus on him.

"I knew a woman named Zahara. A long time ago. She was as lovely as a star." His lips parted into a smile as his eyes met hers, and she did her best to remain upright. She fell into lust on a regular basis, but this was intense. And amazing. "You're beautiful, like she was. That's why you should leave now. I'm not meant for that sort of love."

She blinked a few times, tried to figure out what he had told her, then gave up. After all, she wasn't looking for deep conversation here. He could keep babbling on forever as long as she landed him in bed. "Don't worry, we've all been there. Bad breakup, on the rebound like a rubber bullet bouncing off someone's head—I can totally relate. How about we sit down over coffee and you tell me all about that awful bitch?"

"You are difficult to influence." He tilted his head, as if perplexed, then stared back at the scene across the street. "I must ask you to leave, for your own safety. There are dark things stirring in this city."

Zahara wanted to stir up something in his pants, not continue to go around in verbal circles. He had seemed interested in her for a few minutes. "Any dark things that wanted to stir up a little hell in that house did it two nights ago. Watching it now won't do you any good."

That did it. He snapped his attention back, taking a step forward to tower over her. My, he was tall. A little intimidating, even.

"What do you know about it?"

"Long story." Zahara parted her lips into a wide smile. Like a sheriff in the wild, wild west, she always got her man. "Come with me and I'll tell you all about it."

Chapter Eight

Daniel found Zaid at one of the hotel's poolside tables. His seat had been pushed as far as possible under the shade of a broad-leafed tree. Even from this distance, the jinn looked uncomfortable in the full light of day. His eyes were hidden behind mirrored sunglasses, and the touch of stubble around his face gave him a reasonable chance of being mistaken for a man recovering from a night of excessive partying, not a paranormal creature nursing wounds from a fight with a winged monster.

Daniel made his way past the welcoming phalanx of waiters, the last of whom tugged at his arm and nodded toward the corner. A sheen of sweat shone on Ibrahim's forehead. "Monsieur Al Nemr has been waiting for you, Mr. Goldstein. In the morning, out here in the open. He might not be in the best of moods."

"I had an early meeting, I'm sure he'll understand." Daniel gave Ibrahim a reassuring clap on the shoulder and strolled over to drop in the chair next to Zaid. "Let me guess. You're not a morning person."

"You're late." Zaid tilted his sunglasses down. "And what's that in your pocket?"

Daniel felt the heat rise up his face. He tried to stammer back a response, but Zaid glanced at him and gave a sigh of exasperation.

"I wasn't trying to be cute. I meant it literally. What's inside your pocket? I can sense it from here."

"Oh." Daniel dug around for a moment before producing the hamsa that had saved his life last night. "This. It set that killer angel back on his heels, so I figured I should carry it around in case he shows up again."

Zaid pushed his chair back and grimaced. "Something's changed. Your charm is stronger, more powerful."

"Rabbi Shlomo blessed it for me. He's the one Imam Mohammed told me about. I met him early this morning." Daniel paused for a moment as a nervous Ibrahim swooped in to deposit a carafe of coffee, a glass of orange juice, and a plate of food in front of him. The waiter rested a tumbler filled to the brim with ice and clear liquid in front of Zaid, sweeping away an empty glass. "There's an actual synagogue in the old city. He holds services there and everything." He stuffed some food into his mouth and squinted as Zaid took a sip of his drink. It didn't smell like water. "Is what you're drinking... alcoholic?"

"It damn well better be, or I'll show Ibrahim and the hotel staff what it's like to be trapped in a haunted hotel for a few nights." Zaid tilted the glass back and drained half its contents. He licked his lips. "At least the goddamn Russians have brought some decent vodka with them."

"I thought you weren't supposed to drink."

"I give it up for Ramadan." Zaid placed the glass back on the table. "And I've got news for you, my cousin. That imported French ham you're snacking on isn't exactly *glatt* kosher."

A familiar flounce and wiggle caught Daniel's eye. Zahara had finally made an appearance. She hadn't returned to the hotel the night they fought the angel, or the next. Visiting the world of the jinn to find out more about Harut and Marut, Zaid had said, after Daniel had pressed him. Daniel suspected she had spent the time slinking around local bars and plotting how to further damage his credit card with another shopping trip.

"Well, Zahara's back." Daniel shaded his eyes to get a better look. She was wearing a light floral top and pants, a glowing smile, and had an absolutely gorgeous man on her arm. He looked like he had strolled off the pages of a men's modeling shoot, and she was all but throwing herself at him. "She picked up some random guy on the street and decided to take him home, I think."

Zaid yawned and drained the rest of his drink, scanning the patio for a sign of Ibrahim and another refill. "Since she's supposed to be your wife, perhaps you should step in before the poor bastard ends up as her eternal sex slave. For our sake, not his. She's distracted enough."

"Can't say I blame her." The green-eyed man next to Zahara was drawing closer, and growing more attractive with every step. He made the whole day more beautiful, more wonderful, merely by his presence. Daniel had no idea who he was, or why he had chosen to join them, but he needed to go to talk to him, bask in his goodness, answer any questions he might have…

"*Malak!*" Zaid snarled the word and flung the glass of orange juice in Daniel's face.

Startled out of his daydream, Daniel broke off his gaze at

Zahara's companion and rubbed the pulp off his forehead. "What did you do that for?"

"You're under a spell, you idiot." Zaid jumped to his feet. "Take that cursed *hamsa* with you and let's go. That's no human with Zahara, it's one of the two angels. She led him right to us."

Daniel reached into his pocket and closed his fingers around the amulet. The warm fuzzies flooding his brain vanished, leaving a sick pit of fear in his stomach.

"Okay." He took a deep breath. "This is a very public place. The angel, or whatever he is, can't want to create too big a scene and get the police involved. Let me go over and see if I can get Zahara away from him. Hang back, and try not to escalate the situation if you don't have to."

Zaid gave him a reluctant nod, and a moment later his form blurred and faded into invisibility. Daniel was left sitting next to what appeared to be an empty chair. He rose to his feet, circled around the tables and made his way to where Zahara stood chatting with the angel.

Even with his hand clenched around his talisman, Daniel could sense an overpowering aura from the man, as if a glowing light followed him wherever he walked. He stood, still and silent, his eyes searching the perimeter of the pool, as Zahara giggled and touched the man's chest far more often than was necessary.

"Oh, there you are, honey!" Daniel forced a smile and strolled up to her. The angel's eyes flickered to his face, curious, but with no obvious hostility. "I've been looking all over for you. Zaid's taking both of us on a tour of the Majorelle Gardens this morning, remember?"

Zahara curled her lip. "I have better things to do with my time than check out some Frenchman's cacti collection. Why don't you and Zaid run along without me? My new friend and I are going to have a cup of coffee and chat."

"Sweetie, you know how crazy you get with too much caffeine." Daniel gave his best fake laugh and stuck out his hand to shake the angel's hand. "My name's Daniel, and I'm her husband. And you would be—"

"I am Harut." The angel regarded him from under long eyelashes, as Daniel swallowed hard and tried to maintain a frozen smile. Apparently supernatural creatures weren't too big on elaborate cover names. "This woman is your wife?"

Daniel nodded a vigorous yes as Zahara shook her head no.

"Oh, that. Daniel and I aren't married for real. He's totally gay, believe me." She gave Daniel a quick shove. "And he was just leaving."

"My wife is such a practical joker." Daniel entwined his arm around her waist and yanked her toward him. "I'd offer to have you join us for the tour, but we paid for it in advance with our travel company. Nice meeting you."

Harut's hand shot out and gripped Daniel's wrist. Grimacing, Daniel tried first to turn the gesture into a handshake, then gave up and attempted to pull away. It was no use. He might as well have tried to extricate himself from a metal vise. The guy might look like a male model, but he had the upper body strength of a weightlifter.

"She told me the trouble in the city took place in your clan's house." Harut's eyes wouldn't leave Daniel's face, and the warm fuzzies were coming back. In another minute, he'd be swooning over the guy as hopelessly as Zahara. "Tell me what you know of this."

"Daniel's right, we need to get going or we'll miss the tour." Zaid appeared on the other side of Zahara, one hand resting near his waist, as if ready to draw a weapon not yet visible.

Harut stiffened, his face tensing at the sight of Zaid. "You keep odd company, Daniel. The being next to you is an evil influence. Tell him to leave."

"The name's Zaid," the jinn spat. "And you're the one who's leaving." His sword materialized in his hand. Harut released his hold on Daniel and stepped back.

Something wasn't right. Screams, calls for the police, maybe a few dropped food trays—something should be happening around them. But the lounging tourists around the pool and smiling servers taking drink orders showed no sign of concern at the sight of an impending duel. There was only one exception. Ibrahim. The young waiter stood several feet away, mouth gaping open and a horrified expression on his face.

"What's gotten into the two of you?" Zahara unwrapped Daniel's arm from around her waist and threw it off. She slinked up to Harut and pressed herself against him. Daniel was reminded of a cat that had gobbled down too much catnip. "Maybe Harut and I will skip the coffee and head upstairs to my room."

"Do you work for my brother?" Harut came face-to-face with Zaid, his green eyes now cold and hard. A golden sword with a straight blade appeared in his hand, flames licking up around the hilt. "Bold of you, creature of the night, to show yourself in the light of day. If you and your human companion have deceived this innocent woman and tricked her into helping your dark purposes, be warned. I'll destroy both of you to protect her."

Zaid blinked. "Innocent woman? I guess you *have* been hanging upside down in a cave for a few thousand years."

Daniel pulled the hamsa out of his pocket and shoved the amulet into Harut's face. "Back off. She's with us. Now turn off that Jedi mind trick stuff and get lost."

Harut regarded the amulet with interest but gave no sign of concern over its presence. Zahara, on the other hand, didn't handle its sudden appearance well. She gave a high-pitched shriek that ended in a frantic growl. Out of the corner of his eye, Daniel caught a glimpse of black fur and gleaming claws. Then she disappeared with an angry pop and a swirl of smoke.

The angel lifted the hamsa from Daniel's nerveless fingers. "Two evil jinn adept at disguise, and a human sorcerer who seeks the power they hold. I see Marut has found allies here. I've met your kind before, Daniel, and they all came to a bad end. This is not the time or the place for me to confront you. But I'll be back. Tell my brother I'm coming for him."

Chapter Nine

Z AID CLOSED THE door behind him and indicated the room with a wave of his hand. "Not up to par with the accommodations the two of you had to vacate on such short notice, but here we are. My home is your home."

Daniel wasn't sure what he had expected a jinn's inner sanctum to look like, but his overall impression was that Zaid was a bit of a neat freak. His modest apartment on the upper story of a modern building in Marrakech was sparsely furnished with a few well-cared-for antiques, a hand-knotted tribal rug, and shelves crammed with books. Zahara curled up on a few silk pillows on the couch, her lips pursed into a sullen pout. She had reappeared during their departure from the hotel, after Harut had left by walking over the water of the pool without his feet even getting wet. Ibrahim had passed out cold at that point, and Zaid and Daniel had taken advantage of the sudden tumult to make a hasty exit.

Zaid strolled over to his compact kitchen to set some water boiling. "I'll make us some tea. We should lay low until dark, when Zahara and I have the advantage. Over the years I've either set up or traded for some powerful protections around this space. The safety will be worth the decreased living space."

"It's a good-sized apartment by New York standards,"

Daniel said. "And you have some rather surprising decorating skills."

"I like it." Zaid placed an assortment of candies and pastries on a low table near the sofa, which caused Zahara to perk up. "Only one bed for the three of us, I'm afraid."

"I don't have a problem with that." Zahara popped a chocolate-dipped cookie into her mouth.

"Maybe you don't, but I'd prefer to take the floor." Daniel found himself wanting the tea to be ready faster. He needed something to soothe his nerves and occupy his hands with something other than shaking some sense into Zahara. "You have no self-control whatsoever. I can't believe you tried to put the moves on that killer even after he told you he was one of the bad guys."

"But he was so gorgeous," Zahara protested. "And that charisma spell or whatever he's got going on is awfully good. It's one thing to charm a few dumb humans, but mesmerizing a jinn of my powers is impressive."

"He couldn't figure out you weren't human for a while." Zaid's brow furrowed. "He has some weaknesses, and so does his big brother. And chief among them is that they're not working together. Maybe we can exploit that, use it to our advantage."

"Do you think he could be a good guy?" Daniel asked. "A real angel would want to help some dippy horny tourist who got herself mixed up with the wrong supernatural crowd."

"Neither of them are a true *malak*." Zaid shook his head, then continued at Daniel's questioning look. "When God created the world, he constructed three races. From mud, he made humans, like you. You're born, you die, you decide to obey God's laws or you don't. From smokeless fire, he made the jinn. We have children too, and we're mortal as well."

"But not as mortal as you are." Zahara sandwiched several sugar cubes between some honey pastry and taste-tested it with a lick. "We live a long time."

"And have far fewer children," Zaid added. "When God created angels, he made them from pure light. They aren't mortal, and they have no choice but to obey him."

"So they don't have free will." Daniel thought back to what he had read about the two brothers. "But Harut and Marut asked to be made human. And when they were given a choice between good and bad, they chose bad."

"They chose Zahara." The female jinn flipped her hair back. "I always thought my name was awesome."

"*That* Zahara resisted their advances and ascended to heaven," Zaid pointed out. "A display of self-restraint I doubt you could follow. Regardless of how they got here, the fallen ones need to be stopped, along with anyone who's helping them."

Zaid's commitment to the cause was certainly welcome, especially since Daniel's personal jinn consultant on this crazy quest had been less than helpful so far. Still, they didn't even know what kind of threat the angels posed, much less how to stop them.

"Zaid said you traveled to the Mountains of—that word that starts with Q—to find out more information about what Marut is trying to do." Daniel reached out for the last sweet on the plate before Zahara could get her red-polished fingernails on it. "What did you find out?"

Zahara's attention appeared more focused on the now empty food platter than Daniel's question. "I was about to eat that."

"You ate everything else on the plate." Daniel wasn't that hungry, but he stuffed the pastry in his mouth to make a point. "Come on, Zahara, you went AWOL for over thirty-six hours. You must have found out something that could help us."

A set of sparks began to glow on her fingertips, and Daniel took a step back, remembering Zahara's pyrotechnical hissy fit in his apartment.

Zaid reached out for her arm, clearly thinking the same thing. "Did you speak to your—" his voice caught for a moment, as if he wanted to say a specific name, but thought better of it. "Your mother, after you crossed the *araf* and returned to the Mountains of Qaf?"

"I tried." Zahara blew out the embers on her fingers with a series of annoyed huffs. "She wasn't home. I did hear something about the dev being put out by the whole thing."

Despite Zahara's earlier warning, Daniel had read up on the Persian version of the jinn. Demons who detested humans, the dev were mortal enemies of the peris, who were as beautiful as the dev were hideous. Together, they sort of made up the bad fairy-good fairy dichotomy his childhood of watching animated films had prepared him for. It had bothered him Zaid sensed some sort of dev magic on the oil lamp he had used to summon Zahara. But nothing in his research had shed any light on that mystery.

"That's it? We need some real information about what's going on."

"Shouldn't *you* be able to tell us more about your own grandmother's house?" Zahara rose to her feet and gave Daniel a poke in the chest. Either taking that last treat had ticked her off, or she was acting defensive about something. "That giant angel didn't need those weapons we found, and somebody had to snatch the kid for him. If you were a real sorcerer, you'd scry their location in a reflecting pool of blood."

"Eww," Daniel said. "I'm not sure exactly what you said, but I'm not trying it."

"Let me suggest a course of action," Zaid said, stepping between Zahara and Daniel. "I have a contact in the police who can tell me who owns the house. Since Daniel's probably better at computers than gazing into the Cup of Jamshid, he can do some research when I get the name."

"Fine." Zahara flounced down on the sofa again. "Tell him to look up some nifty ways to kill angels while he's at it."

"When the club opens up," Zaid continued, ignoring Zahara's comments, "we'll go and see what other information we can scare up about the humans helping the two fallen ones. We find them, we find the big guy, Marut. We can take out pretty boy after we've dealt with his brother."

"There's a club for genies?" Daniel asked. "Do you guys get together and swap stories of the dumbest wish you've ever heard, or something like that?"

Zahara gave him a glare that made Marut's eyes of flame look positively friendly in comparison. "Zaid's talking about the nightclub he owns."

"It's a happening place, not to mention a profitable venture on my part." Zaid walked back to the kitchen and returned with the tea. "And the drink selection's a lot better than the one I have in my apartment."

"WHY IS THE music so loud?" Daniel couldn't even hear his shouted question over the pulsating soundtrack blaring out of his laptop's speakers. Zahara stood in front of the computer screen, shifting her weight from one foot to the other. She had changed into a pair of bottom-hugging workout pants and a flowered sports bra. The music swelled in volume, and she flung her hips from side to side, following that move with a swift fling of her arms behind her head and then around her waist. She spun around to face him, switching her arm routine to a mock boxing combination, as Daniel tried to shove past her to reach for the volume button.

On the other side of the electronic divide, a video of a dance class played out on the screen. None of the dancers, male or female, wore a stitch of clothing.

"What are you watching?" Daniel tugged at his tie, trying to loosen it a little. He had dressed in the only business suit he had packed, all for the occasion of tonight's fact-finding mission to Zaid's nightclub. He looked more like an accountant than a club-goer, but he had never dressed for a meeting with a mobster before. Ibrahim had brought over his and Zahara's luggage, and with a shaken expression confirmed Harut hadn't returned to the hotel to walk on water, or to ask any questions.

"Naked Dance Studio." Zahara rotated around in a circle, undulating her hips and bust to the music. "First time I've tried it. I love it."

Daniel resorted to shouting into Zahara's ear as she shoved his hand away from the volume bottom again and turned the music up. "I'm waiting for a Skype call from Anton. He knows the Russian guy who owns my grandmother's house."

Daniel turned to Zaid for help. They had to pull the plug on this dance party and get his ex-boyfriend on the line to get some useful information out of him. Zaid had been able to obtain the records on what Daniel now referred to as "his haunted house." The deed had recently been transferred to a man named Vladimir Borskoi, a name which generated a fair amount of interesting links online, of which "shady businessman" was the least pejorative. Daniel had been pleasantly surprised to find an unguarded wireless account in Zaid's building to use in his research; he had been unpleasantly surprised to find his ex-boyfriend's name associated with Borskoi's financial affairs.

Zaid strolled over and angled the upper part of his body briefly into the computer screen's field of vision. Unlike Daniel, he had elected for a black silk shirt and dark jeans that set off his taut physique perfectly.

"Don't tell me you do Naked Dance Studio, too," Daniel said.

Zaid reached over to adjust the volume level to a hair below earsplitting, and darted out of reach as Zahara tried to slap his hand. "No, but I occasionally *dabka*."

Daniel took advantage of Zahara's inattention to yank

the computer screen away from her and silence the music. The call came in a second later, and Anton's face—handsome, angular and set off by a tasteful gray tie—filled the screen. He didn't waste much time with pleasantries. "What kind of questions do you have about Vladimir Borskoi? If you're thinking about approaching him about a business relationship, I'd advise against it."

"I'm curious about him because he's listed as the owner of the house my grandmother's family owned, that's all." Daniel's tone switched to chirpy and carefree. "Nothing major."

"Are you considering property investment in Morocco?" Anton gave a grunt. "Foreign real estate can be a tricky market, even for someone with good financial sense. Which you don't have."

"It's more personal, actually." Daniel shifted his position and coughed. "I'm enjoying exploring my heritage, and it's a beautiful old home. Maybe this Borskoi guy could be persuaded to sell it me."

"Especially if you like human sacrifice." Zahara pushed her head closer to chime in. "It's got a great set-up for that sort of thing."

Anton squinted at the camera, then shook his head and went on. "Well, he's a business mogul based out of Vladivostok. Made his initial fortune in arms deals. But he's shady, even by that standard. Reputed ties to some militant groups in Chechnya, lots of black market scuttlebutt about his investments. And then there's the matter of some of his business rivals ending up dead at convenient times. Frankly, I could do without him as a client."

"Then why does your company take his money?" Daniel asked.

"Tell you what." Anton sat back in his chair. "Why don't you finish up your consulting work in Marrakech, and when you come home, I can guide you into picking out a condo on the Cape. Maybe in Truro. It's close to P-Town, but much quieter. Great resale potential."

"I'll keep that in mind." Daniel wanted to keep the conversation as short as possible, and he had bigger concerns than buying a vacation home in Massachusetts. Anton had always been obsessed with waterfront property values. "Thanks for the advice," He clicked off the call. "I don't know. Vladimir Borskoi sounds like a dangerous guy. Are you even sure he'll show up tonight?"

"He'll be there," Zaid said. "I sent out a special invitation through the young ladies he retains most evenings. We need to get some information out of him. I know some tried and true methods, of course, but since I've sworn off demonic possession and most of the more entertaining types of torture, my options are limited."

"I can try to chat him up, I guess." Daniel rubbed his forehead. "I'll have to think of some way to start a conversation."

"Wouldn't it be wonderful if you had someone who could help with this plan?" Zahara came up behind Daniel and intertwined her arms around his shoulders. "You know, an alluring seductress who could catch Vladimir's attention, then ply him with alcohol until he spills the beans about everything he knows?"

Daniel struggled to stop Zahara from running her hands

over his chest, then gave up. "You're suggesting you work on him first?"

"Unlike Zaid—" Zahara pressed her breasts against his back. "I have no moral scruples. And my little aerobics workout got me thinking I should bring back my traditional dance work. Long family tradition. I'm sure Vladimir Borskoi will love it."

IT WAS CLOSE to ten p.m. before Daniel made his way through the well-dressed crowd thronging Zaid's late-night dance club and bar. The jinn had arrived earlier, explaining that although he had a full-time manager and a loyal staff, some things didn't get taken care of unless the boss made an appearance. Zahara had disappeared into the back rooms where a small army of scantily-clad performers were preparing for their nightly show.

"Total cultural nonsense, of course," Zaid had told him. "Whatever they're doing out there, it bears little resemblance to any of the real traditional dances in this country. But if the tourists don't get to slip a belly dancer a few bills and ride on a camel, they feel cheated."

Daniel took a seat at a small table near the bar and pretended to peruse the menu as he scanned the room. His research had uncovered articles and references to Borskoi, and included in them were a few photographs. When the man himself walked in, Daniel had little difficulty identifying him.

"Toadlike" might have been a charitable description.

Vladimir Borskoi was heavy-set, bordering on obese, with a bullet-shaped head that sat directly on his shoulders without the benefit of a neck. He wore a gray suit that managed to look garish despite its drab color, and a red and yellow tie that did little for his blotched complexion. Daniel counted six women around him in total, each with heavily plucked eyebrows and generous applications of foundation and blush.

The Russian businessman was ushered to a booth to Daniel's left, and several champagne buckets were wheeled out without delay. Daniel lifted the menu to cover his face and watched as the group lit cigarettes and clinked glasses. Good. They were settling in for a long night of drinking.

"You need to rethink the choices you've made. It's not too late for you to follow the correct path, but time is growing short."

Daniel froze at the sound of the voice. He rested the menu down on the table like it had been printed on plastic explosives and turned to his right. Harut sat next to him, his brilliant eyes glittering in the flickering light of the solitary candle that sat in the center of the table. Aside from the hand-shaped charm that hung from his neck, he had nothing on him to suggest he was anything other than an attractive young man, out enjoying the city's nightlife.

"If that's my hamsa around your neck, I want it back." Daniel tensed his leg muscles, ready to jump up and make a run for it if Harut decided to pull out his sword again.

"It was given a powerful *baraka*, a blessing." Harut touched his fingers to the amulet. "Not only by one holy man, or even two, but by a young life you saved. Perhaps that was a calculated move, another trick from you. But in case it wasn't, I've come here tonight to try to dissuade you from your association with the creatures of the night you've summoned to do your bidding."

Clearly Harut knew the gist of what had happened at his grandmother's house, though he wasn't giving Zaid or Zahara any of the credit. Daniel risked a quick look around the room. There was no sign of his two supernatural allies. Playing it cool and hearing Harut out might be the best option.

"Those two creatures of the night saved that kid, too. And it was your brother Marut who was about to devour him before we showed up."

"Marut *was* my brother. A long time ago." The angel removed the amulet from around his neck and placed it on the table. It shimmered, then resumed its original shape. Daniel reached out a cautious hand and took it back. Harut pressed his palms down in front of him on the table, as if to emphasize he had no intention of lashing out. "Now he's something else—something dark and terrible. He's associated himself with the worst of humanity to achieve the revenge he desires."

Daniel hesitated. Maybe Harut was telling the truth about wanting to stop Marut. And he certainly knew more about his brother's abilities and motivations than they did.

"What's he planning to do?" Daniel asked.

"He wishes to rip open the veil between your world and another, a land where the jinn and others live, mostly as they did before my fall." Harut answered without hesitation.

Daniel had no doubt this angel was also dangerous as hell, but he didn't strike him as a good liar, or even someone who bothered to lie at all.

"He seeks a war between the two sides, and if he comes into his full powers, he'll succeed."

"Full powers," Daniel repeated, unsure if he had heard correctly. "He's pretty damn big and nasty right now."

"His strength is still limited, and will be until the sacrifice to him is completed. The child was marked to die by a powerful spell. The act of saving his life transferred the curse to another. To you, actually."

A cold chill settled inside Daniel. Some of the events of that evening remained a blur, but he hadn't rescued the little boy and beat off Marut on his own. As he remembered it, he had been sprawled out on his back when the child had somehow squirmed away from both the angel's grasp and the plunging chandelier. This was one occasion when getting credit as the hero wasn't doing him any favors.

"I had help with that. Both of the jinn who are with me want to stop Marut as well. Zahara because I summoned her, and Zaid because he wants to do the right thing. If you're trying to stop Marut, let's all sit down and talk. We could join forces, work on the problem together."

Harut was silent for a moment. Daniel held his breath, wondering if the angel was going to accept his proposition or try to kill him.

Then the lights dimmed and the show began. A phalanx of belly dancers marched down the marble steps leading to the bar, swirling and swaying in a riotous display of scarlet, emerald and peacock-blue skirts and veils. A number of more substantially dressed older women in long embroidered tunics balanced entire platters of lit candles on their heads, as their younger counterparts darted around the room, twirling and clanking coin belts to a sudden blast of dance music.

Vladimir Borskoi seemed to be enjoying the display. A lot. He rose to his feet, clapping and shouting, and several of the women fluttered by to accept the bills he stuffed into the tops of their skirts.

The music dimmed in volume, then switched from Western pop tunes to a reggae-style Arabic beat. Zahara made her way down the staircase alone. She had on a pair of translucent black harem pants slit on the sides to reveal the curve of her legs, and an embroidered top that bared her midriff. Henna designs twisted up from her wrists and ankles, and a sheer veil trimmed in crystal covered all but her eyes.

She moved farther onto the floor, closer to Borskoi's table. Daniel was no expert on Middle Eastern dance, but Zahara's moves were stunning, down to a series of serpent-like moves with her hands that alternately covered and exposed her shimmying hips and belly. Enthralled, Borskoi leaned forward, offering her a rolled-up wad of cash. Zahara threw a quick triumphant glance toward Daniel. Then she spotted Harut and her eyes narrowed.

Taking a quick running start, she launched herself onto her hands and flipped over three times in quick succession to land in front of their table. The audience oohed and clapped, some guests turning to each other to whisper in surprise. Zahara posed with one leg bent, resting on the ball of her foot, then reached down to pull her gleaming silver sword out from between her legs. Harut stared back at her, his hands remaining on the table.

Daniel wasn't sure if he should try to tackle the angel or Zahara. He had been so close to getting Harut to agree to at least discuss the situation. Now it looked like things were going to break into a full-fledged battle.

"You come here now!" Vladimir shook the table in front of him, sending glasses flying and shattering on the floor, and the women around him into shrieks of dismay. "You want me to fight him for you? I do it, then!"

Great. Zahara was about to challenge the angel to a duel, Zaid was nowhere in sight, and a lovestruck Russian mob boss wanted in on a bar fight to end all bar fights. Zahara bared her teeth in a tense grin as the shouting behind her continued. She held a manicured finger up to Harut, as if to ask him to wait, then tossed her sword high up into the air. Arching backward, she spun herself into a series of back flips, landing a few feet away from an openmouthed Borskoi. She held up her hand, and the sword fell into her grip. Swaying her hips, she rotated around to face him, extending her hand to beckon him closer. Eyes glazed, he leaned forward. With one quick snap of her hand, Zahara reached out, grabbed his tie, and jerked him face down on the table. She raised her sword and slammed it down.

The stunned silence turned into gales of laughter as she held up the severed remains of Borskoi's necktie. Zahara spun around, and snapped her fingers. The music pouring out of the speakers altered, stretching out to an unfamiliar melody, slow and sensual.

Daniel caught Harut nodding along with the rhythm. He knew the song, and Daniel guessed the music was far older than anything the club's sound system should be playing.

Zahara passed her sword from hand to hand, cutting a few slashes through the air, as the clubgoers around her began to clap in robotic unison. Smiling, she placed the weapon on top of her head, then bent down into a deep knee bend. The angel wasn't the only one mesmerized. As exciting as Zahara's show was, the degree of attention paid to it by the crowd was unnatural. And absolute. Every person in the room stood motionless and silent, their attention focused only on her, as if in a mass trance.

Rising and bowing, Zahara made her way back to Harut, then raised both hands to lift the sword from her head to balance it on her waist. Arching backward, she pulsated her hips toward him, grinding closer and closer, the blade's edge drawing a fine edge of blood on her smooth, bare skin. The golden coins on her belt clinked and flashed, as her vibrations came harder and faster, building up to a climax.

Daniel swallowed hard and squeezed the hamsa. Whatever waves of magical pheromones Zahara was generating, his amulet was barely able to block them. To his right, Harut sat immobilized, sweat beading on his forehead. Daniel caught a glimpse of yellow gleaming in the dim light of the bar. Then a pair of cat's eyes materialized in the air above the angel's head.

Zaid. He and Zahara had played a tag-team approach. She had immobilized the room into a catatonic state of lust, allowing Zaid to place himself in the perfect spot to take out Harut with one swift, final blow. The realization crystallized in Daniel's mind a second after his legs propelled him out of his seat and sent him in a mad rush to tackle the invisible shape behind the angel's chair. He contacted solid flesh with a thump; Zaid cursed. An invisible knee landed in Daniel's abdomen, knocking the wind out of him. Gasping for air, he pressed the hamsa blindly forward. A snarl of pain followed.

Harut rose to his feet, the spell broken. Zahara gave a small shriek and disappeared into a funnel of smoke. The strong arms pinning Daniel to the ground released him, and an acrid scent of brimstone breezed past his face as Zaid and Zahara made their magical exits. Harut strode to the middle of the room, and a pair of flawless white wings are from his back, sweeping forward to extend from one end of the room to the other. The club's patrons, freed from the enchantment, shrieked and began fleeing toward the exit. Only Borskoi remained facing the angel. He slumped at his table, his eyes still focused on the spot where the dancer who had so entranced him had last appeared.

Then the wall behind the Russian exploded, sending blood, bricks and glass everywhere. A ball of fire expanded into the space, and the angel reached out his arms as the flames roared into his chest.

Minutes or hours later, Daniel found himself sprawled out on the floor, hot, warm liquid dribbling down his face. He lifted his head, blinking to clear his vision as smoke billowed around the room, lit now only by piles of burning furniture. Borskoi's bloodshot eyes met his, bulging out in a stare of shock and dismay. His head, remarkably intact after being blown off his body, had rolled to within a few inches off Daniel's own.

A hand shook his shoulder, and Ibrahim's face, covered with soot, appeared above him. "Mr. Goldstein! Talk to me.

Are you hurt?"

"I don't think so." Daniel propped himself up on one arm, as broken glass crunched underneath him. Screams and moans filled the air, blending with the wail of sirens. He wiped away the blood seeping down his face. His own or someone else's, he couldn't tell.

"What happened?" He coughed out some of the ash that had settled into his lungs.

"The terrorists." Ibrahim reached out to lift him up by the shoulders. "They've blown up the club."

Chapter Ten

ZAHARA PARTED THE heavy curtains shrouding the southern-facing window in Zaid's apartment, flinching as a bolt of brilliant light from the noontime sun shone in. Not a hint of cloud cover today, and it would be hours before sunset, and even longer before the pre-moonrise darkness that would mark the optimal time for their departure.

She walked to the couch and sprawled out on the pillows, fanning out a large pair of batlike wings behind her. She had gone so far as to add two fashionably small horns on either side of her forehead. On occasion, she appeared to Zaid with this particular twist on her human manifestation. If he assumed this was her elemental form—well, it wasn't lying, exactly.

Zaid continued his furious pacing back and forth, as frustrated as if he was imprisoned in an iron cage as opposed to his comfortable loft.

"When I get my hands on him, I'm going to tear his balls off and make him eat them."

Zahara picked up the last sugar cube remaining on the tray in front of her, and with a sad sigh, popped it into her mouth. They were low on supplies. Like candy, alcohol, and magical weapons that worked against angels. "Now isn't the time for your romantic fantasies about Daniel. Why don't you curl up next to me? I'll give you a little rubdown to relax you, and maybe throw in a happy ending to boot."

"We were so close to killing one of them." Zaid whirled around and stood over her, his tail twitching. Away from any human presence, he had taken on his preferred half-form, his lower body ending in the powerful legs of a leopard. "Your lust spell was mind-numbing, even by your standards. If Daniel hadn't jumped me with that tinker-toy charm of his, I would've had Harut's head as a souvenir."

Zaid certainly was taking this whole fallen ones situation personally. Which would have been great, if Zahara still wanted to fulfill her contract with Daniel. Since that particular arrangement had turned out to involve not only a fight with two deadly angels, but a confrontation with her mother, she was more than content to chalk this entire experience up to a life lesson learned. Never trust a sorcerer with good intentions.

"Harut does have a nice head." Zahara licked the last crystals of sugar from her fingers. "On top of a beautiful chest, and great legs, and well... I didn't have a chance to check out the most important parts."

"*Cherie.*" Zaid leaned over and ruffled her hair. "You need to start thinking with what's between your two little ears. Whether Harut's for or against his brother, he's come down on the side of trying to kill us."

Zaid needed to be distracted before he thought up something that might bring them into conflict with Harut or Marut again. All they needed to do was lay low for a while, then get far, far away from this mess.

She would love to have left the situation behind her last night. But Zaid had insisted on doing what he could for his staff and patrons caught up in the attacks. And as for Zahara descending through the levels and returning home, that meant facing her mother again. Not to mention it wouldn't do her much good if Daniel chose to summon her back. Best to scuttle out of town with Zaid for protection and hope Daniel had lost his appetite for saving the world.

Zahara added a forked tail to her current manifestation and slithered the prehensile end toward Zaid's belt buckle. She giggled, enjoying his expression as he backed away, pretending to look shocked. "No hands doesn't mean no fun. Come on. I'm bored, and you haven't been all that good lately. We can't get out of town before dark. How about a little roll in the hay?"

"I need to know what the hell happened." Zaid's face darkened again. He turned away and stared at the television in the corner. Aside from herself, Zaid was more comfortable in the human world than any jinn she had ever met. Even so, she had needed to coax him into setting up and turning on the nice high-definition screen she had lifted from a local store last night before returning to his apartment to hunker down before dawn broke.

Zahara had tried rotating through a variety of news sources, but whether in Arabic, French, or English, the channels carried the same feed—images of Zaid's now-destroyed club with blackened walls, screaming patrons being carried out by stretchers, and shattered glass glittering in pools of blood. A claim of responsibility for the bombing had come in from a hitherto unknown terrorist group headed by an English-speaking spokesman. Most of the channels had been making much of his obvious American accent, and the usual round of conspiracy theories had begun to circulate.

Zaid cursed under his breath as he watched. "They hit my property, my source of fortune, and my people. Several of my staff members were hurt, and most of the dead are the working girls that helped get Borskoi out to my club."

The updated death toll, intoned solemnly by commentators in a variety of languages, could have been worse. Only five had died and of them, only Vladimir Borskoi warranted a name. The others were listed as unknown local women. Given the size of the explosion, Daniel and a whole mess of other humans shouldn't have survived. But they had. Harut had done something to protect them.

Well, her mother had said the two brothers didn't see eye-to-eye on this whole end-of-the-world thing. Good. Perhaps the two of them were fighting it out right now, and she and Zaid were the least of their concerns.

"Maybe Borskoi was the target, not all those tourists." She raised her eyebrows at Zaid's expression of surprise. "I can think about something other than sex for short periods of time, you know. What about the two girls who survived? Could they tell us anything?"

"I paid for them to go to the private hospital where they took all the foreigners," Zaid said. "But they're in no shape to talk. Ibrahim told me they're barely hanging on. Humans are fragile."

"Daniel probably went there, too." Zahara stretched out her arms and yawned. All this thinking about other people's problems was tiring her out. "Then right back to New York with his little tail between his legs, I'm sure." Thus solving her problem. There wasn't much wiggle room in the magical contract of the summons, but if Daniel wasn't directly commanding her to try and stop the two fallen ones—well, she wasn't going to keep at it on her own and get herself killed. "That would be a fun little prank to play on him, now that I think of it. Maybe I'll turn him into his elemental form. As a wild guess, I'd go with a Chihuahua with self-esteem issues."

"Only humans with some of our blood are easy to transform." Zaid waved away the thought of such a minimal punishment for Daniel. "But you're right about him taking off. He'd be a total idiot to stay here after what he did to us."

There was a hesitant knock on the door, then another. Daniel's voice came through the wood. "Zaid? Are you in there?"

"On the other hand…" Zaid pulled a wicked-looking knife off his waist. "Maybe he is that stupid."

"Put that away." Zahara bounced to her feet as Daniel's voice grew more muffled, and the sound of clanking buckets and falling objects came through the door. Damn. Daniel hadn't run away with his tail between his legs at all. Instead, he had tracked the two of them down like a poodle with separation anxiety. "You may not follow the old rules anymore, but you know them. He's mine, unless I decide to give him to you as a present. So behave."

"Your so-called sorcerer doesn't even know enough magic to unblock the closet spell I put on the door." Zaid's voice dripped with disdain. "One time I forgot and left it in place on cleaning day. Even the maids were able to figure it out. A little salt and a prayer or two, and they got right in."

Zahara made her tail and wings disappear, and patted her head to shrink back her horns before walking over to swing the door open. Daniel stumbled in, tripping over his feet as he entered. The right side of his forehead was swollen, and a few metal sutures glinted in the mess of half washed-out blood and disinfectant in his hair. All his limbs were intact, however. Considering how close he had been to the bomb's target, he didn't look that bad. Or, at least, as bad as he would if Zaid got his way.

"I don't understand." Daniel spun around in a circle. "I kept opening doors that looked like the one to Zaid's apartment, but when I opened them I walked straight into a cleaning closet. Every single time."

"Magic!" Zahara flung up her arms in mock drama. "We don't want anyone opening up the door, Daniel. Because we're hiding out from the feathered monster you decided to save at the last moment."

Zaid lost any semblance of self-control and grabbed Daniel by the throat. "I wanted that angel's head on a tea tray. But as it stands, I'll settle for yours."

"Stop. Please. I can explain." Daniel tried to pry Zaid's fingers off his throat, giving Zahara a pleading glance. She bared her teeth and growled, and Zaid opened his hand, albeit with a great deal of reluctance.

"Harut came to talk to me." Daniel massaged his throat, his voice hoarse. "Not to attack me, but to try and convince me to follow the proper moral path. He wants to stop his brother as much as we do. I was trying to explain to him we could all work together on this, have a dialogue. But he has an issue with both of you being jinn."

"There's no issue," Zahara said. "He wants to kill us, we want to kill him. That's what mortal enemies do, and it's the way things have always been between our kind and our enemies. We don't sit down together and talk about our feelings."

"Harut saved those people in the club. Most of them, at least. And for all we know, that blast could have killed him."

A rivulet of dust floated down from the ceiling, covering Daniel's head with a fine powder. He brushed it off, then tried to remain upright as the room shook and swayed.

Above their heads, a patchwork of lines expanded across the ceiling. The cracks spread out like tendrils of vines, as more dirt and plaster dropped down on top of them.

Zahara darted backward and pinned herself against the wall for protection. The room's ceiling, along with a good chunk of the top of the apartment building, ripped itself free, leaving a jagged hole open to the blazing sun above them. A wing-shaped shadow flickered across the dust-covered floor, growing larger and larger as its owner dived toward the opening. The blinding sunlight dimmed as a form blotted out the sun's rays, leaving a glowing halo around the shape of a winged man staring down at them from the edge of the yawning hole in the roof.

With a sharp clank of steel, Zaid unsheathed his sword. "Looks like Harut is alive and well. And I don't think he came here to chat."

Zaid sprang upward and onto the roof, as Zahara shrank back into a shadowy corner. Brightness was everywhere, draining her of whatever strength she had left after her performance last night. She should dematerialize and descend through the levels now, leaving Zaid to hold off Harut. But judging by the hole the angel had ripped through both the building and Zaid's best protection spells, the battle wouldn't go well for her fellow jinn.

Her uncharacteristic hesitation to leave other people to deal with a crisis carried a penalty, and a heavy one at that. As soon as she dissolved her lower body into smoke and prepared to exit the human plane of reality for the first of the seven levels of hell, a sharp jolt shook her to the core. She tried again, more desperate than ever to escape, but her solid form remained, stuck to the floor like her legs were made of lead.

Then the whip coiled around her. Gold and braided, it twisted around her arms and legs, then jerked her upward. She made the initial mistake of struggling to free herself before attempting any sort of counterspell. The rope tightened, digging into her flesh. Any curses or enchantments she could half cough out had no effect. Reeled upward like a fish on a line, she found herself tied in a tight bundle on the building's flat roof, her head next to one of the several satellite dishes on top of the building. Sunlight seared her eyes, reducing her breath to short gasps. There wasn't much more she could do other than call for help, but Zaid had problems of his own. The sword battle between him and Harut was close to finished, with the jinn bleeding from one useless arm, and his other barely blocking the blows from the angel's flaming weapon.

A hand gripped the jagged edge of the hole torn in the

roof, and Daniel's head appeared. He pulled himself up, then fell down again, before he could lift his leg up over the edge and inch his body onto the flat surface. He lay there, winded, as Zahara screamed at him to get up and help. He stumbled toward her, then fell to his knees and ran his hands over the golden bonds encircling her.

"What's this stuff made of, and how do I cut it off you?" Another clang of swords rang out, and Daniel glanced up at the fight between Zaid and Harut. His face grew pale.

Zahara gritted her teeth and poked two of her fingers out of the coils. Her sword materialized next to Daniel. "Hurry. Up."

He grabbed the blade and began sawing through her bonds. She held as still as she could, having learned the painful lesson that any movement only tightened the cursed rope Harut had thrown around her. Her legs were free, and she had struggled to her knees when Harut came over and took the sword from Daniel's hand. With his other, he dropped Zaid on the ground. Her friend was breathing, at least, although blood had soaked through his shirt and spattered over the fur of his animal legs. Another golden lariat twisted around his arms.

"The only thing you should do with that sword is cut her throat." Harut pulled Daniel to his feet by his hair, and tossed Zahara's sword aside. He lifted his own gleaming gold weapon and rested the tip on her chest. "One more chance, Daniel. Prove to me you haven't given your soul to this wretched seductress and I'll allow you to live. Kill her and the other jinn with your own hands."

"You're some kind of batshit crazy, you know that?"

Daniel's legs were shaking, but his voice wasn't. Not that it would help the situation or anything, but talking trash like that to an avenging angel about to decapitate all three of them did take a certain amount of courage. "I'm not going to hurt Zahara or Zaid."

"Do what he says." Zaid croaked out the words. He had transformed into his elemental form, and the bloodied body of a male leopard now lay entangled in ropes cutting into his limbs. "There's no sense in all three of us dying."

Now *that* was batshit crazy. If Zahara was going to die tragically young and under violent circumstances, she wanted as many people as possible around her to get it as well. Trust Zaid to come up with some heroic nonsense at the end.

"They're not evil. Your brother Marut is." Daniel whipped out his hamsa and tried to shove Harut away by pressing the object to the angel's chest. It had no discernible effect. He might as well have tried to push an elephant out of the way. "Let them go and focus on stopping him."

"Do you not see the horrible, twisted shapes of the ones we fight against?" Harut gestured toward Zaid.

The angel must have excellent self-control to not just whack Daniel and get it over with. All her human sorcerer was doing was buying them a little time. They were out of options, except for Zahara's one remaining spell. And she had sworn an oath to five demon gods she'd die before using it.

"Zaid is a big cat." Daniel raised his palms up in a pleading gesture. "I love cats. All kinds. I even buy those Big Cats of the World calendars to support the World Wildlife Fund. Leopards are endangered, you know. PETA's going to go all sorts of medieval on your ass if you hurt him."

Zahara didn't get Daniel's strategy, assuming he had one. Was he trying to annoy the angel to death?

"What about the woman?" Harut glared at her. Her fingers were too numb from the ropes to flip him off, so she stuck her tongue out at him instead. "Do you not see the evil that lurks below that attractive surface?"

"Sure, blame it all on the one with the vagina," she said. "Like I haven't heard that before."

"Zahara isn't a bad person." Daniel hesitated. "I mean, not that she's a person, of course. And she can be a little uninhibited. But look, children love her. I mean, they want to hug her and take her home. She has potential. Maybe you could work on morally reforming her or something like that."

"Take your moral reforms—" Zahara spat at Harut, missing his face by a hair "—and shove them up your ass, along with the stick that's already there."

Harut held out his hand to Daniel. "Give me your amulet. I'll show you her true shape, the one she can conceal even from me. When the full horror is revealed, you'll know I'm telling you the truth."

"I've seen the real Zahara." Daniel gave her a few frantic head nods. "Go on, show him the version of you with gigantic boobs."

Zahara shimmered, shifting to the shape and outfit she had worn to Daniel's apartment. In an attempt at added realism, she added in the forked tail and wings.

Harut hesitated for a moment, then swallowed hard, "This form she has now assumed... I don't believe it's her true shape. And it would not be terribly... displeasing to most humans. Especially the male ones."

"Ya think?" Daniel asked.

The angel snatched the hamsa from his hand and came forward to press it onto Zahara's exposed bust line. It glittered in the light, a burning heat emanating from it as it touched her.

She screamed. The flesh she had so carefully created around herself peeled off, stripped away by the power of the amulet. Spots of fur emerged as more of her human persona peeled away like tattered rags. The golden bonds dissolved, unable to continue binding her in the face of the wave of magic coming from the hamsa. She crouched on the ground, shivering in humiliation. She was naked, completely exposed. The lie she had covered up for years was now out there for all to see.

"Don't look at me!" she shrieked, before her voice altered into a high-pitched snarl.

Daniel was facing away from her, struggling in Harut's implacable grasp. He had made a last ditch effort to grab Harut's sword, without success. Both men gasped as they turned in her direction. Beside her, Zaid muttered a quick prayer.

Sinking to his knees, Daniel came up to within a finger's breadth of her face, his mouth hanging open. "You. You're so... so..."

"Don't say it!" Zahara bared her fangs and scraped her claws along the concrete of the roof. "Don't you dare!"

"Adorable!" Daniel's voice raised up to a squeak. He reached out to pet her head as she furiously tossed it away. "The cutest thing I've ever seen in my life. You are so precious!"

That was it. If this was the end, they'd all go with her. She sat back on her haunches, widened her soft brown eyes, and blinked her long eyelashes at Harut. The angel took a step back, shocked, and his sword fell from his hand. Reaching into her throat, she came out with a long, deep purr. Daniel collapsed, and the angel took another step back. With a powerful push from her hind legs, she launched herself forward, striking him in the chest and barreling him backward and off the side of the building.

He fell like a stone, his wings limp behind him, as she soared away. Her stubby little wings couldn't take her far, but she could glide without any difficulty. When he was close to impact on the street, a spark of light came from Harut's center, and the angel disappeared, replaced by a hawk. The bird flapped its wings, its flight erratic.

Zahara wasted little time zooming back over the building. Zaid had freed himself and was back in human form. His shirt ripped and bloodied, he cradled Daniel's limp body in his arms. She folded her wings and dropped down on her paws next to him.

He avoided any direct eye contact with her. Which was for the best. For both of them.

"It's been centuries since I allowed myself to be taken through the levels." Zaid reached out to grasp one of her paws. "But Daniel risked his life for me. I'll do it to save him."

The sharp cry of a bird of prey echoed above them. Harut had recovered from her spell. Daniel most likely would not. Taking Zaid and Daniel into hell with her was the only remaining option.

Chapter Eleven

THE BEAUTIFUL RHYTHM of the chant floated over Daniel's head, each word at once clear and incomprehensible. Even without understanding their meaning, he could sense the words were sacred. Then another prayer broke through, this one in English. A woman's voice, clear and strong. "In the name of the Father, and the Son." A third, deeper voice joined in, rich and resonant. Hebrew, definitely. Too bad he couldn't understand all the beautiful words. They were so soothing. He could lie here and listen to the three voices forever.

A hand slapped his face, hard. Daniel blinked and opened his eyes. Zaid leaned over him, his face tense. He had on a clean shirt, his right arm supported by a sling. The singing and chanting halted, and Daniel lifted his head to find himself lying on a velvet sofa in the Le Churchill bar. Imam Youssef stood to his right, in a white skullcap and a long traditional robe. On his other side, a man with a *kippah* on his head and a *tallit* over his shoulders reached out to squeeze his hand. How had Rabbi Shlomo found him? The third person gathered around the sofa didn't look familiar. She was an older woman with cropped gray hair, warm blue eyes, and a clerical collar.

"Daniel, this is Reverend Margaret Collins, of the

Church of Saint Andrew." Rabbi Shlomo smiled at her.

"Call me Molly," she said.

"You left us for a time. To a dark place." Imam Youssef nodded at Zaid. "Your friend called us to help you come back."

Daniel pushed himself up into a sitting position. "So, a rabbi, an imam, and a priest walked into a bar…"

"To perform an exorcism." Zaid held out his hand, and Ibrahim stepped forward from his spot near the bar to deliver a steaming cup of coffee. The jinn pressed the mug into Daniel's hand.

"Perhaps more like a psychic intervention." Reverend Collins beamed at him. "We're so glad you're feeling better."

"I tried to find a Catholic priest," Zaid whispered, "but on short notice, I ended up settling for an Episcopalian."

"Thank you." Daniel took a sip of coffee and scanned the room, but saw no sign of Zahara. "I think I'm fine now."

The three religious guardians smiled and made their way out after each shook Daniel's hand in turn. Imam Youssef left last, with some additional whispered instructions for Zaid.

"Feel up for some dinner?" Ibrahim came over to the sofa.

"Soup maybe." Daniel's stomach felt quite empty, now that he could focus on it. "What about that tasty one you eat with the special wooden spoon?"

"*Harira*." Ibrahim laughed. "I'll get you a bowl." He began to walk out of the room.

"To go, along with some water and a few snacks," Zaid told him. "We need to hit the road, and soon."

The events on the rooftop came flooding back, with one exception. How had they escaped from Harut? One minute Zahara had been an over-the-top caricature of a sexy genie, and the next she had become... soft. And cuddly. With big, brown eyes that melted his heart.

Zaid slapped him again.

"Ow." Daniel rubbed the side of his cheek. "That hurt. Cut it out."

"You were thinking about Zahara, weren't you?" Zaid hit him again, this time on the head with the heel of his palm. "I don't need you slipping back into your trance again."

"There was fire." More fragments of memory came back to Daniel, all of them dark and terrible. "Then cold, so much cold."

"Zahara took us both through the levels to escape Harut." Zaid handed Daniel the cup of coffee again, making sure he took another gulp. "The sight of her elemental form was too much even for him. You didn't handle it well at all."

So Daniel had been to hell... and back again. Maybe it was for the best that he had been barely conscious through it all, thanks to Zahara's unorthodox method of attack. Horror, panic, fear—he should be able to muster up some reaction to the ordeal, but any attempt to dwell on it brought up dizzying memories of a cute and fluffy Zahara. He pushed both the coffee cup and the memories away.

"She told me her true form was so horrible, it would destroy me if I saw it." Daniel tried to climb to his feet, and Zaid held him around the waist with his good arm to ease him up. "But she wasn't scary at all. She was... adorable."

"I've seen a lot of strange things in my life," Zaid said.

"But her transformation surprised me almost as much as it surprised Harut. We'll have to ask Zahara about it later, if she gets over her embarrassment enough to join us. But for now, we need to get out of town. Between the police and your friend with the fire sword, this city is way too hot for me."

"Harut's working on the same side we are. But convincing him of that might be tough."

"Trying to convince him of anything was stupid." Zaid studied Daniel's face, his dark eyes glinting in the room's soft light. "You should have obeyed him and taken my head off."

"I couldn't do that to you." Daniel reached out and touched Zaid's injured arm. "Or Zahara. That's not the kind of guy I am."

"I didn't say you weren't brave." A trace of a smile played on the jinn's lips. "I'm saying you're an idiot, that's all."

"You're welcome." Daniel returned the smile, then shoved his hands back into his pockets. "So, how are we getting out of town? Camel caravan? Flying carpets?"

Zaid reached into his pockets and showed him a set of car keys. "Try again. My new BMW four by four might be a more comfortable way to travel. Finish your coffee. We're going on a road trip."

ZAID PULLED OFF the highway onto a side road, and the town came into view. Two and three-story buildings glowed a dusty rose color in the late afternoon sun. Groups of children in school uniforms giggled and played in the narrow streets, kicking soccer balls or chatting as they carried their backpacks home.

After leaving Marrakech, they had driven through the night and a good portion of the day, stopping a few times for bathroom breaks and Daniel's intense curiosity about the items for sale in roadside shops, ranging from perfumed oil soaps to a polished ashtray carved from local stone embedded with fossils. "You don't even smoke." Zaid had pointed out after Daniel purchased it, along with several other souvenirs and a few snacks for the road.

As they rounded another nondescript corner, they found themselves face-to-face with a building resembling a castle from an Arabian fantasy film. Walls of red stucco stretched up into square towers and ramparts. Balconies crammed with flowers fronted picture windows decorated with ornate metal screens. The front courtyard was paved with fitted cobblestone, and featured a graceful fountain spraying water over its green and white tiled base.

"This is where we're staying?" Daniel asked. "I thought we might hide out in some sort of mysterious cave of wonders."

"Well, I'd rather stay in a comfortable hotel with a decent restaurant." Zaid stepped out of the car and waved toward a pair of Fez-wearing valets. "The hotel's chef trained in France, and I hear she's fantastic."

Daniel hung around in the lobby and tried to look the part of an ordinary tourist making his way through the country as Zaid chatted with the desk clerk. There had been no sign of Zahara so far, and Daniel had no idea where his personal little evil genie had gone, or how he could find out.

Harut was out there, somewhere, and that meant she was in danger. And they weren't any closer to locating Marut, or figuring out how Borskoi's death and the bombing played into all of this.

He had tried to keep up with the media coverage of the attack on the nightclub. A videotape by the group claiming responsibility appeared over and over on every social media site he checked. Other than that, few concrete details had emerged.

Zaid walked over and handed him back his passport. "It might be helpful to get you a different ID. You can't pass for a local, but a change in name might throw off any interest from the government."

The officers who had interviewed Daniel at the hospital about the bombing while an English-speaking physician had cleaned and stapled the laceration on his scalp couldn't have been more pleasant. Or more persistent. Had Mr. Goldstein frequented the club before last night's regrettable incident? Anything out of the ordinary before the explosion? An oddly dressed person, perhaps. Or an unusual article or piece of luggage. Did Mr. Goldstein travel frequently? Any recent trips to other countries in the region—just as an example, of course, to Israel?

Before the events of the last week, being caught up in a foreign government's investigation of a bombing would have terrified Daniel. Now he was more worried about having his head taken off by a pissed-off angel with a magical flaming sword.

"A name change isn't going to throw off any of your kind." Daniel walked with Zaid up a series of winding stone staircases enclosed by wrought-iron bannisters. The metal key from the desk opened up a room on the second floor decorated in the same lavish style as the rest of the building, down to a mirrored desk and silk-trimmed bed crammed with embroidered pillows. "How are we going to get Zahara to come out of hiding? I'm worried about her."

"After midnight, you're going to cast a pentagram and summon her back." Zaid sat down on the bed and pulled the sling off his arm. He yanked off his shirt, and ran his hands over a knot of scar tissue running down from his shoulder. "She can't refuse. She's still bound by the contract."

"Your arm looks much better." Daniel touched the cut on his head, which still stung. At some point he was going to have to find a doctor to take the staples out.

"I heal fast." Zaid flexed and extended his well-defined bicep. "But I could use some purification after the pounding that so-called angel gave me. Go wash up, and the two of us will go to the *hammam*. I have an acquaintance here that may have some important information. He prefers to meet in locations unlikely to have anyone listening."

"What's a hammam?" Daniel asked.

"Think of it as a spa treatment." Zaid stretched his arms over his head. "I'm sure you'll enjoy it."

ONE HOUR AND one nice, hot shower later, Daniel put on all his clothes except for his shoes, and took a seat at the edge of the bed. Zaid had contacted his mysterious friend in the Moroccan police, and now they had a little more time to kill before heading over to whatever sort of spa Zaid had described as the meeting spot. He supposed he could try to take a quick nap, but once again, the sleeping arrangements in the room involved him and Zaid ... and one king bed. Trying to banish inappropriate thoughts from his mind, Daniel raised his voice and shouted through the wall. "So what's so terrible about Zahara's true form?"

The rush of water from the shower stopped, and Zaid stepped out of the bathroom, wearing a small towel and nothing else. "Her clan is of the old blood—demons you would call them—from out of Arabia. Her mother is one of the most powerful *shaytana* in our world. That family background comes with certain presumptions. Cute and fuzzy aren't among them."

"So Zahara's mother has unrealistically high expectations for her daughter." Daniel tried to break things down into terms he could process. "I can relate to that. My mother's still giving me grief about not going to medical school."

Zaid sprawled out on the small sofa next to the bed, making no effort to put any of his clothes back on. "It all makes sense now. I always wondered why she never chose to return home. Her clan has always refused to intermarry with the dev of Persia, or others of their kind who live in the Mountains of Qaf. It's also not uncommon for some of the jinn to take a human lover, bring some fertile blood into the mix. But they've remained above all that. The mere sight of some of her relatives would turn you to stone. Others could drive you to kill yourself by their speech alone."

"Death by petrification, death by assisted suicide." Daniel rubbed his temple. "But Zahara is death by cute."

"Exactly." Zaid glanced at the open seat beside him on the sofa. Daniel wasn't sure if he should move closer to him, go and take another, colder shower, or continue to stare at his bare feet. He opted for the third choice.

"I thought she was a half-blood human when we first met. Every century our numbers dwindle, and we have fewer offspring. Meanwhile the world of man grows larger exponentially. Mixing is frowned upon, but it works. At least in terms of having a child. What you'll end up with is another question. Magical abilities can skip a generation—or twenty."

"So." Daniel got up enough nerve to meet his eyes. "Are there any little Zaids running around?"

The jinn laughed. "No. But I have two brothers, both married, and one of them has been blessed with two children."

"Do you get to see your family much?" Maybe the conversation had gone a little too far, become too intimate. But Daniel had a hard time stopping. There was so much he wanted to know about Zaid's world, and about the man himself.

"No." Zaid was silent for a long moment. "My family rejects my conversion. Most of the jinn follow the old religions. Pagans, I suppose you would call them. They have many gods, many goddesses. Different tribes follow different ones. Even our enemies, like the peri of Persia, hold similar beliefs. But some of us have accepted the current religions of man. Mostly we live here. It's easier on everyone."

"How did you decide to become—" Daniel searched for a word. *Good* was awfully judgmental. After all, he had several friends who were pagans of one sort or another. Aside from burning an excess of patchouli whenever they came over to visit, they were nice people. "When did you convert?"

"A long time ago." Zaid stared out the window as he spoke. "At least by how you reckon time. It was in your country, actually. I had become involved in a nasty blood feud in this world, and, in the interests of keeping the death toll down, I was asked to take a vacation away from Baghdad. The further away the better, so I decided to take a steamboat and see America."

"This was in the 1800s?" Daniel asked.

"Thereabouts." Zaid sighed. "I was a cocky son of a bitch then. Of course, some might argue I'm the same now. In any event, I was bored and looking for entertainment. I decided to possess a young Muslim I came across in Boston—a freed slave, who worked in a coppersmith's foundry, hoping to apprentice himself. Not much iron there, and some of the metal work interested me, so I had stopped by to shop. His name was Rahman, and God, he was beautiful. Young and pure, with eyes like a doe. At that time, if I liked something, I just took it. He fought me off harder than I would have expected, even after I gave him shaking seizures and drained half the life out him."

"That's horrible!" Daniel broke in, a note of indignation in his voice.

"Zahara wasn't lying when she told you I had been a bad boy." Zaid's face settled into a grim smile. "I was careless. What did these foreigners know of the jinn? Nothing. They had their own spirits to haunt them. But the boy was devout, and he sought help from a wise woman. Half-Iroquois, she was, and could carry out a mean exorcism." Zaid gave a brief shudder. "She was quite a force, and I've been attacked by some of the best."

"So she was able to save the boy?" Daniel moved closer to the edge of the bed, leaning forward to hear how the story ended.

"She expelled me from Rahman, and that put me in a bad spot." Zaid stroked his chin. "In my arrogance I hadn't taken any precautions, and I was vulnerable. She was able to trap me in one of the shop's copper vessels and allowed Rahman to decide whether to destroy me or throw me into the depths of the ocean to rot for a long, long time."

"Sounds like you deserved both," Daniel said. "So how did you get away?"

"I didn't," Zaid said. "Rahman let me go. Told me that the children of smokeless fire were as much a part of God's creation as he was, and his only wish was that I wouldn't inflict the tortures he had endured upon anyone else."

"Wow." Daniel swallowed hard. "I thought only Jews were good at laying on that level of guilt."

Zaid shook his head, smiling. "So I beat a hasty retreat, and licked my wounds for a while. But I had a hard time getting what he had told me out of my head. Eventually I couldn't resist, and visited him again, while he prayed."

"Can't imagine he was too happy to see you."

"He wasn't afraid, or even surprised." Zaid turned back to the window again, and shut his eyes, as if to bring the memories flooding back. "He spoke to me for a while about God, and I went away. Then I came back a few days later, and then again. Eventually, I began to study a little, and learn more about his beliefs. I said the *shahada* a few years later."

"What happened to him?"

"We became good friends." Zaid turned back to Daniel, his face wistful. "But your kind is shorter-lived than mine. He died of cholera as an old man, well into his seventies. A noted imam by then and a force for good in his community. I looked after his extended family for a while, then returned back to my own clan. But my decision was not welcome there, and I'm not allowed to return to the world of the jinn. Sometimes I go the mosque to pray and no one thinks of me as anyone unusual. But sometimes people can see through the facade and recognize me for what I am. Like Imam Youssef's wife. After she told him, he was nice enough to overlook the fact he has a jinn in his congregation."

"So you and Zahara are both exiles." Daniel stood up as Zaid got around to finding his clothes. "I wish I didn't have to wait until midnight. I don't like the idea of her out there alone with Harut and Marut on the loose. Remember not to tease her too much about looking like the latest plushie from the Disney store."

Zaid had stepped into his jeans, and he paused for a moment before pulling a tight gray shirt over his muscular torso. "I'll do my best. As much as I try, totally reformed isn't how I'd describe myself."

DANIEL CLUTCHED THE towel around his midsection and tried to keep his gaze centered on his flip-flops. He wasn't sure what he had expected a hammam to be like. Sparkling white walls and a hot tub, perhaps. Or maybe some neatly dressed women applying algae face masks. He hadn't expected a communal sauna packed with dozens of undressed men, each better looking than the next.

"Are you ready?" Zaid motioned for him to enter into a closed-off room to his right. Steam roiled up the edges of the rock walls around them, giving the jinn's dark skin a fine, wet sheen. He was entirely naked. The chiseled chest and powerful arms apparent even under his clothing ended in a rippled abdomen. His legs were now entirely human, with the same taut musculature as the rest of his body. And as for what was between his legs... well, "decidedly larger than average" was about all Daniel's mind could come up with.

"Sure." Daniel tried to get the words out in a casual tone. "So your friend is already in there?"

"He can't wait to meet you. Now, lose the towel." Zaid snatched it off him and motioned to the entrance.

Daniel mumbled something in response, and opened the door to walk inside. The dripping wet rock walls of the traditional hamman surrounded a few low stone benches. A domed ceiling, topped by a brass grate set into the apex, allowed in a few glints of starlight. The center of the space was dominated by a massive metal brazier holding piles of glowing coals. The man seated on the bench at the far wall reached over to pour a ladle of water over them, sending clouds of white vapor billowing into the air. The steam dissipated, revealing the man's features. He was large—taller than Zaid, with a polished bald head and a well-trimmed mustache. His aging physique still radiated grizzled strength.

"Good to see you again, my old friend." The man nodded at Zaid, then grinned at Daniel, as his eyes examined him closely. "*Asaylumu alaikum*, and *bonjour*. My name is Ahmed. A great pleasure to meet you."

Zaid took a seat on the bench opposite him, and Daniel followed suit. "Peace be with you, brother Ahmed. This is my friend Daniel Goldstein."

"Ah. I should have said *shalom*, then." The man gave a chuckle. "So, what puts you in the company of the infamous Zaid? Are you Mossad?"

Daniel rolled his eyes. He was growing tired of this line of questioning. "Hmm... Mossad. Is that a well-known high-tech firm in the region? Because everyone around here keeps asking me if I work for them."

Zaid winced, but Ahmed broke out into peals of laughter. "Oh, very good. Very good joke indeed."

"Daniel's connection to the incident in Marrakech has more to do with my world than yours." Zaid stretched out his arms into the heat pouring out of the coals in front of them. The scar on his arm had faded further, down to a thin white line. "If this problem involved only the affairs of men, I would take whatever revenge I saw fit and not involve you."

Ahmed stroked the side of his mustache. "What I've heard so far is that the Borskoi incident was a hit—an operation carried out by foreign radicals the Russian had provided some financial assistance to. Of course, it was a major blow against the government as well. The king panics easily over any threat to tourism."

"Anyone who makes money off it panics over a drop in tourism," Zaid replied. "But that's not what I'm concerned about, even though my business was destroyed. This so-called jihadist group answers to someone not from this world. And your friends in the military aren't going to be able to stop him."

"Oddly enough, I've heard a similar theory." Ahmed smiled and raised his hands. Each one was the size of a slab of beef. "From an American, no less."

"A US government official told you they believe in the jinn?" Daniel asked.

"I wouldn't describe this conversation as an official one, no." Ahmed shook his head. "Your state department is concerned, of course, with a bomb blast in a major city here. There's talk of purse strings loosening further, and newer and better technology for us. But this consultant I met with—Donnelly, he calls himself—speaks of more than computers and the latest military hardware."

Zaid leaned back, droplets of sweat on his skin gleaming gold in the glow of the brazier. "Your reputation for connections with the unseen world brings you interesting visitors, Ahmed."

The huge man chuckled. "Perhaps. I played dumb, of course. But he hinted that this... *someone* you speak of was known to his people. As in, he's killed a good number of American ex-soldiers."

"He'll kill again if he gets what he wants," Zaid said. "I have a proposal for you. Daniel and I need some breathing room from your people and whatever insanity the Americans have dreamed up. In return for your help, I'll make sure any human allies of our enemy I come across end up in your capable hands."

"If possible." Ahmed leaned forward to pour more water on the brazier. "One or two of them alive would be appreciated."

"I'll try." Zaid stood up and stretched, motioning for Daniel to follow him. "Far too many humans have developed an unhealthy interest in the affairs of the jinn. Things are going to get bloody, and soon."

Chapter Twelve

ZAHARA PERCHED ON the roof of the hotel like a gargoyle defending her castle, and plotted her revenge.

To protect herself from discovery, she had assumed not only invisibility but her elemental form. In that shape, she was about the size of an undersized lynx or an overfed Maine Coon cat. Her batlike wings gave her a reasonable ability to fly at night, especially if she launched herself off a nice perch, like the one she had chosen. The rest of her, as Daniel had so painfully put it, was *adorable*. Her fangs could do little more than give someone a good nip; only the claws jutting from her padded paws had any ability to inflict real harm. Her wide brown eyes, set off with long lashes, only contributed to her strong resemblance to a child's plush toy.

No wonder her mother considered her an embarrassment to the clan.

It was close to midnight, the time when Zahara's limited skills in magical mischief were at their peak. If she wanted to avenge her humiliation, now was the time. Not to mention that moping around in the hotel spa and raiding dessert platters in the kitchen was getting old fast.

She had fled Le Bar Churchill and gone into hiding seconds after dragging Zaid and Daniel through the seven levels and materializing with both of them in the hotel. A few weeks ago, she might have considered that a triumph. Her family had feared she wouldn't even be able to transport herself through the levels without getting lost, much less take two people—one of them human, no less—with her. None of that mattered now. That awful angel could have killed all three of them, sparing her the humiliation of having her true form revealed. As it was, the only one who had probably been killed was Daniel. And that had been her fault in a way.

She wasn't sure why the thought of Daniel dead or comatose bothered her so much. It was unseemly to care about a sorcerer. And as mortifying as her charisma spell was, at least it had done a certain amount of damage. But not to the right person—the one who had lured her in with his fantastic body, then exposed her secret.

Harut.

Clearly, the angel deserved the worst and most original revenge she could think up. The problem was, she had no idea what to do to him, or how to do it.

She needed to have a chat with the one person who might be able to help her—Daniel's late, lamented bubbe. After all, she was the one with the bright idea to stop Harut and Marut in the first place.

Zahara regarded the stars sparkling above her, stretched her wings out, and soared across the hotel gardens. Within a few minutes, she was flapping her way over the bustling crowds in Jemaa el-Fnaa. Either from defiance or merely in the pursuit of an evening's entertainment, the square remained crowded despite the recent bombing attack. Puffs of aromatic smoke from outdoor carts selling hot street food floated around her, and she dipped lower to inspect the scene, seeing nothing out of the ordinary except for a heavy military presence.

She flew down side streets, twisting and banking to wind her way through the narrow alleys before perching upon the balcony railing of Daniel's grandmother's house. Below, a pair of bored police officers smoked and traded complaints as they guarded the front entrance. Zahara hopped down and used one of her claws to pry open the balcony doors a crack, then squeezed inside.

Nothing looked much different to her in the master bedroom. The official investigation of the property had involved removing the stash of weapons—the pornography had vanished as well; valuable evidence, no doubt—and shifting around some of the furniture, but little else had been touched. After a few cautious sniffs, she left the bedroom and made her way down to the first floor. The hanging goat and most of the blood had been cleaned up, but the room where they had narrowly escaped Marut's rage was still trashed, with splinters of wood strewn over the cracked floor tiles.

Zahara prowled around the perimeter of the room, ears pricked up to catch any threatening noises. Aside from a few odd creaks, silence reigned. She sat down and raised a hind leg to scratch at one ear, uncertain how to proceed. Communication with the human dead was an unusual talent for a jinn, and, although her family had done its share of dispatching humans to the hereafter in a variety of gruesome ways, none of them possessed that particular ability.

"May I speak with you, *lalla*?" Zahara spoke in the Moroccan dialect of Arabic. No harm using the polite form to address an older woman of impressive power, even if she was dead.

"Did Daniel send you?"

Zahara startled as the words echoed through the empty house. "He needs your advice." She thought it best not to mention that in all likelihood, Daniel would be joining his grandmother in the hereafter shortly. "We need to know how to kill Harut."

"Harut's not the problem, my dear." The voice held an edge of irritation. "Marut's the one who needs to be stopped."

"Well, maybe we can take Harut out first and then get his big brother." Zahara paced forward a few steps, her whiskers quivering. Granted, she knew little about ghosts, but Daniel's grandmother didn't sound all that... dead. "Any advice would be nice. A fatal flaw or two, maybe a critical weakness—even a food allergy would help at this point."

A deep sigh filled the room. Maybe ghosts didn't appreciate humor. "Tell my grandson to travel to Ouazarzate. The veil is thin there. My tie to my old home is too weak for him to come here."

Zahara doubted Daniel was in any shape to jaunt off to the south of Morocco. This whole ghost-whisperer mission had been a waste of her time. "I'll be sure to pass that along."

"The letter I sent him has instructions to help him. Tell him to read it again, carefully this time. No offense, dearie, but you're far from the best jinn for this type of work."

Zahara prepared herself to give this obnoxious granny ghost a few choice words, but a faint shudder ran through the floor underneath her, and she slunk back into a corner, alarmed. Maybe pissing off Daniel's bubbe wasn't the best idea. She eyed the large windows on the far wall of the dining room that overlooked the house's central courtyard. She could break one and fly through it to safety, if she had to.

But as she considered the window best situated for a quick escape route, the glass shattered and imploded. The figure of a man appeared in the frame, silhouetted against the night sky behind him. He leapt into the room, landing in a crouch.

Zahara restrained herself from letting out a loud snarl as Harut rose to his feet, pulling out his sword. He held up his left hand, and a ball of pure, white flame floated up toward the ceiling, bathing the room in light. He spun in a circle, poised for attack.

Her fur on end, Zahara crept along the wall, placing each paw on the ground with care. She wasn't as confident of her invisibility spell in the harsh magical light Harut had brought into the space, and she would need to take a running leap to have any chance of getting enough height to fly out the window the angel had broken.

Harut, rather unexpectedly, sheathed his blade and stood under the brilliant light above him with his head bowed. Zahara paused to watch him. She could see his lips moving, as if in prayer. He remained still for a moment, then raised his arms. The light above him intensified, sending blinding beams around the room. She cringed, trying to shrink herself down into the smallest ball of fur possible.

The light diminished, and Harut stood—naked save his sheathed sword—in the center of the room. A pair of wings had sprouted from his back, huge feathered things that swept out on either side of him. Despite herself, Zahara froze in place, entranced. The disorienting high of his charisma spell, which had charmed her like a mosquito to an electrically charged death, wasn't in play here. It was more that he was so beautiful, in a haunting, alien way, that she couldn't tear her gaze away from him. Not only his body, magnificent as it was. No, it was the wings that fascinated her. Each feather was embedded with different eyes, blinking and opening in turn. Some were human, with a rainbow of iris colors. Others were the fierce eyes of birds of prey.

Zahara shook her head, angry with herself. Now was not the time to be swept up in lust, or whatever crazy emotion made her so fascinated with Harut. She needed to get out of here before he finished the job he had started on the rooftop of Zaid's apartment building.

"I know you're here, Zahara." Harut's voice broke the silence. "You're quite clever about hiding, I'll admit, but I can sense your presence."

Zahara's heart pounded in her chest, and the acid chill of panic spread through her. Even Zaid hadn't been able to defeat Harut, and her last and worst weapon, the unbearable cuteness of her true form, had done little more than stun him.

"I'm not going to hurt you." Harut turned in a circle, his eyes searching the room.

No, he wasn't—not if Zahara had anything to say about it. Why was he trying to trick her? Probably to draw her out. He had all but admitted he couldn't pinpoint her location. She bared her teeth and padded behind an overturned side table.

"I need to know more about Daniel." Harut took several steps forward, appearing to focus on the broken window above him. That was the most obvious escape route, and it made sense he would recognize that. The dining room doors were the next best choice, but they were on the far side of the room, and the light from his unnatural ball of fire illuminated them far too well for her taste. "Did he summon you for power, money, lust? Or does he want to stop my brother because it's the right thing to do?"

Now, what possible difference did that make? Zahara had to bite back a sarcastic retort. At least Marut hadn't tried to bore her to death with stupid rhetorical questions before attempting to smash her into the floor.

Then she saw it—a way out of this awful situation and a chance to pay Harut back for all the trouble he had caused.

A dust-covered armoire holding some shattered dinnerware stood to Harut's right, a little out of his line of vision. With a good, strong push, she could topple the heavy wooden antique on top of him. It wouldn't be as spectacular as when she had pinned Marut under the sharpened iron point of the chandelier, but it should be enough to give her a head start in her escape. Maybe even break a few of his bones.

She took the risk of transforming into her human form, still wearing her nightclub belly-dancing outfit. Too revealing and too jingly jangly, especially her coin belt. Fortunately, magic involving material goods, especially clothing, was another of her freakish strengths that perplexed her family. With a whispered spell, she draped herself in a full black *niqab*, similar to the body-enveloping outfit her mother had worn for their lunch meeting. Well, not too similar. Hers clung to every curve, with an embroidered fringe hiding all of her face except for her eyes.

Drawing closer and closer to Harut, she skulked along the wall as he continued to scan the room for her. When she reached the armoire, she stepped behind it and pressed two silk glove-covered hands against the back of it. One shove and the weight of the entire piece should land directly on him. Then she stopped, a tremor passing through her body. She stumbled backward, horrified. No, not now, of all times.

She was being summoned. Her do-gooder of a sorcerer had picked this moment to cast a pentagram and call her to do his bidding. Not only had Daniel survived; he had decided to force her to travel through the levels to join him.

This couldn't be happening. Only a few of the jinn—like her people, or the cunning dev of Persia—could traverse the levels of hell and pop out wherever they wished. It was an awesome, frightening power.

It also had a few serious drawbacks.

For one thing, it was hardly subtle. Black flames licked around her feet with a loud crackling noise, and her lower body began to dissolve. But her upper body was now completely visible, her hiding spell null and void.

Harut spun around and spotted her in an instant, his hand flying to his sword. She tried to frantically beat out the flames and return to the safety of invisibility.

The compulsion hit her again, impossible to resist. She couldn't stop it, and she couldn't speed it up, either. No other magic worked during her dissolution, and none would work until she regained her full form at whatever location Daniel had chosen for this ill-timed rendezvous. Knowing him, he had probably summoned to her rescue a pet cat stuck up in a tree or something like that.

Harut crossed the distance between them in a few quick steps, his sword now in hand. Not only couldn't she dissolve in time—she couldn't even do much to fight him off. Marut had survived Zaid's sword thrust when he was half-formed; she had no such chance against his brother. Harut reached out a hand, his eyes burning into hers and his wings spread out behind him in the awful, horrible shape of an avenging monster. She stared back at him, terrified, as the flames leapt higher.

But Harut never delivered the killing blow. The boom of transition into hell resounded though the room, deafening in its loudness before fading to a whisper, and she dissolved into blackness.

Chapter Thirteen

DANIEL CHECKED HIS watch and drew a single match across the rough surface of the box's lighting strip. The blueish flame snapped and crackled into life, and he bent down to touch it to the wick of the last black candle. He placed the oil lamp inside the pentagram he had drawn out on the tiled patio of the hotel's inside courtyard. Raising his hand, he coughed out Zahara's name. For added measure, he said it another two times. Three times was the charm, wasn't it? Then he stopped, and waited.

Black smoke curled up from the lamp at the center of the pentagram, suspended in the air like a vaporous question mark. Then a harsh crack of thunder echoed overhead as a hot breeze, redolent of jasmine and burnt metal, blew over him. The smoke swirled into the conical shape of a veiled woman. She lifted her head, then took a series of swaying steps toward him, small gusts fluttering the lace fabric framing her face and revealing a flash of oval eyes beneath long lashes.

"What do you want now?" Zahara placed both hands on her hips and stamped her foot. "For your information, this was not a good time to interrupt me."

"I was worried about you." Daniel extended both arms in her direction, then dropped them by his sides as she turned her face away. "We've got two badass angels on our tail, bombs going off in nightclubs, and I've had to do the shopping for both of us. We need to stick together."

"You're not dead." Zahara made the statement sound like an accusation. "I warned you my true form would overwhelm the most heroic of humans, much less someone like you. I don't how you survived, but I'm sure the shock of it wiped all memories from your consciousness."

"It was hard to forget." Daniel winced as soon as he said it. Zahara's shoulders slumped, her entire body appearing smaller. "I mean, you almost did me in. It took a major interfaith conference to rescue my immortal soul. Not to mention that you saved all three of us from Harut. I owe you. Zaid owes you."

"Zaid." Zahara drew her breath in with a sharp gasp. "He saw everything. Is he here now, with you?"

"He was the one who suggested I summon you again." Daniel held out his hand. "I don't understand why you're so upset."

"You saw the real me!" Zahara's eyes glistened with tears. "How can I command respect from wretched sorcerers so desperate for power and gold they endanger their souls by summoning me if I look like a... a..."

"An adorable baby gargoyle with fuzzy ears and cute little dragon wings?"

"I'm not a gargoyle." Zahara reached out to shake him as hard as she could. "Try to get your imperialist Western paranormal concepts out of my culture. I'm a *lamassu*, you idiot."

"Of course you are." Daniel leaned forward to engulf her

in a hug. "And an extremely scary one at that. Far more terrifying than those crazy French colonial gargoyles. Which, by the way, also scare the hell out of me."

"You really think I'm awful and terrifying?" Zahara slipped her arms around his neck and he squeezed her back as hard as he could.

"Absolutely." Daniel stepped back from her, smiling. "Now let's get back to Zaid."

"He'll make fun of me." Zahara wiped a tear from her cheek. "I know him. He won't be able to resist."

"Don't worry." Daniel took her arm in his and began to walk her back to the hotel room. "I had a long talk with him about sensitivity, and being in touch with other people's feelings. I'm sure he'll be very understanding."

DANIEL KNOCKED ON the door. He had an extra key, but he wanted to make sure Zaid knew he was coming in with Zahara. Now that they were all back together, he needed to keep the group as harmonious as possible. They were in too much danger to quarrel among themselves.

Zaid swung open the door and beamed at Zahara. "*Cherie*. You're back, and safe. I'm overjoyed. Come in and relax. I told the kitchen to send up a dessert platter, just for you."

Zahara chewed on her lower lip for a moment, giving Daniel a questioning look. He waved his hand toward Zaid and they walked into the room.

It took a few seconds for Daniel to notice anything was

wrong. After all, the hotel's interior decorator had been fond of colorful pillows and soft throws. So the added effect of hundreds of plush toys strewn over every item of furniture in the suite didn't register for a long moment. He bent over to pick one up. It was in the shape of a black cat, adorned with pink glitter wings and a dragon tail.

"Where did these come from?" he asked.

"You!" Zahara's voice rose several octaves into a shriek that shattered the facade of the mirrored desk, along with every other glass surface in the room.

Zaid backed away from her, bent over double in mirth. "I thought you might feel more at home surrounded by some of your cute little friends."

"I don't look anything like this!" Zahara snatched the stuffed animal out of Daniel's hand and threw it at Zaid. "That's it. I'm challenging you to a duel." She stripped off her veil and outer garment, revealing the belly-dancer outfit she had worn in the nightclub. Her ornate sword flashed into her hand.

"A duel?" Zaid choked out the words between laughs. "I taught you how to fight, darling. Before you met me the only thing you knew how to do with that sword was balance it on your bosom."

"I have news for you, Zaid." Zahara thrust her chest out and shimmied her substantial cleavage into a blur of movement. "This amazing rack is going to be the last thing you ever see."

"What can I say?" Zaid's own sword, a curved blade with a simple cross hilt, appeared in his hand. He raised it up to his face, then flourished downward in a formal salute. "I couldn't ask for a better way to go."

Eschewing such formalities, Zahara charged forward with her blade raised.

Daniel hopped up on the bed to get away from the clash of metal. This was not how he had intended the group reunion to go. "The two of you are going to trash the hotel room. We're trying to be undercover here, remember?"

He jumped off the bed a second later as Zahara took a flying leap onto it, then used the mattress as a springboard to charge at Zaid. The male jinn fended off one, then two blows and made a half-hearted attempt to strike the sword from her hand. She did a handless backflip out of the way, then hopped onto the cracked bureau to gain a height advantage over him, slashing in a blind rage.

Daniel found himself backed up against an open closet door, unable to do much but watch the bout progress. He knew nothing about sword fighting, but Zaid didn't seem to be breaking a sweat in this match. Both he and Zahara were lefties, but Zaid flipped his sword from one hand to the other, blocking his opponent's increasingly furious blows with ease.

"I'm not cute, and I'm not adorable." Zahara leapt off the dresser and back onto to the bed, kicking off most of the collection of toys strewn over it before doing her best to decapitate her opponent. "You take it all back, now!"

Zaid stepped smartly to one side to dodge a particularly wild blow. "It's not my fault your elemental form looks like a cross between a pussycat and a fruit bat."

Zahara screamed in fury and attempted to use her sword as a skewer. Zaid lost his focus, laughing, then struck out with a more serious blow aimed at knocking her sword from her hand. Instead, his leg gave way with a high-pitched squeak as he stepped on one of the more musical of the many toys he had hauled into the room. The stumble gave Zahara an opening, and her next blow opened up a slash on Zaid's right arm.

The two of them paused for a moment, as if neither of them believed she had succeeded in landing the hit.

"I have to admit, *cherie*." Zaid admired the blood welling out through his shirt sleeve for a moment. "You're a much better fighter when you're angry."

His sword spun into a blur, and with a flurry of blows he forced Zahara back toward the closet door Daniel was half-hiding behind.

So much for group unity and so much for their deposit on the hotel room. The floor was strewn with shards of broken mirrors. Zahara's slashing attacks had left dozens of the stuffed animals decapitated, with a high toll among the decorative pillows as well. Feathers and white stuffing drifted in clouds around the room, falling around the two battling fighters like drifts of artificial snow.

"She's a *lamassu*," Daniel shouted at Zaid. Unless he wanted to end up like one of the mutilated plushies, there was no way he could get around the two jinn to run out the front door. Even the path to the room's balcony, which sat above a two-story drop to the ground outside, was blocked.

"The smallest *lamassu* I've ever met was the size of a house," Zaid yelled back at him. "Body of a lion, giant eagle wings, head of warrior king. Does that sound like anything we saw last night?"

"Maybe she's small for her age." Daniel dropped into a crouch as a sword splintered the flimsy wood of the closet door inches above his head. "Anyway, let's cut out the swordplay and agree to disagree on the subject."

"The three of you have an odd way of settling your differences." Harut's voice, calm and dispassionate, silenced the frenzied noise in the room like a stereo plug had been ripped out of the wall. Zahara and Zaid froze, swords in hand, as Daniel crawled into the open. The angel stood in the doorway of the outside balcony. He was dressed in a white shirt and pants, without any visible weapon.

"I've come here to propose a *hudna*, during the time of your greatest power." Harut waved a graceful arm in the direction of the stars sparkling above the broad-leafed tree outside.

"Great. You'll be easier to kill, then." Zaid leveled his sword at the angel and Zahara followed suit.

Daniel scrambled to his feet and dashed over to plant himself in front of Harut, arms extended. "No! He's offering a truce." He turned back to Harut, hoping that's what *hudna* meant. "He isn't carrying a weapon. Are the two of you going to attack an unarmed man who came in peace?"

Zaid paused at this. Zahara gave Daniel a perplexed look.

"Yes." She charged forward to attack Harut, who raised a hand. Both she and Zaid flew backward in the air against the wall, their swords clattering to the ground.

"I said I came unarmed during the time of your greatest power." He folded his arms. "Not that I'm helpless."

Zahara recovered first, picking herself up off the floor and tossing aside the eviscerated plush toys that had cushioned her fall. "One more step, and I show you the real me again."

"Please don't," Daniel groaned. "It was like watching thirty-six hours of adorable kitten videos."

"Odd, I would have assumed you'd try to push an item of furniture on top of me." Harut's comment was lost on Daniel, but Zahara didn't seem surprised by it. What had she been up to before he had summoned her back?

"Moving on to more important matters." Daniel glared at Zaid to stop him from grabbing his weapon. "Harut, you're here because you want to work with us, right?"

Harut regarded Daniel for a moment, his expression unreadable. "Is it painful, the injury to your head?"

Daniel touched the cut on his scalp, unsure what that had to do with anything. "Still a little sore, I guess."

With a quick fluid motion, Harut took a few steps toward Daniel, and rested his palm on his forehead. Daniel couldn't decide whether to pull away, or accept this as an odd version of a handshake. Harut drew his hand back, and the metal staples that had been used to clip Daniel's scalp together fell to the floor. Daniel ran his fingers through his hair, now unable to find any evidence of the cut—not even a faint tenderness.

"The righteous, I can heal." Harut pointed to a bloodied Zaid, who had retreated back to lean against the wall, watching the angel with narrowed eyes. Zahara crept up next to him for protection. "My powers cannot help those who are not righteous."

"As if I'd ever let you lay hands on either one of us while my heart was still beating," Zaid snarled.

"Look, I appreciate the hands of healing trick, but you need us as much as we need you." Daniel gave a quick sideways glance to ensure Zahara wasn't positioning herself for another sneak attack on Harut. "You can't stop Marut on your own, or you wouldn't be here. And if you want to work with me, you have to work with Zahara and Zaid as well. We're a team."

Zahara made an outraged noise, somewhere in between a snort and a soft growl.

Harut gave a slow nod. "Very well. I accept your terms."

"I'll tell you who's a team," Zaid said. "The two so-called angels who've been hanging by their feet for a few thousand years, waiting for revenge. Maybe Harut's here on Marut's orders, and this hudna is nothing more than a trick."

Harut gave both Zaid and Zahara a hard look. "As for my brother's true intentions, you're welcome to ask him about them, seeing as he'll be here shortly. He might even answer, before he kills all of you. I didn't come here only to form an alliance; I came to warn you. Marut knows where Daniel is, and he's planning to kill him and anyone else who gets in his way."

Chapter Fourteen

ZAHARA LEANED BACK against the car door and narrowed her eyes into another evil glare at Harut. She had spent the ride keeping as far away from him as possible. A difficult task, since they were both back seat passengers in the same car. Under normal circumstances, if she had been in a confined space with a man even half as attractive as Harut, someone would have had to peel her off his lap.

After a quick and prudent departure via the balcony from their hotel, the four of them had sped off toward the mountains in Zaid's SUV. Dawn had broken around them, followed by the full light of day, and still the ride dragged on. At least she wasn't the only one in a foul mood after Daniel's insistence Harut join the team. Zaid drove on in silence, one hand on the wheel and a sullen expression under his dark sunglasses.

She squirmed in her seat, unable to decide what irritated her more—that her newest archenemy was sitting comfortably only a few inches away, enjoying the view, or that he wasn't paying any attention to her.

"Aren't you tired of ogling piles of brown rock?" Zahara had never been good at keeping quiet, and the silence in the car got the best of her. "You act like you've never seen a mountain before."

"Well, I haven't seen these mountains before." Harut's serene gaze remained fixed on the dizzying drop of plunging slopes below them, their rocky brown surfaces interspersed with a handful of goats nimbly devouring patches of grass. Zaid continued to weave the car around the narrow road spiraling up in elevation, slowing just enough at each bend to avoid local traffic whizzing in the opposite direction. "I was thinking they would be lovely to fly over."

"I think it would be lovely to be over them and back on a flat surface." Daniel had both eyes shut tight, his head plastered back as far as possible in his seat. Zaid gave him a brief grin and accelerated around the next curve.

"What about you?" Harut gave her a sideways glance, a faint smile playing over his lips. "Do you like flying, in your odd little winged form? Most of your kind prefer slithering underground, or perhaps sniffing around at human garbage dumps."

Zaid flashed him an irritated glance from the rearview mirror. "Apparently, you've never tried to outfly an ifrit. Maybe I could introduce you to a few of them. I hear they're partial to roast hawk."

"Daniel's evil *jinnayah* isn't an ifrit, certainly." Harut turned back to the window. "And she has a most unusual method of defense. A charisma spell so powerful the viewer is left catatonic. The only beings I've heard of with a similar effect are infant *cherubim*."

"How dare you insult my clan." Zahara wasn't about to sit there while Harut insinuated she had mixed blood. "I'll have you know my family traces its lineage back to Iblis himself."

"You think Zahara's kitty-cat gargoyle shape looks like a cherub?" Daniel opened his eyes and peered around the seat rest at the two of them. "I'm still recovering from the trauma of it all, but what I saw of her didn't remind me of a cute naked baby flapping his wings around."

"You're thinking of a *putto*." Harut's tone turned icy.

"You wouldn't think the little bastards were all that adorable if you'd been bitten by one," Zaid broke in. "Damn beasts were zooming around all over Sicily when I visited there last."

"The *cherubim* are a higher order of angel," Harut said. "I'm using the Hebrew term for them, since I thought you might possess some rudimentary knowledge of the beings described in your religious texts. *Karabu*, I suppose, might be the term the two jinn would be familiar with."

"My father was a *lamassu*," Zahara snapped. "An awful, terrifying creature with eagle wings who gobbled up anyone who came near the treasure he was guarding."

"Is that so?" Harut sounded unconvinced.

"Yes, it's so, because I said it was." Zahara could have come up with a few better arguments if her mother had ever bothered to tell her who her father actually was. Granted, there were an unwieldy number of possibilities.

Zahara folded her arms and turned away from Harut. Maybe *she* would stare out the window for a while. She peeked over her shoulder to check if he had noticed she was ignoring him.

"Are there any mixed marriage situations in your world?" Daniel asked. "If an angel and a demon ever decided to get busy, what would happen?"

"Nothing," Zaid said. "Because true angels obey God. Harut can call himself whatever he wants, but he and his brother are no different than us jinn. He may appear as different from us as a dev is from a peri, but he's as capable of mortal sin as we are."

"From what I've heard," Zahara added as much malice as she could into her words, "the two of you managed to work your way through quite a few of the traditional sins during your initial visit here. Let's see, drunkenness, idolatry, adultery, murder—am I missing anything?"

"Not much, no." Harut's gaze turned back to the mountains. Good. Maybe she had found a topic of conversation that would shut him up.

"What happened to the real Zahara?" Daniel asked. "In the versions I found online, she ascended up to the heavens and became a star or something like that."

"Not the heavens, certainly." Harut's tone indicated he considered that particular topic to be closed. "Since my release, I've seen some of the human texts you speak of. There's a kernel of truth in the stories. My brother and I were sought out by would-be sorcerers greedy for magic. I would warn them we were an infernal temptation, and to leave at once. If they did not heed my warning, Marut would grant them one power, which always came at an awful price."

"How many listened to you?" Daniel asked.

"Very few," Harut said. "Did you listen to any warnings about the price you would pay Zahara for the request you made of her?"

"No one warned me about anything," Daniel said. "Maybe my grandmother did, in the written instructions she left, but I freaked out and burned them."

There were a few moments of silence in the car. Zaid tilted his sunglasses down and turned to Daniel. "Did you even *try* to negotiate with her?"

"Sort of." Daniel's greenish skin tones turned pink around the edges. "I wanted three wishes. She said one, and then I told her if she helped me I'd follow all the rules." He rotated his head around to stare at Zahara, who did her best to feign interest in counting goats. "So, what are the rules?"

"The arrangement is always the same, unless you're absolutely specific in your conditions," Harut said. "Which you weren't."

"There is a strategy to these things, you know." Zaid mumbled something underneath his breath about human stupidity and punched the accelerator again. "Even I was outfoxed a few times. If your request is something the jinn is already honor-bound to perform, for example, you're off the hook."

"Okay, so I didn't think of anything like that." The car swerved around a speeding truck traveling in the opposite direction. Daniel closed his eyes and pressed his head back against the seat before addressing Zahara again. "So what is it you want when and if we stop Marut? A year's supply of cotton candy, maybe unlimited discounts on designer shoes. Oh, I know. More jewelry."

That same, odd heaviness Zahara had felt when she had seen the child sacrifice set up by her mother's magic settled into her chest. Maybe she needed to be checked out by a healer if she made it through all of this. Before she could think of anything to say, Harut answered for her.

"If we succeed and stop my brother, you owe Zahara your soul."

Daniel swallowed once, then leaned back into his seat. He didn't yell or curse at her, or try to come up with a way to weasel out of the arrangement.

Instead, he spoke to Zaid. "You could have said something."

Her friend cursed again, this time louder, and took the next few curves at an even faster pace. "Yes, I could have told you. But there's nothing I can do to help you."

"You can help yourself, you stupid idiot." Zahara found an empty water bottle and threw it over the seat at Daniel's head, since he wouldn't turn back to talk to her. "Run away. Do you think I *want* to go up against some giant winged monster who'll be unstoppable once he munches on you?"

They drove on for several long minutes, no one saying a word, before Daniel spoke again. "Running away isn't going to do any good if Marut needs to get to me before he can do some real damage. So I'll take all the help I can get. And that includes you, Zahara. Like it or not, you're working with the good guys on this one."

ZAHARA SPENT THE next few hours sulking. The men around her persisted in chitchatting with one another, discussing various options for defeating Marut. All the while, they ignored her sensible suggestion to run away and leave her out of the entire mess.

Try as she might, she couldn't tune out the conversation.

Harut shared some depressing information about his brother with Daniel and Zaid, most of which fit in with what she had learned from her mother. Marut could barely tolerate the sun's rays, and remained within the cave during the day. At night, he could roam the earth at will, traveling through the levels much as she could. That meant they had to travel and work in the sunlight, when she and Zaid were at a disadvantage.

Finally, the three men shut up as they reached their destination. Apparently, their late arrival was also her fault. Zahara had forgotten all about her conversation with Daniel's bubbe, and when she had thought to mention it, Zaid had already taken them a good few hours in the wrong direction.

Zaid pulled the car onto the wide thoroughfare running through the town. Adorned with elaborate street lights, the boulevard featured palm trees and pink buildings, some of which had been designed to resemble the local earthen brick *kasbahs*. Zahara now knew this useless fact, along with many others, thanks to Zaid. The jinn had gone on and on, explaining to Daniel the importance of the small southern city to the tourist industry, due in part to the presence of the country's largest movie studio. Why Zaid felt obligated to play tour guide to soothe Daniel was beyond her. It wasn't like he hadn't played his fair share of nasty games with wannabe sorcerers, back in the day. He had even gone so far as to reassure Daniel they should have little trouble finding a comfortable place to spend the night.

Unless Marut decided to pay them them a visit. That wouldn't be quite so comfy, now would it?

"Nice town." Daniel peered out the window in evident fascination. "What's it called again?"

"For the fifth time, it's Ouarzazate." Zahara hated that Daniel refused to give her the satisfaction of moaning and whining about being tricked. Clearly, he was going to see this stupid quest to the end if it killed him. And her. "Is it that hard for you to remember one non-English word?"

"It has a lot of vowels in it." Daniel wiggled out of his seat belt as Zaid parked the car. His rather entertaining shade of green had lightened after they had passed over the mountains and returned to a lower elevation.

Zaid turned off the ignition and opened his door. "I'm going to contact Ahmed again. I'd like an update on the Americans he warned me about."

He exited and slammed the door behind him without so much as a glance in Zahara's direction. Daniel scrambled out to follow him. Like a puppy. Why was he scampering after Zaid? He was *her* sorcerer. "Where are the two of you going?"

"I'm not staying in this car one minute longer than I have to." Daniel poked his head back inside. "Maybe you and Harut could compare notes about Marut's vulnerabilities. You know, do your job for a change."

Then he had the nerve to smile at her, before jogging off to catch up with Zaid.

"This is the town your companion spoke of, where the theater dramas are held?" Harut tapped her on the shoulder, interrupting her in the middle of choosing an appropriate revenge curse.

"It's called a movie studio." Zahara folded her arms and

leaned back in her seat. Harut's haphazard knowledge of the modern world was one of his few weaknesses. Unfortunately, she couldn't figure out a way to turn his naiveté about the latest film production techniques into a fatal flaw that allowed her to get rid of him. "Want to take the backstage tour?"

Outside the car, Zaid slowed down to let Daniel catch up, then gave him a slap on the back after a whispered conversation.

Zahara sat up straight. Was Zaid *happy* Daniel wanted to go ahead with this insane plan?

She let the two men get a little further down the sidewalk, then began to chant a spell. Maybe she'd start by giving Zaid a pair of donkey ears. Or think up something entertaining to do with the more sensitive areas of his anatomy.

"No." Harut placed his finger against her lips. Not the most unpleasant of sensations, of course, but how dare he try to shush her? "You must not attack your allies. This is dishonorable and devious."

Zahara snapped her teeth shut, and Harut pulled back his fingers just in time to avoid being bitten.

"He deserves it. And you have no business trying to stop me from playing a good trick on him. You tried to kill both of us, remember?"

"Things are different now." Harut motioned outside the car. "I'd like to take you up on your earlier offer to me, in fact."

Now that was more like it. Enemy or not, a lewd suggestion from Harut was quite welcome, given the rough day she'd endured. She reached out to run her fingers up his thigh. "Now, that might be exciting."

Harut caught her hand before she succeeded in getting anywhere interesting. "I meant the tour of the theater. This is something I wish to see."

HARUT LIFTED THE massive boulder over his head. It appeared to weigh as much as a baby elephant. After a moment of contemplation, he rested it back on the ground.

"Most interesting." He turned to Zahara. "And you say such artifices are nothing compared to this movie magic you speak of?"

So far, Zahara had driven Harut to the movie studio, endured a lackadaisical guided tour of the highlights, and provided the fascinated angel with plot synopses of all the major cinematic masterpieces filmed there. Now they were exploring the set's collection of movie props, including the giant foam rocks.

And she thought the car ride had been tedious.

"Oh, yes." Zahara leaned against the inner wall of the current set they were visiting—a rather convincing underground dungeon that had served in a number of productions she was familiar with. Too bad she couldn't tie up Harut inside of it and try out a few punishment techniques. That would make this silly side trip worth it. "Say 'CGI' three times and a giant wise-cracking marid appears to grant your every wish."

"You're mocking me." Harut sounded more amused

than irritated, which was not what Zahara had been going for. "Your knowledge of the modern world of man is quite extensive. I suppose for someone so young, adapting to such change is not difficult."

"I've been around." Zahara had no intention of telling Harut her true age. Jinn as young as herself were viewed as little more than children by most of her kind Zaid's age, let alone someone as old as Harut. He and his brother must be from her mother's youth, maybe even more ancient, if that was possible. No reason to reveal any more information to her enemy than she had already. "So happy to serve as your tour guide. Is this movie studio the real reason you and your brother decided to come here? Maybe the two of you are both frustrated Hollywood producers."

"Why Marut chose this country to begin his revenge is a mystery to me." Harut tilted his head back to look up at a scrollwork grill set in the ceiling, which let in streaks of light from the sunbaked grounds above. They had spent an interminable amount of time walking around there, as Harut had examined fake ancient Egyptian statues, some replicas of Roman siege devices, and a dusty fighter jet. The chatter of other tourists walking over the roof of the dungeon floated down into the artificial prison cell. "When I learned where my brother planned to obtain the sacrifice that would give him the power he seeks, I flew here to try and stop him."

"Do you mean that literally?" Zahara asked. "Not as in, 'I upgraded to business class and chose the shortest layover times?'"

"I used my elemental form to travel here, yes."

So he had turned into a hawk and headed out to track

down his big, bad brother. Zahara tried to imagine flapping her little wings all the way from Iran to Morocco. Truly, Harut was crazy.

"Our bond as brothers is broken forever, but the blood he carries is still close enough to mine that I can track him, if I perform a blood spell."

"Can he find you the same way?" Zahara asked. "That doesn't give me a warm and fuzzy feeling as I'm standing here next to you."

"Above all, he's drawn to the sacrifice that was denied him," Harut answered. "Daniel has become the one Marut wants."

"Well, he can't have Daniel, he's mine." Zahara paused, her curiosity overcoming her caution. "So why did you go back to his grandmother's house?"

"A new blood spell revealed one of my kind there." Harut came up to her, his gaze intense. "I thought my brother had returned. Instead, I found you."

Zahara didn't like that implication at all. "For one thing, my invisibility spell was working perfectly until Daniel blew my cover. For another, your angel radar is way off."

"My brother's blood wasn't what drew me there." Harut didn't lower his gaze. Any man who spent that much time looking into her eyes needed to make a pass at her or try to kill her. "Yours was."

"Keep it up." Zahara worked to keep the surprise out of her voice. "In another thousand years you might come up with a pickup line that works on me."

"I'm not making an indecent proposal." Harut leaned in closer. "I've told you about my past, now I want the truth from you. Who was your father?"

Even if Zahara knew the answer to that question, she wasn't about to tell Harut. She could either storm off in a fury to end the conversation, or lean forward and kiss him. That should shut him up.

Zahara pressed her lips against his, expecting him to pull away, or maybe smack her and give her a long talk about morality.

Instead, he grabbed her and kissed her back. Hard. Pushing her shoulders up against the cold stone of the wall behind her, he crushed her mouth against his. It was rougher than most frantic embraces that had come her way, and she liked that. A lot. Squeezing her eyes shut, she darted her tongue into his mouth.

Harut slid his hands up her shirt, cupping her breasts as he pressed her against the wall. Zahara slipped her own hands lower, tugging at the front of his pants. She arched her back, enjoying the feeling of his skin against hers.

An odd sensation buzzed along her spine. Zahara did her best to ignore it, wiggling her fingertips over Harut's belt and yanking it off.

"Foul spirit of smokeless fire, I summon you. Zahara, come forth."

She knew that voice from somewhere. But who would try to summon her here in Morocco? By name, no less.

"I call up the one known as Zahara. Reveal yourself to me as I command."

Anton. Daniel's bothersome and boring ex-boyfriend. Zahara opened one eye and stared up at a slim shadow looming over the metal grill set in the ceiling. What in the seven levels of hell was *he* doing here, and why was he attempting to summon her with one of the cheesiest incantation spells imaginable?

Anton's attempt at a summoning spell had no significant power over her, except to annoy her to the point where she would appear in front of him. With her sword at his throat. With some reluctance, she opened both eyes and pushed Harut off her. He pulled back, face flushed and panting, as she walked under the opening in the ceiling to confirm her suspicions.

"I'm sorry." Harut buried his face in his hands. He did have a flair for the dramatic that was for sure. All he had done was kiss her back. "I shouldn't have accosted you like that."

Zahara felt cranky after a week or two without someone naughty to spice things up for her. She couldn't imagine how she'd feel after hanging in a cave for a few thousand years without getting lucky. "Sorry about the interruption. But Daniel's about to get his revenge wish against his ex-boyfriend, whether he wants it or not."

She faded away into invisibility, leaving Harut searching the room for her, and ran out of the dungeons and onto the outdoor grounds of the movie theater. Sure enough, Anton stood directly above where he had so rudely interrupted her little underground tryst with Harut. Daniel's red-haired ex focused all of his attention on the crystal ball in his hand, polishing it with the stiffly-pressed cuff of his sleeve—as if cleaning it might help reveal her secret location.

A fortune-teller's *schtick*, really?

"Looking for me?" Zahara popped out into visibility. Anton gasped and took a step back. She snarled a spell, and the polished clear sphere cracked and shattered in Anton's hand. "Nice trick. You've found me. I'm going to make you regret that."

Anton turned a few shades paler than his usual coloring, which was quite an accomplishment. "I came here to find out what happened to Daniel. I know you're not human. But I can still cause a good deal of trouble for you if you've harmed him in any way."

Actually, he couldn't. His halfhearted attempt at a summons had put him in a precarious position. Without so much as a salt circle around him for protection, he had opened himself up to whatever Zahara wanted to do to him. Even better, the movie lot around them had emptied of tourists.

"You're trying to help Daniel Goldstein?" Harut came up to stand next to Zahara. Now, where had he come from that fast, and why was he butting in? "This woman and I are traveling with him, and he's under my protection. Why do you seek him?"

"Who are you?" Anton had his hand in his pocket, and Zahara didn't think he was doing anything entertaining with it. A gun wasn't going to work against her anyway, and if he attacked her first she had an even better excuse to resolve Daniel's emotional rebound issues. Permanently.

"His name's Harut, and he's gorgeous." The words slipped out of Zahara's mouth as her simmering rage at Anton faded. Standing there in the sun, with his hair ruffled by a faint breeze, Harut was utterly beautiful. She could lose herself in his emerald eyes for hours. And everything he said made so much sense, it was all so *right*, the way things should be.

Wait, *what?*

Zahara reached up and hit herself on her head with her palm. Harut might be trying out his charisma spell on Anton, but she was the one swooning over every word from the angel's lips. She needed to work on something to counter this persuasion thing Harut could pull off, and fast. At this rate, he was going to talk her into doing all sorts of things she didn't want to do. Like letting Anton live.

Anton, oddly enough, wasn't buying it. He grimaced and pulled his hand out of his pocket. Zahara's sword materialized in her hand, and she readied it for a quick slash across his neck. Daniel's ex thrust a necklace into Harut's face. As jewelry went, it looked pretty cheap—a braided string with a glass trinket dangling from it. The flat surface of the amulet resembled a large eye, with concentric circles of dark blue, white and light blue surrounding a black center.

Zahara shrieked when she recognized the object. She dashed behind Harut and pressed herself against his back. "Take that horrible thing away from him this instant!"

Harut reached out and took the item in his palm. "A *nazar*, with a small blessing upon it. Interesting. My companion would prefer you put it away, however."

Anton swallowed hard. "With what I paid for it, I was expecting it to have more impact."

"You were sold a talisman against the jinn," Harut said. "It won't help you against me. But if you're trying to help Daniel, you don't need to fear me."

"Is he all right?" Anton asked. He twisted the lapel of his

starched shirt, now damp with perspiration. "I never should have told him anything about Borskoi and that house in Marrakech. He isn't cut out for this sort of business."

Now, *that* sounded like a confession. Zahara peeked out from around Harut's shoulders. "I should have known a creep like you would be up to his investment-firm eyeballs in this entire mess."

"It's not like I had much of a choice." Anton gave a sigh and tucked the *nazar* back into his pocket. "Vladimir Borskoi was my uncle."

Chapter Fifteen

D ANIEL LIFTED HIS glass and took another sip. The white wine, crisp with a hint of mineral flavor, was quite good. He wasn't as much of a connoisseur as Anton, but he liked this one. "I had no idea Morocco had a wine industry."

Zaid glanced up at him from under his dark eyebrows. "You have no idea about most of what's going on in this entire part of the world."

"I'm learning, aren't I?" Daniel asked. "Like I learned I'm either going to get killed or become Zahara's eternal sex slave."

The two of them sat on a rooftop terrace overlooking the town's main street, with Zaid opting to push back his chair into the limited shade of the table's umbrella. The restaurant was perfect for the tourist crowd, with a menu in multiple languages and decorative urns overflowing with fragrant flowers.

The weather was sunny and dry, the food was delicious, and Zaid was a fascinating, if sometimes prickly, lunch companion. The experience was almost pleasant enough for Daniel to forget the impossible situation he had placed himself in. He dug into the vegetables and seasoned meat of his *tagine*, which had been served in a glazed clay dish with a conical cover so intriguing, he had asked the waiter if he could buy one before Zaid had been able to stop him.

He might as well enjoy the meal, seeing that it might be his last.

"Took you long enough to figure it out." Zaid glanced over the edge of the terrace again, at the unobstructed view of the now-empty spot where he had parked their car.

After Zaid had held a brief, tense conversation with Ahmed on a phone "borrowed" from a careless pair of tourists, the two of them had returned to find the car gone, along with Zahara and Harut. Zaid seemed less concerned about this than Daniel thought he should be. Zaid was also a good deal less sympathetic about the whole eternal slave situation than Daniel thought he ought to be.

"So what makes you so sure Zahara didn't say 'to hell with it' and run off home to the Mountains of Qaf?"

"In the first place," Zaid said, "she might be able to run off and travel through the seven levels to get away from us, but she couldn't take Harut with her. Or my new car, fortunately."

"She took me and you." Daniel furrowed his brow and tried to see if he recalled any details of the trip. Not that visiting hell had ever been high up on his bucket list, but it was a pretty unique travel experience. All that effort got him was a flashback to Zahara's paralyzing cuteness. Zaid had to snap his fingers to get his attention.

"I agreed to go with her," Zaid said. "And the two of you are joined in a magical contract. Harut isn't one of our kind and I'm confident even Zahara couldn't lure him into that mode of transportation." He took a bite of his dish, a flaky pastry filled with pigeon meat and cinnamon. Daniel hadn't been quite brave enough to try it. "Zahara has to return if you summon her, and she has to help you stop Marut. Even her mother couldn't get her out of a contract like that, although I'm sure Zahara asked her to."

"You sound nervous when you talk about Zahara's mother," Daniel said. "Is she that scary?"

"I'm not nervous about Lilitu, devourer of souls." Zaid paused to murmur a quick prayer under his breath. "I'm absolutely terrified."

Daniel reminded himself to try and worry only about the horrible supernatural monsters he was directly responsible for stopping. "So how do we contact my grandmother? So far, the only one she's talked to is Zahara, and we didn't learn much from that."

"We learned your *jeeda* wanted you to come to Ouarzazate." Zaid pointed a fork in his direction. "And if you hadn't burned her letter, we'd know what to do next."

Daniel winced. That had been an act of inspired idiocy on his part. "You don't know any magic to raise the dead?"

"Even back in the bad old days, I'd have thought twice about that sort of nasty business." Zaid shifted in his seat. "Besides, my clan is known for our swords, not our spells."

"Maybe we could call in a consultant." Daniel poured more of the wine into Zaid's glass, then his own. Zaid made no move to stop him. Could the jinn even get drunk? "You could travel to your world and bring back some magical reinforcements."

Zaid toyed with the stem of his wine glass. "That's not an option."

"How long has it been since you've seen your family?" Daniel wanted to take back the question as soon as he asked it. He could tell at once it was too personal.

An expression crossed Zaid's face, more of regret than anger. "A long time. Zahara did me a favor and took a message to them, to ask if I could return to present my case. They refused. My conversion isn't acceptable to them."

"It's all about religion, then?" Daniel felt he had pressed too far, but he continued. "Not about liking men."

A smile returned to Zaid's face, and he sat back and took a sip of wine. "You do manage to change the subject to sex easily, don't you? No, my clan has little interest in which lovers I choose. Marriage is different. That's about alliances and offspring, not love."

"That's a little rough." Daniel decided it would be a good idea to drink more wine as well, so he did. "For love to be off the table, I mean."

"How about you?" Zaid asked.

"My family is supportive." Daniel tried to figure out how much actual truth there was in that statement. "Actually, the first person I came out to was my grandmother. Somehow, I knew she'd accept me no matter what."

"She sounds like an extraordinary woman." Zaid studied Daniel's face, thoughtful. "But was there anything else about her, anything unusual?"

"Everything about my grandmother was odd and fantastic." Daniel reached for the wine bottle at the same time Zaid did, and their hands touched. Neither of them pulled away. "She and my grandfather acted like lovestruck teenagers, even after all those years. They were each the only thing the other wanted."

"When all your desires are distilled, you will cast just two votes—to love more, and be happy." Zaid grinned at Daniel's surprise. "A quote from the great Hafiz of Persia. I've always regretted never meeting him in person."

Their hands rested together, touching for a long moment. Then Zaid stiffened, and leaned forward to look over the edge of the terrace. "Well, well. Our two traveling companions have returned, and with a new friend."

On the street below, Zaid's car had pulled into its original parking spot, and three occupants were exiting the vehicle. Zahara stepped out from the driver's side, tapping her foot as she waited for Harut to join her on the sidewalk. The next person to exit the vehicle was the last individual Daniel had expected or wanted to run into while in Morocco—his ex-boyfriend, Anton.

"What's *he* doing here?" Daniel asked.

Zaid took a closer look and grimaced. "Damn Americans are overrunning the country. Perhaps you should tell him I'm your tour guide." He gestured to the waiter and spoke to him in Arabic.

Left with little choice, Daniel stood up and waved at the group. Anton's head shot up, relief washing over his face as he spotted Daniel.

The waiter had pushed another small table against the one Daniel and Zaid were sharing, and added additional chairs before the three of them made their way onto the restaurant patio.

Anton came up to Daniel, jaw clenched. "No one's been able to reach you. Not even your parents. What the hell were you thinking?"

"I was thinking I was on vacation and didn't need to worry about you." Daniel shot Zahara a questioning glance. She tilted her head toward Harut, then flounced down into her seat in a full sulk. The angel sat down next to her, his face serene.

"Please, join us for lunch." Zaid stood up and pulled out a chair, his best hospitality smile plastered on his face. "I'm Zaid, with the tour company."

"Daniel." Anton's voice had the grating quality it developed when he was lecturing him on some particular failing. "Perhaps you could ask your guide to take a break for an hour or so. You and I need to talk."

A muscle in Zaid's face twitched, but the smile remained.

God, Anton could be a pompous ass sometimes. In fact, all the time. "Anything you have to say to me you can say in front of him."

"This is serious." Anton's face reddened. When was the last time Daniel had point-blank told him off when he had made unreasonable demands? Probably never. "This country is too dangerous for you, and you can't trust these people."

"These people?" Daniel shoved the table in front of him. He never did that, never physically showed his anger. As luck would have it, the light plastic table shook wildly, sending the dishes clattering and toppling a few wine glasses. He hadn't meant to make that much of a scene. "Let me tell you something, Anton. Zaid isn't my tour guide, and he's not leaving."

Zaid fixed Daniel with a long, hard look. Right. Daniel couldn't tell Anton the truth, and he had just talked himself into a corner.

"Not that it's any of your business." Daniel drew in a deep breath. "But Zaid and I are together. I met him here and decided to extend my business trip to spend more time with him."

Zahara spit out a little wine in a giggle and Anton's face deepened to a dark purple color. As for Zaid, Daniel couldn't tell much. He had expected derision, or perhaps annoyance, but Zaid merely sat there, regarding him with mild surprise.

Harut leaned forward. "Your human friend knows about the unseen world, Daniel. In fact, he has knowledge that may be valuable to us. Perhaps you could set aside your earlier differences given the urgency of the situation."

"Oh." Daniel sat back in his chair. "Great. Well, I wish someone had clued me in to that a little earlier."

Anton shot an uneasy glance at Zaid. "Well, if everyone here is part of this unpleasant business, I suppose I can speak freely."

Daniel couldn't process that his ever-practical, jaded ex-boyfriend would accept any supernatural explanation for recent events. Come to think of it, he had trouble wrapping his head around the concept that Anton had flown in from New York to check on him. Or that Daniel had just claimed he and Zaid were a couple in front of the entire group.

"Vladimir Borskoi was my uncle, not just a client," Anton began. Daniel blinked in surprise, but Zahara and Harut nodded as if they had already heard this information. "It's not that I was unaware of the unsavory aspects of his business dealings, believe me. But blood is blood, as they say."

Zaid gave a grudging grunt of assent at the comment, and Zahara brightened at the mention of any sort of exsanguination.

"I hoped the hints I dropped during our phone conversation would have been enough to dissuade you from talking to him, but I was concerned. So I called Vladimir, planning to warn him not to try anything with you. We weren't close, but he was a relative, and the services my financial group provided for him were quite valuable."

"What's the word you humans use for that sort of thing?" Zahara snapped her fingers at the waiter, who arrived with some additional bottles of wine and a towel to clean up the mess Daniel had made. "Coin-washing, gold-cleaning…"

Anton waited until the waiter departed, his teeth gritted in irritation. "Money-laundering. In any event, he told me your grandmother's property held significance to certain organizations in this country. Anti-government groups. Unfortunately, I let it slip that your interest in the property related to your family ties. That was a mistake."

Daniel gave a little shiver, despite the sunbaked air around him. "Why was it a mistake?"

"Vladimir became quite interested in you." Anton reached out to pour himself some wine, and knocked it back with an alacrity Daniel had never seen in him before. "He started talking about your grandmother having powers, and said they often skip a generation or two. Well, he believes in all this nonsense, you know."

"What nonsense?" Zaid's voice was close to a growl.

He and Anton hadn't hit it off, that was for sure.

"He believed we were descended from a *rusalka*." Anton

twisted in his seat, as if embarrassed. "Family legend has it that our great-grandfather in the Ukraine avoided being drowned by one by offering to marry her."

Daniel gave Zaid and Zahara a questioning look. He had tried to diligently research any references to Middle Eastern mythical beings the two jinn had thrown around in casual conversation, which was enough to set off a week of nightmares, but that name hadn't come up.

"Think lovely Slavic lake mermaid, then think serial killer," Zahara suggested.

"The *rusalki* are quite stunning, if you're partial to redheads." Zaid gave Anton a tight smile. "Which I'm not."

Anton pressed his lips into a thin line and continued. "When I heard about Vladimir's death, I assumed he had made a deal with the wrong group and paid the price. But when you didn't rush home after the bombing, and then left a message with that Ibrahim fellow at the hotel in Marrakech that you had gone off to the mountains, I got worried."

"But Vladimir Borskoi's dead," Daniel said.

"His business associates are alive and well," Anton said. "And they want to find you. Vladimir backed out of a major deal because of your grandmother. As crazy as it sounds, he told me she had spoken to him in the house."

"Having been to the house, it doesn't sound all that crazy," Daniel said.

"I think he was killed because he crossed both his business partners and the group they were financing." Anton wiped a few beads of sweat off his forehead. "And they know about your connection to the house. That's why you need to go home."

"I'm not leaving." Daniel felt a small sense of satisfaction at the look of surprise on Anton's face. "My grandmother spoke to me as well, and I have a job to do here. What I need to do is talk to her and get some advice on how to do that."

Anton fell silent for a moment. "I might be able to help you with that, if it'll get you out of here faster."

"*You* have some sort of deep connection to the spirit world?" Daniel asked.

"You'll be connected all right, if you try that crystal ball trick again to track me down." Zahara used one of the knives on the table to point at Anton. "You're lucky Harut was there to save you."

Harut himself spoke, his voice carrying a tone of command. "You're not the only human here with the blood of evil spirits, Daniel. Let Anton help. It's time for us to speak with the dead."

WHAT BETTER PLACE than an ancient temple to hold a séance?

Maybe one that hadn't been built as movie set. Daniel leaned against the oversized door frame leading to the stage used for filming biblical epics and waited for Zaid. The jinn had sent all of them ahead to set up tonight's talk-to-the-dead extravaganza while he parked his car in a less conspicuous location.

Zaid gave him a nod as he approached, and Daniel felt the heat rise up in his face. It was his first moment alone with Zaid since he had created one of the worst cover stories imaginable. Of course, he had bigger things to worry about tonight.

"So Ahmed finally got back to you?"

"He had bad news and worse news." Zaid looked uncharacteristically somber. "There haven't been any leads on catching anyone connected to the nightclub bombing."

Daniel knew how personally Zaid took the attack on his club. "And the worse news?"

"Ahmed warned me this American he spoke of—Donnelly—has flown in an entire group of American counterterrorism private contractors to investigate the bombing."

"That doesn't sound unusual," Daniel said. "The government here has close relations with the US, and an attack on a major city might lead them to ask for help."

"Except that Donnelly asked more questions about the jinn than about local jihadist groups," Zaid said. "He and his men also carried antique weapons on them, concealed in modern packs. Ancient swords, crossbows, that sort of thing."

"I don't get it. Are they planning to get into a sword battle with terrorists? I thought that's what drones were for."

"Bombing the hell out of everything, and solving nothing, would be a typical military response, yes." Zaid frowned. "I think these contractors came prepared for a fight with the jinn. A human could use a weapon from our world against us. I've seen it a few times. From what Ahmed told me, these men know ordinary guns won't work on us."

"Not even if they had silver bullets in them?" Daniel asked. "Like you'd use to stop a werewolf."

Zaid chuckled. "Our local ones are called *qutrub*, and you'd need more than a little silver to stop one. From what Ahmed told me, I'm sure these were the guys connected to the release of Harut and Marut."

"Well, they must want to stop Marut, then." Daniel felt quite out of his depth fighting an angel-turned-monster. Military experts who wouldn't fall on the floor laughing when he told them about his grandmother's instructions and who had magic swords of their own sounded like the answer to his prayers. "After all, they're the good guys."

Zaid didn't say anything in response. His withering glare of disbelief at Daniel's statement made words unnecessary.

"Or they could be more interested in using whatever powers Marut has for their own benefit," Daniel added. He thought some more, and came up with even worse possibilities. "Then the rest of you would be in their way and I'd be the dumb schmuck who knows too much to be kept alive."

"Congratulations," Zaid said. "You're not quite as hopelessly naive as I thought." He motioned to the door in front of them. "They should be ready by now. Let's go in and see if we can talk to your grandmother."

"I guess I'm ready to talk to a ghost." Daniel stepped closer to the door, then hesitated. "About this afternoon. I didn't mean to embarrass you. I wanted to get rid of Anton, and it was the first thought that came to mind."

"That's all it was, then—an off-the-cuff excuse?"

"It might have been that." Daniel hesitated. It had been more than that. "It might have been a little… aspirational."

A smile played over Zaid's lips as he pushed Daniel through the door. "Tell you what. When we stop running for our lives, bring up your aspirations again. I'd like to hear more about them."

The remainder of their party sat cross-legged in a semi-circle inside the room, dwarfed by the fake columns and stone steps around them. Harut and Zahara sat a little distance apart, engaged in a whispered conversation that didn't involve any theatrics from the jinn, which was a first. To Daniel's eye, the angel appeared oddly uncomfortable. He lifted his head and moved away from Zahara as Daniel and Zaid approached.

That left Anton, who sat holding a fresh crystal ball, face flushed and legs jammed into an awkward crisscross. For once, Daniel could sympathize with his irritability. He'd be in a bad mood too, if he looked that ridiculous.

"There's camp." Daniel came closer and took in Anton's attire from all sides. "And then there's a crime against fashion. You'd get laughed out of a drag queen revue in that outfit."

Anton turned around, his turban slipping off his uncharacteristically ruffled hair. He slammed it back on, the ostrich feather affixed to the top wavering dangerously in the air.

He raised one arm, clothed in a canary yellow sleeve, and pointed at Zahara. "Your paranormal consultant over there told me the séance won't work unless I'm dressed up like this."

Zahara, for her part, did a masterful job of keeping her expression bland and unrevealing. She widened her eyes and gave an innocent shrug. "He can't be the vessel for an otherworldly spirit in poorly-fitting Brooks Brothers, now can he?"

"For your information, the suit you had me take off to put on this ridiculous outfit was an Armani," Anton snapped back.

Daniel plopped down next to Zaid, trying to prevent the image of his ex-boyfriend dressed as the world's least convincing fortune-teller from being seared into his mind. The bizarre location of the movie studio had been Anton's idea. He had even gone so far as to bribe the studio's nighttime security guards for them.

Anton hefted the crystal ball in his hand. "I've only tried something like this once, with a recent suicide that had died taking critical financial information with him."

"How did it go?" Daniel asked.

"Two of the people in the room died in drowning accidents within the next six months."

"Well, that's cheery." Daniel turned to Harut. Anton didn't sound like he was joking, and this entire séance idea was sounding like a worse idea by the minute.

"Call out to your kin." Harut's voice resounded with a deep echo.

Daniel cleared his throat. "Solikis Botbol, I, Daniel Goldstein, your grandson, have created this spirit-friendly environment in the hope of receiving a sign of your presence. Please feel welcome in our circle and join us when you're ready."

Anton turned to stare into the ball, his expression more of anxiety than spiritual enlightenment. The rest of Daniel's companions met his remarks with more stunned silence than approval.

Well, maybe someone else could give it a try. Weren't

there three ancient mythical beings with magical powers in attendance? They would have a much better chance of turning a muumuu-wearing Anton into Daniel's dead Jewish grandmother.

The shocked stares continued, and Daniel threw up his hands. "Okay, I admit it. I looked up 'How to Perform a Séance in 15 Steps' online, and this is what popped up."

"Your bubbe's real name is Solikis?" Zahara pushed herself back a little from the circle. "You never told me that."

"You never asked." Daniel didn't know what his grandmother's first name had to do with anything.

"Was she named after *the* Solikis?" Zaid leaned forward, his eyes intent. "The enchantress of the sands?"

Daniel opened his mouth to tell Zaid that name sounded like bad video game backstory, but as he did, Anton's eyes rolled back and he slumped to the ground.

Daniel jumped to his feet to rush over to him. Anton's right hand clenched, then released. His spine arched into a semicircle, his mouth open as grunting noises forced themselves out of his throat. Uncertain of what to do, Daniel knelt beside him. The shaking worsened, and Anton's arms and legs flailed against the floor.

"We need to call an ambulance. He's having a seizure." Daniel looked around for some support, but Zaid and Zahara had vanished. Out of the corner of his eye, he caught a faint rustle of movement in the shadows cast by the columns around them. This was no time for their jinn invisibility tricks.

Harut rose to his feet, ignoring the spasming man and Daniel's pleas for help. Instead, he bent down in a low bow.

Left with no support, Daniel reached out with a hesitant hand toward Anton's head, which kept slamming against the ground. His cheeks had turned dusky, and a trickle of blood trailed out the side of his mouth.

Dim memories of a CPR course Daniel had taken in his teenage years at the local Jewish community center kicked in, and he used both hands to pull Anton's jaw forward and up. The awful snoring noises stopped, and air rushed into his ex's mouth. Daniel released the chin thrust and rested Anton's head on the ground. Then he climbed to his feet, searching the room for Zaid and Zahara. He needed them to get Anton medical help.

"Good to see you again, duckie." His grandmother's voice, rich and throaty, came from the floor.

Daniel turned to see Anton climbing to his feet, a smile on his face. Only it wasn't Anton in there.

"Is that you, Grandma?" Daniel's throat tightened, the words coming out with difficulty.

He had loved his grandmother, had been hit hard by her death. But she had been so lost and forlorn after his grandfather passed, and she had lived a long, wonderful life. Was it right for him to call her back to his world, even if he desperately needed her help?

"In spirit, dear, but not in the flesh." Solikis regarded the body she appeared in with interest. "This is your special friend, duckie? A little overdressed for this occasion, I would think."

"I tried to follow your instructions," Daniel began. "I didn't summon a marid, like you asked me to. But I did get a hold of Zahara—she's around here somewhere. Zaid's helping us, too. Oh, and we picked up one of the angels. The good one."

Solikis spoke again, this time in a language Daniel was quite sure he had never heard before, and Zaid materialized to Daniel's left. His sword was now slung sideways across his waist, and his hand rested near the hilt as he gave a short and cautious bow in her direction. Zahara reappeared as well, peeking out from behind a column. Granted, listening to his grandmother's voice coming from Anton's mouth was unsettling, but his supernatural companions seemed more than a little nervous around his bubbe. He would have thought a dead spirit or two wouldn't have bothered them so much.

Harut spoke, in what Daniel assumed was the same language Solikis had used, but she shushed him. "Best to let everyone in on the conversation, no?"

He inclined his head to her in a gesture of respect. "My apologies, *lalla*, and peace be upon you. I know your time here is short, but we have need of your help. My brother's strength grows with each passing day."

"Well, then, you should get around to stopping him sooner rather than later, I would say." Solikis gave him an irritated wave. "Your skills aren't likely to be much use. Not like appealing to Marut's better nature will get us anywhere."

She gave Zaid an appraising glance. "I see that one of the *hamar* accompanies you. The clan of the red jinn would be of some help in a fight." Anton—no, Solikis—gave Daniel a wink. "Not to mention he's awfully easy on the eyes."

"Regrettably, *lalla*, I cannot call on my family to come to our assistance." Zaid spoke in a courteous, deferential tone, but kept his hand close to his sword. Why was Zaid, of all people, afraid of Daniel's grandmother?

Solikis sighed. "What about the little *shaytana* you called up, duckie? You should have paid better attention to my instructions about negotiating with a jinn, but that's a discussion for another time. Tell her to stop hiding behind that hideous misinterpretation of a temple pillar and join the discussion."

Zahara leaned out farther. "This is quite close enough, thank you very much."

Solikis narrowed her eyes, and a shiver ran through Daniel. An electric charge seemed to crackle across the room. "Now I recognize her blood. Some of it, at least. How is your mother, dear?"

"She's good," Zahara called out from behind the pillar. "Or bad, depending on your point of view. Anyway, she'd be awfully annoyed if you killed me. So if it's all the same to you, I'll hang out back here, waiting for your words of wisdom."

"Quite the motley crew you have as allies to defeat the fallen one, duckie." Solikis clucked her tongue. "My, but what a mess I've gotten you into."

"I need to know what to do," Daniel said. "We don't even know how Marut plans to start a war between the human and jinn worlds, much less how to stop him."

"First he has to free himself from the curse of the cave he and his brother were trapped in, for all those years." Solikis nodded at the crystal ball resting on the floor beside her. It bounced up into the air, as eager as a puppy showing off a new trick. The globe spun, light reflecting off its surface sending dancing prisms around the room.

"After centuries of waiting, the cave of Marut and Harut received new visitors." The rainbows of light faded, and the room around them altered, darkening into a soaring cave marked by stalactites above and stalagmites below. Daniel had the impression of being trapped inside the mouth of an enormous beast, about to be snapped in half by needlelike teeth. "But these were not the sorcerers of old, coming to ignore Harut's warning words and seeking a dark spell or two from Marut."

The gloom of the cavern lightened enough to make out two massive shapes hanging suspended from the ceiling. Their feet were high above, bound by great chains to the hanging icicles of stone. Their wings were crushed against their bodies by hissing ropes of snakes, and their mouths hung open. A stream of water poured down from the ceiling, splashing just beyond their cracked, bloody lips.

"The modern-day seekers of the cave were warriors," Solikis continued, as mist swallowed up the two hanging giants and the image shifted to a group of men in camouflage rapelling down long ropes from an opening in the top of the cave. "American sellswords—mercenaries who seek money and glory in fighting the children of smokeless fire and others like us. They sought knowledge that could help them win their wars. Instead, they released a monster upon themselves and the human world."

The mists swirled up and cleared again, illuminating a massacre. The soldiers lay scattered on the floor, ripped apart like stuffed dolls. Marut, even more massive than he had appeared in the house in Marrakech, strode amongst severed limbs and clumps of eviscerated intestines, his face triumphant. A naked Harut knelt, praying, in a shadowed corner of the cave.

Daniel squeezed his eyes shut, trying to block the images out long enough to stop himself from vomiting. When he opened them again, the image of the cave had begun to fade away. Solikis snapped her fingers and the crystal ball floated back down to the floor. The room's lights once again illuminated the silent, grim audience around her.

"The broken curse gave each brother what he didn't want." Solikis gestured to Harut. "Your new friend here wanted to stay and endure his punishment so he would be redeemed in the afterlife. So he received both his freedom and a mortal form."

"And Marut remained partially trapped." Daniel found his voice, somehow. "And he needs the sacrifice to have both his freedom and his full powers."

"He needs to devour the person who willingly took that sacrifice's place." Solikis raised her eyebrows in Zahara's direction before turning back to Daniel.

"That would be me." Daniel wasn't thrilled he had a giant magical target on his back, but he didn't regret taking the place of the young boy.

"Until then, Marut has some weaknesses," Solikis continued. "He's far weaker in the day than even we are, and can be halted by objects of faith and power, even killed by the righteous."

"And *that* would be me." Zaid raised his eyes to Solikis, as if in defiance, but she only gave him an amused smile.

"Why Morocco?" Daniel asked. "The cave is in Iran."

"As are the dev of Persia," Solikis replied. "Marut's plan to rip open the barrier between the human and jinn worlds is too drastic even for them. But Marut has a powerful magical ally who arranged for the sacrifice to take place here, far from their influence. The selection of my old home for this was no coincidence."

"So how do we stop him?" Zaid spoke again, his gaze lowered and voice low, but he sounded bitter. "Far more powerful jinn than those standing before you have good reason to oppose Marut. Who from the Mountains of Qaf will stand with us?"

Solikis's eyebrow twitched, and for a moment her face became blank and stupefied. Daniel could sense Anton was struggling to return, probably not handling this channeling thing all too well. Then the sharp glint in the eyes returned. "I will. But I need Daniel to come to the *hiloula* first." She held out her hand toward Daniel. "Until then, stay safe, duckie."

The figure in yellow robes and the turban gasped, then collapsed to the floor. Anton's voice came from the mound of garish clothing. "That was by far the most unpleasant experience of my life. I hope you learned something important out of all that."

"We did." Zahara popped out of her hiding place and walked over to them. "Daniel's grandmother isn't a ghost. She's a jinn."

Chapter Sixteen

Z AHARA STRODE OUT onto the starlit grounds of the studio lot, glaring through the shadows cast by assorted props at Daniel and Harut as they assisted a limping Anton out of the fake temple they had used for the séance. They needed to get out of this amusement park of cinematic junk and back to the limited safety of the hotel room. The protective spells around it were better than anything she could have come up with, thanks to Harut.

"Hurry up." She risked another stage whisper order at the three of them. It was no use. Anton wasn't going any faster, even with Daniel and Harut holding him on each side. He had come out of Solikis's possession without much sign of aftereffects, but as soon as they had tried to exit the building, the energy had drained right out him.

How could she have been so stupid? She should have figured out long ago that Daniel's beloved and ever-so-dead bubbe was actually a jinn. Not just any jinn, either, but Solikis, enchantress of the sands. Having that sort of pedigree was the only way he could have gotten this far. Up until now, she had chalked it all up to dumb luck.

"We're coming as fast as we can." Daniel paused for a moment as Anton's legs wobbled. "It's going to take Zaid a few minutes to bring the car around, anyway."

"Try faster." Zahara scanned the area, checking for signs of Zaid. The surprise revelation that Daniel's grandmother was a living, breathing, dangerous jinn sorceress had made a bad week even more terrible. "I want to get out of here, now."

"Anton's having a hard time." Daniel took another step forward, then tripped over a fake boulder. Somehow, a staggering Anton maintained his upright posture despite the loss of support. "Not to mention it's dark, and I can't see where I'm going."

"You don't even have night vision." Zahara jabbed a finger at a brilliant swath of stars above them. The lights of the nearby town dimmed some of their brilliance, but the studio lot wasn't even comfortably gloomy, let alone pitch-black. "A grandmother like that and you get the short end of the magical talent stick."

There was one positive outcome from this evening's activities. At least she wasn't the only one who didn't live up to family expectations.

"I still don't believe my grandmother was a jinn. I had a hard enough time thinking she was a ghost."

"*Is* a jinn," Zahara corrected. Out of the corner of her eye, she saw Harut's free hand hovering over his sword hilt. He had summoned his blade as they exited the séance chamber. Zahara wasn't the only one spooked by tonight's revelations. When would Zaid get back with the car? "After her human husband died, the enchantress of the sands headed back to the Mountains of Qaf and her tribe. She's there now, which is why she needed your slowpoke friend there to have a conversation with you."

"My grandmother mentioned she knew your mother." Daniel stared at a point a meter to the left of Zahara and blinked. And she wasn't even using her invisibility spell. "Are they friends?"

"Not exactly." Zahara bit off the words with a snap. In fact, "mortal enemies" might be the best description. She'd never met the famed enchantress of the Jewish jinn in person, but her name had come up in family chats. The sort where her mother waxed nostalgic about her top-ten list of enemies, and interesting ways to kill them.

Zahara shook her head. First she had to put up with Harut, and now she had to face down a jinn sorceress strong enough to give her mother a run for her money. This was the worst summoning ever.

Ahead, the sign marking the main entrance to the movie studio loomed. They would have been there already, if Daniel had put as much effort into dragging Anton along as he did asking dumb questions.

Anton groaned and slumped to the ground. Both Harut and Daniel bent down to help him up.

Zahara turned around with a loud sigh. Great. Now what was wrong with him?

"Freeze or we'll shoot." The words, in English, boomed out in deep baritone.

Zahara whirled around, a curse slipping from her lips. Two men stood between them and the exit. Both wore desert camouflage attire, set off with matching balaclavas and accessorized with semiautomatic weapons. The guns weren't pointed at them, however. Instead, each man aimed a crossbow in their direction.

Harut reacted first, striding toward the two men as his wings flared out behind him to protect the rest of them. Both men followed through on their threat and fired, the arrows directed toward Harut's chest.

As the bolts flew, Anton jumped up and darted away from the group. Either he had experienced a miraculous recovery, or their slow departure from the séance had been his plan all along.

Zahara was willing to bet candy on the latter.

The arrows froze in the air an arm's length from Harut. He waved his hand and the projectiles burst into flames and floated to the ground in a puff of ash. Their attackers took only a few seconds to recover from their shock before bringing up their semiautomatic weapons and opening fire on all of them.

The hesitation gave Zahara enough time to take action. As the shooting began, she flung herself toward Daniel, toppled him over, and sprawled out on top of him. The men firing aimed at chest level, so most of the rounds streaking toward them whizzed overhead anyway, but a few stray bullets that came near her froze in midair and dropped to the ground.

Harut never so much as flinched. The arcs of light from the ammunition streamed toward him, then clattered at his feet in clumps of metal.

The two attackers paused, their eyes bulging in fear and disbelief. Then both of their heads came together in a satisfying clunk as Zaid rose up behind them and slammed their skulls together. They both collapsed to the ground, their weapons landing next to them. Zaid kicked one of the guns away and pressed his sword point against the throat of the less-dazed attacker.

Zahara rolled off Daniel and stood up, brushing dust off her clothes. She approached the men sprawled on the ground, pushing at one of the crossbows with her foot. An odd choice for studio lot guards who hadn't got the memo—and the bribes—not to show up tonight. A faint vibration came from the weapon. Magic, weak but present. Someone had armed human thugs with weapons that worked against the jinn. Well, maybe a jinn like her. Harut was another story.

She scooped up the gun instead of the crossbow and trained it on the two men. These guys weren't jinn, and bullets would work just fine against them if they tried anything else.

She cast a side eye at Zaid. "It's about time you showed up."

"Our friends here found our car before I did." Zaid bent down and ripped the mask off the man he had pinned down with his sword. It wasn't an attractive face, and it wasn't local. "I want to know who these guys are, and I have a feeling Anton can tell us. Where is he?"

"He's hit," Daniel called out.

Anton's move to ditch them had backfired. Badly. Several meters away, he sat on the ground, a dark stain spreading across his chest. Daniel crouched beside him. One of Harut's glowing orbs of light hovered over the two of them, illuminating the sheen of sweat on Anton's forehead.

"We need to get him to a hospital." Daniel lifted his head as Harut approached. "Call an ambulance. Do something."

"I'm not going to make it to a hospital." Anton stared down at the blood soaking through the garish yellow of his fortune-teller muumuu. His face had a gaunt, hollow look, as if he had begun to waste away in mere seconds. Daniel wadded up a ripped-off strip of his shirt and pressed it against the oozing wound.

Harut motioned to Daniel to move back. He pulled off the already-soaked wad of fabric and placed the palm of his hand over the blood welling from Anton's chest. Zahara watched, fascinated, as his hand began to glow. A breeze blew past her, warm and redolent of grass and rich earth. Some of the peris had the power of healing, a magic utterly alien to her. The spreading stain stopped, but Anton continued to grow paler, his breath coming in harsh gasps.

Harut pulled his hand away, his face grim. "My powers can only help the righteous."

"What are you talking about?" Daniel asked. "You were able to heal me."

"That's the problem, you see." Anton's face continued to change, growing long and lean. His hair lengthened into a thick mane around his shoulders, gleaming red in the starlight. "I'm not like you, Daniel."

Daniel reached out to touch him and Anton flashed him a now-fanged smile. "I'm sorry, I really am. That part about the rusalki—I think I got most of the family blood. Like you got most of your grandmother's. Maybe that's why we got along, for a while. Not like we had much else in common."

"You're becoming a sort of... merman?" Daniel pulled back his arm, shaking. A dull gray tail flopped under the edges of Anton's long gown, where his feet should have been.

"A river or lake is what I want to die in." Anton licked his cracked lips. "Terrible luck to find out I got all the water monster family heritage, here in the middle of the desert."

Daniel turned to Zahara. "You were able to take me away with you in your puff of smoke. Can you bring him to water?"

"I could take him through the levels." Zahara hadn't encountered a rusalka before, since she didn't tend to wander around Eastern European lakes much. From what she could recall, the rusalki enjoyed decorative aquatic plants and luring passersby to a watery grave. Definitely people like her mother and her relatives. And Harut either couldn't or didn't want to use his healing magic to help her kind.

"Ouzoud." Zaid kept his sword poised above their two captives and motioned for her to walk over toward Anton. "The waterfall there houses a small clan descended from Aisha Qandisa. But I think Anton needs to answer a few questions before we grant him any dying wishes."

Zahara checked the two men lying on the ground again. They were either too smart or too concussed to make a move. "First things first." She stalked over to Anton. "You knew we were going to be hit. This was all a setup."

Anton hacked up a clot of blood. "I'm not working for Marut, if that's what you think. Neither do those two men."

"Then who do you work for?" Zaid asked.

Anton closed his eyes for a moment, then began by not answering the question. "My uncle Vladimir had a bad habit of dabbling in black magic when it suited his business interests. A few months ago, he received a visitor who promised him access to the legendary sorcery of Harut and Marut—if he provided access to a certain property he owned in Marrakech."

Solikis's old house in the *mellah*. Daniel was right—it was haunted, but by jinn and sorcerers, not ghosts.

"A human visitor?" Harut sounded puzzled. "I doubt my brother would condescend to appear as a child of mud."

"Vladimir only told me it was a woman who reached out to him. I warned him no good would come of his obsession with using the occult to line his pockets."

"And you only pick up your cheesy crystal ball for charity, I assume." Zahara didn't like where the conversation was headed. Only one person came to mind who would go seeking human allies to help Marut.

Anton coughed again. "I've done some consulting work myself with a rather unusual US government contractor—a company that specializes in supernatural threats and opportunities. I reached out to a contact I have in the organization."

"Let me guess," Zaid called out. "His name's Donnelly."

Anton didn't even blink in surprise. Then again, it looked like much of his energy was being spent on the few shallow breaths he could take in. "Yes. We told Vladimir to play along. His first task was to offer the house and some weapons to a group of men who came to him with a wild story about an angel who appeared to them in their dreams. Told him if they sacrificed a little kid they'd have more power than they could imagine."

It had to have been Lilitu. Who else would have set everything in place for Marut's release and return to power? No wonder she was so furious; in her mind, Zahara had messed everything up. But as it turned out, someone else was interfering with her mother's beautiful, diabolic plans—the mercenaries who had released Marut in the first place. Too bad they also wanted to kill Harut and any jinn unlucky enough to be with him.

"So the guys who kidnapped the little boy in my grandmother's house were also responsible for the club bombing," Daniel said.

"From what Vladmir said, these guys were bit players, legends in their own mind." Anton's skin grew gray; his new tail flapped weakly against the ground, sending up a cloud of dust. "The plan was for them to summon Marut, and Donnelly and his men would be ready for him."

The odd and convenient location of the iron chandelier made a lot more sense, now. The mercenaries who had originally freed Marut and Harut by mistake planned to rectify their error by taking out the fallen one as he took the sacrifice. They had known the little boy would die, too, and hadn't cared.

"Vladimir was told the wrong date for the sacrifice deliberately." Anton's voice was little more than a croak. "So Donnelly and his men weren't there for Marut's arrival. I didn't put all the pieces together about your involvement until after Marut's men killed Vladimir." Anton spat out more blood, and gave Daniel a pleading look. "Please, tell Zahara to take me to the water. It's better than drying out here in the dirt."

"I'd like nothing better than to dump you into a nice, deep lake." Zahara kept a snarl in her voice, but she had heard enough of this touching deathbed confession. If Anton didn't kick the bucket soon, the conversation could get back to the topic of Vladimir's original visitor.

Daniel didn't jump up and tell her to take Anton away, as she expected. Instead, he stared at Anton as if he had never seen him before. It didn't seem to have anything to do with his ex having a tail, either. "So why did you call a bunch of mercenaries in to kill me?"

Anton reached out to touch Daniel's arm. His hand had transformed, with rubbery gray skin and webs between his fingers. "I thought I might be able to protect you. Donnelly and his people hold Marut and Harut responsible for the deaths of their comrades. They'll stop at nothing to take them both out. If I gave them Harut and the two jinn, I thought they might leave you alone."

If it had been up to Zahara, she would have walked away, leaving that backstabbing Slavic merman to die in the dust. But she wasn't surprised when Daniel gave her a slow nod.

"Hold on tight." Zahara pulled Anton close as her lower body dissolved into flames. "One rushing waterfall, coming right up."

Chapter Seventeen

I F DANIEL CONCENTRATED, he could sense a reassuring presence in the room. Somewhere off to his left. Or maybe to his right. The drab office deep within the local police station contained little in the way of furnishings, except for a battered desk and two chairs, but Zaid didn't need anything physical to hide behind. He had promised Daniel he would stay close by him during the entire interrogation process, and Daniel knew the jinn hovered somewhere in the room, sword in hand. Hopefully he wouldn't need it.

Daniel squirmed in the uncomfortable chair he had been directed to by a nervous Ahmed. The Moroccan policeman—Daniel had a strong impression Ahmed was a good deal more than that—had arrived at Daniel's hotel room in the predawn hours bearing bad news. Donnelly and his team knew where Daniel was, and there was no way he could get Daniel out of an interview with the American.

The door swung open to admit a man with broad shoulders, a buzz cut, and a travel mug in each hand.

"Sorry to keep you waiting." He placed the cups in front of Daniel on the worn metal desk and extended a hand in greeting. Daniel didn't believe the friendly smile plastered across his face for an instant, but he rose to his feet and did his best to return the man's viselike handshake. "Brought you some real coffee. Not a big fan of tea. How about you?"

Daniel thought hard and decided this was probably not a trick question. "I love coffee." He sat down, squared his own shoulders and did his best impression of a manly American male who most certainly did not sip tea.

"Great." The man took a seat across from Daniel and leaned back in his chair.

He certainly didn't need to work on *his* image as an example of the ultimate American heterosexual. Well over six feet in height, with the cleft chin and blue eyes of an action hero, he radiated physical confidence. And a hint of menace.

"Not sure if the locals mentioned my name. It's Donnelly."

First name? Last name? One of several secret agent aliases used as he jetted around the world looking for monsters to take on? Well, it didn't matter much.

"I'm Daniel Goldstein." Daniel smiled so hard his face hurt. "But you probably know that already."

"That I do." Donnelly took a sip of his own coffee. "I understand you do IT work. Cybersecurity? I've got a few friends from New York in that field."

"I make up computer games." Daniel felt obligated to try his own coffee. It was piping hot, and a lot stronger than he liked. He drank it anyway.

"I work in security consulting," Donnelly said. "To reassure you, I'm not here in any sort of official capacity. My firm has been asked to give the locals a hand with the terrorism investigation, and I understand you were an eyewitness."

"I spoke extensively to the authorities in Marrakech after

the club bombing. Not sure if I can add much more."

"Some odd stories from that attack." Donnelly shook his head, as if in amusement. "Some of the people I interviewed told me they had seen an angel with wings covered in blinking eyes. They say he stood up and took the force of the blast."

Somehow Daniel doubted Donnelly found much in the story to laugh about. "I guess surviving a trauma like that might cause people to think they were saved by divine intervention."

"Are you religious yourself?" Donnelly asked. "Many American Jews come here to reconnect with their heritage, I understand. Because you're not here on a business trip. At least not according to your colleagues at work."

Daniel tried not to let his surprise show on his face. Donnelly had done his homework. "That's right. My grandmother was from Morocco."

"It's nice to find out more about your family," Donnelly said. "Is that why the woman you shared a room with came here as well? Zahara. You listed her as your wife when you checked in."

"Oh, that." Daniel did his best to chuckle. "We thought it would be more discreet to say we were married. She's only a friend. I don't know her well enough to have met her family."

Based on what Zaid had told him, meeting Zahara's family could be downright hazardous to his health.

"And you don't know where she is now." An edge of sarcasm crept into Donnelly's tone. "Or where your friend Anton Koval is. He flew into in the country only a few days after his uncle Vladimir Borskoi was killed in the bombing."

Despite their best efforts, covering their tracks after last night's horrific events had been difficult. Anton—it was so hard for Daniel to wrap his head around the fact he was dead—had vanished with Zahara, taken to the watery grave he so desperately wanted. The two mercenaries had been a bigger problem, until Harut had agreed to use his charisma spell to give them amnesia. Hunkering down until dawn and leaving town had been the plan—at least until Ahmed had come calling.

"Anton's in Morocco?" Daniel asked. "I had no idea."

"Anton told us you planned on meeting him at the movie studios last night." Donnelly's tone turned icy. "Along with three new friends of yours. Today's he's gone, and the two men I sent to check things out can't remember what month it is, let alone what happened."

Donnelly placed both arms on the desk, taking up far more space than was strictly necessary as he leaned over Daniel. "Everywhere you go in Morocco, trouble seems to follow right behind."

"I have no idea what you're talking about." Daniel folded his hands and forced himself to meet Donnelly's gaze. "I came here to tell you what I saw the night of the bombing. Believe me, I have every reason on earth to help the authorities here catch the terrorists who almost killed me."

"Our mutual friend Ahmed told me you were quite cooperative with the investigation." Donnelly gave a nod toward the door. "I can't say I agree with him."

"Unlike you, he has some legal authority here." Daniel stood up. He felt a hand on his shoulder. Zaid was giving him a warning not to push this Donnelly guy too far. "Speaking of which, I'd appreciate it if we invited Ahmed in on this discussion. Seeing how you're only a consultant and all."

Donnelly's eyes hardened. For an instant, his gaze flickered to a point behind Daniel's shoulder. "I'm not sure what you've gotten yourself into, but keep one thing in mind. I'm on the side of the angels here."

Donnelly probably did believe that. Trouble was, everything he and his men had done so far had helped the wrong angel.

Daniel made a move toward the door, and Donnelly didn't try to stop him. Instead, he stood up and offered him his hand.

Daniel accepted another handshake, surprised to feel a firm object pressed into his palm. He glanced down to see that the American security consultant had given him a curved dagger, complete with an intricately embossed sheath.

"A little souvenir for you."

"Thanks." Puzzled by the gift, Daniel turned the object over. It was a little longer than his hand, the pale metal worn, black tarnish bringing the crevices of the design into sharp relief.

"Berber handiwork." Donnelly clucked his tongue. "I should say Amazigh, actually. Pure silver. The replicas in the souk are based on antiques like this."

"It's beautiful." Daniel had an odd feeling about accepting it, but pissing Donnelly off when he was so close to getting away from him didn't strike him as a good idea. "I'd guess you and your coworkers have some higher-tech weapons to work with than this."

Donnelly's face twisted into a grin. "Never bring a knife to a gun fight." He took the dagger back, and unsheathed it. The curved blade had a series of markings engraved into its surface. With a quick, fluid movement, he raised the blade up, then swung it down with a savage cut. "Unless a knife is what you need."

The blade cut nothing more than air, but the action made Daniel jump. Behind him, he heard Zaid curse, and felt his presence fade away.

Daniel stood facing Donnelly, uncertain about what had happened, except that Zaid was no longer there to protect him.

Donnelly handed the weapon back to him. "Old superstition around here. If you encounter a jinn, drive a silver blade through the air and you'll drive him away."

"I guess that means any jinn hanging around have left the building." The joke felt hollow. Daniel wasn't fooling anyone.

Donnelly had known Zaid was here, even if he couldn't see him.

Daniel waited for Zaid's hand to reappear on his shoulder. It didn't.

The two men faced each other for a long moment. Donnelly leaned forward. "Tell you what, Daniel. Since your mysterious friend has decided to leave you here, maybe you should enjoy our hospitality for a while. For your own good."

Chapter Eighteen

ZAHARA POPPED OUT of invisibility and got right into Ahmed face's seconds after he stepped out of the car at their prearranged meeting spot—without Daniel *or* Zaid. He jumped back a step, his hand going to his suit pocket. Zahara could tell he had a gun in there and didn't care. It wouldn't do any damage to her, even if he was brave enough to try and shoot her.

"Where are they?" Zahara raised her hands and allowed flickers of flame to dance along her fingertips. That was mostly for show, but if Zaid's so-called friend Ahmed had sold him out along with Daniel, she would find a way to make him regret it. "Zaid told me he trusted you."

"We shouldn't talk here." Ahmed blotted away some sweat from his brow, and stared up at the sky. "The Americans have eyes in the sky, as they say."

Zahara bit her lower lip. The man might be telling the truth about that. She had to get him away and find out what had happened. After Ahmed had tipped them off that the American contractors knew where they were staying and wanted to talk to Daniel, Zaid had decided that Daniel should meet with the head of the mercenaries and play dumb. As a human—even one they now knew had some impressive jinn blood—Daniel couldn't move through the country unnoticed as easily as they could.

"If the conversation takes an unpleasant turn, I'm more than capable to handling a few human sellswords," Zaid had told her as he left with Daniel. "Let's try to resolve this without smashing more heads together if we can. Donnelly and his group are fighting the same enemy we are, even if they don't realize it."

Something had gone wrong with that plan and Ahmed knew something about it.

Zahara extinguished the flames from her fingers and reached out to grab Ahmed's arm. He stiffened, his gaze wary. "Tell me you want to be unseen."

Ahmed repeated back the phrase, and Zahara dragged him down the street, then took a series of turns down several streets at a fast jog. Along the way, they brushed past several people who spun in surprise, staring blankly at them. A van accelerated toward them as they darted across a street, but Zahara pulled Ahmed out of the way and kept moving. The two of them ended up behind an empty building under construction, under the shade of a plastic tarp that had been stretched out to protect tools and equipment.

"No one could see us." Ahmed stared down at his hands, as if surprised he could see himself. "We were invisible?"

"Unseen, invisible—it's all the same to you humans." Zahara was in no mood to explain jinn magic to the man. "Tell me what you know, or no one will ever see you again, at least alive."

He held up his hands in a placating gesture. "I did as Zaid asked. Donnelly interviewed Daniel in one of the local police offices here in town, but his men were the only people in it. Zaid told me he would stay with Daniel, undetected by the same magic you've used on me. But something went wrong."

What could have gone so wrong that Zaid couldn't handle it? Zahara tried not let her panic show on her face as she glared at Ahmed. She expected him to continue, but he paused and patted his pocket.

"It would be better to show, not to tell." Ahmed pulled out a knife, slowly and with great care. Zahara took little solace in Ahmed's fear of provoking her. A feeling of dread was settling over her, like a blanket of smog descending upon a city in the stifling heat of summer. Ahmed held out a curved *Koummya*, sheathed in a silver scabbard with an upturned tip. He pulled it out by its contoured handle, the double-edged blade slightly curved at the tip. With a twist of his hand, he rotated the blade vertically, as if to slice it through the air between them.

Zahara gave a snarl and gripped his arm, her usual flawless human disguise wavering in panic and anger.

Ahmed winced as her claws pierced through his shirt into his skin, but made no sudden move to pull away. "This is what I think Donnelly did. But not with this one. A different dagger, with more magic in it. The American sent Zaid away, then took your Daniel with him."

Zahara regained some control over herself and retracted back her claws, then reformed her human hands, down to her cherry red nail polish. "Where did they take Daniel?"

Ahmed shook his head, and clutched at his arm. Dots of blood stained his sleeve, and Zahara didn't feel bad about that at all. This might not have been Ahmed's fault, but he still deserved to be treated like a bearer of bad news. "Daniel was alive and well when they them took him from the station, and I don't think even this Donnelly is crazy enough to kill a fellow American here. When Zaid comes back from your world, the two of you can find him, no?"

Zahara set her jaw and settled her face into a mask of fury and menace, battling the temptation to let her tears flow. She couldn't show any weakness to this human, or any other one. Zaid was gone, back in the Mountains of Qaf. Daniel had been spirited away by the group of mercenaries who started this whole mess in the first place. That left her with— Harut. Just when she thought this summoning bargain she had made couldn't get any worse, it did.

"If anything happens to Daniel or Zaid, I'm going to find you." Zahara allowed her claws to reform again, and drew a light scratch along Ahmed's neck before his hand could fly up to protect it. "And you're the one who'll be leaving this world."

A FEW MINUTES of invisibility later, Zahara arrived at a battered car parked on a side street not far from their hotel. Harut sat in the passenger side, his expression one of definite disapproval. Even Zaid had agreed his new SUV would need to be left behind to make it more difficult to follow them, so Zahara had helped out by stealing them a new means of transportation and making sure their belongings—especially her suitcases full of the latest human fashions—had been tucked away in the trunk. Harut had taken a dim view of all of her excellent work on this, not surprisingly.

She jumped into the driver's seat, slammed the door shut and revved the engine to send the car hurtling down the road, all without a word to Harut. He might be all she had left for support, but she wasn't about to pretend she was happy about the situation.

"I take it, then, that this conversation with the men who freed myself and Marut from Mount Damavand did not end well." Harut's tone indicated that all of this was somehow her fault.

"They used a magic dagger to send Zaid back to the Mountains of Qaf." Zahara couldn't keep the shaky tremble out of her voice, as much as she hated herself for it. "Then they kidnapped Daniel. And they're after us. Any suggestions on what to do next?"

"Leaving the city at this rate of speed would be wise, if we survive your means of transportation." Harut frowned as he watched the landscape flash by as Zahara accelerated even faster onto the highway going south. As far as she could tell, the angel had little concept of what a phone was, much less how to drive a car, so he shouldn't be making snarky comments about her lack of respect for speed limits. "The *hiloula* Solikis mentioned is near the desert. When your fellow jinn returns from across the veil, he will expect us to be there."

"Zaid wasn't supposed to return to the Mountains of Qaf. Ever." Zahara tightened her grip on the steering wheel and punched the accelerator. "He might not be able to come back.

"He is far older than you, and I will admit, quite skilled with his sword." Harut glanced over at her, and Zahara blinked furiously to disguise the tears that threatened to well up in her eyes. "I'm familiar with the magic used to force him away, and if the blade went through air and not his flesh, he will arrive in his own lands of Jinnestan, unharmed and with his weapon."

"His family has sworn to kill Zaid if he returns from exile." Zahara wracked her brain for what Zaid had said about the Solikis's parting words. Something about the city of Merzouga, known as the gateway to the Sahara. But what good would come of going there now? Daniel wasn't with them, and Zahara certainly wasn't going to strike up a conversation with the enchantress of the sands if she could avoid it. She was already stuck with one archenemy; she didn't need to arrange a lunch date with another one."

"We need to focus on Daniel." Harut tilted his head up to stare up at the skyline.

What was he doing, admiring cloud formations? Zaid could be under attack right now, and there was nothing Zahara could do to help him. Or herself. Jinn-hunting human mercenaries, bomb-throwing zealots, and a giant fallen angel with a boulder-sized chip on his shoulder were all after her, and the moralizing bore next to her was her only source of support.

"These mercenaries will have taken him as a lure to draw my brother into an ambush. You need to help me find him."

Zahara opened her mouth to tell Harut off in no uncertain terms, then felt her teeth chatter shut as the car sputtered and jerked back and forth. She slammed her foot down harder on the gas pedal, and gripped the steering wheel tighter. What was wrong with the car she had stolen? She should have grabbed the newer van that had been parked in a more conspicuous location. This piece of junk was falling apart on her.

The grinding engine noises settled into an ominous silence, and Zahara was forced to steer the car into a halting stop at the edge of an abrupt drop-off into a palm grove. Zahara let out a few curse worlds spanning a wide range of the human languages she was familiar with as she punched the steering wheel. Nothing was working, even their stolen escape vehicle.

Zahara slammed her head back into the car's inadequate headrest, in a furious sulk. A second later, Harut was on top of her. Now, Zahara wouldn't normally criticize someone for being overcome with lust, but Harut couldn't make up his mind. After their steamy makeout session in the fake dungeon, he had gone out of his way to reject her advances. Was there something about a car engine sputtering into oblivion that turned him on?

Apparently yes, because there he was, his chest and hips pressed against hers, pinning her to the sweaty vinyl of the seat. He smelled fresh and bitter at the same time, like crushed green herbs and citron, and the weight of his body on hers was warm, heavy and solid. Startled, she didn't have enough time to reciprocate with a nice thrust of her pelvis before he unlatched the door and tumbled the two of them out of the car and onto the ground. They rolled down the steep slope next to the road, finally coming to a rest in the dust and stone of a dried-up creek below.

He collapsed on top of her, panting. Zahara gave him a moment, then pivoted and flipped him over on his back, rubbing her body against his with a delighted purr. "That wasn't bad. A little quick, maybe, but we can work on your technique later."

Harut pushed her off and straddled her, his knees planted on either side of her hips as he supported his weight on his muscular arms. His glistening white wings beat the air above them, sending crystals of sand swirling into the air. As sexual positions went, it wasn't terribly practical, but she gave him points for effort.

A moment later, a ball of flame erupted on top of the rise, and glass shards and chunks of metal from above rained down over them. Zahara choked back an involuntary shriek, but Harut's feathers fanned out, shielding her from the debris.

"We were tracked from the sky by Daniel's captors." Harut climbed to his feet, shaking dust from his wings. "I'll follow the mechanical automaton that attacked us and try to find him."

His shape shimmered in the air, like heat rising up from asphalt, and a fierce brown hawk appeared in his place. The bird shot upward, wings flapping as he climbed into the cloudless blue of the sky. Zahara stood, shading her eyes to try and spot him. What did he expect her to do? Fly after him?

Around her, parts of the car and burnt items from their luggage littered the ground. They had been drone-bombed. Wonderful. She bent over and picked up the charred remains of a particularly fetching pair of heels and swore again. Whoever had blown up her favorite shoes was going to regret it for the markedly shortened rest of their lives.

Adopting her elemental form, she took a few quick hops forward and stretched her wings out. She always had trouble taking off from ground level, and with the sun shining overhead, it was by no means assured she would get into the air at all. After a few struggling flaps, she climbed high enough to catch a rising current from the ground and soared after the hawk.

Her attempt at daytime flying didn't last long. There was no way her stubby wings were going to carry her high enough to catch up with Harut. Exhausted, hungry and grumpy, she glided down to rest on the broad stalks of a date palm. If that angel wanted to soar off and attempt some sort of rescue, he was going have to do it by himself.

Panting, she squeezed herself into a comfortable shaded spot and eyed a nearby cluster of dates, golden brown and redolent of rich, dark sugar. There were worst places to wait it out until dark, certainly.

A half hour and several delicious dates later, Zahara lifted her head and scanned the leaves around her, suddenly alert. She would have missed the snake's approach entirely had it not been for the contrast of its reddish-brown body against the green palm stalks. An African puff adder. Nasty bite on those things. The thick-bodied reptile was responsible for most of the snakebite deaths on the continent of Africa.

The serpentine shape drew closer, the animal's true length revealed to be a full meter. Zahara gave a long sigh and gave up any hopes of snacking on more delectable fruit any time soon.

"Hello, Mother."

The snake paused, then raised a wide head to regard her

with copper eyes. "I told you to stay away from Harut, my daughter."

"We're on opposite sides on this one, remember? I need all the help I can get to kill Marut."

Lilitu drew back into an *S*-shape and a let out a hiss like steam escaping from a pressure cooker. "You compound your foolishness with mistake after mistake."

"Daniel's not totally helpless, you know." It felt odd to be defending her do-gooder sorcerer, but Zahara had about had it with her mother's withering criticism of her every action. Maybe name-dropping might bring her down a peg or two. "His grandmother sends her regards. Solikis, or something like that."

"I'm now well aware of Daniel Goldstein's background." Her mother allowed a forked tongue to slither in and out of her mouth. "In retrospect, my choice to use my enemy's former dwelling to complete Marut's transformation may have been a miscalculation."

"Getting worried?" Zahara was in no position to declare victory. Zaid was gone, Harut had flown off to gods-knew-where, and for all she knew, Daniel was already dead. But bluffing was the only weapon she had left.

"Hardly." Lilitu slid closer. "The foolish human sellswords have taken your sorcerer to lure Marut into an ambush he will have no trouble turning against his enemies. At midnight, Marut will drink Daniel's blood. Then the fallen one will be unstoppable."

"His brother might have something to say about that."

It was as unsettling to hear a laugh coming from a puff adder's mouth as it would have been from the gaping maw of her mother's true form. "Harut has been misdirected to another location entirely. He'll never find Daniel in time. At least, not without help."

Zahara arched her back, her fur standing on end. She shouldn't be surprised. Her mother was always several steps ahead of her opponents, positioning her moves against them perfectly.

"I've almost resolved this debacle you've created for me." Her mother inched forward, her scales gripping the surface of the palm leaves. "You can get out of this alive, Zahara, if for once you listen to me. Harut can't find Daniel without your help. Vanish into the levels and return home. We'll discuss your disobedience and unreasonable behavior at a later date."

A low growl began in Zahara's throat. A thought, unbidden, came to her mind. Honey badgers ate puff adders with relish, and she was at least as tough as one of them. Not to mention far more adorable.

"Are you listening to me?" Her mother's tone sharpened. "This affair is all but settled—*if* you behave. What of the apostate, Zaid? He's long since outstayed his welcome. Is he someone I need to trouble myself with?"

Zahara knew all too well what her mother meant by that. Lilitu was ruthless with her enemies. Hell, she was ruthless with her own daughter. Zaid wouldn't stand a chance if her mother went after him. As much danger as he was in from his own clan back in the world of the jinn, he was in far more danger from her mother.

"No." She flattened her ears and buried her head in her paws. "He wasn't trapped like me. Those nasty Americans were the last straw. He left us."

"Useful idiots, that crew." Her mother's serpentine shape crept backward, muscles constricting and releasing to pull her long body backward down the palm tree. "I've endured this cursed sun and the wretched world of mud people for long enough. See that you follow my instructions. Perhaps your narrow escape from this affair will teach you caution in the future."

The snake slid away, and Zahara waited until her sharp ears picked up the distant crack of thunder that marked her mother's passing into the levels. That was what she needed to do as well—disappear when Daniel needed her most, leave Zaid to be killed if he returned to help, and listen to whatever stories would be told of Harut's eventual brutal death at his brother's hands. Oh, and be grounded for about a hundred years.

Or she could sit here, and enjoy a nice bunch of dates until Harut got back.

HARUT FINALLY GOT around to finding her hours later, as she sat and used the talons on her padded paws to skewer the golden dates hanging in giant clusters from the tree and pop them into her mouth.

The hawk landed next to her, folded his wings, and tilted his head, his beady eyes fixed on her with disapproval. The unbearable cuteness of her form had little effect on real animals, and it had never had much impact on Harut. "Your human charge is in danger, and you're making no effort to help him."

"He's more of a mark, actually." Zahara licked the last speck of flesh off the date seed with her rough pink tongue and flicked the pit in Harut's direction. This conversation had to be handled with a little delicacy. She didn't want to seem too eager to rush to Daniel's aid. After all, her mother had expressly forbidden her to do so. "These sorcerers think they're so clever, using a spell to force a jinn to serve them. Once the bargain is set, they're so excited about the power and riches coming to them that they overlook the fact they'll end up a slave for the rest of their lives."

"I see." Harut edged closer to her along the stalk, his claws gripping the green surface. "And do you have many of these wretched thralls suffering in your evil clutches?"

"Well, not that many." Zahara cleaned her paw with another few laps of her tongue. "Okay, Daniel will be my first. After all, I'm awfully young, by demon jinn standards. Have to start somewhere."

"Shouldn't you try to preserve his life, then?" Harut was nothing if not persistent.

"I don't know where he is. And you said you were flying off to save him, with that flaming sword and sourpuss attitude of yours."

"His captors drove him west, into the desert." Harut's bird head bobbed up and down, as if in frustration. "Then a sandstorm arose and I was forced to break off the search. It was no coincidence, I assure you. Marut has partnered with evil itself to achieve his goals."

Evil itself. Her mother would all but blush at this shameless flattery if she heard it.

"Daniel has to summon me, and order me to do something." Zahara decided to explain things slowly, like she was instructing a small child to pour cayenne pepper into his father's jockstrap. "Don't you know anything about my kind? Now, if I was an evil sorcerer with a jinn under contract, and I was kidnapped, I'd call her for help."

"Daniel's not evil, and he might not be able to manage a full summoning while being held captive." Harut ruffled his feathers, his voice tight. "Reach out and contact him before it's too late."

Anxiety gnawed away at her date-filled stomach. If she listened to her mother, she'd be safe, but miserable. She stretched out her wings and pretended to yawn. The sun had begun to dip behind the bare rock mountains surrounding the lush valley they were in, but it wouldn't be dark for a while yet. Daniel was safe until midnight, wasn't he? Plenty of time. "Still too much light. We need to wait for nightfall. Maybe Zaid's back and looking for him."

That was unlikely. Zaid's exile had come with a death sentence if he tried to return. Her attempt to take a message to his clan to even discuss the matter had been met with cold refusal. If Zaid had been forced back into the Mountains of Qaf, he would have his own problems to deal with. And her mother to face if he dared to try and rescue Daniel.

"Why would he risk himself for Daniel?" Harut asked.

"Daniel chose death over harming him." Zahara drew her answer out, with an emphasis on each word. Defying her mother openly terrified her. Falling into her usual role of the family's great disappointment would be so much easier. "Now Zaid is obligated to him. Plus, between the two of us,

I think Zaid's getting a little soft as he gets older. He actually likes Daniel."

"So among the jinn, a life saved is a life indebted." Harut bobbed his feathered head. "Well, I saved your life when we were attacked, so you're now obligated to me."

Took him long enough to figure it out, didn't it?

Zahara's tail twitched, and she gave an exaggerated growl of protest. "I don't owe you anything."

Harut stretched out his neck, his hooked beak a whisker away from her nose. "I saved your life, and for payment I demand a favor in return. Help me find Daniel."

There it was. She couldn't refuse Harut's demands after he had saved her, or risk offending the gods. Only rescuing him in turn would get her out of that obligation. So, technically, she had no choice *but* to help Daniel.

"Fine." She spread out her wings, crouched, and prepared to spring into flight. "Let's go find some candy."

HALF AN HOUR later, an exhausted Zahara rearranged the piles of wrapped candy for the last time and finished the spell. She had transformed back into her human shape and salvaged a few bags of emergency treats from the burned and exploded contents of their car. All in all, it was an awful lot of work. She needed a stiff drink and a good nap.

"There." With a sigh, she tossed a handful of the sweets on the ground and scrutinized the result. "Give me a minute, and I'll figure out how far away he is."

"We're running out of time." Harut crouched next to her

in the scorched earth, staring down at her magical construct with a great deal of skepticism. "And this method you've chosen to find Daniel is most unusual."

"Keep your pants on," Zahara snapped, annoyed at the interruption. Then she glanced over again at Harut, who had also transformed back into his all-too-heavenly human form. "Or go ahead and take them off. I promise I'll only peek a little."

"Why do you employ these sugary confections in your dark magic?" Harut asked.

"I'm casting the bones, dumbass." She pursed her lips. If this was correct, Daniel was close to two hundred kilometers away. That was a problem. There was no way she was flying that far, and their only method of transportation had been blown sky high.

"Cleromancy is hardly unknown to me," Harut said. "I know all of the versions that can be used as a conduit for seers, and those to mete out justice as well. But care must be taken in the selection of the lots, and these items have no magical power. They're little more than colored sugar."

"I know." Zahara unwrapped one of the candies and popped it into her mouth, closing her eyes to savor the taste. "I'm supposed to be using the clean-picked bones of my enemies, after I've roasted them alive and fed on their flesh. But it's hot and bright outside, you're in a big hurry, and this candy is as close as I can get, okay?"

Harut folded his arms. Honestly, even his eyebrows screamed disapproval. "So where is he?"

"West." She pointed at the setting sun. "Which is tha-taway. About two hours by car, several days by foot, and never if I have to fly there."

"We'll need to purchase one of the mechanical vehicles we used to travel here, rather than resort to the unsavory methods you used to procure our earlier means of transportation." Harut rose to his feet. "Perhaps I can speak to one of the local people and impress upon them the purity of our mission. Then they'll allow us to borrow one of them."

"If we need to score a new whip, leave that to me." Zahara scrambled to shove as much of the candy as possible into a makeshift purse created from a torn piece of silky fabric she had recovered from the wreck. She took a closer look. Probably Daniel's underwear. "And I'm doing all the driving. If I leave things up to you, you'll get suckered into buying a lemon and drive the entire distance several kilometers below the speed limit."

ZAHARA ADJUSTED THE clutch into fourth gear and accelerated down the darkened road, the car's headlights penetrating the late night gloom. Now this was much better. It was dark, she had a powerful engine humming underneath her, and Harut was the one who was annoyed. To irritate him even further, she had transformed her clothing back to her belly-dancing outfit.

"We could have offered the two some gold or other wealth to part with this vehicle." Harut ran his fingers over the inside of the Range Rover, frowning. "You didn't need to use your ability to stupefy humans to steal it from them."

The two French tourists Zahara had singled out as likely

candidates to provide her with her new sweet ride had been left behind at the gas station, staring out at their surroundings with beatific smiles and no memory of the adorable brown eyes that had rendered them incapable of stopping her from grabbing their rental car keys and taking off down the street.

"Do you have any money on you?" Zahara asked. "Because I don't. So it wasn't like we could buy a car. Anyway, once I *do* get money, I need to spend it on something fun to wear. All my clothes were blown up by Donnelly's pathetic minions. I was quite fond of a number of those outfits, you know."

"Your current attire reveals too much of your skin." Harut's gaze remained fixed on the road ahead, as if he preferred not to spend too much time confirming his concerns. "Since we may encounter others who don't know our true form, you should adopt modest dress."

Zahara reached down to undo her coin belt and shook it to make a musical cacophony of clattering metal before tossing it in the air to land on Harut's head. He allowed it rest there for a moment before removing it, as if unsure even how to respond to such a childish antic.

Well, Zahara had a few more tricks like that up her non-existent sleeves. "Keep complaining about what I'm wearing and I'll take more of it off." She raised her eyebrows. "Unless that was your plan all along."

"Certainly not." Harut shifted in his seat. "Are you sure you're competent to handle this device? Our rate of speed appears unsafe."

"I'm a great driver, for your information." Zahara

punched the gas pedal to make her point. "And since you've been hanging upside down in a cave for the last several centuries, I'm not letting you behind the wheel."

"I'm confident I could learn the procedure to handle this machine in a short period of time." Harut leaned forward to examine the dashboard dials, then sat back. "I would have thought your kind would try to avoid being surrounded by iron."

"Lots of plastic and refined steel in these newer cars." Zahara rapped her knuckles against the car's interior. "And human technology doesn't bother me much. I've been here for so long."

"Why do you live in the world of man?" Harut asked. "You could cross through hell and select a victim anytime you chose."

"I like it here, that's all." Zahara considered turning on the radio to drown out Harut's constant questions.

"You also spend an inordinate amount of time seeking out sugar in any form," Harut noted. "In Persia, candy and fragrances were used to drive away demon jinn like the dev and your kind."

"Well some of us prefer the dripping raw blood of a fresh sacrifice and some of us have a sweet tooth." Zahara craned her neck to get a better look at a faint glow in the skies above. A plane, maybe? The light was either growing brighter, or the object it was on was coming closer.

"You live among humans because you can't stand to stay with your own kin." Harut spoke softly, but his voice carried conviction. "Your mixed blood compels you to seek out sweetness to drive away the evil inside of you."

Zahara ignored the road in front of her and took both hands off the wheel as she turned in a fury to face Harut. "That is, hands down, the most ridiculous thing anyone's ever said to me."

She had more to say, most of it a string of profanities, but she never got to scream them in Harut's face.

The faint glow in the sky expanded into a giant sphere of light. That better not be another drone again. Zahara slammed on the brakes and swerved the car to the left. The right wheels came off the ground for several seconds before the vehicle fishtailed into a spin and came rattling down on the ground.

Zahara clung to the steering wheel, her heart thumping in her chest. The front windshield had shattered into a spiderweb of cracks that blocked any forward vision.

"What the hell was that?" She turned to her right, but Harut was gone. She jerked open her door, sending smashed pebbles of safety glass flying.

Whatever it was, they weren't driving themselves away from this. The car's front tires were shredded, ripped apart by a line of spikes set into the road. Hardly the tactic of a nonhuman enemy. Another light flashed into her eyes, blinding her. Search beams. The light swung away from her, illuminating first the disabled car and then the ground around it. As the spots in her eyes receded, she saw a circle of men in army fatigues advancing upon their position.

Zahara faded into invisibility, and after further consideration, transformed into her elemental shape. She and Harut could have randomly run into a military checkpoint, or been suspected of some nefarious behavior by the authorities—

motor vehicle theft notwithstanding, she'd been remarkably well-behaved on this trip. If so, it was an awfully inconvenient coincidence.

She chose to scamper forward on all four paws, rather than fly, and succeeded in darting through an opening in the ring of armed men drawing closer to the car. One turned as she slinked past him, a pair of night-vision goggles on his face and a recurve bow in one hand. There was a whiff of magic on it, like the weapons they had taken off the two men at the movie studio.

Somehow, Donnelly and his band of merry mercenaries had tracked them down. Again.

Confident of her invisibility skills, Zahara ignored the man as she surveyed the scene by the desert road. An array of armored cars had been concealed behind a crumbling mud brick structure, and an even larger group of soldiers huddled near them, scanning the area with an air of anxiety. None of them carried any antique weapons. Local troops for back up, probably.

She hopped up onto the hood of one of the vehicles, thinking she might get a better view from the roof. Plus, she could use the height as a launching pad for a nice slow glide over the scene to figure out what was going on.

A rope slithered through the air, and within an instant, her entire body was encircled by coils that constricted with her every breath. At one point, Zahara might have thrashed about from surprise, but the memory of the cursed whip Harut had used against her and Zaid was fresh enough that she froze in place.

The soldier with the bow approached, one bolt notched

and ready to fire in her direction. As he drew closer, he returned the arrow to the sheath behind his back and pulled out a *hamsa*. Zahara cringed. This one wasn't as powerful as Daniel's, but it had enough strength to make her flinch.

"Got you." The man spoke in English, with an American accent. "I can't see you, but I've got you."

Chapter Nineteen

DANIEL GAVE UP fighting against the plastic zip ties digging into his wrists and did his best to meet Donnelly's eyes.

"That's all, then?" The mercenary raised his hands up in a questioning gesture, then let them fall by his sides. He had added a side holster with the butt of a gun sticking out from his right hip to his original version of the military casual look he had worn when he had started interrogating Daniel in the police station. The silver knife that had somehow cut Zaid out of this reality entirely was tucked into his belt on his left. "Your original list of lies was quite impressive. Maybe there are still a few more details that have slipped your mind."

Daniel gave a shake of his head as he scanned the room again. It held assorted crates and long duffel bags, and was lit by a string of electric bulbs running off a generator, if the humming noise outside was what he thought it was. Aside from Donnelly, the tent held four other men, all dressed in desert camoflauge fatigues and armed to the teeth.

Daniel had been taken out of the station with a hood thrown over his head, then loaded into a car for the drive to this new interrogation center. Hours had gone by, as Daniel breathed in the unwashed sock smell of the fabric blocking his vision, and played out every possible awful scenario for his captivity in his mind. The hood had been removed after Daniel had been placed in a chair in the center of the tent, with no opportunity for him to glimpse any clue outside that could help him figure out where he had been taken.

Judging by the darkness outside the tent's flaps, and the relief from the oppressive heat that had built up inside the white canvas walls, it had to be late at night. Prime hunting time, if the fallen one wanted to track Daniel down. And fancy dagger or not, Donnelly wasn't likely to have anything in this tent like the magical protections Harut had placed around their Ourzarzate hotel.

"I'm telling you the truth about Marut." Daniel had done that, even though he had left out as many details as he dared, especially any information about Zahara. He didn't have any other option than to try and talk himself out of the situation. Only Ahmed knew what had happened, more or less, and even if the Moroccan intelligence officer shared that information with Zahara, Daniel had no idea how she could locate him. Not to mention that taking on five mercenaries would probably require more than magical dancing and her skill in decapitating plushies with an overly-decorated sword. Harut might be his best option for a rescue, but if a fallen one could locate him anywhere he was taken, Daniel was worried the wrong one would find him first. "I'm trying to stop Marut, and so are the people with me. If we don't work together on this, he's going to be the only winner."

"Your new friends aren't human, Daniel. They come from the same hellhole this baby came from." Donnelly patted the dagger on his waist. "I don't want any help from their kind. I lost a lot of good men in Iran thanks to Harut and Marut. Both of them are going to die for that, along with anything else that's helping them."

"Marut wants to start a war, and Harut is trying to stop him." Daniel strained his ears, trying to hear anything outside the tent over the rumbling of the generator. "You're going to need help to stop that from happening."

"War isn't the problem." Donnelly gave him a cold smile. "In fact, most of the time it's the solution. Not to mention that it's good for business, after all. All I need is a clear shot at Marut and it's all over."

"Like your giant chandelier of iron trick?" Daniel tried again to make out the new sound outside. A car engine, maybe? "Because we dropped it through his chest and all it did was slow him down a little. You're out of your depth here, even if you don't realize it."

Donnelly laughed, and a few of the men standing around him chuckled as well. "I don't think I'm as out of my depth as a video game geek trying to play with real monsters." He turned, and another fatigue-clad person strode inside. She looked to be in her early thirties, with close-cropped hair under a camo baseball cap emblazoned with what Daniel assumed was the mercenary company's logo. She spoke quietly into his ear, and a smile spread across Donnelly's face.

"That's two more down, and only one to go." Donnelly and the woman exchanged looks of self satisfaction, and Daniel felt his stomach sink. The head mercenary had to be referring to Zahara and Harut. Either they were dead, or as captive as Daniel was. Meanwhile, Marut was now free to roam the darkness outside, and Daniel was sitting here like a neatly wrapped package of take-out fallen angel food.

"Congratulations, Daniel, you get to play a starring role as bait. Our best intel is that Marut wants whoever stopped the sacrifice alive. There's some controversy about whether he needs to rip your heart out and eat it, or if drinking most of your blood will work. Personally, I'm willing to take a wait and see attitude about those options." Donnelly took the silver knife off his belt and tossed it to a heavily bearded man who had a good half a head on the mercenary commander's tall frame. "The dagger's going to stay here if your pet jinn shows up. But if Marut comes for you here, we've got him. If it's his brother he's after, I'll have those bases covered as well."

"What makes you think your men can do anything to him if he does show up?" Part of Daniel wanted to believe that Donnelly and his gang could take on Marut and come out victorious. Then he'd at least have a chance to survive, assuming Donnelly didn't intend to kill him no matter what happened. But that would mean that Harut would also bear the brunt of the mercenaries' revenge, along with Zahara. "Semiautomatics and bullets don't work on any of the jinn, much less someone as powerful as the bad apple of the two fallen ones."

Donnelly paused as he strolled toward the tent's entrance to kick at a rectangular crate on the floor. It reminded Daniel of a long, skinny coffin. "We have surface-to-air missiles that can take down an airliner. If Marut can take a hit from one of those and come back, I might start taking you seriously."

Donnelly waved a hand at the giant with the beard who

had taken custody of the dagger. "Whether or not the target makes an appearance, I think we'll need that video recording of our guest here for public consumption."

He and the woman disappeared through the tent's front flap, and Daniel slumped back in his chair. Donnelly's casual aside about filming him brought up several distinct images to mind, most of which involved Daniel growing shorter by a head.

The giant grunted at one of his compatriots, a clean-shaven man with a head like a bull and biceps the size of bulk-store soup cans. Bull Man sighed and left his position of looming ominously to retrieve several objects from the crates piled in the corner. He dragged out a folding screen and set it up behind Daniel. With a quick glance over his shoulder, Daniel recognized a familiar shade of green. His suspicions were confirmed when Bull Man unfolded a laptop and set up a high-end video camera to face Daniel.

"Juan's the expert on this, not me." Bull Man frowned at the laptop and tapped a few keys before giving the giant a sour look.

The giant grunted. "Juan's not here. Let's just get this done."

Daniel tried to swallow away the panic that rose up in his throat and threatened to choke off his breath. He twisted his hands behind his back. The plastic ties were as tight as ever, but at least he wasn't physically bound to the chair. Still, standing up and rushing four professional mercenaries with his hands behind his back wouldn't end well. He tried to think of anything he had on him that could help him, and came up with nothing. The men had quickly searched him, but had left his hamsa in his pocket, along with his wallet and the watch on his wrist. Petty theft wasn't their style, but a fake video of a real execution just might be.

"You're setting up a CGI scene just for me?" Daniel put as a cheery a note in his voice as he could, under the circumstances. "Seems like a lot of work if you're planning to let Marut snack on me."

"Too much work." Bull Man grumbled in agreement at Daniel's statement.

The giant glared at Daniel. "If you're smart, you'll play along with this particular production. We need an explanation for the disappearance of two Americans here. A kidnapping video where you cry tears about your dead boyfriend Anton and beg to be rescued will do the trick. It's your choice whether or not you show up later on the news alive thanking the heroes who got you out or fly back to the States in a coffin."

Daniel wasn't sure he believed Donnelly would take a chance with option one—letting him live, maybe making him sign a nondisclosure agreement—but at least he had the two men talking to him. He needed to keep the conversation going, and try to figure a way to get out of this.

The rustling noise started up again, and a gust of wind blew a thin stream of sand into the tent. The grains whirled into a circle in the air, then collapsed at Daniel's feet. The sense of the reassurance he had felt when Zaid had stood behind him, invisible, returned. Could the jinn be reaching out somehow to him?

Both Bull Man and the giant were hunched over the laptop now, with the silver dagger gleaming dully next to it. If

Donnelly had used it to send Zaid away, maybe Daniel could use it to bring him back.

"I'm willing to help." Daniel sucked in his breath as the two mercenaries looked up and glared at him. Then a flicker of a glance between them confirmed his suspicion that they might just fall for his crazy plan. "Not in filming my own execution, but a fake kidnapping video I'm totally cool with."

"How much do you know about this technology, gamer boy?" The giant wasn't exactly on point with his insults, but he wasn't stupid, either. Daniel had to convince him he could be useful to them.

"For one thing, your background color is off." Daniel twisted around and gave the blank screen behind him a critical look. "More Kermit the Frog than true chroma key green. The folds in it will give you image artifact, and you've placed me so close to it there'll be shadows all over the place."

Bull Man left the keyboard and strode over to him and Daniel tensed, sure the man was about to slap him upside the head, or worse. Instead, he jerked Daniel up to his feet and pushed him toward the laptop.

"What are you doing?" The giant grabbed Daniel's shirt as Bull Man produced a pair of wire cutters. Daniel winced as the man pulled on his already stiff wrists and, for a moment, wasn't sure if he intended to use the cutters to sever the plastic ties or take off a few fingers. His hands were so stiff and painful he had to bring his fingers up to his face and wiggle them to convince himself they were all still there.

"Saving myself a few hours of work." Bull Man kicked a

crate over and motioned for Daniel to sit in front of the laptop. "Try anything and you'll regret it. Our orders are to make sure you're here and alive if that feathered monster shows up. But no one told us you couldn't spend the wait time screaming your head off."

"Come on." Daniel finished shaking out his hands and placed his fingers on the keyboard. To his left, the ornate scabbard of the dagger glinted into the corner of his vision. "I'm a video game designer, and I'm not trying to play hero. What I told your boss was the truth. I want to take out Marut as much as you do."

"Talk less and type more." Bull Man hit him between the shoulder blades hard enough to make a point, but not to the point of stopping Daniel from doing his work for him.

An idea popped into Daniel's head. It was insane, but it was an idea. He got to work on the keyboard and nodded at Bull Man. "Like I said, you need to stretch out the green screen fabric tighter and move your talent—that would be one of your well-armed comrades taking my place for now— a little further away from it.

The giant grunted at one of the two remaining guards in the room, and the man walked over to rearrange the chair and screen. He took Daniel's place in the chair, with an irritated expression on his face. Apparently no one liked playing the hostage in distress role. Daniel used those precious moments to check for anything on the computer that might help him. No internet connection, not surprisingly, but he at least now knew what time it was. He hunched over the screen, made sure the video feed uploaded properly into the computer and set to work on the CGI effects.

Fortunately, the mercenaries had an impressive array of video-editing software loaded onto their computer. Whoever Juan was, he had some serious computer skills.

Daniel finished, then checked the clock again. It flashed military time. Twenty-three forty-five. Close to midnight, the same hour Marut had attacked the last time. He glanced up at his captors and pointed to the screen. As he had hoped, both men leaned to watch the show. The green background behind the chair disappeared, replaced into a landscape straight out of Dante's Inferno. Bubbling lava spat out of crevices in black rocks, as a chorus of screams wailed in the distance. A hellish version of Marut came forward—or at least the version of a fallen angel Daniel would have imagined before meeting a bona fide, murderous version in the flesh. His wings, covered in jet-black feathers, swept up behind him. His face was obscured by a dark hood, his chest bare and heavily muscled, and he carried a sword with flames flickering along its entire length. The virtual Marut advanced upon Daniel's stand-in, slicing off his head, and sending a shower of blood out to splatter the hellish landscape with scarlet drops.

Considering the short span of time Daniel had put into the special effects, not to mention the guard's nonexistent acting skills, the interface of the CGI software with the mercenaries' hostage film setup did achieve a certain level of artistic impact. But unless Daniel could take advantage of the mercenaries' temporary distraction, the playacting in front of him would become all too real when Marut showed up.

Daniel slid one hand toward the dagger. What the hell would he do with it if he could grab it? He didn't know, but there had to be a way to use it to get Zaid back.

Bull Man snorted as he watched the screen. "Nice special effects, gamer boy, but we need a hostage video that will look like it came from an authentic jihadist group, not one of your geek sword fighting epics."

An explosion roared on the screen and it dissolved into the face of a blond, blue-eyed man aiming a sniper rifle at the screen. The virtual fighter fired, and the effects Daniel had set up made the screen appear to shatter into hundreds of fragments.

As his captors jerked back in surprise, Daniel's fingers closed on the cool scabbard of the dagger. He had a vague idea that he could somehow slide it up his sleeve, but the motion of his hand attracted the giant's attention.

"What the hell are you doing?" He chose to land a punch alongside Daniel's head rather than grab his hand, and Daniel pitched himself backward, avoiding most of the impact of the giant's fist. He succeeded in pulling the dagger free of its sheath as he fell, but at the cost of a deep cut in his palm. The giant and Bull Man both pounced on him and the pain in his hand became the least of his concerns.

Bull Man hit him first, a solid punch into his abdomen that drove the breath right out of him, and sent a fireball of pain into his gut. Daniel dropped the dagger and tried to struggle to his feet, but Bull Man forced him into a kneeling position, twisting his good arm behind him. Daniel tried to gasp in enough air to say Zaid's name, to try something like the magic he had used to call Zahara, but nothing came out.

Daniel's computer game soundtrack switched again, this time to eerie music intermixing with howling winds. A tiny part of Daniel's mind, free of the chilling panic that gripped the rest of him, wondered why it sounded so unfamiliar. The giant loomed over Daniel, his semiautomatic rifle in hand, and Daniel knew he was going to die. As his heartbeats pounded in his ears, the only thought in Daniel's mind was Zaid. He could *see* him in his mind, as plainly as if he were close enough to touch. His dark eyes focused on Daniel's, and his lips moved, giving silent instructions. Daniel clenched his fists, feeling the slick wetness of his own blood from the cut he had given himself with the dagger. The image of Zaid dissolved, blurring into a twisting dust devil of sand.

The giant's face went slack, an expression of stupefied horror replacing contorted fury. His arm holding up his weapon went limp and his rifle dropped to the floor. Behind him, the green screen flickered to life, as if a high-def movie had been projected onto it. A roaring sandstorm boiled over moonlit dunes, and a dust devil spun outward toward them. Virtual reality became actual, as hot air seared Daniel's skin, and he needed to blink away the particles of sand that swirled into his eyes.

The giant collapsed on the ground, convulsing. A dribble of foam oozed down the side of his mouth. His limbs jerked uncontrollably.

"Shit." Bull Man released Daniel's arm and lifted his own weapon, swinging it from side to side as he searched for a target. The two other mercenaries in the room backed away from the screen, guns at the ready. One of them yelped out in panic, as an electric cable on the floor reared up like a cobra and struck at him with a jolt of blue fire. The tent rattled, howling winds whipping its cloth sides.

The funnel of sand loomed closer to fill the green screen, then swirled into the tent itself. A glowing pair of yellow eyes materialized in the center and Zaid's body shimmered into view. He wore a long, sweeping white robe with a scarlet sash around his waist, and a turban set with a single large ruby. He raised his blade and slashed it through the air, shifting his sword from hand to hand.

One of the mercenaries made a run for it, maybe to call for help or possibly to save his own skin. The other mercenary recovered from his shock, throwing down his semiautomatic rifle and pulling a short sword out from his waist. Zaid grinned and leapt forward with his blade slicing through the air in a blur of silver. The mercenary's attempt at hitting him failed miserably, and Zaid stepped to the side, using the flat of his blade to whack the man's buttocks as his momentum carried him forward to sprawl on the floor.

"Drop the weapon or your friend here gets it." The Bull Man yanked back Daniel's head, and the sharp edge of a blade pressed against Daniel's neck. The remaining guard lurched to his feet and stumbled over to aim a gun at Daniel's head.

Zaid stood stock still, his sword gripped in one hand, as the blade at Daniel's throat pressed in harder and a gun safety clicked off. The sword in the jinn's hand dropped to the floor, and Bull Man's knife pulled back ever so slightly from Daniel's skin.

Then Zaid faded away, leaving a pile of sand where he had been standing. Bull Man cursed softly and released his hold on Daniel, shoving him to the ground. Daniel looked up in time to see the sudden movement as both men's heads connected with a satisfying crunch. They both fell down, and didn't get up.

Zaid reappeared, his hand held out to help Daniel to his feet. "That part when I told Zahara we should try *not* bang their heads together? I'm going to take that back."

"That was incredible." Blood dripped down Daniel's arm from the slash on his hand, but he didn't care. "How did you cross over and find me?"

Zaid tore a strip of cloth from his robe and took Daniel's hand in his own, wrapping the fabric around the wound. "I didn't. You called me to you, from the Mountains of Qaf."

Daniel stared down at the bloodied dagger at his feet. Somehow, he had used it to bring Zaid out of his world and into this one. He bent down to pick up the dagger and its sheath from the floor. He held it out to Zaid, but the jinn shuddered and motioned for him to take it back.

"I'd rather not deal with that magic again, and that blade has no business being in the hands of Donnelly's thugs. You clearly know how to use it, so you should keep it."

"What about Zahara and Harut?" Daniel made sure the blade was tucked into its scabbard and stashed it his front pocket. "Donnelly got a message while he was here. I think they grabbed both of them, somehow."

"It would take more than this lot to kill Harut." Zaid patted Daniel's bandaged hand. "And I know how we can find out about Zahara."

Daniel nodded; the rush of adrenaline and fear washing out of him, and leaving him shaking and relieved. Then he felt it. A vibration underneath him, as if feet heavy with the burdens of thousands of years of sin and death were slamming into the earth, coming closer with each step.

"Marut's coming." Daniel reached for the knife at his belt, as if he could somehow defend himself with it. "Don't ask me how I know. I just do."

"I believe you." Zaid grabbed Daniel's arm and pulled him toward the tent flap. "Let's pull a Zahara, steal a ride, and get the hell out of here."

Chapter Twenty

MAYBE AN HOUR had passed. Or six. If anything, it felt like Zahara had been tangled up in the ropes for days. One thing was certain—the midnight deadline for saving Daniel had drawn near, if it hadn't passed already.

Remaining motionless, channeling her energy so she could stay invisible, and cursing her decision to answer Daniel's summons had taken a lot out of her. She would have only one shot at her plan to escape, and with this level of exhaustion, she might not be able to pull it off.

The soldier with the night-vision goggles who had sprung the trap on her had pulled back quickly, then called in reinforcements. A large group of his comrades gathered around the vehicle, and proceeded to engage in tense conversations with one another using a variety of communication devices. They encircled the truck she lay on with a ring of weapons and gear, then talked some more. At one point, an odd little machine on tire treads rumbled close to her, raised up one hinged arm and gave the ropes binding her—and her invisible ribs—a good poke.

A military robot, seriously? The humans' utter paranoia about her limited fighting skills would have been flattering if she wasn't on a deadline. And time was ticking away.

Her unusual discipline in remaining utterly immobile

had produced one tangible benefit. Just as the ropes tightened with any movement, they relaxed over time in the absence of any struggle. She had a small, precious amount of space to move in her bonds. She needed the right moment to press that advantage.

After yet another huddled meeting, the original soldier who had captured Zahara approached her, his posture wary. His companions aimed a variety of weapons in her direction—a few crossbows, a spear or two, and an assortment of more standard modern military rifles.

The soldier thrust his amulet closer to the tangles of rope. Loath as she was to relive her recent humiliation during Harut's attack, Zahara had no other choice.

She sparkled into visibility and opened her eyes wide, letting out a soft purr. The man froze, the *hamsa* dropping from his hand. With a quick exhalation, Zahara flattened herself into as small a shape as possible and slipped a paw out of whatever cursed material made up the ropes trapping her. One slash of her claws was all it took to sever enough of them to wriggle free.

A group of men rushed toward her, swords drawn, as the man who had faced her true form crumpled to the ground. Zahara scrambled up to the roof and took off with her wings outstretched.

The group gathered around the fallen man, and a few scanned the air above with similar goggles, but none of them had enough perception to pick up her small shape flapping through the air. Some sort of heat-sensing technology, maybe? Invisible or not, the children of smokeless fire were warm-blooded enough for that sort of human trick to work, but only with an operator who had some degree of the sight. Her unbearable cuteness had taken care of that particular soldier.

Zahara banked toward the road and looked down to see a thick black net stretched over a bird, its wings outstretched. It was no ordinary trap. Even this far above, Zahara could sense a dark force emanating from the material that not only entrapped Harut, but forced him to assume his elemental form.

She rode a thermal updraft rising from the asphalt and turned in a slow circle as she pondered the situation. She had some familiarity with items used against the jinn. The *hamsa*, the *nazar*, along with various blessed objects and sayings— fraud or truth, weak or powerful, they all aimed to repel people like her. What she knew far less about were objects cursed to harm anyone like Harut. She had spent most of her life in the human world by choice, and had little knowledge of what it took to harm someone like him. Now *this* was a situation where her mother's extensive background in maiming and killing enemies might come in handy.

A fascinating magical mystery, if she was into that sort of thing. Zahara wasn't, and all this thinking was making the little horns on her head ache. Harut had used up the favor she owed him when he demanded she help find Daniel. Lifting as much as a paw to save Harut from whatever awful fate his captors had in store for him wasn't required. Or wise, given she was facing a band of humans armed with both magical and automatic weapons.

Not to mention that Daniel needed saving and fast. She couldn't come out of the levels to some vague location based on her interpretation of a few scattered candies; flapping her way there was the only way to do it. Zahara swerved to fly west, then looked behind her. Due east, opposite the direction the sugar bones had told her Daniel would be, a faint light glowed on the horizon.

Dawn.

Hours had passed, and the midnight deadline had come and gone. Daniel was dead.

It was over, then.

No contract, no command to stop Marut. Nothing to do but leave Harut in the hands of the humans who had captured him, and slink back home to her mother. Who had won. Again.

She glided lower, watching as a group of men dressed in some crazy spacesuit outfits loaded the net-entangled bird-form of Harut onto a military truck. What she shouldn't do, under any circumstances, was follow the vehicle and try to figure out a way to outwit a small army and free him.

Chapter Twenty-One

THE SUN NOW blazed high in the sky, and Zahara still hadn't figured out why she was doing exactly what she had promised herself she wouldn't do. Namely, clinging to the side of the armored vehicle transporting Harut and his captors by her claws, without a clue how she would rescue him.

They rumbled by a peeling white sign announcing their arrival at an air force base. Ahead, a single runway stretched out over the baked brown earth, surrounded by a small cluster of aircraft hangars and low office buildings.

The truck squealed to a stop outside a structure that didn't fit in with the others. For one thing, it hadn't been built during the Cold War. The triangular shape and thick walls made little sense to her. Then she glanced over a fighter jet parked nearby.

Apparently the building was a giant protective dog house for a pet airplane. Humans and their odd attachments to machines. Glancing further down, she spotted several more of the armored hangars. None of them had aircraft parked outside. The jet had been taken out of the fortified structure to make room for something else.

Several men jumped out of the truck, opened the back of the vehicle and proceeded to move the netted bundle into the hangar. A pair of massive concrete doors, fronted by steel scaffolding, began to close. The men rushed back out, and the doors slammed shut.

With any luck, the men would grab some cold drinks and settle in to congratulate themselves on placing Harut into their cozy high-tech dungeon. Then all she would have to do was sneak inside the hangar, find Harut, and get them both out of here.

Like most battle plans, Zahara's didn't last long after contact with the enemy. The hangar had been inconveniently outfitted with enchanted objects embedded into every possible entrance. After trying and failing to squirm into her last option—a small air vent in the back—she made an attempt to jump into the levels and pop inside. No luck. The magical protections around Harut's prison blocked that option as well.

Exhausted, she flew down to the shade of a nearby jeep and crouched under the front wheel. A quiet rustle behind her gave her a start, but as she whipped her head around, she saw nothing more alarming than a Fennec fox. The giant-eared canine gave her a cautious sniff. Invisibility didn't work so well with animals, especially those with an excellent sense of smell.

She deduced the fox was a male, and responded to the hopeful tilt of his head and his throaty trill with a growl.

"Can you grasp the concept of anatomic impossibility?"

Well, all right. Maybe in her current form it wasn't entirely inconceivable—merely quite ambitious on the animal's part. The Fennec lowered his ears in disappointment and trotted out from under the jeep, only to encounter a man and woman in uniform carrying boxes and heading in the direction of an office building adjacent to the hangar. He scrambled a few feet away, then hesitated. Fennec foxes in the wild fed mostly on insects and small rodents, but some animals that lived near inhabited areas accepted scraps from humans. Zahara's own sense of smell was heightened in her elemental form, and the rich aromas of the food the two were carrying made her stomach grumble. The woman laughed at a comment from the man, and as the door to the building opened to admit them, she tossed a small piece of bread to the fox.

Zahara perked up her ears, watching as the pair entered the building. Top secret building or not, everybody needed to eat. And despite her limited knowledge of magical alarm systems, there was one thing she did know. There was nothing like an invitation to disarm the most powerful protection curse.

It took her a while to make the necessary arrangements. She found a spare army uniform in the back of one of the trucks as she crept around, keeping mostly to the shadows under the vehicles. Not exactly what she needed, but there were all types of magic, and clothing enchantments happened to be one of Zahara's specialties. Finding a box to mimic a food delivery wasn't much of an issue, but figuring out what to put inside it was. For that, she needed a little help from her new foxy friend.

Preparations complete, she shimmered into visibility behind one of the military vehicles parked near the entrance. It was close to noon. None of the jinn she knew would dare consider an appearance, let alone an attack, at this hour.

With any luck, Harut's captors wouldn't be expecting any trouble. The Fennec fox at her side tilted his enormous ears and gazed up at her. Zahara was back in human form, her hair yanked into a tight bun. She wore a smartly pressed military policewoman's uniform offset with a white belt and matching holster. Long leather gloves and a jaunty visored cap completed the ensemble.

"One long arm of the law, coming up." Zahara reached down to give the fox a pat on the head and picked up the box on the ground beside her. "I suppose you preferred my earlier look. Hope it was good for you."

She strode over to the entrance with her package tucked under one arm and gave the two soldiers on guard a smile and her best salute. Both were obviously Americans, wearing desert camouflage fatigues and mirrored sunglasses. In addition to the semiautomatic weapons they carried, both had short swords strapped to their waists. The magic coming from their weapons sent a chill through her. Not that the swords were anything like the blade Zaid carried, or Harut's flaming sword, but they were more than she could take on in a fight.

"My colleagues missed part of the food order." She took care to add a Moroccan accent to her English. "The best part—dessert!"

One of the men chuckled, lowering his glasses to give her a better appraisal. His companion gave a disapproving grunt. "There's a table inside on the right for deliveries."

"So I can enter, yes?" Zahara asked. She resisted the urge to try a compulsion spell too soon. Her skill in those was better than average, but if these guys knew enough to protect their command center with cursed objects, they might be able to figure out what she was doing.

"Go on in." The first man puffed his chest out and opened the door for her. "I'll be right behind you."

Zahara gave him a modest flutter of her eyelashes and walked inside. For a moment, she felt a wave of resistance, stretching like an invisible elastic band. The pressure snapped and she stepped into the inner room.

The building had appeared simple and utilitarian from the outside, and the foyer didn't hold much. The space resembled an airport security check point, with a body scanner inset with hamsa symbols that arched in front of a second, reinforced door that had a lighted security pad to the right. No other entrances or exits, and no windows.

"Right over there." The friendly guard scrounged around and located a rather low-tech clipboard and pen. A security badge of some sort dangled from the metal clip. Now that was awfully careless of him. He nodded toward a table pushed against the wall and gave her a wink. "I'll write this up for you. Don't want you to get in trouble for missed paperwork or anything."

If this was what passed for killer pickup lines in the US military, she was most unimpressed. Adopting her best wide-eyed innocent look, she held out the box. "I was told all packages must be inspected."

He grinned at her formality and reached out to open the box. Zahara had given it a little shake first, just for fun. The enraged cobra inside reared up, hood flared, and sank its fangs into the man's hand. His scream of pain and surprise trailed off into a strangled gurgle as Zahara's knee hit his groin. She snatched the badge from his hands and dashed for the inner door.

Passing through the scanner made her flinch, but the broad invitation to enter had been open-ended enough to allow her to get through, albeit with some difficulty. Skin crawling, she pressed the card against the light pad and darted inside. She gave a quick glance back in satisfaction at the guard writhing in pain on the floor before slamming the door behind her.

So far, so good.

Zahara wasted little time transforming back to her elemental form and fading away into invisibility. Surprise attack or not, the response to her breaking and entering ploy was quick and organized. After a few shouts, a group of soldiers rushed forward toward the door she had entered through. Two took up positions inside, brandishing swords instead of guns.

They already knew she wasn't human, and they wanted to keep her inside. Well, she would have to figure out the escape part of the plan after she found Harut.

After some wrong turns and a few close misses from clomping feet, Zahara's search led her to a group of five or six men guarding a door at the end of a corridor. Protecting something important, obviously. During her endless attempts to get into Harut's prison, she had circled this office building multiple times. There was no external door on this side. Instead, it abutted the hangar. A service tunnel, maybe?

Zahara sat back on her haunches and peered around a corner at the guards. A muscular man in fatigues approached them. Everyone straightened up and saluted. This had to be the boss—Donnelly, the "security consultant" who had banished Zaid to the Mountains of Qaf and taken Daniel away to be killed by Marut.

Her insides twisted again—that odd little feeling that kept happening to her. Daniel hadn't made it. Zahara was free. So why was she here trying to save Harut?

She shook her head, vowing to stop all this deep-thinking nonsense. Time to focus. Invisible or not, she had no way to fight off that group of armed-to-the-teeth guards. She needed to move on from the minions and focus on the top dog around here.

Donnelly took off at a brisk pace down a hallway and she followed. At one point, he slowed, his eyes scanning the space around him. Zahara plastered herself against the wall, her pulse racing. She could hide better than anyone she had ever encountered, but this guy made her uneasy. The sword at his waist held more power than any human had a right to carry. After another quick inspection of his surroundings, he walked on, before swiping a card to open a door to his right. He didn't close the door after him, so Zahara crept up closer and peered in. The room held a desk with a computer on top of it, and little else. Donnelly had his back to her, and spoke in clipped tones on a phone.

Whatever he had sensed in the hallway wasn't bothering him now. Zahara sauntered in, giving the commander a once-over as she came up behind him. He wasn't bad-looking, if one went for tall, muscular, and nasty. Which Zahara didn't—or at least not that often.

The door behind her slammed shut, and she startled, whirling around to check out what had happened. Another man had entered the room, armed with a heavy crossbow. And she could have sworn it was pointing in her direction. She snapped her head back and found herself facing the point of Donnelly's sword.

"Awfully good at disappearing tricks, aren't you?" The man in charge of the blade at her throat gave her a cold grin. "But you'll show up fine when you're dead. Which is what you'll be in another minute if you don't reveal yourself."

She had been led into a nice little trap.

Out of options, Zahara resumed her human shape and her visibility. The hard-eyed commander let out a brief breath of surprise at her policewoman's outfit. "That's quite a convincing human transformation."

"Glad you like it." Zahara tipped the brim of her hat in his direction, taking the opportunity to get a better sense of the awful situation she had put herself in. The hulking soldier with the crossbow had a bolt aimed at her chest, and Donnelly held his sword close to her neck. A quick scan around the room confirmed the presence of a few wall-mounted cameras aimed in her direction. The two men could kill her before she managed to dematerialize to travel through the levels, and she certainly wasn't going to fight her way out of the situation. Her reticence to transform into her embarrassing elemental form had diminished considerably over the past several days, but even that wasn't likely to work. The paralyzing effect of her true form wouldn't work on anyone watching her on a TV monitor. "You strike me as the kind of man who enjoys a good spanking from a girl in uniform."

Donnelly didn't appear amused. His eyes narrowed further, as if he were trying to look through her and figure out exactly what she was. "Your magic has no force here, unclean spirit. Reveal your true form and tell us from what jinn clan you hail from."

It was Zahara's turn to be puzzled. He had spoken the words in the dialect of Arabic widely used in the land of the jinn. With an atrocious accent and more than a few grammatical mistakes, but still—for a human, he knew far too much. And what was with the formal insults? He must be thinking he was dealing with an ifrit, or a marid. They loved to spout this nonsense back and forth before getting down to any real fighting.

She rested her index finger on her lips, feigning deep thought. "Well," she said in her best computer dating video voice, "my name's Zahara, and I like long walks along bombed-out beaches and quiet afternoons on the computer carrying out drone attacks. Just like you."

One corner of Donnelly's mouth twitched up, then he gave a nod to the soldier holding the crossbow. The man kept the weapon trained on her as Donnelly sheathed his sword and went over to his desk. He pulled out a simple clay bowl and a lighter. Zahara didn't know what he was up to, and she didn't like that.

"Not *the* Zahara, I presume." Donnelly gave up his attempts at Arabic, mercifully, and walked back toward her. "Or are you the one who led to Harut and Marut's downfall in the first place?"

"Before my time." Zahara fanned her fingers over her mouth and mimicked a yawn. "And speaking of the two bad boys, where's the one I have dibs on? Give me Harut and I'll

261

go easy on you."

Donnelly did laugh a little at that. And here she had been thinking he didn't have a sense of humor. "Whether you're here to kill him or save him, you're not getting what you want. His brother took out some of our best men, and I intend to see both of them pay for it."

The good news was that the crazy mercenaries with borrowed magical weapons were after Marut, not her. The bad news was that they wouldn't believe she and Harut were actually on their side. In fact, by taking out Harut and preventing her from saving Daniel, they had probably ruined any realistic chance of stopping Marut. Armed to the teeth and too stupid to realize what they were blundering into. Useful idiots—for her mother, at least.

"Here's a thought. Next time you wander into a cave with two tortured monsters giving out magical secrets, don't let the crazy one loose."

"So hostile." Donnelly shook his head and held the bowl up to her face. "And I brought you flowers and everything."

Zahara's nose told her what was in the bowl before she recognized the dry, shriveled petals heaped inside. She coughed, trying to get the thick scent of rotting cocoa beans and black cardamom out of her throat. Her lungs burned as he passed the bowl back and forth.

"Syrian rue." Donnelly apparently felt the need to explain the details of the torture to her, as if she hadn't figured it out already. The weedy plant with yellow flowers had been used from time immemorial to repel the jinn. Zahara hadn't thought it was too popular with ex-US military types—but this Donnelly had just enough magical knowledge to make him dangerous. "Didn't do much to your friend Harut, but we found something to help with that. Seems to be doing the trick on you, though."

He flicked the lighter open and touched the flickering blue flame to the dried petals. Plumes of thick, suffocating smoke rose up, and no amount of coughing stopped the painful squeezing of her chest. Her eyes filled with water, and Donnelly blurred into an ominous shape looming over her.

"I have a few questions I'd like you to answer." Donnelly pulled the bowl back far enough to let Zahara take in a few gasping breaths. Her body shook uncontrollably, and it was all she could do to remain standing. "Let's start with what you really look like, and what the hell you are."

That first part wasn't going to be difficult. The pungent smoke from the rue had drained most of her strength, and she transformed despite herself.

She couldn't bring herself to attempt as much as a purr, but she flickered her eyes open long enough to catch the surprised gaze of Donnelly's crossbow-carrying companion. He froze, then dropped his weapon to the floor, a dazed smile wiping away the tension in his face.

"Here kitty, kitty." He sank down to his knees and extended a hand toward her. "Does little Miss Mittens want a scratch behind the ears?"

It took all of Zahara's self-control not to sink her teeth into him and break the spell. She struggled to her feet and dodged his outstretched fingers to face Donnelly. He was a much tougher nut to crack. The bowl of smoking rue gave him protection his companion lacked, and she suspected he had never had a Miss Mittens in his life. In fact, if anyone had ever given him a kitten or a puppy, he probably would have strangled it to death if the order to do so came through a proper chain of command.

Still, her cuteness had some effect. Rivulets of sweat ran down Donnelly's face. He forced his eyes away from hers and tried to push the bowl closer. Zahara wrinkled her nose and gave a tiny sneeze that sent the other soldier into quivers of admiration.

"Get. In. Here. Now." Donnelly barked the order into a microphone set into his shirt and reached out a shaking hand for his sword. With the last of her strength, Zahara lashed out with her claws, scoring a long cut along his arm. He switched tactics and reached out to grab her by the throat. Her powerful back claws dug into his chest, and he fell backward, a hissing and squirming Zahara on top of him. She broke his hold on her neck, but his fingers still gripped one of her wings, even as she shredded his fatigues and the skin underneath. Reinforcements were on the way, and she was running out of time.

"You little freak," he croaked. With a sudden twist, he rolled over and pinned her underneath him, his hands once again finding her throat.

Zahara thrashed, her windpipe closing as her already pained lungs strained for air. Fury burned inside of her. She wasn't a freak, no matter what her family thought. And she wasn't going to die like this, throttled by an oversized, boneheaded human who didn't realize she was on his side, for once. An image flashed into her mind. Her mother, wearing an expression of tired disappointment, trying to decide the optimal time to avenge the death of her daughter, the great failure of her long and terrifying career.

No.

She was the daughter of a horrible, soul-sucking demoness, and it was time to act like it.

She stilled her thrashing limbs and went limp. Donnelly's hands loosened, and a trickle of air entered her chest. She focused her mind, trying to recall half-remembered instructions from her mother, and pushed.

Not physically, not with any muscle in her body. Instead, she felt her sense of self slipping away as she entered Donnelly's mind.

And took it over.

A second later, she rolled over, her lungs filling with air. The bowl of burning rue rested next to her, and she sent it flying across the room with a powerful kick. A very powerful kick, in fact. She climbed to her knees and stared down at her muscular arms, her huge fists. Inside her head, the real Donnelly screamed uselessly in protest. She had done it. After all the mocking and the snide comments from her relatives about her lack of any appreciable demonic talents, she had possession of a human's mind. And not just any human, either.

Zahara was now in charge.

Chapter Twenty-Two

IT WAS EARLY afternoon before Zaid pulled the van over to the side of the road and turned off the engine. He pointed toward a nearby hill, where a small masonry structure, topped by a dome, shone white as bone against the dry brown earth around it. "That's the saint's tomb up there."

Daniel had tried correcting Zaid when he said they were traveling to the grave of a Jewish saint.

"We don't have saints," he told him.

An hour later, after Zaid had lectured him on several hundred years of North African religious history, Daniel had a better idea of what the tomb in front of him represented. Both Muslims and Jews in Morocco traveled to visit the graves of certain pious individuals, loosely termed "saints" in English translation. A *hiloula* was a combination of a festival and pilgrimage to their grave sites. Zaid had known immediately what Solikis was referring to when she had told Daniel to go the *hiloula*, since this particular celebration was to be a major event, with both local and foreign worshippers expected. Hundreds of people would arrive tomorrow morning, maybe more.

And Marut planned to kill them all.

Helped by his mysterious supernatural ally, Marut planned on ripping open the boundary between the human and jinn worlds at this site, using the blood of the worshippers to aid in the magic involved. But Marut needed his full powers to pull it off—which meant he needed to devour the sacrifice first.

Simple, really. Daniel needed to not die and save the world. Or, at least, a good part of it.

"I understand why my grandmother told me to come here." Daniel shaded his eyes against the sun. The temperature was scorching, and his hand and most of the rest of his body hurt like hell. "But I have no idea how to contact her."

"Maybe we'll find answers inside the tomb itself," Zaid said. "Speaking of contacting people, I'm going to see if I can get a message to Ahmed through a less-than-official channel. Start climbing up the hill, I'll catch up."

Daniel nodded and started up the incline. The climb up the hill soon grew far steeper than it had appeared from the base, and he paused for a moment halfway up to catch his breath and survey his surroundings. The area around the tomb was largely uninhabited, but at this height he could make out a small town in the distance. Back at the van, Zaid was crouched down in the limited shade provided by the vehicle. Daniel squinted, and was able to make out a small feline shape sitting at attention beside him. Either Zaid was more of an animal lover than he let on, or he had contacted one of the local jinn who could take on the appearance of a cat.

Daniel continued the climb and reached the white-washed facade of the tomb several minutes later. It was humble in appearance, with the only opening a sealed door in the front. A flat marker had been affixed to the right side of the door. He came closer to examine the writing.

"This is in Hebrew," Daniel said out loud. He heard a low chuckle beside him, and an invisible, powerful shape slid by him, soft fur over rippling muscle.

"That's because it's the tomb of a Jewish saint. A woman, in fact." Zaid materialized to Daniel's left, only the upper part of his body human. "But both Muslims and Jews come here."

"Why do they come to the *hiloula*?" Daniel asked. "To pay their respects to the dead, honor their good deeds, that sort of thing?"

"Yes." Zaid rested his hands on the sealed entrance to the tomb. "And some also come to ask the saint to provide them with an important *baraka*." He continued to press his palms against the surface. "A blessing for a good marriage, a speedy recovery from an illness, healthy children—that sort of thing. And a saint can provide protection, too."

"Against what?"

Zaid grinned, a pair of fangs visible under his lips. He hadn't bothered to transform his eyes, and they glowed sulfurous and catlike, setting off the arch of his eyebrows. "Creatures like me, mostly."

The stone in front of him shifted and he pushed harder. The door swung inward with a groan. Daniel fumbled in his pocket for the mag light he had found in the van and aimed the beam inside the opening.

Zaid hesitated at the threshold. "Something's wrong. There's power here—it's holy ground. But there's something else inside."

That didn't make Daniel feel much better about going

in, but when Zaid slipped through the entrance Daniel followed, flinching as a stale smell of decay hit his nose. His light flickered along the walls of the tomb. Windowless, they stretched up into an enclosed dome above them. On the far side, Daniel could make out a quick movement, like a fine piece of fabric fluttering against the stone. But when he aimed the beam in that direction, he saw nothing but a blank wall.

Zaid snapped his fingers and his ball of light meandered into the space, drenching the inside of the tomb in a blood-red aura.

The mosaic tile of the floor had a rectangular opening in the center. Zaid and Daniel crouched down to stare at its empty stone walls.

"The saint's body is—gone?" Daniel asked.

"Or it wasn't here in the first place." Zaid stood up and folded his arms across his chest.

Daniel straightened up as well and flicked his flashlight off. Zaid's statement didn't make much sense, and he wanted to ask him what he meant by it, but something else had caught his attention. He stared again at the far side of the tomb, the eerie red glow inside the small space distorting his vision. The wall's surface waxed and waned, like the mirage of an oasis beckoning a thirsty traveler in the desert. It looked so insubstantial, like he could walk right through it. Before he even knew what he was he was doing, he had taken a few steps toward the wall.

Zaid's solid, muscular grip clamped around his arm before he reached it. "You can see it, can't you?"

"See what?" Daniel blinked, trying to tell if the shimmering surface of the wall in front of him was some trick of his vision.

"The *araf*, the veil between worlds." Zaid pulled Daniel closer to him, away from the stone. "Certain locations in your world—holy places, mostly—are connected to the world of the jinn. A few humans who have our blood can cross over at these points."

"Does Solikis want me to come to her?" Daniel found himself trying to escape Zaid's grip, as pleasant as the touch of his arm was. "Maybe that's what she wants me to do."

"This is her space." Zaid swept his arm to indicate the room around them. "That's why it's an empty tomb. Solikis was the saint. She's lived in your world before."

"I need to go to her." Daniel tried to take another step toward the wall. The compulsion to go to it was so strong, like a magnetic force was drawing him there.

"This is your gift." Zaid's voice dropped to a whisper. "Not magic spells, not the sight, but the ability to cross over to our world. And you also have an even more unusual power. You can help our kind come here."

"I do?" Daniel thought back to Zaid's rescue, and a sudden realization clicked. Not only had he communicated with Zaid when he was in the Mountains of Qaf, he had helped him cross over to this world. He needed to do the same with his grandmother. "We'll go there together, get help, and come back to stop Marut."

"I don't belong there anymore." Zaid pulled Daniel toward him. "Listen to me. The dagger Donnelly used sent me across the *araf*, back to the home I was exiled from. My two brothers disobeyed my clan's orders and didn't kill me. But only on the condition I never try to return again."

"I want to go." Daniel turned again to the fluttering barrier. "I have to, I think."

Zaid pulled him by force toward the tomb's exit, and gave him a strong push to get him through the tiny door. "You might be right, but now isn't the time. As much as I hate to admit it, I need Harut's help. You need to summon Zahara. Hopefully she's okay and with him. Then the three of us can hold off Marut while you go to Solikis."

Chapter Twenty-Three

Z AHARA STRUGGLED TO her feet a few seconds before four soldiers crashed through the door, armed with a collection of mismatched swords and other assorted antique-style weapons. Leaving nothing to chance, two of them aimed semiautomatic rifles in a sweeping motion around the room, looking for monsters that weren't there. Whatever trove of magical weapons they had either stumbled upon or been given consisted mostly of trash. Donnelly's sword, which rested on the floor beside her, was the only weapon of significant power.

Not that it mattered how stupid they were. She couldn't take on this many human fighters, poorly armed or not, and while she inhabited Donnelly's body, she would suffer any injuries he did. She needed Donnelly alive and obedient, at least for now.

She held up a hand to stop the men, trying to strike an authoritative pose. Moving the military commander's limbs for him felt like guiding a clunky, oversized puppet. A simmering brew of fear, hatred and frustration bubbled up in the back of her mind. Donnelly didn't like being possessed, apparently. Served the lunkhead right for waving that Syrian rue in her face.

"At ease." Zahara wracked her brain for military stock

phrases she had overheard while perusing the more salacious human entertainment that usually caught her interest. She coughed her voice into a reasonable approximation of Donnelly's. "The creature that attacked us is unconscious. No threat to us now."

Her legs swayed for a moment, and one of the men rushed up to her. "Are you hurt?"

My, isn't this touching. And unwelcome. Zahara tried to shove him away. "Just need to get my sea legs under me, matey."

The soldier blinked at her in confusion.

Wait, that wasn't right. Perhaps she could order all the men in the room to line up, or tell them to strip and head to the showers. Come to think of it, that last one might not have come from a completely realistic cinematic portrayal of military life.

"What's that thing Carpenter's holding?" Two men bent over the soldier she had mesmerized with her elemental form. He had crawled over to her true body to cuddle it, and now her furry form lay in his arms, snoring gently. Meanwhile her mind rattled around in Donnelly's head, trying to fight off his attempts at breaking the possession and hold herself upright at the same time.

"Whatever it is, it's precious!" The excited words came out in a squeal from one soldier.

"Let me see!" Three of the men pushed and shoved to get a closer look. Since Zahara no longer had any control over her real body, the effect of her magic was diluted. Most of the men close to her elemental form were acting like idiots, but they weren't immobilized, and their bizarre behavior alarmed the man she had been talking to.

"Something's wrong." The unaffected soldier turned to her, face tense with suspicion. This wasn't good. If they knew enough to use jinn weapons, they probably had some concept of possession, even if they hadn't seen one before.

Zahara grabbed the man's shirt and concentrated on a compulsion spell. Her new, masculine fist was huge, and she could hear the man's teeth rattle as she shook him. "Get a grip."

His eyes widened as he nodded. "Yes, sir."

Now, that was more like it. "I need you to focus. There may be more of them in here." She released him, and the man gave her a quick nod. "The one with the wings we caught, where is he?"

Confusion flickered across his face again. "In the hangar."

Zahara winced at her slip, and the lack of focus set off Donnelly, who succeeded in wresting control of his left hand for a moment. She reached out to grab it with the right hand. This internal wrestling match was getting old, and fast. "Do you *know* he's still in there?"

He swallowed. "I'll check it out. Now."

"*We'll* check it out." Zahara bent down to grab Donnelly's sword and pushed the soldier toward the door, admiring the rippling biceps in the arms of the body she inhabited. This possession thing could get interesting, if she had the time.

They left the group of milling soldiers behind them, most of them reduced to babbling about how her elemental shape reminded them of childhood pets or favorite stuffed animals. Several other soldiers came up to her, shouting various questions, and she gave them an imperious wave. The entrance to the service tunnel for the hangar remained guarded by several men. They gave her a quick nod in greeting.

"Open it up." Zahara took the risk of adding yet another compulsion charm to her words. Holding Donnelly in check was exhausting enough. Too much more magic, and she wouldn't have the strength to go into the levels. Her spell, spread out over too many minds at once, wouldn't have done much to them if they had been prepared for it. Combined with the sight of Donnelly glaring at them, however, it had the desired effect. One of the men slid a bolt across and opened the door.

"I'm going in to find out what he knows about this."

"I think you should go in with backup." The man who had helped her find the room rested his hand on his weapon, a muzzleloader decked out with ivory and brass that looked like it dated from the Ottoman Empire. Seriously, how could any magical object that new do much of anything?

"I work alone." Zahara's attempt at a steely gaze wasn't helped by a mad twitching of her eye. Damn that Donnelly. She opted to mimic a quick salute, hitting her head in the process, which actually hurt.

"But we have procedures for this. We need to follow them."

She turned on him, voice raised into a snarl. "You're talking to me about standard operating procedure? We're at color threat level burnt orange."

He stared back at her, blinking. Her spell was having

some effect, since her un-Donnelly-like behavior hadn't raised enough suspicion in his mind for him to take action. "What's a situation burnt orange?"

"One step above turquoise and two below chartreuse." She jabbed a finger into his chest. "And believe me, you *never* want to see a situation chartreuse."

The spell held, despite the nonsense she was spouting. His face went slack, and she wasted little time pushing past the soldiers and through the door, slamming it behind her and pressing her back against it.

She let out a long breath of relief. Securing the door behind her was crucial. A curse to seal the entrance with dripping molten rock would have a certain amount of flair. Or the door could be enchanted to open up into a dank maze, crawling with scorpions.

Too bad both of those options were well beyond Zahara's magical abilities.

Spotting a large wheeled cart at the far end of the tunnel, she settled for ramming the heavy device against the entrance. Then she ducked back through the passage, climbed a short ladder and pushed open a hatch at the top.

She climbed out into the hangar and locked eyes with the room's only other inhabitant.

Harut hung suspended from the ceiling, and he didn't look good. Bare-chested, with his wings tangled into the black net that held his body dangling in the air, he lifted his head only a fraction at her entrance.

"I'm sorry to disappoint you." His voice cracked with agony. "My brother's whereabouts are unknown to me, and holding me here will not help you stop him."

"I'm disappointed too." Zahara allowed her true voice to come out of Donnelly's throat. She glanced around the space. The concrete structure was shaped like a hexagon, with strips of lights glowing along the walls. The far end had been blocked off by the massive doors she had seen slammed shut after they had brought Harut in. The roof above her must be the most reinforced section of the shelter, with no obvious exit points. "If you're half-undressed and all tied up, I should have been the one to do it."

Harut's eyes, glazed with pain, widened. "Zahara?"

"I'm trying out a new look." She came closer to him, puzzling over how on earth a group of humans had succeeded in keeping him locked up in here. Then she understood. The netting consisted of intertwined circles, each in the shape of a snake devouring its own tail. The bonds constricted around his body and wings, and at every contact point, the flesh underneath bubbled and oozed. Then the snakes shifted and twisted, leaving the damaged area and moving on to untouched skin and feathers. As she watched, one of the slashes healed over, as another cut opened up near it.

"Now that's a nasty piece of work." Zahara tried to sound casual, but the sight of Harut tortured and flayed alive made her throat constrict in rage. Donnelly *would* pay for this.

"Don't try to free me." Harut stared down at the writhing snakes searing his skin. "They are the *ouroboros,* and touching them will kill the human body you now inhabit."

She should have been impressed instead of horrified. Using the sacred *ouroboros* as a torture device was a trick worthy of her mother, and Harut's amazing ability to heal made it all that much worse. A jinn like her would eventually die of the wounds; he could be kept like this for a long, long time.

Then a thought struck her. The *ouroboros* was more than a torture worthy of her mother—it was yet another part of her plan to take out Harut. Lilitu had blocked Harut's attempt to rescue Daniel, then given the soldiers the tools they needed to track him down and keep him captive. While Donnelly's men were busy trying to torture Marut's location out of Harut, the fallen one would face no further obstacles in achieving his goal.

Zahara gave a low growl. "The only problem with using the *ouroboros* to kill Donnelly is he'll die too quickly."

"No." Harut returned his gaze to her, fierce and angry, like that of the hawk whose shape he took. "The men here aren't my enemies. They're the comrades of the warriors my brother killed to free himself when they found our cavern. They seek to stop Marut, and I cannot convince them I have same goal."

"Well, having spent far too long in this asshole's company, I can assure you he completely deserves whatever awful fate I can think up for him." Donnelly fought back at that, and her left hand reached up to try to grab her throat. She pried off the fingers with her right hand. This was taking far too long, and the men outside would shake off her spell and smash in the door at some point. Letting the *ouroboros* kill Donnelly sounded appealing, but it would force her spirit to return to her true body, currently being cuddled in another room. That wouldn't solve anything.

"My punishment was to hang suspended, ever thirsty, ever wanting." Harut closed his eyes. "A stream of the purest water flowed only a sword blade's thickness from my lips. I endured that, I will endure this. You must not harm the human you have put under your spell."

"Oh, please. Stop it with the martyr act." Zahara hesitated for another moment, then decided. There was no other way. "I'll ask the *ouroboros* to let you go, nicely."

A flicker of a smile played over Harut's pain-stricken face. "I'm not sure why you came to save me, Zahara, but theirs is an old magic, and a powerful one. Leave me. You're not safe here."

He was seriously giving her a lecture about dark magic. Like she didn't know anything about it.

There were many ancient languages once spoken by humans that were now only used as a form of communication by the jinn and other paranormal beings of this world and hers. Then there were those languages whose syllables had never crossed the lips of a human, the sound of which would drive most of them mad.

Like the language Zahara spoke at home. Hopefully Harut couldn't understand it.

"Release the winged one you bind and burn, O Great Ones." No such thing as casual slang in her mother tongue, that was for sure. "For he is mine, and I alone decide his fate."

One of the snake heads spit out its tail and wiggled upright, puffing into a cobra hood shape. "Says who?"

Zahara folded her arms across her chest. Disrespectful little thing, even downright rude. "Perhaps you didn't hear me command you in the tongue of the *shaytan*. Release the one you hold, or face the consequences."

The snake hissed a laugh. "You can barely keep hold of the weak-minded human you caught, much less deal with one of the two fallen ones."

"Release. Him. Now." The words echoed through the room, dark and resonant, and Harut shuddered.

"I ask you again." The snake gave up trying to jibe her. "Who commands me to release my prey?"

Zahara drew in a deep breath, shooting a quick glance at Harut's face, pale and wracked with agony. He couldn't understand what she was saying, and it wasn't like she had much of a choice, anyway.

"It is I, Zahara, daughter of Lilitu, devourer of souls, scourge of men, serpent of blindness, deliverer of the desolation." She paused. There were at least another hundred names or so to go, but that should do it. "Give your prisoner unto me, or prepare for her wrath."

The serpent's head deflated. "Well, now that you put it like that—"

Each of the hundreds of encircled snakes released their hold on their tails. Harut collapsed to the floor; the wriggling black shapes slithered off him, swarming to the hatch leading to the service tunnel. The one who had spoken to Zahara crept up to her shoe and gave a low bow before sliding away to a safer distance. "Kindly give my regards to your mother."

Zahara held her hand out to Harut to help him up. "Told you I could talk them out of it. Now come on. I'll make you unseen, and we'll slip past the guards to pick up my real body. Then we get the hell out of here. No pun intended."

He ignored her outstretched arm and climbed to his feet,

his face set like a stone. "The *ouroboros* would not be swayed by a falsehood. I knew you were the spawn of a demoness, but now I see why you refused to reveal your clan to me. Lilitu herself birthed you."

"You got all that?" Zahara had never heard of anyone other than demon jinn speaking her native tongue. "Fine. So now you know. Let's go."

"When Marut and I fell, Lilitu was there, laughing." Harut's voice grew thick with hate and grief. "She still held the shape of the woman I thought I loved, that I would do anything for. Cheat, lie, even kill. The first Zahara wasn't a woman I fell in love with. She was a monster. Years later she gave birth to another monster—and gave you the name of the human woman she claimed to be."

Great. Her mother and Harut had some history together. From the sounds of it, an entire love triangle's worth. Then a thought struck her, and she choked back a gag. "*You're* not my father, are you? Or maybe my uncle? I'm not sure what would be worse."

Harut paused, his cold fury turning to irritation. "My brother and I fought over your mother's affections millennia ago. If you have a century of living behind you, I'd be surprised."

She hated that Harut had come so close to guessing her true age. "So my mother was the original Zahara. Who cares? I'm trying to stop her from starting a war between the worlds, and I need your help. Stop pouting and come with me."

"I'd rather die here than be dragged through hell by the likes of you."

How *dare* he?

"Look around, you ungrateful bastard!" Zahara swung her arm around the room, miscalculating the force of her new muscles and whacking herself in the head. Taking Harut with her through the levels was their only way out—assuming they could get away from the building's magical security system. She needed him to help her. "Do you see any other way to escape and find the much bigger and badder monster you're responsible for? Marut is still out there."

A section of the floor exploded, effectively ending the discussion. A tall form climbed out of the hole, long wings dragging behind him.

Marut was no longer out there. He was in here. With them.

Zahara took a swift step back toward the wall and, for once, Donnelly didn't fight her. Harut straightened and moved forward to confront his brother. Given the restrictions of the space they were in, Marut had taken on a shape only a few inches shorter than the hangar ceiling, which didn't make him an iota less intimidating than when they had faced him in the old house in Marrakech. The fallen angel's sword hung at his side, though he made no move to draw it. Zahara doubted he needed it to deal with the soldiers guarding the service tunnel entrance.

She considered releasing Donnelly from the possession. He'd be a better fighter that way. But that would be a whole lot easier if she had ever done it before. She had been in physical contact with Donnelly when she had taken him over, and she wasn't sure how to get back to her real body.

Marut raised a hand in Zahara's direction, then let it fall. "Is this what you now call an ally, my brother? You too join forces with the jinn."

"I haven't become more evil than the worst of them, like you." Harut swayed on his feet. He was still weak from the torture, and he hadn't called up his own weapon. Zahara wasn't sure he could, in his condition.

She kept one hand on Donnelly's sword. It was all she had, but she doubted it would do much against Marut. Besides, she had trouble walking in a straight line inside the soldier's body, much less fighting.

"I have become more than I ever was." Marut's eyes were black and lifeless, without the sheen of fire that had glowed in them before. "And I can become greater yet, and raise you up to stand by my side."

"An oathbreaker like you is lower than filth." Harut gestured towards Zahara. "At least the one beside me keeps her word."

How generous of him. Zahara was still seething over Harut's ingratitude, and she was in no mood to listen to insults from both brothers. Pressing herself against the wall, she tried to sidle along toward the gaping hole leading to the service tunnel. The hangar had no other open exit, and she couldn't leave through the levels trapped in Donnelly's body.

Marut laughed. "That you needed such a pathetic creature to help you escape from this human rabble demonstrates how low you have fallen. The children of mud have no love for you, brother. Give me the sacrifice and I will forgive all."

Why was Marut still searching for the sacrifice? Her mother had set everything up for him. He should have shown up for the late-night, all-you-can-eat Daniel buffet hours ago. But he hadn't, which meant Daniel could still be alive. For some crazy reason, Zahara's heart lightened at the thought.

"Forgiveness is what we bargained for." Harut's hand tightened into a fist at his side, but no sword appeared. "Our punishment on earth paid for redemption after death. You had no right to take that choice from me."

"I set you free!" Marut's voice grew into a roar. "From an eternity of service to the vilest of human scum. You should be on your knees, thanking me."

Good luck with that. Zahara could have told him that appreciation wasn't high on Harut's list of skills. Taking advantage of Marut's inattention, she took a few steps to her right, inching toward the hole. The oversized angel wasn't as far away from it as she wanted, but there was enough space behind him and the blasted-out opening to allow her current, larger body to dash past him.

"The children of mud may choose good over evil, as do the children of smokeless fire." Harut circled to his brother's right, and the larger angel turned to watch him, his attention now fully away from Zahara. "When we faced the same temptations they do, our resolve lasted mere months. Our fall was greater, and so should be our punishment."

Zahara scooted a little closer to the hole in the floor. So close. One more long rant from Marut and she could slip right past him. Pity she couldn't make Donnelly invisible.

"I saw little good in our miserable cave, and neither did you." Marut's back was to her now, as he snarled at Harut's hectoring. "If you wish to live and die as little more than a peri, I'll allow it. Why won't you give me the sacrifice? Is it because you desire the little demoness who's so besotted with you?"

Now that was unfair, and totally wrong. She didn't have a crush on Harut; in fact, she didn't even know why she had shown up here to save him. With one last silent movement, she moved past Marut, just steps from her escape. Her real body was in the adjacent building, completely vulnerable if Marut trashed the place after he crushed Harut like a bug. There was a reason most of her kind possessed humans only while their bodies remained in a secure location. Exorcism was a real risk for even a powerful jinn, much less a beginner like her. A jinn could be expelled from a victim by any smelly little magician with some black seed oil and a few prayers. More sophisticated sorcerers could even trap a jinn inside an inanimate object, which could make for a quite uncomfortable few hundred years.

But Zahara couldn't blame a human sorcerer for putting her into this mess. She had done it herself. If she left Donnelly and didn't make it back to her real body, her soul could wander around untethered to anything, including her own sanity. She had to protect her true form. It was here, and in danger. She would die when and if her body did.

Unfortunately, Marut decided to punctuate his suggestions about Harut and Zahara's relationship status by inclining his head in her direction. When his gaze fell on a blank wall, he spun around and spotted her creeping into the opening. With a roar, his eyes flashed into fire and his sword appeared in his hand.

A rush of fear hit her hard in the stomach and she stared

down at Donnelly's sword, now clenched in the hand she had controlled until a few seconds ago. Donnelly had taken his body back, and she felt herself being pushed out. The decision had been made for her. She released all of her control over him at once, in direct violation of every rule of possession. She didn't want him to suffer as much as a twitch, much less full-blown seizures. Harut needed all the help he could get. The last glimpse she caught through Donnelly's eyes was Marut charging forward in her direction, as Harut raised his own sword to his brother's back.

She popped her eyes open and found herself curled up on the lap of the soldier she had first bewitched. He was rocking back and forth, mumbling something about tummy rubs, as he stroked her fur. She restrained herself from giving him a solid nip, stretched out her paws and gave her tail a wiggle. Everything worked. Not bad for her first demonic possession.

Donnelly's office had become a command center of sorts for the surviving soldiers. Close to a dozen of them crouched in positions around the walls, clutching weapons and staring up at a monitor on the wall. Marut's battle with Harut and Donnelly played out on the screen. One of the men, pale and perspiring freely, held a small device in one hand. It resembled a TV remote, which made little sense to Zahara. She failed to see how hiding in this room and switching channels would do much to stop the pissed-off giant angel in the hangar.

The sweating soldier clicked the remote and dove flat to the ground; the entire group followed suit. Even the entranced soldier holding Zahara was flung down by one of his comrades, and she ended up squished underneath him.

Whatever the new channel was, it had some great special effects. A massive explosion rocked the room, and dust clouds swelled around them. Her black fur was now coated entirely in white. Zahara sneezed out the worst of the chemical stench of burning plastic and squirmed out from under the soldier. As the swirling powder settled into piles, coating every surface, bright beams of sunlight broke through above her.

Zahara took to the air, her wings carrying her above the dust. The fortified hangar had lost its roof, and taken a good part of the adjacent office building with it. The crazy bastards had blown up their dungeon and part of their headquarters. She took in the entire scene with a measure of admiration for the glorious destruction of it all. Marut stood in the center of the blasted-out hangar, his arms thrown up to shield himself from the searing light flooding over him. Harut lay crumpled at his feet, sword still gripped in his hand. Donnelly wasn't dead, which was quite an accomplishment. The mercenary commander lay slumped against the remnants of a wall, blood streaming from a cut on his arm, in addition to the scratches she had inflicted on his chest. Her timing in leaving his body had been impeccable.

The remaining soldiers, their faces and clothing caked in white, rushed out to encircle Marut, whose form grew less and less distinct as the dust blew away and the light around him brightened. Several arrows flew through him, and his shape faded away entirely.

Marut still couldn't handle a few rays of sunshine. He had failed to devour the sacrifice. And if a few human soldiers could scare him off, maybe he could be stopped permanently. But that would take require a team approach, whether Harut liked it or not. As the soldiers milled around in the wreckage, Zahara took advantage of the distraction to zoom down and drop on Harut's chest, transforming back into her human shape.

"Will you go through the levels with me now?" She slapped his face hard, eliciting a weak groan. Close enough. Black flames licked up around her, and she grabbed him, pressing his body against her as hard as she could. "I'll take that as a yes."

Chapter Twenty-Four

D ANIEL LIT ANOTHER sizzling emergency flare and rested it at the final point of the pentagram he had scratched out in the dirt. He said Zahara's name again, then held his breath, afraid something had gone horribly wrong with his summoning. He didn't have the lamp, or even real candles. Zaid had been confident Daniel didn't need any magical accessories; if he'd been able to reach Zaid across the Mountains of Qaf with a video game app and a little blood, he should have no trouble calling up Zahara, who was bound to him by the contract. Whether Zahara knew or cared where Harut could be found was another question.

It was also hardly the witching hour. The sun had only begun its slide toward the horizon, and the tarp Daniel and Zaid had stretched over several poles to shade the area of the pentagram did little to hold off the sweltering heat of late afternoon or the brightness of the light. Waiting until dark to call Zahara wasn't an option—they needed to bring Solikis back from the Mountains of Qaf before Marut arrived.

Two soot-covered figures shimmered inside the pentagram, then faded, like a campfire struggling to stay alight in a windstorm. They reappeared again, this time in solid form, and Zahara rolled off Harut with a groan. She climbed to her feet and gave the angel a kick in the ribs. He stirred, coughing out a cloud of ashes. A few singed white feathers floated in the air. Harut looked terrible. Raised red welts covered his bare chest, and his wings were gray with soot.

Zahara, on the other hand, had adopted the quite inappropriate persona of a female police officer, complete with a stiffly-pressed uniform and a holster for a baton at her side.

"Thankless son of a bitch." She tore off the visored hat covering her hair and threw it at Harut. Then she turned to stare at Daniel. "You're not dead." It wasn't an accusation this time, and her eyes had become a little misty.

Had Zahara been *worried* about him? And what had she and Harut been doing while Daniel was busy getting kidnapped and Zaid had almost been killed by his family?

Zahara wiped at her eyes, then stalked up to Daniel and Zaid and began complaining about Harut. "He fought me like a madman through every level. Nice timing with the summoning, by the way. Changing direction to suit your little whims and beating him into submission at the same time was close to impossible."

"You were able to take *him* through the levels?" Zaid jogged over to Harut and tried to help him sit up. "I thought you needed consent to do that."

Harut coughed out some soot. He didn't look capable of speech, much less able to fight off his far more fearsome and deadly brother.

"I was out of options!" Zahara threw her hands up. "That human creep Donnelly drone-bombed all of my best outfits, messed up my rescue plan for you, and then I had to save that birdbrain over there from a net of ancient snakes and our least favorite angel."

"*You* had a rescue plan for *me*?" Daniel had more questions, mostly about what Zahara and Harut had been up to before the summoning, but they had bigger issues to deal with. "Marut's attacking a religious festival here tomorrow. You and Harut have to help us stop him."

Zahara pushed out her lower lip and surveyed her surroundings with an air of skepticism. She raised her eyebrows at a rectangular crate propped against a wheel of the Humvee Daniel and Zaid had stolen from Donnelly's camp, then came over to examine its contents. Her initial reaction was pretty much what Daniel would have expected.

"This looks like a giant penis."

"It's some sort of rocket that can be fired from over the shoulder," Daniel explained. "We found one in the back of the Humvee we stole. Donnelly thinks they can stop Marut."

"I know what a MANPAD is." Zahara flipped her hair back and lifted the missile partially out of the box, giving a knowing nod.

Daniel's mouth dropped open, and Zaid, still trying to revive Harut, appeared mystified.

"You know about modern military hardware?" Daniel finally got out.

"Unlike *some* people, who want to remain stuck in the eighth century"—Zahara pointed at a still gasping Harut—"I've developed an appreciation for the finer points of the human technology of destruction. And, yes, I don't think it looks like a giant penis by accident."

"We found something even more interesting in the saint's tomb," Zaid said. "A crossing point over the *araf.*

Daniel can see it. Which means he can cross over and find his grandmother. We'll have the enchantress of sands by our side."

Zahara bit her lower lip. "Daniel can't go to the Mountains of Qaf."

"Thanks for your expression of confidence in my survival skills," Daniel said.

"Believe me, I'm not crazy about the plan either." Zaid gave the angel a solid whomp on the back, and Harut coughed out more ash. "But we can only stop Marut before he devours the sacrifice. Now that you've brought Harut back, he and I can hold Marut off and protect the festival. You can go with Daniel to the Mountains of Qaf and bring Solikis back with you."

"Daniel can't seek his kin in the world of the jinn." Harut's voice, hoarse and weak, echoed through the heat of the air with a solid finality. "Zahara's mother will cut him down as soon as he sets foot there." He climbed to his feet and pointed at Daniel. "Had I known you summoned the spawn of my old enemy Lilitu, I would never have agreed to join forces with you."

What the hell was Harut talking about? Daniel turned to Zahara. Her eyes were cast down to the ground, and her cheeks flushed.

"Lilitu is the power behind Marut?" Zaid came up to Zahara, his voice low but harsh. "I expected you to run to your mother for help when you realized you were in over your head. But why didn't you tell me we were up against not only Marut, but the devourer of souls?"

Zahara shifted her feet and flicked a quick glance at Zaid

from underneath her long lashes. "What was I supposed to tell you? That I screwed up and blundered into one of my mother's great schemes? That she's still going ahead with her plans, even if I die? No one can break the contract I made with Daniel, not even her."

"Lilitu is pulling the strings that allow my brother to advance his plan," Harut said. "It was no accident Zahara was the one to answer Daniel's summons."

"I was set up!" Zahara turned to Daniel. "My mother doesn't trust me to fill the vat of bloodwine before a family dinner. She wouldn't have sent me for something this important. This is what Solikis wanted all along."

Daniel tightened both his fists and walked closer to her. "So you think that my grandmother lured you into a contract with me so Lilitu would have to see her own daughter murdered if she wanted her side to win?"

"Who else would have sent you a lamp, of all the stupid clichés?" Zahara asked. "It was brilliant strategy on Solikis's part. Exactly what my mother would have done, if the opportunity came up."

"My grandmother is nothing like your mother."

"You need to go home, *cherie*." Zaid's tone softened, but as Zahara reached out to him, he pulled his hand away. "Lilitu wouldn't have allowed you to be here if it wasn't something she wanted. You don't belong here, with us."

Zahara lifted her head, her eyelashes wet with tears. "You don't understand. I don't belong there, either."

Daniel steadied his breathing and faced her. "I release you, Zahara, from my request to battle Marut for me. I command you to return to the world of the jinn." He reached into his pocket and pulled out his *hamsa*, holding it up to her and taking a threatening step forward.

Black flames licked around Zahara's feet. Fire and smoke rose higher, boiling up around her in dark clouds that obscured her bowed head and the sobs shaking her chest. Then a sharp clap of thunder echoed off the hills around them, and the last wisp of smoke faded away.

HOURS LATER, AFTER the chill of a desert night had driven away the last remnants of the sun's warmth, Zaid walked up to Daniel's chosen hiding place behind the van, the silver dagger Donnelly had used to banish him to the Mountains of Qaf in his hand. "Here." He showed Daniel the narrow strip of red cloth he had fashioned into a sling of sorts for the weapon. The two ends were knotted into small rings set on each side of the dagger's sheath. He draped the fabric over Daniel's shoulder, so the knife hung from his left waist. "This is how you wear it."

"Thanks." Daniel glanced at his right wrist. He still had his watch, which hadn't even suffered a crack through everything he had gone through. After their frantic preparations to set up an ambush for Marut, the remaining minutes until midnight had ticked by at a glacial pace. "The moon will pass into the House of Al-Ghafr soon. Not exactly an auspicious mansion."

Zaid cocked his head. "I thought you didn't have any formal training in that sort of magic."

"I didn't." Daniel tapped his watch. "But I had some

time to do a little research, and there's actually an app for it."

Zaid laughed, then grew serious. "Harut's planning on waiting out in the open for his brother. That might give me a chance to hit when he's not expecting it. Harut's a good fighter. If the two of us can take Marut, stay put. If it's not going well, retreat into the tomb itself. It's hallowed ground, and may give you an advantage."

"And if all else fails, I'll cross over the *araf* and take my chances." Daniel stared down at the hamsa in his hand. The skin of his palm bore no mark or scar, and even his stomach felt fine. Harut had healed the cuts and bruises from his captivity with a simple touch. "I know Solikis is waiting for me."

"So is Lilitu." Zaid reached out a hand and brushed Daniel's cheek. "Stay safe. I'm still waiting to hear about those aspirations of yours."

He faded into invisibility, his eyes smiling in the starlight as his body dissolved into the gloom.

MINUTES LATER, MARUT arrived.

The angel made no effort to hide his approach. Daniel spotted him striding down the road leading to the tomb, his shape that of a man more than twice Daniel's height, with wings that dragged behind him more like grim burdens than means of flight.

He paused as he approached the van, then raised his hand to send a ball of flame into the air to illuminate the surrounding area. The spinning globe cast a sickly yellow glow over the landscape.

"The human warriors of this age differ little from those of the past." The angel's voice was low and soft, nothing like the ominous rumble Daniel had expected. "Courage can only take them only so far."

He reached into a large sack he carried and tossed two objects out onto the road. The giant's and Bull Man's heads, each bearing the startled expression of the freshly dead, rolled along the ground for several feet before coming to a stop.

Daniel choked back a rush of nausea as he peered around the back of the Humvee. Marut ignored the body parts he had thrown on the road, instead focusing on a point outside the circle of light he had created. Harut stepped forward, his own wings spread behind him, the embedded eyes in his feathers wide open and glaring.

Marut held out a hand toward him, making no move to draw his weapon. "Give me the sacrifice, my brother."

Harut unsheathed his sword, and flames licked up the blade. "You and I are no longer kin."

As Marut raised his own weapon, Zaid gave a shout and charged forward to attack the angel from the side. The jinn focused his attention on Marut's left leg, slashing at the angel's dead gray skin with his blade.

Marut staggered and fell into a kneeling position, his sword toppling to the ground. Zaid jumped in to swing at his exposed neck, but a single blow from the angel's fist sent him into a crumpled heap on the ground. Harut stepped in to block the jinn's prone body from further assault, and drove the point of his sword into Marut's left eye. The angel roared in surprise and anger, his orbit now reduced to a smoking crater.

Marut's next move was swift—and impossible for Harut to dodge. He reached out with an enormous hand and gripped his brother around the chest, his fingers clenching to crush the life out of him. Zaid darted forward to strike at Marut's blind side, but the angel thrust out his opposite fist, knocking the jinn backward and sending his sword flying. Marut opened his hand and let Harut's limp body slide to the ground.

The angel reached out to retrieve his weapon, then climbed to his feet. His next step would be to finish Harut off, then Zaid. Daniel couldn't let that happen. He stepped out from behind the van and gave a shout. Marut turned toward the sound, his one-eyed gaze meeting Daniel's.

In a few impossibly long strides, the fallen one strode up to the van and tossed it aside with a crash of metal and broken glass. His sword, the blade crawling with fire, came down over Daniel's head.

Daniel threw his arms up to protect himself. The *hamsa* in his right hand grew hot enough to burn his skin, and the blade stopped less than a foot from his skull. Marut staggered back a few steps and gave a grunt of disbelief.

The amulet shattered into dust.

He tossed the powdery remains of the *hamsa* at the angel and took off at a dead run. He had nowhere to go but the tomb, and he scrambled up the slope through the darkness, his lungs burning before he reached the halfway mark. An acid rush of adrenaline pushed him onward, and he half-ran, half-stumbled onto the flat plain surrounding the structure.

Even in the black of night, the whitewashed dome reflected enough starlight to be visible. He staggered forward, his breath ragged. They had left the door closed but not secured, and inside was the only safe haven available. Both Zaid and Harut were at best badly injured, and the only possibility of help lay on the other side of the tomb's far wall, past the fluttering shadows and into Zaid's world. If there was any chance of getting help, he had to try and cross over, no matter what was waiting for him on the other side.

Only steps from the door, a sudden flare of light blinded him, and he shrank back. Marut, reduced to the still-unmanageable height of a professional basketball player, leaned against the wall of the tomb. The flames dancing over his sword dimmed, and he regarded Daniel with his remaining eye, dark and devoid of light or pity.

"You're not much of a sorcerer." The angel came closer, and neither Daniel's mind nor legs were capable of escape. "And you continue to deny me my sacrifice."

"Back off, tall, dumb and ugly." Zahara's voice rang out behind Daniel, and he turned to see her step out of the shadows into the unearthly light of Marut's sword. Wearing nothing more than her belly dancing outfit, she posed with her gem-encrusted sword held high in the air, henna tattoos writhing on her exposed arms and abdomen like a nest of baby snakes. "Pathetic or not, he's *my* sorcerer."

Marut sent a stream of flame from his sword in her direction. Daniel jumped back, plastering himself against the side of the tomb.

A fireball blasted the earth where Zahara stood, scorching the ground and sending out an expanding sphere of heat that made Daniel gasp despite his distance from it.

Zahara's form remained unaffected save for a brief flicker, as if a glitch had struck a video game character. Giggling, she balanced the sword on her chest and sank to her knees. She arched backward, thrusting her hips up from the ground, before rising up like a dancing cobra, the blade remaining in perfect position above her breasts.

Confused with her ability to withstand his strike, Marut stepped forward, grunting. The angel swung his sword at the dancing girl with a savage, two-handed blow. The blade passed through her, causing no apparent injury. He stabbed again and again, frustrated, but Zahara was as unaffected by his blows as a puff of smoke would have been.

"What magic is this?" He brushed at his face in annoyance as a darting red light jumped from his face down to his chest. "No weapon of the jinn can kill me."

Laughter rang out, this time further away, and a slender form became visible on a nearby hilltop, silhouetted against the star-strewn sky. The real Zahara had a cylindrical object balanced on her shoulder.

It looked, for all the world, like a giant penis.

Daniel dove for cover as the shoulder-fired missile shattered the night with an explosion of sound and arced toward the laser sight on Marut's chest. It exploded upon impact, sending plumes of smoke and fire streaking up into the night sky.

The towering giant of an angel remained standing for a long minute as charred hunks of flesh broke off and rained down over the ground. Then he toppled forward, landing with a crash as dust and sparks floated into the air.

Daniel picked himself up, coughing out soot and wiping

ash from his forehead. A small furry shape flew toward him, and he knew enough to shield his eyes before Zahara transformed back into her human shape, a triumphant smile on her face.

"I have to get another one of those. That was awesome."

"Is he dead?" Daniel covered his mouth, gagging at the stench of smoldering flesh. Whatever Marut had been was now little more than a mix of ash and white threads that resembled a mound of maggots. A half-dozen small fires burned in the perimeter around the missile's impact.

She darted over and jabbed her sword into a charred remnant of an arm. "Well-done and crispy, I'd say." With a flourish, she sheathed her sword and wagged a finger at him. "You suck at this sorcerer gig, Daniel Goldstein. For one thing, when you told me to go back to the Mountains of Qaf, you neglected to order me not to turn around and come right back."

A breeze blew by them, surprisingly cold even given the late hour. The remnants of Marut's corpse stirred in the wind, and the pale threads of flesh in the center began to squirm.

Daniel raised a hand to point at the movement, squinting in the hazy light of the smoldering fires.

"And second, all those things you thought I wanted instead of your soul—cotton candy, jewelry, *all* the shoes." Zahara's voice swelled into a triumphant crescendo. "You are *so* going to give me every one one of those."

The wind blew by him again, cold and hard, and a flurry of white flecks flew into the air. They writhed and twisted, forming a human shape. Marut reappeared, now a man of normal height, without wings or a shred of clothing. He held his sword in one hand, the smooth skin of his newly-formed body glinting in the starlight over his tense muscles.

Zahara whirled around, pulling out her own sword, but the restored angel knocked it out of her hands with a jolt from his weapon, then plunged his blade into her abdomen.

Choking and gasping, Zahara fell backward as Daniel jumped forward to hold her in his arms. Blood welled up in her mouth, a dark, liquid pool, and spilled over her chin. A spasm wracked her body, and Daniel found himself facing Marut's blood-drenched blade as the angel held it to his throat.

Marut smiled. Reaching out with his other hand, he stroked Zahara's face, coating his finger in her blood. Then he brought his hand to his mouth, licking and swallowing every drop.

"At last," he said, "my sacrifice."

Chapter Twenty-Five

A SNARLING MASS of bloodied fur hit the angel from one side, the leopard's claws reaching to rake the angel's face. Knocked to the ground, Marut gave an enraged scream of surprise as he and Zaid rolled in the dirt, the fully transformed jinn clawing and biting at his face with relentless fury.

The night disappeared, and a blinding light drenched the ground around Daniel. It took a few seconds, and the roar of a helicopter's rotors overhead, before he processed that this wasn't another paranormal event. The cavalry had arrived, in helicopter gunships instead of on horseback. Marut threw Zaid off him, then retrieved his sword and disappeared into the glare of artificial light to confront the new threat.

Daniel lowered Zahara to the ground, tearing off part of his shirt and pressing the fabric against the bleeding hole in her abdomen. A hand gripped his shoulder, and Harut stood over him; searchlights from the Blackhawk helicopters overhead framed his battered body and bloodied wings in a halo of light. Behind him, men dropped down from the sky on long ropes like spiders descending on spun silk.

"The humans who captured me have arrived to fight my brother." Harut pulled Daniel to his feet, despite his efforts to fight him off and remain with Zahara. "They will fail, and so will we, without help. Go into the tomb now. Cross over. Solikis is our only hope."

The earth shook under Daniel's feet, a sickening jolt like an earthquake. Towering above them, an enormous Marut, now as tall as a two-story building, reached out to bat two circling helicopters out of the sky. Twin explosions lit up the night, sending streaks of light arcing to the earth. Daniel ran forward, chunks of burning metal falling around him, and wrestled open the door to the tomb.

Inside, the blackness cut off his vision, leaving only blotches of light seared onto his retinas by the firefight outside. Then the details of the interior swam into focus, and he saw it. Directly ahead, something fluttered, like a tattered curtain behind a shattered window. Daniel hesitated, the warnings about Zahara's mother—more terrible and awful than the monster killing people outside—playing out in his mind.

With a creak and a groan, the dome of the crypt shattered. Chunks of plaster fell around him down as starlight spilled onto the floor. Above, a massive, dark shape stood silhouetted against the night sky. Marut had cracked off the tomb's roof like an eggshell.

Daniel's decision had been made for him. He muttered a half-forgotten prayer and ran headfirst into the wall.

He winced, squeezing his eyes shut, as he waited for contact that never came. His legs kept running, kept moving, and he had the sensation of falling a great distance at the leisurely pace of a dropping leaf. Then he hit the sand, hard.

He was lying flat on his back, awash in bright sunlight. Bright, *hot* sunlight, so brilliant and warm that it lit up the inside of Daniel's eyelids like he was staring at a fire through a grimy furnace window. He blinked a few times, his eyelids cracking open only a hair, as he tried to block out the pain of the light.

When his vision cleared, the face of the man holding a sword against his throat swam into focus. His resemblance to Zaid was obvious—he had the same striking cheekbones, dark eyes and even the same turbaned outfit. One of Zaid's brothers had found him—and was planning to cut his throat.

Another face, similar to the first, leaned over him and barked what Daniel took to be a question, if he could have understood the language it was asked in.

"Are you working for Lilitu, too?" Daniel had nothing to lose at this point. "If you want a war that badly, come back to my world and fight Zaid and me on our turf."

The first man's face darkened in anger, and he responded by pressing the tip of the sword against his skin. The blade was so sharp Daniel felt no pain, only the trickle of blood that dripped off one side of his neck.

"You accuse us of allying with the devourer of souls?" The second man, older and with a trace of gray in his beard, spoke to him in English. "Her last servant sent here died at the point of our swords in this very spot."

Harut had warned Daniel Lilitu would be waiting for him if he crossed over. It sounded like that plan had gone awry. The trouble was, he could end up as dead as Lilitu's minion if he couldn't convince these two that he wasn't working with her as well. "I'm fighting alongside Zaid, and he's in trouble."

"Our brother has been banished for centuries." The first man continued to hold his blade against Daniel's throat. "Using his name will not help you."

"I know you disobeyed your clan and let him live when he returned here." Daniel caught the glint of surprise in his captor's eyes. "How would I know that if I worked for Lilitu?"

The older man reached over to push the sword away from Daniel's neck. The two stepped back, and Daniel climbed to his feet. His clothes had disappeared, replaced by a *jellaba*—a long hooded robe. His dagger still hung at his waist, but the rough band of knotted cloth that held it had been transformed into a scarlet sash.

Around him, dunes of golden sand stretched out in every direction toward toward a horizon dominated by towering mountains. Their slopes were a vivid green, even at this distance, and their peaks disappeared into frosty clouds. The mountains had to be of staggering height, like Everest or K1, not anything like the ranges in Northern Africa. Or anywhere else in Daniel's world, for that matter.

He was standing in the Mountains of Qaf, the world of the jinn.

"I need to speak to Solikis." Daniel turned to the older man. "She's the only one who can help us."

The younger man laughed. "Who are you, human, to seek out the enchantress of the sands?"

"Her grandson." Daniel watched as the smile on the man's face faded.

He raised his hands, and his form swirled into a twisting funnel of sand.

Zaid's older brother produced a leather-wrapped bottle from his waist and handed it to Daniel. Still staring at the sandstorm roaring away from them, Daniel tilted the container up and poured the contents into his mouth. The water, cool and flavored with lemon and honey, slid down his scratched, dry throat.

Golden grains of sand fell into a pile next to Daniel as he finished off the last of the water, then rearranged themselves into the form of the younger jinn. He nodded at his brother, and the two of them indicated the air in front of them with a wave.

One minute the open expanse of desert in front of him stretched out into an empty sea of rippling dunes. The next, the air blurred into a haze, and the clan of Jewish jinn appeared.

There were about a dozen in all, several men with long beards and flowing white caftans, and a few children who jostled to get a better look at him. Two younger women stood at the center of the group, with oval eyes and dark eyebrows beneath beaded headdresses set off with silver spikes.

The group parted, and an older woman strode forward, her head covered in an indigo wrap decorated with ropes of silver discs. Faint lines creased around her dark eyes, and her face had been painted white, with black markings forming vertical lines on her forehead and cheeks, and a hashed line under her chin. Other than the strange getup, his grandmother looked fantastic. Years younger, in fact.

"Peace be upon you, *ya sayyidati*." The taller of Zaid's brothers inclined his head in a polite bow to Solikis, but kept a hand resting on the hilt of his sword. "Is this human here at your invitation?"

"He is." Solikis lifted her hand, each finger ornamented by glittering rings, and gestured around to the people grouped around her. "Even my clan's mixed-blood mud children come under our protection."

"Grandma." Daniel began, then faltered. "Zaid and Harut are trying to hold off Marut. He didn't want me as the sacrifice, he wanted Zahara. And he got her." He hesitated, wanting so badly to hug her. "I need your help."

"Oh, duckie." Solikis came forward to kiss him on his forehead. "We need your help as well." She beckoned for Daniel to follow her as she strode off through the sand. He jogged to keep up; Zaid's brothers spoke in low tones to each other and trailed behind at a respectful distance.

As the reached the top of a low dune, Solikis waved her arm, her bracelets tinkling like wind chimes, and the air grew hazy again. A grove of palm trees stretched out before them, with blue-green grasses clumped under the shade of their swaying, broad leaves. Deeper inside the oasis, sunlight reflected back from a rippling body of water.

"Is that a mirage?" Daniel asked.

Solikis laughed. "It's a real *wadi*. A long time ago, even by our standards of time, it served as a place of worship. An open, natural temple, for gods even the jinn have forgotten."

Daniel walked into the oasis, the soft sand under his feet giving way to packed earth, then lush grass. "You've been to my world before. Why couldn't you return earlier?"

"I can't cross over to the world of man without you." Solikis nodded, and the clan of jinn moved through the swaying vegetation to gather at the water's edge. Zaid's two brothers followed, then stood a distance apart, their arms folded across their chests. Neither took his eyes off Daniel as his grandmother spoke.

"I loved your grandfather, Daniel. So much so, I wanted to have his child. But for a jinn and a human to do this requires much magic, and a price must be paid. When your grandfather passed on, I had to return to the Mountains of Qaf, and leave my daughter and grandson behind."

Daniel thought back to his grandfather's funeral, and his grandmother's proud and grief-stricken face as she had embraced him and helped him say goodbye. An impossibly long lifespan and great power came at a price.

"My enemy Lilitu chose to use the power of my old home in Marrakech to assist Marut in his plan." Solikis reached out to touch his arm. "She thought I had no magic strong enough to return to the world of man this soon. But she was wrong. I have you."

Solikis took his arm and brought him closer to the pool. The water was so clear he would have been sure he was looking at air, had it not been for a solitary palm leaf floating on the surface. The inner walls of the pond were plunging rock, and a stone archway lay on the sandy bottom. It looked tiny, like a toy bridge. From this perspective, he couldn't tell if it was that small, or the water so deep he was seeing it at a distance.

Solikis crooked a finger, and the leaf skimmed along the surface of the water toward her, carried on an unfelt breeze. It washed up onto the rim of sand and rocks at the pond's edge, close to Daniel's feet.

"Follow the leaf, duckie."

Solikis murmured to the jinn gathered around her. The women and children came closer to hug her. One of the older men produced a roll of parchment wrapped around two gold shafts, studded with diamonds and rubies. It was the most beautiful Torah scroll Daniel had ever seen. The rabbi read out a short prayer, and Daniel somehow understood the power of it, if not the exact words.

Then his grandmother walked into the water, gliding forward and down until her head sank under the surface.

The leaf stirred, then glided away from him. Daniel glanced at the group, his jinn cousins. They gave him encouraging nods, and he took a few steps into the pond. The water, cool and clear, lapped around his feet and soaked the long folds of his jellaba.

"Wait." Zaid's two brothers approached the water's edge. The taller of the two raised his hand. "Tell us why Zaid fights the fallen one, and why he risks death to defend a world not his own."

"Because he's brave," Daniel turned his back on them to slog deeper into the pool. "He wants to do the right thing, even if it costs him everything. And because he belongs in my world, more than here."

Daniel was up to his neck in the water now. The leaf spun in lazy circles beyond his reach, then slipped under the surface.

Two flashes of white ran past him, as Zaid's brothers charged across the pool's surface, sprays of glittering waterdrops kicking up around their feet. They reached the center and spun to face him.

Daniel took one more hesitant step forward, and the gentle slope downward vanished into an abrupt drop. He sank to the bottom as if made of stone. Panic filling his chest, he struggled to slow his descent, then held his breath until his lungs burned in agony. He gave up and opened his mouth to suck in the water and drown.

But he could breathe. Quite easily, in fact.

He bounced forward, his feet striking the sandy bottom and pushing him in long, weightless jumps. Light from the white-hot sun above diffused into a soft glow. He turned his head from side to side, his hair swirling in all directions as his robes billowed out around him. Then he spotted the leaf as it floated by, drifting toward the stone arch he had seen from the surface.

Solikis stood to the left of the structure, a massive half-circle covered in runes and symbols all but worn away by time. Zaid's two brothers waited across from her. The leaf glided through the dead center of the arch, then disappeared. Daniel tried to follow it, but the water grew thicker and more viscous with each step. Dragging his arms and legs, he pushed forward until he stood under the arch. The imprint of a hand with an eye embedded in the palm had been carved under the very apex of the structure. Then all resistance gave way, and Daniel found himself lying facedown on cold, hard stone.

Disoriented, Daniel came up to his knees. He was back inside the tomb, still wearing the ankle-length jellaba and soaking wet. An unnatural blue light lit up the sky above the now open-air tomb, illuminating the palm leaf resting on the floor in front of him. A gust of wind sent it spiraling up into the air and above the shattered stone walls.

Follow the leaf.

It was as good a plan as any.

Another explosion sent the earth shaking under his feet. The tomb's doorway was blocked by rubble, and lacking either wings or the magical know-how to grow them, Daniel was left with the less glamorous option of climbing over the piles of rock and plaster. He yanked the silver dagger free of its sheath and prepared to join the fight. Easier thought than done. Crawling out of rubble with a knife in one hand was not as easy as every cheesy swashbuckler he had ever watched made it out to be.

Solikis had started without him. His grandmother's form flashed in and out of view as fire and light from her battle with Marut reflected off a canvas of dark clouds above them. She stood on the nearby hilltop where Zahara had launched the missile, her arms raised to send bolts of blue fire toward the angel.

Marut, now back in his smaller human form, stood in the center of the ring of azure flames Solikis had used to trap him. Zaid's two brothers and a limping but still battle-engaged Harut encircled him, striking at him with the last of their strength. Their deadly angel enemy was badly outnumbered, but his opponents' blows glanced off him without leaving a mark. The three men around him had not fared as well. Each bore at least one bloody slash from his weapon.

Chunks of twisted metal and bodies in military fatigues littered the ground. Daniel approached two injured men resting against the outer wall of the tomb. Ahmed held a Koran in one hand and *hamsa* in the other, alternating what sounded like curses and prayers at the circle of fire. Donnelly sat next to him, a tourniquet wrapped around one leg. He glanced up as Daniel approached.

"No air support, no communications, no nothing." Donnelly raised his hand and dropped a radio unit on the ground beside him. "We don't have any other backup options."

"Prayer." Ahmed grunted. "That is what we have." He tucked both the book and the amulet into his fatigues and accepted Donnelly's sword from him as he climbed to his feet.

Daniel stared at the burly Moroccan soldier's back as he limped to the circle of fire, and certain death. He hefted his small dagger in one hand and wondered what the hell he could accomplish with it.

Then he spotted Zaid. The jinn knelt on the ground several feet away, beside a small, crumpled shape. Daniel walked toward him, breaking into a run as more flashes of light flickered the scene in and out of bright relief. Zahara lay on the ground, transformed into her catlike gargoyle form, and in a dark pool of her own blood. Zaid was by her side, his hands cupped in prayer, a cut gaping open on his forehead. Daniel dropped to the ground and reached out to stroke Zahara's soft, dark fur. A faint, shuddering breath rose and fell under his hand.

Zaid lifted his eyes, reddened from more than the smoke blowing around them. "I've completed a *dua* for her soul. There's nothing I can do for her body." He gazed out on the battle taking place in front of them. "Now I will join my brothers in our last battle."

"You're in no shape for that fight." Daniel reached to touch the swelling on Zaid's forehead. "Solikis will stop him."

"Marut's too powerful now, with Zahara's blood to give him full form." He patted Zahara's head. "I never saw what Zahara did in that house to save the boy, and I'm not sure if even she understood why she did it." He reached out and gripped Daniel's hand. "Stay with her for me. At least I'll die with my family fighting by my side. She's all alone."

Zaid rose to his feet. In the center of the circle of flames, Ahmed lay groaning on the ground, and one of Zaid's brothers had fallen next to him. The blue fire burned lower, and some points flickered out entirely. The jinn turned to walk into the battle, while on the hilltop across from the tomb, Solikis fell to her knees, spent.

Daniel gripped his dagger in his hand so hard his hold slipped, slicing his palm in an identical cut to the one Harut had healed for him. He watched the blood pool, and closed his hand into a fist. Maybe they would all die. But Marut would, too, if he had anything to say about it.

He cupped his hand around the wound in Zahara's abdomen, mixing his blood with hers. Then he crawled forward and marked out a crude pentagram on the packed earth around him. The sounds of the battle near him grew louder and more anguished, and he could tell, without turning to watch, that his side was losing. Words poured from his lips, forming a singsong blur of sounds. He had never spoken or heard the language he was using. He wasn't sure if any human had.

He added a name to the spell. *Lilitu.*

He crouched over Zahara, covering and protecting her body with his. Inside the pentagram, smoke rose up to the sky, and black flames outlined the five-pointed star. A crack of thunder shook the ground around him. The flames darkened and solidified, forming hundreds of wormlike wings, each studded with sets of glowing eyes that fixed their awful stare upon him. Inside the swirl of writhing movement, a raw maw of teeth and mucus gaped wide to draw him in.

Daniel clawed at his face, trying to rip the image before him out of his vision. A voice, high-pitched and screaming, bored into his mind, threatening to destroy what little sanity was left.

"Who dares summon the devourer of souls?" The question was a long, drawn-out screech, like fingernails ripped to shreds as they were dragged against granite. "And what is it you ask of me?"

"My name is Daniel." Each word required incredible effort, as the pain in his head intensified and he struggled to push the fractured images of what he had seen out of his mind. He sat back, holding his hands out to show her Zahara's bleeding body.

Daniel cracked open his eyelids, catching a glimpse of fluttering dark tentacles draping themselves over the shape in front of him. He sensed loss. And grief. Horrible as the creature in front of him was, she could feel emotional pain, and know the ache of losing someone she loved.

Then the stabbing began, a searing burning in his head, worse than any he had ever experienced. He screamed out in agony.

"No. This cannot be her. My silly, foolish girl is safe, back in our world. You were the one who interfered. You should have been the one to die."

"She came back to help us." Daniel gasped out the words. "And she saved that child, not me."

The pain increased, mounting to a level where Daniel would have gladly slit his own throat if he'd had the strength to pick up the dagger beside him.

As abruptly as they'd begun, the noise and agony stopped. The world was reduced to nothing except for the dark, hard words that echoed in his mind.

"Tell me, then, what is it you dare ask for?"

With tremendous effort, Daniel lifted up his hand and pointed at Marut. "I want you to avenge your daughter's death."

Then he was cold and shivering, as wet tendrils dragged across his body, sucking out every last flicker of warmth, of joy, of hope itself. Lilitu passed over him, leaving him alive. For now.

Chapter Twenty-Six

ZAHARA FELT DANIEL'S hand stroke her fur for the last time. After another whispered word of comfort, he stood up. She cracked her eyelids open with great effort, watching as he grasped his dagger in his bloodied hand and stumbled toward the circle to join the fight.

Stupid, brave Daniel.

She needed to follow him, try to protect him from Marut somehow. That was why she had returned, wasn't it? To save him, like she had saved that little boy. To do something silly and foolish, something her mother would never do. Something for the greater good.

She reached out with one front paw, her claws digging into the ground to pull the rest of her forward. She had no feeling in her body below her chest, and she couldn't move her back legs. The awful, searing pain in her abdomen had ceased with the chill of her mother's touch, but with the relief had come paralysis.

Her body smeared the outline of the pentagram Daniel had drawn to summon Lilitu as she dragged herself a little further. Daniel couldn't pull off a card trick, much less a real magic spell, but his jinn blood—and his stubborn determination to do the right thing—had brought Solikis, enchantress of the sands, across the veil between the worlds to join the fight. And when that wasn't enough, he had called up someone even more powerful and terrifying. Lilitu, the devourer of souls. So why had he gone to join the fight himself? He didn't have a chance against Marut. She had to do something.

Every rock, every slight incline blocked her path toward the circle of fighting. Given the amount of blood leaking from her abdomen, the ground beneath her should have grown a little slippery. Enough to ease her way, at least. No such luck. Another slope loomed up before her, as staggering an obstacle as a mountain. She dug her claws deeper into the packed earth and crawled up to oversee the battle.

It wasn't going well.

There was no sign yet of her mother. The remaining fighters had retreated or lay motionless on the ground. Dead or exhausted—she couldn't tell. Zaid crouched next to the collapsed form of one of his brothers, his mouth moving in a final conversation. Or maybe a prayer. On the far hilltop, Daniel's grandmother knelt, her arms reaching up more in supplication than attack.

That left the two angel brothers alone to fight. Marut's naked, smooth skin gleamed red and perfect in the light of burning clumps of debris around him, unmarked by the blows leveled against him. His sword danced in his hand, inflicting cut after cut on his staggering brother, who continued to circle him, attempting to land a blow. One of Harut's wings dragged behind him, and half-healed gashes and new oozing wounds covered his body. His brother was toying with him, using Harut's ability to heal himself to draw the battle out into a slow, torturous death.

Daniel lay in a heap a few meters from her. Maybe he had tried to position himself behind the fallen one, out of his line of vision. He hadn't counted on the waves of heat rising off Marut's body, or the clouds of red vapor that hung in the air. Even from Zahara's protected position close to the ground, the harsh sting of sulfur burned her nose and lungs.

As she tried to creep closer, Harut fell to his knees. The fallen one raised his sword to Harut's neck. He touched it lightly once, to draw a line of blood only, then gripped it in two hands to deliver the blow that would sever his brother's head from his body.

Zahara dug into the earth with her claws, trying to drive herself forward. Daniel lay unmoving, and Harut was about to be decapitated in front of her eyes. She had no spell, no trick, no last clever idea to save either of them.

Tendrils of black smoke rose around Marut's feet. The fallen one ignored them, his single-minded focus on Harut's imminent execution blinding him to the threat at his back. He screamed as Lilitu formed around him, her multi-eyed limbs humming over his exposed skin, extinguishing his red glow in streaks of frost and leaving bloody gashes on his flawless body. Her circular mouth, filled with endless rows of pointed teeth, opened wider, hovering over his head and chest.

Somehow, despite her mother's grip on him, Marut fought back. He swung his blade with his free arm, severing grasping tentacles and leaving them writhing on the ground at his feet. Her mother's lifeblood, inky black, seeped from the stumps of her appendages and pooled in the dirt.

No, this couldn't be happening. She had wanted to show

her mother she could do something on her own, that she belonged in her family as much as her older and far more powerful relatives. Instead, all she'd managed to do was set up her mother and her friends to be killed by Marut.

Zahara scratched at the earth again, her movements growing frantic. Her claws pulled her paralyzed legs forward over the ridge, and the weight of her body sent her tumbling down the slope. She came to a stop against Daniel, who gave a low groan. Marut's fire and Lilitu's ice had combined to lower the temperature to a level where they both could breathe. But he needed to wake up.

Raising her head, she searched for the nearest spot on his body to deliver that message. He was lying face down, and that made for an obvious choice. She bared her fangs and bit his butt as hard as she could.

Daniel grunted, his hand coming down to push her off him. He twisted his head to stare at her, then back at the scene in front of him. The few seconds it took him to make a decision ticked by, as Zahara tried to cough out a scream, a curse, a plea for him to try and help her mother.

He climbed to his feet, dagger in his hand. One hesitant step followed another, and Daniel stood within an arm's length of the fallen one before Marut sensed his presence.

Marut turned his focus from his fight with Lilitu and rotated to face Daniel. The dagger Donnelly had given him gleamed in Daniel's right hand, raised in the air for a downward strike not through air but through flesh. The fallen one met Daniel's gaze for a long moment, handsome amber irises transforming into roaring flames of fury. He raised his sword to strike, but a tentacle shot out to rip the sword out the angel's hand.

Daniel buried his knife blade into Marut's heart.

The fire and light extinguished, and more of her mother's black tentacles rose up, dragging Marut down into a void in the earth itself.

Daniel fell down with him.

Zahara cried out, the last gasp of air she could force from her lungs. A large feline shape vaulted forward, leaping through the swirl of ice and gleaming eyes. Zaid transformed into human shape as the roiling mass began to involute upon itself. He reached down with both arms in a last, desperate attempt to save Daniel's life.

Zahara couldn't make out anything in the swirling mass of dirt and dust. Daniel had no chance to survive in whatever deeper level of hell Lilitu was dragging Marut off to. If Zaid had been pulled down with him, even he wouldn't last long in the presence of her mother's furious spasm of revenge. To avenge her daughter's death, tradition demanded she draw out Marut's death into as long a torment as possible. And Zahara, who still had a few heartbeats of life left in her, would die alone.

The black mists dissipated. Around Zahara, the temperature rose. Solid earth replaced the gaping pit Marut had fallen into. On top of it, Zaid knelt beside Daniel, his battered face breaking into a smile as the young sorcerer stirred and sat up. A palm leaf floated down to rest beside the two men, then disappeared as Solikis appeared in its place. The enchantress of the sands reached out, her smile warm and proud, and touched her grandson's face. Beside her, Harut staggered to his feet—wounds oozing, posture triumphant.

They were alive. All of them. Her friends, her mother's enemy who had come to their aid, and Harut. All together, and happy. Zahara was happy too, but so tired. The rush of energy that pushed her this far had ebbed, and she needed to close her eyes and sleep. She struggled to fight against the cloud of fatigue. A few more seconds awake was all she wanted. To see them all alive and happy.

A pair of arms encircled her, strong and comforting. Zahara looked up to see her mother, brown eyes dark and wet with tears.

Such a good human transformation, for a change.

Everything was fine now. Zahara wasn't alone anymore. She could close her eyes and sleep forever.

She heard Daniel call out her name. He limped back to her, supported by Zaid. Solikis came up behind the two of them, her face tense and hard. The enchantress of the sands was ready for another fight.

Zahara tried to push herself upright in her mother's lap. This wasn't good. The battle had ended, and this would be an excellent time for everyone to get far, far away from her mother.

Harut took a few running steps and came to the front of the group to confront Lilitu. "You spent much time arranging for my brother and I to fall, all those years ago." He raised his hands, the cuts on his exposed arms sealing over as he spoke. "I'm sure you were all too pleased to assist him to do even more evil in this world. Why did you stop him, at the end?"

Lilitu gestured at Daniel. "Your sorcerer's wish has been

fulfilled. Perhaps after I take his soul I'll force him to kill all of you, to make his infinite torture as my slave even more painful."

"Actually." Daniel held up his hand, the cut from his blood offering to Lilitu gaping open. "I don't think so. I asked you to do what your honor demanded—avenge your daughter by destroying her killer."

Her mother's body stiffened. She hated to be outmaneuvered. And by a human, no less. She spat back her reply to Zaid. "Clever little toy you have, apostate. No matter. After I mourn my own, I'll return for all of you."

"Give Zahara to me." Harut held out his arms. "I can help her."

Lilitu laughed, a harsh crackle that failed at being entirely human. "You can only heal your kind."

Harut reached out to rest his hands on Zaid and Daniel at the same time. Daniel clenched and unclenched his fist, staring down at his now healed palm. Beside him, Zaid gave a small gasp of surprise, then straightened up.

The angel walked over to the prostrate bodies lying on the ground around them. He touched Ahmed first, then Zaid's two brothers, and a soft light glowed over them. He even stooped over a moaning Donnelly, reaching out to clasp him on the shoulder. Then he returned to face Lilitu.

"The righteous, I can heal." He held out his hands again.

Zahara's mother tensed, clutching Zahara even tighter. Her family never asked for help, never gave or expected mercy. Maybe Harut could heal her, maybe he couldn't. It didn't matter. She knew him well enough to understand this was no trick. Lifting her head, she coughed out a few short phrases in her family's language. So hard to say *please* with the words they had available.

Her mother's grip around her body loosened as Harut pulled Zahara into his arms. His hands were warm and soft, and she breathed in his faint scent of citron.

Light enveloped both of them, blinding her with its radiance. The brilliance around them dimmed, and she stood upright in Harut's arms. He had transformed her into her human form—and he hadn't. She still had her long black hair, human legs, and feet that rested on the ground, whole and uninjured. But a pair of wings arose from her back, and they were nothing like the leathery appendages she added on for Zaid's benefit. As her eyes opened wide and wondering, hundreds of others embedded in her wings did as well. These eyes were different from those on Harut's wings—odd, like her mother's. Some belonged to reptiles and insects, and some to creatures utterly alien to this world.

Zahara's hand came to her mouth in a gasp, and she pushed away from Harut. She whirled around to face her mother.

"And you are correct, Lilitu," Harut said. "I can heal my own kind."

Zahara stretched out a trembling hand for her mother. Lilitu shrank back, staring. There couldn't be many things the devourer of souls hadn't seen in her long lifetime, but the transformation of her daughter had shocked even her. Zahara choked back a sob. She had never been anything like anyone else in her family, but she hadn't been anything like one of their enemies, either.

Then Lilitu made her decision, and the aging woman in

black reached out to take Zahara into her arms. The two clung together for a long moment. Lililtu whispered a short prayer into her ear, then spoke the words that would send both of them swirling into the levels of hell. Back to the Mountains of Qaf. Back home.

Chapter Twenty-Seven

ZAHARA TOOK IN a breath and tried to ignore the gaping pit of anxiety her stomach had become. She *could* do this. After all, she had faced down a monstrous fallen angel and lived to tell the tale. Barely, but she had still done it. Not to mention her other recent achievements. Her first demonic possession, dragging rather unlikely companions through the levels without killing them, and tricking and fighting a whole host of villainous humans.

How hard could it be to talk to her mother and finally ask the question she'd been holding back all these years?

She smoothed the embroidered folds of her long tunic, a pale spring green designed to contrast with the rose silk trousers gathered at her ankles. Her favorite human shape and medieval garments worked together to give her the appearance of a courtly lady who had stepped off the enameled surface of a Persian miniature painting.

None of this was by personal whim, although Zahara rather liked her look. Her mother was hosting an emissary from the dev, the powerful jinn of Iran. The opening of the cave in Mazanderan and the escape of the two fallen angels had happened right in their backyard, and they had requested a meeting to hear the details of Marut's defeat. And Zahara, having been at the center of the entire mess, needed to make an appearance.

Hence the outfit, and her human manifestation. If Zahara appeared in her true form, especially to such an important sometimes-ally, sometimes-enemy, her mother would be mortified. There was a new option, of course—the most irregular and horribly frightening shape that Harut had managed to transform her into after inexplicably saving her life.

She pushed that thought out of her mind. Her mother, true to form, declined to discuss the matter further. After their arrival in the family fortress, Zahara felt fine, and was able to transform into either her original, adorable shape or appear human without any difficulty. The only remaining side effect was that she could become that *other* shape, that terrible angelic form, at will. She had done it a few times, in secret, twirling about and trying out her strange and awful wings. Ultimately, she concluded it was best to let the matter rest, and focus instead on her mother's new concern—the arrival of a special visitor.

The dev lord had enough human blood in his family tree that direct contact with Lilitu's elemental form could be hazardous to his health. That gave Zahara's mother the diplomatic out of hosting her honored visitor while wearing her own human shape, and demanding the same of her daughter. Given the reputation of the dev as masters of political intrigue and covert information gathering, Zahara had no illusions that their distinguished frenemy didn't already know her family's not-so-hidden, shameful secret.

Zahara stepped into the large antechamber of her clan's vast fortress, a room reserved for the entertainment—and, if necessary, quiet elimination—of important guests. Lilitu despised the excesses of decoration so dear to Zahara's heart, and the hall reflected her mother's love of minimalism and intimidation. Vast arches of translucent peridot stretched overhead, with hidden flames embedded deep inside that cast a greenish glow over an obsidian floor devoid of anything save a single carpet. Even this textile was stark, woven in a primitive style from white wool, with only a few scattered geometric designs. The current favorite from her mother's harem of husbands, a young-looking incubus, lounged at the far end of it. He reclined next to several drinking vessels and plates of food, and his slender fingers caressed the strings of a lute.

Her mother sat erect, completely veiled in her *niqab*, on the left side of the carpet. Directly across from her sat their guest. He rose to his feet as an extra trill from the lute announced Zahara's arrival.

If this was the dev lord's true form, Zahara could see why her mother had been so disparaging about his mixed blood. He was only about a head taller than the average human, with a thin patrician face framed by long white hair. The only features that distinguished him from a handsome older human man were the horns jutting from each side of his forehead and a pair of leathery wings hanging from his back. Like Zahara, he had chosen to wear ancient Persian clothing straight out of an illustrated book of Hafiz poetry.

"I'll need to set the lights extra bright for his human eyes so he doesn't trip on his way in," Lilitu had scoffed. "That, and be prepared to listen to a two-hour dissertation about the superiority of Persian culture."

"Peace be upon you, Zahara bint Lilitu." The dev lord swept his hand to his heart and gave her a deep bow. His fingers were far too long to be wholly human. Pale and thin, they spread over over his chest like a spider web. "My greatest spies have whispered to me of a beautiful ruby hidden deep within the fortress of your feared clan, a fair maiden of unsurpassed allure and magical charms." He inclined his head in her mother's direction. "I fear I'll need to chastise them. They failed miserably in their description of your youngest daughter's beauty and grace."

Lilitu, who had remained seated, gave a deprecating wave of her gloved hand. Zahara allowed herself to preen a little, despite her anxiety. It was all a show, of course, but she couldn't help but be charmed by such outrageous flattery. Quite the silver fox, this one.

"My dear Reza, my youngest child has only recently re-turned to the bosom of her worried family." Lilitu clasped her hands to her chest and batted her eyelashes at him. As part of the elaborate charade of the meeting, her mother referred to their guest by the name he used when he adopted a full human manifestation. "We have much to discuss, as mother and daughter. I'm sure you understand, having children of your own."

This was a polite invitation to get the hell out, and Reza ignored it.

"Five sons and one pearl of a daughter." He was leaving out that two of his male heirs were dead, one by his own hand if rumors could be believed. "So precious and so draining are our blessed offspring. I had heard that, despite her youth, your beautiful Zahara acquitted herself most honorably against the fallen one."

"Our ancient foe was a formidable enemy indeed." Lilitu's eyes creased into a hard smile above her veil. "But Marut is now trapped in a level of hell he will not be able to leave for eons to come, as I've assured you multiple times."

"Yet his brother Harut still roams the world of man." Reza turned back to Zahara, his black eyes boring into hers. Charming and deadly, like a viper. No wonder her mother was fond of him, after a fashion. "I understand your human sorcerer compelled you to seek his aid in defeating Marut."

Great. Even the meddling dev of Iran knew all about Harut saving her life. Hopefully they didn't know anything about his odd trick of transforming her shape after he did it.

"Most unpleasant, I would imagine, to spend time with one of his ilk." Reza gave a sympathetic sigh. "In this, my people could be of service. Harut is little more than one of the peri now." He drew out the Persian name of the winged jinn with a sneer of disgust. "We have much experience killing his kind. Do you have knowledge that could assist us in this regard?"

Zahara gave her best wide-eyed, dumb virgin look. "No clue." She wagged her thumb and little finger by her ear in a mock phone shape. "If I see him around, I'll give you a call."

Her response only caused his thin lips to break into a wider smile. "I'm sure you will." He turned back to her mother. "Quite fortunate, that your daughter inserted herself in the sorceress Solikis's clever plan to use her half-blood descendent to stop Marut. Was this interference a technique of your own devising?"

Lilitu stiffened. "Certainly not." She gave Zahara a hard

glare, as if accusing *her* of some elaborate subterfuge.

It hadn't been her fault. How could she have known what a mess she would start by answering Daniel's summons?

"A most auspicious happenstance." Reza turned back toward Zahara, the tips of his fangs now visible within his smile. "Of course, had the clan of Lilitu decided from the beginning to support Marut's position, it would be a most devious trick indeed, to arrange for a young child from the family to agree to a contract to fight the fallen one. That would have placed your dear mother in the terrible position of having to choose between killing her own daughter or stopping Marut."

Zahara stared back at him, mouth agape at the audacity of it all. Nothing had been an accident, and Solikis hadn't been the one to lure her into the trap. Her mother's allies, the dev of Persia, had sent a backup plan in the form of a cursed lamp to Daniel. A little insurance, in case Lilitu had lied about her repudiation of Marut's plan to pit the human and jinn worlds at war. Which, of course, she had.

Her mother's eyes had long since turned to those of a snake, and tendrils began to squirm out of her heavy black clothing.

The dev lord appeared unconcerned with Lilitu's transformation. "Bear in mind, this plot of Marut's to open the barrier between the human world and our own is not an isolated one. Our peri enemies have broken millennia of tradition and shared our secrets with certain humans of considerable military prowess. This represents a danger to us all."

Donnelly and his company had been busy, hadn't they?

"When the houses of the dev and the House of Lilitu have mutual interests, we will speak again." Zahara's mother gave him a wave of dismissal. "May you have a safe journey through the levels."

Reza inclined his body into a gracious bow. "With deep regret, I will take my leave of this most charming of feminine company." Flames leapt around his feet, and his body dissolved into smoke, then flowed away into an invisible vent as thunder rocked the antechamber.

Zahara's mother snapped her fingers and her lute-playing husband leapt to his feet, bowing his beautiful head toward both of them before beating a hasty retreat. Zahara and her mother were left alone in the vast emptiness of the hall.

"Did you hear that?" Zahara asked. "He was behind this the whole time. It wasn't Solikis at all."

"Devious, despicable, and brilliant." Lilitu gestured toward the rug for her to sit. "If I approved of mixed-blood unions, which I do not, I would propose an engagement. You need to start thinking about getting married."

"There's no way I would get hitched to the likes of him." Zahara sputtered.

"Of course not." Lilitu pointed again to the rug. "He's much too old. Close to my age, in fact. He does have a nephew, however, who might be a possibility."

Zahara gave a groan and sank down into a cross-legged position. She had just come back from the dead, and her mother was already complaining about her single status. Two *rhytons*, conical, horn-shaped drinking vessels, rested on a platter in front of her. A wide-mouthed ceramic carafe stood next to them, and Zahara crinkled her nose at the red fluid inside. She had hoped the occasion of the dev lord's visit might mean a decent vintage. No such luck.

Lilitu dipped her preferred drinking vessel—the skull of a beast with three eye sockets lacquered in gold—into the bloodwine to fill it to the brim. She kept one finger pressed over the hole in the base, where the creature's snout ended, and lifted out the dripping *rhyton*. "To your health and the honor of our clan, my daughter."

Zahara reached out for her own cup, a far less ominous replica of the head of a lioness, and submerged it into the liquid, trying to scoop in as little as possible. Both of them raised their respective skulls and removed their fingers from the end of the spout, allowing the drink to pour into their mouths. Zahara got down about half of the spiced blood mixture and coughed out the worst of the taste in her mouth.

Across from her, Lilitu continued to drain her vessel, the bloodwine forming a series of inhuman lumps that moved down her throat like a suffocated animal being swallowed by an anaconda. She set down the *rhyton* and regarded Zahara with concern. "Do you not feel well enough to complete our toast? The gods are displeased when the cups are not drained."

Zahara gave in and chugged the rest of hers, gagging as she did so. "Can we stop with the drinking contest, already? You know I hate this stuff."

"You're right, dear." Her mother waved at the open vessel. "We should be drinking the raw blood of our enemy, as he hangs suspended and flayed above us. Alas, that isn't possible."

"Maybe you could have taken a nip or two out of Marut on the way down to that level of hell."

"I'm speaking of Harut. He could have had Marut's power, perhaps more, since he's the brighter of the two. But he's vulnerable now. Some will seek his knowledge, many more his demise. But I can no longer raise arms against him. He saved you, and thus we are obligated to him. A most distressing state of affairs."

"I'm so sorry I'm not dead." Zahara tried to rub the taste of the toast off her lips with her sleeve. "And for your information, I saved *him* once, too."

"I'm not saying you didn't acquit yourself better than I expected." Her mother's tone indicated some uncharacteristic, if grudging approval. "The dev may take care of Harut for us, in any event."

Zahara dug her fingernails into her palm. If she ever saw Harut again, she needed to warn him. But he had slipped away after bringing her back to life and cradling her in his arms. One brief, beautiful embrace, devoid of any argument or games, and then he had gone, probably forever. After all, why would he stick around? He knew what she really was, and there was no way they could ever be together. Marut was taken care of, more or less, and there was no need for Harut to work with her any longer.

"Let's move on to more pleasant topics," her mother said. "Your acceptance of a contract with this sorcerer, ill-advised as it was, succeeded. He belongs to you now. You should bind his soul to yours in eternal servitude as soon as you can. Tricky little creatures, these humans."

"Oh, that." Zahara tugged at the translucent veil partly covering her hair, pretending to adjust it. "Well, I thought we could spend some quality time together first, Mother. Not to mention that Daniel doesn't strike me as a promising thrall."

"He has Solikis's blood in him." Her mother's tone sharpened and Zahara gave up playing with her clothing. "Even though he's a supposed novice to the dark arts, he was able to summon *me*, who has not been called forth in centuries by even the most powerful of magicians. He used a dread weapon of magic to help me drag Marut away. You must crush his spirit and bring him into line early, before he becomes any stronger."

"Sure," Zahara said. "I'll get right on that. But I was thinking of giving him to Zaid." This wasn't a complete lie. If she let Daniel go, he'd wander on back to New York, and there was a good chance Zaid was interested enough to follow him there. Daniel would have someone to keep him out of trouble, and Zahara wouldn't lose her friendship with Zaid or have to deal with this horrible new emotion of guilt that kept afflicting her.

"The apostate? You would give your sorcerer to *him*?" Her mother sputtered in outrage. "Zaid could set him free, with those insane ideas of his, and then where would we be? Solikis will welcome him to her clan, and he'll become a weapon our enemies could use against us."

Oh, her mother was in high dudgeon now that was for sure. This was going to deteriorate into a complete hissy fit.

"Solikis and the Jewish jinn, Zaid and the red jinn, *and* Daniel were the ones who helped us defeat Marut, remember?" Zahara couldn't tell if she felt like throwing up because of the bloodwine, or because of how much she hated being yelled at. It would serve her mother right if she puked all over the carpet. "Daniel didn't want money, or power, or revenge, or anything but a little help to do the right thing. He saved us, and he doesn't deserve to be trapped and crushed or whatever you want me to do with him."

There was long, uncomfortable silence. Maybe high dudgeon was preferable to the low dungeon her mother might throw her into for disobedience.

"I suppose Harut convinced you of this, during the time you spent with him."

"It certainly sounds like you spent some time of your own with Harut, back in the day." Zahara folded her arms. "Back when *you* were Zahara."

"I enjoyed showing that moralizing bore he was no better than the jinn he scorned." Her mother regarded the *rhyton* resting on floor near her, contemplating another drink. "But Marut was different. I cared for him once, on some level."

Zahara wasn't sure she had heard her correctly. "But they were both stuck in that cave for centuries because of you."

Lilitu nodded, then scooped up more bloodwine and took a drink. "We all make our choices, my dear. And now it's time to make yours."

Well, this was it. The moment she had been waiting for.

"Who was my father?" Zahara blurted before she could lose her nerve. "Was he something... like Harut, way back then?"

Lilitu lifted up her eyes, now the gold gleaming irises and slit pupils of a reptile, to meet Zahara's. "That's not information I wish to share with you, and I doubt any good would come of you possessing this knowledge. Still, if you must know, I'll propose a fair exchange. I will reveal your father's name if you force Daniel to become your thrall, then deliver him to me."

Zahara's mouth grew dry. For a moment, she even considered taking another sip of the spiced blood in the vat between them to moisten her tongue enough so she could speak. Her mother kept to her bargains. As much as Lilitu didn't want Zahara to know who her father was, she would tell her the truth in order to get Daniel.

There was only one thing to do, then.

Zahara uncrossed her legs and stood up, then bent down into a low bow before her mother. "Perhaps you're right. No good would come of me knowing the truth." She straightened up and held out her hands, preparing to dissolve herself and enter the levels. "I ask your leave to depart, Mother. Forever, if that's what you want. I'm going to return to the world of man and tell Daniel he's free."

Rather than fury, faint smile lines creased around her mother's eyes. In the next moment, the human form she had assumed dissolved into the dark, many-eyed tendrils of Lilitu, devourer of souls. "As human babes grow into adults, so does my youngest leave her childhood behind. Return to your adopted world for now, Zahara. Know you are still part of my house, and may return to my welcome embrace. But this conversation cannot be revisited. You will not learn from me the knowledge you seek, and you will not find a way to discover it on your own."

Lilitu's long arms reached out for one last caress of Zahara's cheek before her lower body dissolved into flames and smoke, and her mother's last hissing words of farewell faded into the roaring flames of the first level of hell.

Chapter Twenty-Eight

Z AHARA MATERIALIZED INTO Daniel and Zaid's hotel room in a swirl of pink smoke and a crackle of fireworks, instead of the usual brimstone. For added celebratory effect, she sported a black minidress and enough jewelry to blind anyone within twenty feet. She topped it all off with a diamond tiara.

Given the unsettled situation when she had left them, it was reassuring to find Zaid and Daniel holed up in their original hotel in Marrakech, not under arrest by the Moroccan authorities or whisked off to some black-site prison by Donnelly and his buddies. After spending a little time deciding on the perfect outfit for such an auspicious occasion, she had popped in to visit them without warning. Because surprises were awesome. And because she didn't want to give either of them a chance to tell her they didn't want her to come.

"I'm back!" She struck a pose, hands on her hips. "The party can start now."

Daniel's face broke into a grin as he ran over to hug her as hard as possible, and Zahara felt the unaccustomed and unwelcome presence of tears welling up in her eyes. She tossed her head back and blinked them away. Her mascara was perfect and no matter how relieved she was that the closest people she had to family in the human world were happy to see her, she wasn't about to ruin her makeup.

"I'm having a hard enough time walking, *cherie*, much less partying." Zaid remained curled up on the couch, a blanket around his legs, but his eyes lit up at the sight of her. His face still held a trace of pallor, but Harut's healing powers had resolved most of the damage from Zaid's fight with Marut. Daniel had fared better, with little more than a few scattered bruises.

"I ordered up extra desserts when I heard you were coming." Daniel bustled over to the room's mini-kitchen and came back with a steaming silver samovar. "And Zaid taught me how to make mint tea. Want some?"

"Try not to get too crazy too fast," Zahara said. "After the past week, I was hoping for something more festive than hot water and green leaves."

Daniel placed several tea glasses on a small table in front of Zaid, then pointed to a bowl of sugar cubes and a plate of baklava. "Come on. I know what you like."

"You were expecting me?" Zahara couldn't see how either of the two men could have guessed why she had left her mother's protection, and she hadn't spent that much time shopping, dressing, and procrastinating before this reunion. "What spell did you use for that?"

"Solikis told me," Daniel said. "She's back in the Mountains of Qaf, but we can communicate now. I mean, without enchanted cockroaches, or a séance."

Daniel's sorceress grandmother was keeping tabs on her, apparently. At least she wasn't in the hotel room, ready to pop out of a closet. Zahara had enough trouble with her own mother.

She piled some sugar on the pastry and gave it a lick. "Mmm, yummy. I missed the sweets. I have a hard enough time scoring a drop of honey back home. That whole drinking-the-blood-of-your-enemies thing gets old fast."

"Is your mother well?" Zaid asked. She could tell he was trying hard not bring up her striking transformation after Harut had touched her, and Lilitu's reaction to it. "And Marut not so well?"

"He's not dead, exactly." Zahara crunched away at her dessert and left her mother out of it. "Trapped in some weird circle of hell I've never visited, or something like that."

"So now that Lilitu, devourer of souls, knows her little baby is safe and sound, she's not planning on coming back over to kill us, right?" Daniel asked.

Zahara threw up her hands. What was this, twenty questions? "Well, she's not planning on tracking you two down any time soon. But on to more important matters. What do you think of my dress? Stunning, isn't it? And the shoes? Check them out. Manolo Blahnik, from the new spring collection."

Daniel circled around her as she showed off her ensemble. "A micro-mini with sequins isn't quite what I imagined as standard attire in a household of jinn demons."

Zahara gave him a withering stare. "Hardly. I picked up this up in one of the lobby stores using your room credit. I'm so glad we're back in Marrakech."

"So am I." Daniel poured tea into the glasses, stretching out the liquid stream and not spilling a drop. "Although I'll be even happier when I'm back in New York. The whole mess is being described as a tragic military aircraft accident. Marut's human allies are in custody for the nightclub bombing, and Ibrahim and Ahmed make sure Zaid fades into the woodwork whenever Donnelly visits and offers me a job with his so-called security consulting company. All in all, I think we should be able to fly back by the weekend."

"As long as Zahara doesn't require you to fulfill your part of the bargain, Daniel." Zaid sat up straighter on the couch and gave her a stern look.

Zahara ignored the hint and popped more cubes into her mouth. "That was what was supposed to happen. But Daniel did such a stellar job conjuring up my mother and helping finish off Marut that she was quite impressed."

"Lilitu was impressed." Zaid spoke every word as if it were Daniel's death sentence. Actually, eternal service to her mother would have been quite a bit worse than death.

"Impressed enough that she agreed to tell me who my real father was." Zahara finished off the last of the sugar and gave Daniel a fingernail jab in the ribs. "Provided I turn you over to her as her slave, of course."

Daniel's eyes widened, and the color drained from Zaid's face.

"So who was your real father?" Daniel asked slowly.

"I have no idea." Zahara threw her arms into the air. "Because I told her no!"

Zaid broke into a smile. "You refused her? I can't believe you got away with that."

"Neither can I." Zahara grinned at them. "I'm not even exiled, much less dead. But she pretty much told me I'll never find out the truth. No biggie. I've got more important problems to deal with. Like buying a new wardrobe, for example."

Zahara had practiced this line over and over again, so her voice didn't shake at all when she dismissed her only chance of ever knowing the truth about her father.

"So I'm not the devourer of souls' thrall or your personal sex toy." Daniel held up a finger. "Just so we're all clear on this."

"What I should do is give you to Zaid for helping me out," Zahara said. "You're way too boring for my tastes."

Daniel gave Zaid a nervous look, and the jinn responded with a wicked grin.

"Given the recent events in my club and my apartment…" Zaid stood up and came over to put his arm around Daniel's shoulder. "I'm a little short on dungeon space. So I'll pass. But the next time you have the urge to play with black magic to entrap a jinn, I suggest you lie down until the feeling goes away."

"How about a return of hospitality, instead of my immortal soul?" Daniel smiled up at Zaid, who gave him a squeeze back. Zahara had never seen her friend look that… well, *happy*. "Ever been to Cape Cod?"

"Not since whaling was a major industry," Zaid replied. "Sounds like fun."

A soft knock on the door interrupted the touchy-feelies, which threatened to veer into pure schmaltz territory. If it wasn't room service, she and Zaid might have to do a quick disappearing act. That creep Donnelly was still around.

As Daniel rushed over to the door and peered through the peephole, Zaid gave Zahara a quick kiss. Not with tongue, which she would have preferred. But it was still nice.

"Guys, guess who's here?" Daniel slid the deadbolt sideways and threw the door open. "Harut's back."

"What!" Zahara whirled around in a panic, and Zaid grimaced and summoned his sword into his hand.

"What are you doing?" Daniel came up to them, his arm around Harut's shoulders. "He's a friend."

"The enemy of my enemy is still my enemy after the truce is over." Zaid gripped his sword and nodded at Zahara. She sighed and produced her own weapon. This fighting was getting tiring. And there were more interesting things she'd rather do with Harut than whack swords with him.

Harut raised his hands. "I've no issue with you, Zaid. I came here for Zahara."

"You try anything and I'll call Mommy back." Zahara darted behind Zaid. "Even your big, bad brother didn't handle her too well, did he?"

"I didn't come to fight you." Harut came up closer to her, his deep green eyes meeting her own. She lowered her sword and resisted the impulse to jump into his arms. After all, now that Marut was gone, he was officially enemy number one. Or something like that. "I came back to insist you honor the favor you owe me for saving your life."

Zahara drew in a deep breath. Technically, she still owed him. But she had hoped he would keep that particular chip in reserve to prevent her mother from coming after him.

"I can ask her for anything and you know it." Harut gave Zaid a fierce glare, and her friend took a step back, leaving Zahara to face the fallen angel. The power of that obligation transcended anything Zaid could possibly do to help her.

Zaid couldn't have done anything to stop Zahara from delivering Daniel to her mother, and he couldn't do anything to stop Harut from demanding payment for saving her life.

"This is my demand. Release Daniel from your evil contract to take his soul, and let him continue his life in peace."

"Oh, that's not a problem anymore." Daniel would have said more, much more, if Zaid's muttered spell inflicting a painful and invisible squeeze around his neck hadn't choked some sense into him. He reached up to pry off the invisible vise around his throat and coughed out, "I mean, now that you've arrived in the nick of time to save me from a horrible fate."

Zaid turned to Zahara, one eyebrow raised in a faint twitch only she could see. The two of them faced Harut, their faces sullen as they sheathed their swords with sighs of resignation.

"You're no fun at all." Zahara stomped her foot in mock outrage, to add to the drama of it all. "All right. So we're even."

Harut turned to each of them in turn, as they all choked back laughter. He furrowed his brow with confusion and not a little suspicion. "I must say, I expected a little more opposition to my request."

"We jinn know when we're beat." Zaid gave Harut a bright smile and picked up a glass of tea. "Since you're not planning to kill us, stay and have a hot drink. Daniel is released from any and all demonic contracts, and Zahara and I will try to stay out of your way in the future. Deal?"

Harut accepted the cup and took a sip. He locked eyes

with Zahara, who did everything down to biting her inner lip to stop herself from laughing. "My visit here wasn't necessary. You've already released Daniel from his contract."

Zahara did her best to look indignant, then gave up. "Okay, so maybe I did. Does that mean I owe you another favor?"

Harut considered this for a moment. "I plan to use my remaining time on this earth ensuring my brother's plan to pit the human and jinn worlds against one another never comes to pass. In the future, I might ask for your assistance in helping me navigate this modern existence."

Zahara had hoped for a far naughtier request. Still, it was a start. "For one thing, you need to watch your back. The Persian dev already have your number, and they can cross over to the human world to get you like that." She snapped her fingers for emphasis. "Not that you heard it from me."

For the first time, a smile crossed Harut's face. "That sounds like you're concerned about my safety."

"You're my new archnemesis." Zahara flipped her hair back. "No one else is allowed to go after you."

"I'll keep that in mind." Harut finished his drink. "I can't imagine your mother was too pleased with your decision to release Daniel."

"She's not too pleased about a lot of things I do. But she's still my mother. And I'm still not her."

"You're right. I was wrong to think you were." He set his empty glass on the table and walked to the door. "I have unfinished business to attend to, but I'll take your advice about the dev."

"So you're leaving?" Zahara asked. "After all the grief you

gave me about Daniel, you could at least stick around long enough for a quickie."

Harut paused at the threshold. That last one scored another smile from him. "I'm sure we'll meet again, Zahara bint Zahara. And I hope when we do, it won't be as enemies."

He was gone before she could come up with one last snarky retort, or say something to make him stay. Maybe her real father had been something like Harut, and maybe the one remaining fallen one could tell her what her mother had sworn to keep secret from her. But now he had left, after giving her a second chance at life and a new look that frightened even Lilitu.

Zahara tore herself away from staring at the door and turned back to Zaid and Daniel. "So far, my first attempt to entrap a human's soul has been a dismal failure."

Daniel handed her a tea glass, reached into his pocket, and produced a secret stash of sugar cubes. Now *there* was a magic trick he needed to keep up. "Don't worry. With all the shopping you've done on my credit card, I'll be a slave to some debt company soon enough."

Zahara waved her hand. "I'm sure Zaid can find a haunted treasure spot not far from here to rectify that problem."

"As long as a portion goes to charity," Zaid said. "Imam Youssef has many needy cases, and I'd like to ensure the club ladies are taken care of, too."

"I'd like to give some to Rabbi Schlomo and Reverend Collins." Daniel beamed back at Zaid.

Okay, this Daniel-Zaid couple thing was already getting too cutesy for her to handle. Besides, they hadn't even bothered to include her in their gift-giving plans. Not that charity was something she had ever considered. But somehow, it didn't feel all that... wrong.

"I suppose that little munchkin I saved could use a treat, too." Zahara had expected Daniel and Zaid to be a little surprised that she planned on giving up potential shoe money, but the gaping shock on their faces was way over-the-top.

Daniel recovered first. "That's the most adult and responsible thing I've ever heard you say." He used the same congratulating tone pet owners might employ with a puppy that had learned to pee on a pile of newspapers. "You could bring him and his family new clothing, or maybe school books."

"Hello, demon jinn here." Zahara called up a crackle of flames from her newly manicured fingernails, and watched Daniel jump back with a good deal of satisfaction. She was still the daughter of Lilitu, scourge of men, deliverer of the desolation, and owner of a hundred or so other terrifying honorifics. She had a reputation to protect. "We don't give little mud children age-appropriate reading material. I was thinking more along the lines of making the sky rain candy over his town, and then sending in a herd of enchanted goats quoting poetry.

"Here's to Zahara's first demonic charity event." Zaid raised his teacup in a toast. "Given the chaos that will probably follow, we should set up a quick getaway plan."

"Then let's get to work," Zahara said. "After that, Daniel, I need you to buy us all plane tickets. Remember, I don't fly coach. And make sure we lay over in Paris this time. I'm in need of some serious retail therapy."

The End

If you enjoyed this book, please leave a review at your favorite online retailer! Even if it's just a sentence or two it makes all the difference.

Thanks for reading *Summoned* by M.A. Guglielmo!

Discover your next romance at TulePublishing.com.

TULE
PUBLISHING

If you enjoyed *Summoned,* you'll love the next book in....

From Smokeless Fire series

Book 1: *Summoned*

Book 2

Available now at your favorite online retailer!

About the Author

M.A. Guglielmo is a neurosurgeon, mother of two awesome daughters, and a life-long fan of speculative fiction. Her Italian grandmother may or may not have been able to cast the evil eye on difficult neighbors, and Maria loves telling a good story, especially if magical curses and witty villains are involved.

Her interest in Middle Eastern politics and culture inspires her to incorporate mythology and folklore from the region into her writing projects. After having the wits scared out of her by ghost tales told to her over a campfire in the Moroccan Sahara, she's come up with a plan to travel to all the potential settings for her novels. Since those include the mountain-ringed home of the Jinn and a modernized version of the Greek Underworld, some items on her bucket list might be harder to achieve than others.

Maria was born and raised in Rhode Island, and graduated from Yale University with a degree in biology. She completed her M.D. degree at Brown University, and went on to finish her neurosurgical residency there. After several years enjoying the company of sunny friends and overcast skies in Portland, Oregon, she moved back to Rhode Island, where she's a neurosurgeon in academic practice. She lives there with her two daughters, assorted pets, and is always dreaming of the stories that can come out of her next travel destination.

Thank you for reading

Summoned

If you enjoyed this book, you can find more from all our great authors at TulePublishing.com, or from your favorite online retailer.

TULE
PUBLISHING